Shadows on the Moon

ZOË MARRIOTT

WALKER
BOOKS

For the amazing writers of the Furtive Scribblers' Club.
Without you this book would never, ever, ever
have been finished.

First published 2011 by Walker Books Ltd
87 Vauxhall Walk, London SE11 5HJ

This edition published 2016

2 4 6 8 10 9 7 5 3 1

Text © 2011, 2016 Zoë Marriott
Cover illustration © 2016 THERE IS Studio /
illustration and creative lettering by Sean Freeman

The right of Zoë Marriott to be identified as author of this work has
been asserted by her in accordance with the Copyright,
Designs and Patents Act 1988

This book has been typeset in Berkeley

Printed and bound in Great Britain by Clays Ltd, St Ives plc

British Library Cataloguing in Publication Data:
a catalogue record for this book is available from the British Library

ISBN 978-1-4063-6757-7

www.walker.co.uk

The Great Britain
SASAKAWA
FOUNDATION
グレイトブリテン・ササカワ財団

Author's note

Although *Shadows on the Moon* uses many Chinese and Japanese terms, the story is set in a fantasy realm called the Moonlit Land, or Tsuki no Hikari no Kuni. Most of the details of this country are pure invention, and this book is not intended to represent a historically accurate picture of any Asian country at any period in history.

Love comes like storm clouds
Fleeing from the wind, and casts
Shadows on the moon.

Suzume

One

On my fourteenth birthday, when the sakura was in full bloom, the men came to kill us. We saw them come, Aimi and me. We were excited because we did not know how to be frightened. We had never seen soldiers before.

Aside from the anticipation of gifts and special food later on, the morning began just as a thousand others had. Aimi woke me, burrowing under the covers to poke me in the ribs when I refused to leave the warm futon. After I had done shrieking and laughing, we helped each other dress, Aimi sighing as always over my badly folded obi. I slipped my favourite *kanzashi* pin, with its carved bone flowers, into her hair, because I knew she loved it.

We breakfasted with Father, who was smiling and

mysterious when I teased him about what presents I might open that night.

"A poor father you must think me, to spoil your fun so early, Little Sparrow," he teased back. And then his smile turned down at the corners as he said, "Your mother will be upset that she is not home in time."

"Maybe she will arrive today, Oji-san," Aimi said, trying to comfort.

I slurped a mouthful of miso soup and said nothing. I missed Mother too – it was weeks since she had travelled to comfort my great-aunt over the death of her husband – but I could not help feeling it would be a more relaxed birthday without her scolding me for doing all the things that made such times fun, like trying to guess what my presents were, and eating too much, and wearing my formal *furisode*, which Mother said must be kept for best.

When breakfast was done I went to my room and took out my three-stringed shamisen. I put the little cloth cover on my hand and picked up the tortoiseshell plectrum, handling each item with respect. My instrument was not a fine one. I knew its sound was not very good. Still, it gave me pleasure to play and sing. Since it was one of the few ladylike pursuits I would sit still for, I had been allowed to continue, so long as I did not disturb the family. But I was restless that day. After two songs and a little more than half an hour, I put my instrument away and went to look for Aimi.

The serving girl told me that my cousin was outside, but I did not find her in the formal garden that ringed the house. I knew what that meant. I sighed and went to search the orchards. They were much larger than the garden and sloped all the way down to the road that separated Father's land from the forest. The translucent pink cherry blossoms and the white apple blossoms were just starting to fall, and the scent of them was wild and sweet. I trailed my fingers carefully over the black and silvery-grey bark as I walked through the trees.

I found my cousin at the farthest tip of the orchards, overlooking the place where the road emerged from the woods. There was a little bench there, concealed by the foliage, so that you could look down on passers-by without being seen. Not that many interesting people passed on this quiet country thoroughfare – but if they did, we would be in the right place to see them.

I sat down beside Aimi on the bench and watched the empty road for a few moments before speaking. "Did Father's talk about Mother at breakfast upset you?"

"Oh no. Of course not." She took my hand and patted it but did not look at me. I waited.

She sighed. "It is silly to feel sad, when I have been so lucky."

"It is not," I said firmly. Aimi was a year older than me, and so lovely that next to her I felt like a squashy brown toadstool. But she was gentle and sensitive and she needed someone to look after her. "How could anyone feel lucky in your position? You have a right to mourn."

"Oba-san would say I was being sullen."

"Mother says a great many things I do not agree with—" I broke off and giggled. "I sounded like her then, didn't I?"

"A little," Aimi said, with a watery smile.

"Well, do not worry. *I* will not give you indecipherable instructions to pass on to the cook, or send you to find a book that does not exist, or ask you to unravel all the threads in the embroidery box. I think that Mother is sharp with you because you remind her of herself. Father said it devastated her when her own parents died. She has never forgotten. But that is not your fault."

"Sometimes I wonder…" she whispered.

"Wonder what?"

"Why I lived, when everyone – Mother and Father, even the baby – died of the fever. Why I lived to come here, and annoy Oba-san, and be a burden to Oji-san."

I pressed my lips together to hold in the angry denial that wanted to escape. Instead I put my arm around her and hugged her fiercely.

"Perhaps," I said, when I had control of myself. "Perhaps the Moon took pity on me…"

"What do you mean?" she asked, surprised.

"I was so lonely before you came. I used to pray for a brother or sister – someone to talk to and play with. Most especially I prayed for a sister: a kind, beautiful sister. Perhaps the Moon heard my pleas and spared you when my aunt and uncle died, not for your own sake but for mine. If so, I cannot be sorry. Though *you* might be, to have such a sister forced on you, and *such* a mother as mine."

"Suzume!" she said, a little amused and a little shocked. "What would your father say?"

"Oh, he never says anything. That is part of what makes Mother so cross all the time. Father knows that if he scolds me I argue, and arguments are so noisy, and—"

"'A quiet house is a happy house,'" she chorused with me.

She was smiling now, the sweet, happy smile that I loved to see. I congratulated myself, though I had said nothing but the truth. I was about to suggest that we walk back to the house, when I heard hoofbeats on the road. Lots of them. Travelling at a gallop.

We exchanged interested looks. Mother? No – why would she be in such a hurry so close to home? Besides, we could not afford so many outriders.

As I leaned forward to look down at the road, the troop of riders broke out of the forest. Aimi made a sound of wonder. There were an even dozen of them, and they wore black lacquered armour and rode dark horses. The spring sunlight gleamed on the horses' gear and on the silver edges of the armour. They made a glorious picture.

I expected them to carry on along the road, but instead the leader, who had a crest of white feathers on his helmet, pointed, and they wheeled their horses and turned onto our little road. The thunder of hooves shook the ground as they rode under the ranks of blooming trees, and pink and white petals showered down, catching in the dark flowing manes and tails of the horses. They looked like an illustration from one of Father's books.

Yet, as the leader passed us in our hidden place, a cold finger touched my back and I shivered. I did not like the feeling. Sometimes it came when we were about to get bad news.

"They are from Tsuki no Ouji-sama," Aimi said, awed, once the horses had galloped past. "Only his men may wear such black armour."

"Oh," I said, relieved. If something had happened to my mother, the Moon Prince would hardly send his men to tell us. My mother was not even in the city, let alone at the Moon Court.

"They say the Moon Prince comes of age soon, and he will hold his first Kage no Iwai, to choose a favoured companion," Aimi said dreamily. "Do you think…?"

I clucked my tongue. "Why would Tsuki no Ouji-sama invite *us* to his Shadow Ball? The Shadow Bride is always a rich daughter of some high-up nobleman, just as the Moon Prince always has to marry someone who is a princess herself."

"Then what about Kano Akira-sama?" Aimi said challengingly.

"Oh, you and that fairy tale!"

"It isn't a fairy tale. It is a true story and it only

happened ten years ago. I think it's beautiful."

"Of course you do, Little Dancer," I said, and Aimi blushed. Mother had caught her dancing in our room recently and scolded her, telling her that only nasty, common women moved their bodies like that. But Kano Akira-sama had danced at the Shadow Ball and won the old prince's heart with her beauty, even though she had had nothing but the clothes on her back. The old prince had chosen her as the Shadow Bride, the highest-ranking woman at court, save the Moon Princess herself. So dancing could not be that bad.

"And anyway," I went on, "this new prince has never seen either of us. He doesn't know the Hoshima family from … from … the cleaners that sweep his path."

"Well, why have they come, then?"

"Perhaps the prince has seen some of Father's poetry, and has found it so beautiful that he intends to invite him to court," I said, not really believing it.

"That would please Oba-san!" Aimi said with a laugh.

"But not Father. Mother says he is the least ambitious person she knows." And whenever she said it, she made a face like a woman who has bitten into a sweet dumpling and found fish guts inside.

"Well, there's only one way to find out for sure." I jumped to my feet. "Come on!"

I caught her hand and when she rose, I began to run, forcing her to trot after me. She protested breathlessly, laughing as she tried to pick up the hem of her kimono.

"Suzume! I'll rip something. I'll fall."

"Run faster then, *baka*," I said.

But I was much more used to running than Aimi was. I was punished for it all the time.

A thrush sang in the trees above us, and I slowed to a walk as I listened, letting Aimi get her breath back.

I opened my mouth to make some comment about the bird – and heard a scream.

We jerked to a halt, Aimi catching her balance on one of the trees. The screaming voice was cut off as suddenly as it had started, but I had already recognized it. It was the little serving girl Chou. The iciness touched my back again, colder and more insistent this time. I looked up through the dancing leaves and flowers at the blue sky, as if there might be reassurance there.

A cold voice spoke inside me: *Something is wrong...*

"An accident?" Aimi asked. Her fingers tightened on mine.

"I don't know. Come on."

We ran properly now, our hands still clasped. The thrush was still singing, but now there were other noises. Noises that made my mouth dry.

Metal clashing. Horses screaming. People crying out.

My father's voice, raised in anger.

I ran faster, almost towing Aimi along, but she held me back when I would have burst out of the trees onto the open area of moss and flat stepping-stones before the house.

"Let go—" I began angrily, but Aimi pressed her

clammy fingers over my mouth and shook her head, eyes wide. She put her face close to mine and whispered, "We mustn't make a sound."

I took a deep breath and nodded. She took her hand away from my lips, and together we crept around the edge of the orchard, keeping behind the thick tree trunks.

Our few servants were nowhere to be seen and the human screaming had stopped. I could still hear, distantly, the sound of whinnying and kicking from the stables. Someone was hurting the horses. Why?

So we cannot get away, said the cold voice. My stomach turned.

We stopped dead when we saw the black-clad soldiers ranged by the side of the house. Their horses were tethered at one of the long stone garden basins.

Aimi made another shushing gesture, and I nodded. I could not have spoken now if I had wanted to. Where was my father?

What had they done to him?

As if in answer, I heard his voice again. He was shouting. He never shouted.

"This is ludicrous!"

Two soldiers dragged him into view. They held his arms bent painfully behind his back; his tall, lean frame and pale grey kimono made him look weak and vulnerable between the black-clad men. My heart seemed to struggle in my chest, fighting against my ribs just as Father fought against their hold.

The leader of the troop, with his white-feathered helmet, made a movement with his hand, and the two men forced Father down to his knees and held him there.

"You are Hoshima Daisuke-san?" the leader said, formally, emotionlessly.

"You know who I am." Father bit the words out, his eyes burning like coals in his white face. "I want to know exactly what I have been accused of and who has laid the charges, so that I may defend myself. I am innocent, and I intend to prove it."

"You have been found guilty." The leader's voice was final. He nodded at the men holding Father, and they released his shoulders. Father sprang to his feet.

The leader unwrapped a bundle in his hands and held it out to Father. Father recoiled as if the man had offered him a hissing snake.

I bit deeply into my lip, whimpering. It was Father's katana. I recognized the green wrapping on the hilt. They wanted him to kill himself, to commit seppuku with his own sword.

That was the way a man died when he had been utterly dishonoured. When he had forsaken his house. When the only way to regain his honour was to destroy himself.

It was a traitor's death.

They were accusing Father of plotting against the Moon Prince.

"Oji-san," Aimi whispered, her voice breaking.

"I refuse," said Father, proudly. "I am innocent."

"Very well." The leader dropped Father's sword as if it were trash.

One of the men unsheathed his own sword. Sunlight gleamed on the blade as he lifted it. Father did not see. He was still staring at the leader.

I wrenched my hand away from Aimi's and stumbled forward, screaming, "Father! Look out!"

He turned as he heard me, his face filling with relief. His lips moved as if to speak my name.

The sword behind him flashed out. I screamed again, a cry of horror, as Father crumpled to the ground.

"Get the girl," the leader ordered.

The soldier who had killed my father took a step towards me, bloodied blade still drawn.

"Run!" Aimi reached out from behind the tree and grabbed my hand, crushing my fingers with the urgency of her grip. "They're going to kill us. Run, Suzume!"

She dragged me with her, running under the cover of the trees. After a few faltering steps, my legs began to work and I caught up with her.

"Father … Father…" I sobbed. I turned my head, stray strands of hair whipping across my face. The black-armoured soldiers were coming after us, spreading through the trees like monstrous shadows, petals scattering across their path.

"Don't look," Aimi panted. "Don't look—"

There was a low whistling noise, and something flashed past my face.

Aimi grunted. Her fingers spasmed around mine, then slipped away as she sagged down onto the grass.

A black fletched arrow protruded from her back.

She did not move. Her hand lay in the grass like the brittle white branch of a dead tree. She did not move. There was another whistle. An arrow thudded into the tree trunk next to my head. I did not blink. I could not look away from my cousin, my sister, my friend.

Something shifted inside me. It was like a candle flickering to life. Suddenly I was very hot, and the sunlight was very bright, and everything was slow, as if the world had stiffened. I turned to look at the soldiers, and they seemed frozen in that bright, hard light, like insects trapped in amber.

Heat thrummed under my skin, pulsing, demanding to be let out, making me twist and bend with the strength of it.

"Run!" Aimi had said. *"Run, Suzume!"*

I must run.

As if a star had exploded in my mind, I knew it. I pulled the heat and the brightness out, drew them around me like a cloak. They surrounded me and I felt as though I changed: became small and fleet. My clothes seemed to fall away. My feet were silent on the grass. I was like a hare.

Run, little white hare. Run and run, and no one will catch you.

The trees towered around me. Leaf shadows dappled my naked back. The only sound was the soft hum of my own heart. Black shapes moved around me, but they did not see me. They were too slow.

I ran.

Soon I was out of the trees again and by the squat, brick-built kitchen. It was set a little way from the house. My house.

As I saw it, I seemed to burst upwards, out of the small, silent place, and suddenly there was noise again, and fear. Men shouted behind me. My breath rasped. I was shaking, exhausted, as if I had run a hundred miles, and my mind was fogged with grief.

All I knew was that I had to hide.

I went through the open doors of the kitchen. The interior was dark and deserted. The fires had gone out. The massive, low stove, built of stones and clay, sat in the centre of the room.

I went down on my knees, the packed earth floor ripping away skin as I scrambled into the biggest hearth. I burrowed into the ashes. Sparks glowed around me like dying orange suns. They burned and stung my hands, my arms, my back, my belly. Black debris rose around me like a pall of smoke.

The space inside the fireplace was just big enough to hold me, if I curled up, pressing legs tightly to my torso, burying my face in my knees.

I closed my eyes and waited.

Two

The ashes settled around me, drifting over my skin with feather-light touches. The heat in the stove's clay walls made sweat trickle down my back and legs and sting the burns. Outside, the soldiers' voices grew louder, closer. My throat scratched, and I bit down on my already bitten lip, trying to stifle the cough with pain.

"Search that place." It was the leader's voice.

I cowered, curling myself into a tighter ball.

Metal clinked and heavy footsteps crossed the dirt floor towards the stove. My muscles twitched and shuddered, like a chicken with its neck wrung. My throat burned. I dug my teeth in harder, trying to hold my breath.

"That little—!" a deep voice suddenly spat. "Where is she?"

Footsteps moved closer. I saw again the bright red spurting from Father's neck. I saw the arrow sticking out of Aimi's back. I waited for the man to see me, to hear me. I waited to die.

The ashes seemed to sigh, moving, surging up and swirling into a thick, furry blanket. Their darkness settled over me, concealing the whiteness of my skin. They stroked me soothingly, as if to say: *It is all right. Do not fear.*

The soldier swore again, as if in surprise. There was a resounding slap, a heavy thud, as if someone had fallen.

"Where were you hiding, old man?"

The answer came from near by, as if the speaker was lying on the ground too. The voice was weak and quavering with fear. "I—I was not hiding, honoured soldier-sama. My apologies. I always sleep behind the stove."

"Where is the girl? The little one? She must be in here; there's nowhere else." There was another harsh thud and a choked grunt of pain. "This house has the mark of the traitor on it, do you understand? We can kill anything that moves here, right down to the fleas in your bed. If you lie to me, I'll slit you open."

"I—I do not know — no, no, wait! Perhaps ... perhaps I can help you." The old man gasped painfully.

I squeezed my eyes shut.

"I heard that the younger girl is punished sometimes for climbing and hiding in the orchards." He wheezed again. "She is very small, and the trees are in bloom…"

In my hiding place, I jerked with shock. I hated heights. I had never climbed a tree in my life. The old man was protecting me.

The mantle of ashes seemed to tighten, as if in warning.

The soldier drew in a sharp breath. "That must be it. No wonder she seemed to disappear. Search the trees!" he shouted out. "She must be hiding in the flowers!"

Hasty footsteps crossed the floor, and the door banged open and shut.

There was another pained wheeze and a shuffling noise, and the old man's voice came again, much closer this time. "Little Mistress, come out. You must hurry. They will come back soon."

"Than–thank y–you," I choked out. I scrabbled at the rough ground, pulling myself forward against the drag of stiff, protesting limbs. A hand, dirty and calloused and wiry with muscles, thrust into the hearth to help me. As he dragged me out of the tiny space, I felt the strange blanket of ash flutter and fall away.

The old man was surprisingly broad and strong looking but bent with age. His hair was wispy silver and his eyes bright. He was nearly as covered in ashes as I was.

Before I could feel shamed at kneeling there, naked, before the stove – and it was blurry now, what had happened to my clothes – he shrugged off his filthy outer *haori* and put it around my shoulders. The man grimaced with pain at the movement. He had taken so many kicks lying before my hiding place, lying to protect me.

"I'm so sorry," I said, clutching the *haori* to me. It covered me from neck to knees. My voice was a low, toneless croak. "Are you all right?"

"I will live. Can you stand? We must find a better hiding place."

I nodded, though I was not sure. Supporting each other and terribly conscious of the time it took, we both managed to gain our feet.

"This way," he said, moving ahead of me. To my surprise, he seemed to be leading me into the blank wall of the kitchen.

"This is where the cook hides most of the ingredients, in case of a theft," the old man said. He slipped sideways and somehow disappeared into the wall. I lurched after him, scared of being left behind, and found that this wall had been built about a foot out from the real, outer wall. The narrow space between was filled with boxes, bottles and sacks. It was just wide enough for a man to sit down – or a man and a small girl, if they were desperate.

We crushed ourselves inside. The only light came from the slim gap through which we had entered; we had no candles and would not have dared to light them if we did. We worked by feel, bumping elbows and stubbing toes as we shoved boxes and sacks up, blocking the entrance as best we could and clearing a space in the corner, while trying desperately to be quiet.

"What is your name?" I asked him.

"Youta. I am the cinderman," he whispered, spreading empty sacks on the floor and then lowering himself onto them with a sound of effort. I huddled down next to him.

"Thank you, Youta," I said.

"Hush, now. They could return at any time. We must be silent."

He was right. Twice more that day, soldiers came into the kitchen. We heard their cursing and swearing when they could not find us, and the smashing and crashes as they destroyed anything they could find in their fury.

After the second time, Youta whispered to me, "It must be close to nightfall. They will have to make camp here now. Try to sleep."

I could not. I knew I could not. I was too frightened to even close my eyes, in case I saw what had happened again, saw it in my head.

But after a time my exhaustion must have sucked me under, for I woke I knew not how long later, a scream of mindless panic on my lips. Instinctively I swallowed it. Youta was just settling back down beside me.

"Where did you go?" I asked, my fingers reaching to clutch at his ragged clothes. I was ashamed of my behaviour but could not stop. He was the only person I knew now, and I was terrified of being alone.

"To see if they had left. It is morning, but the horses are still there. We must stay hidden."

For another day we lived in the tiny space, until the

air inside was barely breathable with the stink of us and our dirt. Youta broke open some of the boxes and sacks, and made me eat, though the sight of food made me sick, and I gagged when I tried to swallow. The only liquid was alcohol, which set fire to my throat without soothing my thirst. It sent me swiftly back to sleep.

I woke to the sound of people shouting near by again. I pressed closer to Youta, trembling.

Then I recognized one of the voices.

"Suzume! *Suzume!*"

It was my mother's voice.

I leapt up, sending boxes and sacks flying, skinning my hands on the rough floor again as I clambered out of the alcove.

"*Mother!*" My voice was a dry, scratchy whisper, but I kept trying. "Mother! I'm here!"

My legs, folded under me for so long, could barely support me. I stumbled out of the kitchen, eyes closing against the sunlight. Hot tears streamed down my face.

A slender blue form, rippling with my tears, raced through the trees towards me. I held out my arms, like a baby begging to be picked up, and was caught in a familiar embrace, enveloped in a familiar perfume, and held tightly and kissed. My legs gave out, and she sagged to the ground with me, not letting go.

"Oh, my baby, my only baby," she whispered. "I thought you were dead."

"Aimi," I said. "Father."

"I know, I know," she said, voice distorted with tears. "Hush, now, hush."

"They killed—"

"Hush, hush, don't speak of it."

I was seized with dry, raking sobs that shook my whole body. Mother rubbed my back and stroked my ashy hair, and whispered over and over, "Hush, it's all right now. You're safe now. Hush."

"She's … she's really alive," a man's voice said above us.

I stiffened, then slumped in relief when I realized the deep voice belonged to Terayama-san, one of Father's oldest friends. In my confusion I did not wonder why he was there, what he was doing with my mother.

"It is a blessing from the Moon," Mother said.

"Is she injured?"

I shook my head against my mother's shoulder, unable to look up. "I am not hurt."

"What happened here?" Mother implored him. "Daisuke—" Her voice trembled and cut off.

"Things are worse than you know," Terayama-san said. "This was no random attack. The soldiers came from Tsuki no Ouji-sama."

"They wore black armour," I mumbled. "They called Father a traitor."

"*What?*" Mother pushed me back, taking my shoulders and shaking me hard. "What did you say? How dare you say that!" I thought she would strike me.

"Yukiko-san, the child is right," Terayama-san said, dropping to his knee next to us. His massive shoulders blocked the sun enough so that I could squint at him, and make out the grave, unhappy lines on his handsome face. "I have seen the black crest nailed to what is left of the door. The mark of the traitor is on the Hoshima house."

Mother stared at Terayama-san as if he were the traitor. "Daisuke would never—!"

"I know that," he said. "He was my friend. But it does not matter. The mark is there. The House of Hoshima and all who lived here are forsaken. If anyone offers you shelter or comfort now, their lives are forfeit. If anyone ever finds out who you are, they will have to report you, or risk sharing your fate."

We both stared at him, shocked into stillness by the stark reality of his words. We had lost everything. Everything. We had no place to live, no way to support ourselves. We were completely alone. Outcast.

"The Royal Guard do not forgive traitors, ever. They butchered everyone here, even the servants. The only person who could spare your lives is the Moon Prince himself, and it is his seal upon the door, his order that you be executed. It is a miracle that the girl survived," Terayama-san went on. "It is a miracle that you were with me and not—"

Mother stiffened again and spoke swiftly, to cut him off. "What are we to do, Terayama-san? Where will we go, Suzume and me? Will … will you abandon us?"

31

"How can you even ask it?" he said, low and fierce. There was a throb of emotion in his words that made me cringe in shock. I had never heard him speak like that before. His eyes flicked to me, barely seeing me, and returned to Mother as if he could not help himself. "You must come with me, back to my home. We will change your name, make up some story to allow it. The mark means nothing to me."

"Ryoichi."

She said his name as if it hurt her and I was shocked again. I had never heard her speak so informally before, without using surname or honorific. She had never spoken to him so in Father's presence.

"Please," he said, and it was a true plea. "Come with me."

Mother's eyes closed. She nodded once.

His face lit up. In that unguarded moment I saw triumph in his eyes. And something more. Something I could not name – a sort of hunger that was as hot as fury. I dropped my gaze as if that look had burned me, thankful that he seemed to have forgotten I was there.

When I peeked next, his face was composed again, solemn and sad, as if the other look had never been.

"We must leave at once," he said, standing. "This is a cursed place now. I want to be off the lands before nightfall." He reached down to help us both to our feet.

My legs wobbled as I rose, and he steadied me. "Careful," he said, holding onto my shoulders. I did not want to meet his eyes again. I looked past him, at the squat beehive-shaped kitchen.

Youta stood there, in the doorway. *Youta!* How could I have forgotten him, after everything he had done for me? We had nearly left him behind.

I opened my mouth to call out to him, to tell Mother and Terayama-san of my saviour.

Youta shook his head and put his finger to his lips. I hesitated, mouth still open, and he bowed to me, wincing at the pull to his poor ribs and stomach. Then the shadows of the kitchen seemed to shimmer and darken around him, and he was gone.

Three

We travelled for four days to reach Terayama-san's estates. The journey, unprepared as we were, should have pushed us hard, but somehow it was all very easy for Mother and me. Mother explained that she had called on Terayama-san on her way home from her aunt's, and he had escorted her back to Father's lands. He had provided a palanquin, carried on the shoulders of six of his men. And that was why they had arrived together.

I barely listened to Mother's words through my haze of exhaustion and grief; I could not think why she was telling me something about which I cared so little. When I saw the palanquin, though, it was so grand that I could not help but wonder at it.

It was gilded on the outside – the expense of which was beyond my imagination – and shining with newness.

Fit for a princess. The hangings, cushions and silks inside were all in Mother's favourite shades of blue and silver. It was almost as if it had been designed and built just for her.

But how could that possibly be?

We hardly spoke to each other during those four days. I wanted to; I wanted to spill everything out, to tell Mother what had happened to Father and the servants and Aimi, what had happened to me. I wanted to tell her what I had seen and how I felt. The feelings bubbled up in my throat, burning like acid in my mouth, desperate to be expressed.

Only Mother would not let me speak. She shushed me, and told me I did not need to remember – but I could not help remembering. She stroked my hair or held my hand tenderly and whispered, "I know, I know," – but she did not know.

She was not there.

No one knew except me.

The only time Mother asked me a question about that day was when she realized, as I climbed into Terayama-san's shining palanquin, that not only was I filthy and covered in ash but also half naked. She bundled me inside, slammed the golden door and drew down the silvery silk hangings at the windows.

"Suzume, where are your clothes?" Her voice had gone shrill and tight.

"I–I don't know," I said. As I tried to recall, my forehead

began to ache. Everything else that had happened was horribly, painfully, clear in my mind, but as I tried to remember how I had lost my kimono, how I had fled from the soldiers, there was just a blank. "I think," I said slowly, "I think I had to take them off to run. They were getting in the way."

"Is that all?" she demanded. "The soldiers did not take your clothes?"

"No. They did not catch me. If they had, I would be dead, like—"

Mother put her arm around me, cutting me off with "It is all right. We will not speak of it any more. Just remember, Suzume, that you should never do such a thing. Never shed your clothes like that again. It is not decent."

Better naked and alive than decent and dead, I thought. Then all the defiance went out of me, and I cried and cried, the weight of sorrow pressing down on me until I could barely breathe. Mother covered me with blankets and stroked my hair, and shush-shush-shushed me whenever I tried to speak.

I could not stop being afraid. Tiny sounds, like a horse whinnying, or one of Terayama-san's men unexpectedly coughing, would send me into a paroxysm of shivering. I had to squash myself into a ball in one corner of the palanquin and bury myself in blankets, unable to blink, to move, to make a sound, in case it sent me back there, back to that place of death.

It was unreal to me, that journey. Like a dream, or a

nightmare. Nothing was right. Mother petted and cosseted me as she had never done before – at least, not since I was tiny. Yet at the same time she seemed always distant, preoccupied, as if she was constantly straining to hear something I could not, see something I could not. Was it fear that occupied her, as it did me? Fear of the future that awaited us, or of the black-clad soldiers?

The only time Mother seemed to come back to herself was in the evenings, once the palanquin had been safely deposited on the ground and Terayama-san's men had made camp. Terayama-san would visit the palanquin then, sharing our evening meal and talking to us about his plans to ensure our safety.

We were to take the name of Nakamura, a name that belonged to a distant branch of the Terayama family. We would be a widow and her daughter who had fallen on hard times and had written to Terayama-san for assistance.

I could tell Mother did not like that. It wounded her pride to think that she, the beautiful Yukiko, descendant of the House of Yoshinaga, should take the role of poor relation. That was, after all, the role she had made so uncomfortable for Aimi.

I surprised myself with the bitterness of that thought, and swiftly forced it away. Of course she was uncomfortable taking on another name and playing the role of a different person. So was I.

I could not understand how such a lie would even

be possible. It was true that Terayama-san always visited Father, rather than the other way around, and that I had never been to Terayama-san's estate. But Mother had only just been there – would not all the servants know her as Hoshima Daisuke-san's wife? They could not have forgotten so soon, surely? Unless ... unless Mother had not visited Terayama-san at his estate. Unless they had been somewhere else ... alone ... together?

Such thoughts made me feel ill, and, forcing them from my mind, I kept my objections to myself. I was keeping most things to myself by that time. Since Mother would not let me talk about the things I so desperately wanted to, it seemed easier not to speak of anything. I was surprised at how easy it was to live in silence. Overnight I had turned from a twitterbird into someone who could hardly find the words for good morning.

Soon, I told myself. Soon we will be safe at Terayama-san's house. Soon she will let me speak, and we will mourn together. Soon.

On the last night of the journey, Terayama-san came to visit us as normal. But instead of entering, he passed in the trays of food to Mother and then beckoned her to the door of the palanquin.

They spoke in low voices. Terayama-san reached out to touch the hand that rested on the frame of the door. She jerked it away as if he had given her a static shock, but as their conversation continued, her hand gradually crept back to its original position, and the second time he touched her, she turned her hand so that their fingers entwined.

Terayama-san's smile flashed, brilliant white, over Mother's shoulder. "Suzume-chan, I must speak to your mother privately for a few moments," he said, leaning in. His words were for me, but his eyes never left Mother. For an instant I was reminded of the intent, unblinking stare of a cat waiting at a mousehole. I shuddered.

"Try to eat something while I am gone," said Mother – and she did look back at me, but only for an instant.

He helped her to step out, and the door closed behind them.

I could only manage a few mouthfuls of food. I was frightened to be alone, with the noises outside and the light getting dimmer and dimmer. My feebleness disgusted me. Who was this trembling idiot of a girl? How had such a weak, stupid little creature survived when others – so much braver, cleverer and more lovely – had not? But the fear lay on me like a second skin, smothering and cold. I fumbled to light one of the lamps, and then, burrowing down under layers of pillows and furs, sang to myself, my voice tiny and wobbling, until I finally fell into an uneasy sleep.

I woke later to find the lamp extinguished. Moonlight fell through the piercings in the window screens, splashing silver onto Mother's back as she lay curled up on the opposite side of the palanquin.

I thought she was asleep. Then I heard a muffled

noise – an unfamiliar noise. A sob. She was crying. I shifted onto my side, groaning a little with the effort, as I reached out to her. She stiffened, her narrow shoulders hunching up defensively, as if she expected a blow to fall.

I hesitated, my hand curling into a fist. Then I settled back down, snuffling a little, as if I had only been moving in my sleep. She sighed – in what sounded like relief – and I saw furtive movements as the tears were wiped quickly away. Then, pulling a pillow closer, she turned onto her back. I closed my eyes, so no telltale gleam of moonlight falling on my face would give me away.

She sighed again and gave an odd, hiccuping little laugh. And said Terayama-san's name.

I pressed my knuckles to my mouth and bit down. The sound of my mother's voice in that moment made me want to flee, to hide in some silent, safe place far away. I wanted to run, but there was nowhere to go. *What was happening?*

My eyes stayed open for a long time that night, long after Mother's slow, deep breathing told me sleep had claimed her. I fixed my eyes on the pale blur of her dreaming face and tried to tell myself I had nothing to fear.

Four

My new room was high on the second floor. I had never even been in a house that had more than one floor before. I had a balcony, and when I pushed back the screens, I could look out over the still green lake, or the forested hills. If the view bored me, I could walk in Terayama-san's enormous gardens, where there were ferny streams with half-moon bridges and ponds with white koi darting in the shadows.

I had a maid of my own. Her name was Mai, and she was five years older than me, and moved as quietly and quickly as those white fish. Each morning and each evening, Mai would brush my hair without snagging a single strand and hum gently to herself. I would listen to her soft voice and wonder if, somewhere deep inside, she was screaming too.

It had been real. I *had* been real. I knew what had happened. I saw it whenever I closed my eyes.

Yet I had no proof. No one but me had seen. No one but me seemed to care.

In that quiet, golden mansion, surrounded by strangers, I felt as if my old life had never existed. As if the low, thatched house, drowsing among the apple and cherry trees, had been no more than some odd fantasy, and my dear, beloved father and cousin had never even lived, let alone died in front of me. Had I really screamed and wept and run and hid? Had I really been Hoshima Suzume, of the tangled hair and untidy obi and skinny, bruised legs?

That me – the real me – was trapped in a dark place behind my eyes. Nakamura Suzume was in command of my mouth and my body.

Nakamura Suzume was quiet and respectful. She did not run or click her tongue or get into mischief. She lowered her eyes modestly and blushed. When Terayama-san smiled, she drew the image of Aimi's sweet, innocent face into place over her dry, cold lips and smiled back, for she knew that Terayama-san was all that stood between her and exile and death and darkness, and she was afraid.

When, a mere six weeks after we had arrived at the home of my father's dearest friend, Nakamura Suzume's mother told her that Terayama-san had asked her to marry him, and that her mother had said yes, Nakamura Suzume said, "I am so pleased for you both."

And deep inside, the real Suzume, who had told herself

that such a thing could never happen, that Terayama-san and Mother would never do it, screamed louder and louder.

The morning after I had been informed of their engagement, I had an accident. A silly, clumsy accident, nothing more. As I peeled fruit at breakfast, my knife slipped, opening a long, shallow cut on my palm.

Blood welled up as I stared in shock, and pain sang through my hand. Then there was a rush of ... something. Something like happiness, or peace, or relief. It made me dizzy.

"Suzume." My mother reached round the table and caught my arm. "What have you done?"

"It is nothing," I said, softly.

"Wrap it in this," Terayama-san said, passing me a cloth. He sent the serving woman to fetch a girl from the kitchens who knew how to dress wounds, and when she arrived, she cleaned the cut and applied a salve and assured my mother that it would not scar.

Terayama-san sat back with a nod. "There," he said. "There is nothing to worry about."

"Be more careful," my mother said severely. "You could have—"

"Don't fuss, my dear. Suzu-chan is sorry." I would have been grateful for the interruption, except that he did not look at me, did not see me. He interrupted not because he wished to shield me from Mother's fussing but because he wished all her attention to be his. Skilfully he drew her into a conversation that, as usual, excluded me.

For once I did not listen to them with resentment. I was listening to the quiet inside me. For the first time in weeks, the screaming had stopped.

"I will go to the stables and look at the new mare," Terayama-san announced casually a little while later.

"Then perhaps I should look at the fabric for my new gown..." Mother said, half to herself, a look of secret happiness on her face. I guessed the new gown was expensive. Far more expensive than anything that my father had been able to afford for her.

Terayama-san's eyes sharpened and his face went blank. "Do you not wish to come with me?"

Mother blushed, a little flustered, but not frightened. "Oh! I—I do not pretend to know much of horses. I do not think I would be useful."

"Your opinion is always useful to me," he said, gaze fixed, unblinking. I was reminded again of the cat at the mousehole. Any time Mother displayed a lack of interest in Terayama-san, he acted as if she had challenged him. The more she pulled back, the more he wanted her with him. It was as if it were a game. He stalked his prey carefully, giving it the illusion of freedom without ever truly risking its escape.

When had this game begun? I wondered. In the ruins of Father's house, when Terayama-san had offered so generously to save us? Or before that? Perhaps it had been during Mother's mysterious visit to Terayama-san's house, before she had returned home to find everything destroyed.

The visit she had found time for when she should have been visiting her aunt, or at home with her husband and family celebrating her daughter's birthday. The visit that was supposed to have been here at his house but which none of his servants seemed to know anything about.

"If you would really wish for my company," Mother said finally, smiling and pleased.

She had never looked so at my father. But then, I realized, my father had never wanted her with him when he worked. He had shut himself in his study and demanded complete peace, and Mother had been left to the business of the house alone. The only person who had been allowed to interrupt Father while he worked was me...

At her agreement, the tension left Terayama-san's face. "Of course. Come along, my dear."

They left, Terayama-san holding Mother's arm with a grip that could have been possessive or protective. Alone and with nothing else to do, I decided to take a walk in the garden.

The parasol cast a pink shade over my face as I left the shadow of the house and went into the sun. The garden was very quiet: no servant children running errands or cats sunning themselves. No escaped chickens. Normally the quiet here bothered me, but now I did not let it. I revelled in it. I felt distant, as if nothing could touch me. In this mood, I was able to run back over this morning's scene calmly.

How much of Mother's apparent desire for Terayama-san was fear that, unless she pleased him, he would cast

45

us out and we would starve or be killed? And how much was because Terayama-san flattered her, paid attention to her, demanded *her* attention, as my father had never done?

Was it my place to judge? Terayama-san had saved us. I must try harder to be grateful and fond of him, as Mother expected.

From the corner of my eye I detected a movement, a human movement. This happened rarely enough – Terayama-san's servants were so well trained, they seemed to have the ability to be invisible – that I turned to look. A servant, a bent old man, was framed in a circular opening in the wall that hid the kitchens from the rest of the grounds. He was drawing water from the well there.

My parasol hit the ground and tumbled away in the breeze. I flew down the path and through the circular gate, crying out, *"Youta!"*

My impetuous greeting did not make him drop his wooden pail, or even flinch. He calmly set his burden down and smiled at me. "Little Mistress. You have grown."

"Youta – oh – how … what are you doing here?" I babbled, flustered and out of breath.

He indicated a little stone bench against the wall. "Will you sit with me?"

I laughed as I sat; I was so pleased to see him that I could not keep it in. "I have thought about you. All the time. I hoped you had recovered and were doing well. But I don't understand, Youta. You would not let me tell my mother and Terayama-san about you and what you did, but you came here anyway."

"Ah, well," he said, sitting next to me. "I thought it might be better – simpler – if Terayama-sama did not know the details of what happened."

"*Simpler?* What do you mean by that?" I asked slowly.

"Nothing, really. Sometimes I have feelings that I cannot explain, but I have found it best to pay attention to them. Let us just say that I did not wish for their thanks. I made my own way here and gained employment in the kitchens without telling anyone where I had worked before. Cindermen are not usually required to provide references." He smiled a little.

It seemed presumptuous to ask, but Youta had already hinted at it, and I wanted to know. "Did you come all this way for me?"

"I have an interest in you now, do I not?"

It struck me for the first time that Youta spoke keigo: formal, educated speech. That seemed very strange for a man who worked in the kitchens. I wanted to ask about it, but instinct held me back.

"I thank you," I said at last. "I have no other friends here."

"Except your mother," he reminded me gently.

I laughed again, but this time the sound was harsh and bitter.

Youta reached out – a little hesitantly, I thought – and touched the back of my hand with the tip of his index finger. It left a dark smudge. "I am here," he said. "I sleep in the kitchen at night, and no one else is there. If you ever need me…"

I could not reply. My throat had gone tight. I sniffed and nodded.

He stood, picking up his pail again. "Good day to you, Little Mistress."

He walked back towards the kitchens. I sat for a moment, blinking rapidly, then went to find my parasol.

The feeling of peace stayed for most of the rest of the day, but by breakfast the following morning I could hear the real Suzume starting to talk again, her voice angry and raging. My head ached with trying to ignore her.

After dinner, Mother, Terayama-san and I gathered in one of the rooms overlooking the gardens. They were discussing their wedding trip, talking and laughing – Mother delicately flirting. As the evening went on, a ruddy colour began to darken Terayama-san's cheeks, as if he had been drinking – but he had not. The heat, the hunger, reappeared in his face. Cat. Mouse.

I plucked at the edge of the bandage on my hand. I hardly needed it, really, but Mai had insisted it stay on for another day at least. I pulled at the loose threads, winding them around my fingertips until the ends of my fingers went purple.

Something is wrong between them. She doesn't see it. Doesn't see the look in his eyes – or doesn't care. Doesn't she remember how Father looked at her? Doesn't she remember him, miss him, at all?

"Terayama-san," I said suddenly, trying to drown the screaming out. "May I ask something?"

I looked up from my bandage to see my mother and Terayama-san both staring at me as if they had forgotten I was in the room.

They wish you weren't in the room, the real Suzume said. I pushed her voice away and continued. "I am sorry if I have disturbed your conversation. I was lost in my own thoughts."

"You have not disturbed us," Terayama-san told me. His voice was perfectly friendly, perfectly sincere. His eyes looked through me as if I were rice paper on a screen. "What did you want to ask, Suzu-chan?"

That is not my name! My name is Suzume, and no one, not even my father, ever shortened it.

"Before," I began cautiously, forcing myself to sound calm, "I was very fond of music. I wondered if I might be allowed to take up the shamisen again."

"No," said my mother before Terayama-san could answer. The blunt interjection was so unexpected that we both looked at her with surprise.

"But, Mother, why?"

"You must learn to leave things from the past in the past," she said, "and be happy in your new life instead. You have much to be grateful for. I do not want to hear you speak of it again."

Terayama-san nodded at that, already looking away. "Your mother is right, Suzu-chan."

They went back to their talk as if I had never spoken. A moment later, I stood and left the room.

My feet shush-shush-shushed on the tatami mats as I went down the corridor. I was walking too quickly. Almost running. Mother would have scolded me. But Mother was not here, was she? She was back there, with him, leaving her past behind. Leaving me behind. I would run if I wanted.

I put back the screen to my room, startling Mai, who was kneeling in the corner, folding clothes into a cedarwood chest.

"Nakamura-sama?"

"You may leave," I said coldly. Never would I have spoken to a servant at home like that. Never – before they were all killed. "I do not feel well."

She climbed to her feet, coming forward. "Oh, then I—"

"I do not want help. I want to be alone."

"Yes, Nakamura-sama."

I slammed the screen shut behind her, and went to the square recess in the wall, the bottom part of which was taken up with a cabinet with a sliding door. There was a blue cloisonné vase on top of the cabinet that Mai had filled with delicate, scented golden orchids this morning. I wanted to pick up the vase and fling it across the room, but instead I opened the cabinet and drew out a long box of gleaming cherrywood. Terayama-san's gift to me on the day he and Mother had announced their betrothal.

The box was filled with hair ornaments – *kanzashi* pins and combs: coral, mother-of-pearl, silver, ivory and tortoiseshell. They were more beautiful than anything I had ever owned before. Every time I looked at them I remembered my old favourite with its little white bone flowers, and sliding it into Aimi's hair that morning, and the way that Aimi's hair had swirled in the grass where she had fallen.

My hands shook as I selected a long, sharp pin. How to clean it? I lifted it to my mouth and sucked it, grimacing at the metallic taste.

I held the pin between my teeth as I rolled up my sleeve and selected an area at the side of my elbow, then I touched the now warm pin to the skin and pushed it in.

I hissed, tears springing to my eyes as I dragged the sharp end across my arm. Tiny beads of bright red welled up against the white skin. Then the most glorious sense of relief filled me; I let out a long, ecstatic sigh. I had done it. It worked.

This must be why Moon Priests starved and beat themselves, I thought. The pain did something to you: set you free. Gave you control. I had caused the pain. I had chosen the spot, and I had applied pain. The pain was mine and no one could take it from me. It made me feel … real.

I used one of the cloths set aside for my monthly bleed to wrap my arm. I would remove the cloth before Mai came to help me undress for my bath, and if she noticed the mark, I would say I had caught my arm on something. No one would guess. No one would know. I cleaned the pin, dried it on the edge of my kimono and set it back in the box. My hands were steady now as I put everything away.

How much easier life was once you learned how to lie. I had got into trouble by speaking out of turn, arguing and answering back so many times. Not any more. Now I would do what I wanted, and no one would stop me.

Five

Mother looked beautiful in white. Of course, women always look beautiful on their wedding day. Someone told me that once.

"Terayama-san is a lucky dog."

I didn't blink as the man behind me spoke but kept my eyes on my neatly bended knees as the Moon Priests chanted in low voices and the thick blue incense billowed across the room. Most of Terayama-san's friends seemed to believe that because I was still and quiet, I was also deaf. I was growing used to it, though. If I pretended I did not hear, I did not have to be embarrassed, and that spared me the need to blush. I had never known how to blush until recently. Yet another newly acquired skill.

A second man chuckled. "Lucky? My dear friend, she is thirty at least, and has not a copper piece of her own. Her family are not even well connected. *She* is the lucky one."

"So old? With that face?"

"Oh, she may even be older. Have you seen her daughter? The girl must be fourteen or fifteen."

"There's a daughter? If she looks anything like Yukiko-san, I should have thought he would marry her instead. If he's after an heir, that is."

"Ah, well, there is a romantic story behind it all. Apparently Terayama-san wooed the lady long ago, but she chose another: picked the penniless poet over the wealthy eldest son. From what Terayama-san hints, she soon regretted it, but by then it was too late. So the wise Terayama-san bided his time, watched her from afar, and when the first husband finally had the grace to surrender his soul to the Moon, Terayama-san swooped in and got her straightaway."

"Seems like rather a lot of effort on his part!" The man laughed. "Like a child returning to the festival year after year, trying to win the goldfish prize."

"Precisely. One does wonder if he will be quite so pleased with his bargain once the shine wears off. I pity the woman then."

They moved on to discuss other things while I sat as still as a statue, watching Terayama-san and Mother. They were knelt formally side by side, facing the room; she in the stiff white robes and headdress of a bride, and he in black, with a white *tomoeri* collar that made the skin of his throat glow. They sipped from ceremonial cups of sake as the Moon Priest nodded benevolently at them.

The ceremony was almost over now. The triumph was there on Terayama-san's face for all to see. Mother's face was less easy to read. It was blank, white with nerves or excitement. There was a brilliance in her eyes, though. A glitter, like stars in the deep night sky. Every now and again, her fingers reached out across the little gap between them to gently touch his knee.

She turned her head suddenly to look at me and smiled, an awkward smile of stiff lips and rapidly blinking eyes. I smiled back. My smile was much more natural. It was the one I had stolen from Aimi. Mother nodded and turned her attention back to – I forced myself to think it – her husband. If she looked away from him for too long, he would notice. He always noticed when she was looking at something other than him.

It was so easy to fool her now. Once she had seen through my every excuse, detected my every disobedience. Once I had been unable to keep anything from her.

Once, she had known me.

I could hardly wait to be alone that night, hardly wait for the dinner to be over, so Mother and Terayama-san would climb into their flower-hung palanquin and be borne off on their tour of Terayama-san's lands. When the chattering guests finally departed, Mai accompanied me to my room. It was not thought proper for a maiden to be unattended at night, but while Terayama-san and Mother were off on their wedding trip, I had the power to ban Mai from my room, and I did, sharply.

That night one cut was not enough. I broke open the scabs of other cuts, old wounds that I had made over the past three months, and made new ones, slashing again and again with the curved silver blade I had stolen from Mother's manicure tools. I felt no relief. I heard nothing but the shrill cries inside me.

The blade slipped from my fingers and rolled across the tatami mat, leaving a wet trail behind it. I stared, panting. My throat was dry and sore, and my lungs were tight, as if I had been screaming, but the only screaming had been inside, I was sure of that.

Head swimming, I reached for the blade. There were soft plopping noises as I extended my hand. Fat, dark drops spattered the mats. I stared for a long moment before I realized I was looking at blood. My blood.

It had spilled over my pale pink kimono and snaked down my arms. My hands dripped. The gashes gaped open like red mouths. Too confused yet to panic, I tugged down my long sleeves with weak fingers and wrapped the thick layers of fabric around the wounds.

The pain was coming now. It grew with each movement, throbbing and burning. It cleared my head, and I looked in horror at the mess I had made. I had to clean this up. I had to get rid of the blood, or else everyone would know what I had done. I began to use the edges of the kimono to mop up the sticky trails, but more blood was already trickling down my arms. Wetness pooled at my elbows and dripped onto my legs. My sleeves were soaked. I had not known there was so much blood in me.

There isn't that much blood in you. Not any more.

I needed help.

Youta would help me. He would keep my secret. He was alone in the kitchen at night, he said.

I staggered to my feet, the ground shifting uneasily under me. I could not even put out an arm to catch myself. Keeping upright with an effort, I nudged back the shoji screen with my foot and went unsteadily down the corridor.

The pain in my arms was worse with every moment. They felt molten, as if the flesh might simply drop off the bone. It was merest luck that got me down the stairs and outside without falling.

I pushed open the heavy kitchen door with my shoulder, gasping, "Youta?"

Inside it was empty, only the orange glow of the triple-hearthed stove visible. The walls seemed to loom miles above me. I could not hold myself up for much longer. Darkness threatened at the edges of my vision.

"Youta?"

I am going to die, I thought, and closed my eyes on a surge of relief. *At last.*

Then strong arms wrapped around me. They swung me up, making everything spin and whirl inside my head.

A harsh intake of breath and then a shocked whisper

in my ear: "Little Mistress, what have you done?"

I could not answer. I did not know if I were moving or lying still, or even who was speaking to me. Then one of my arms was lifted up. I whimpered in protest. The sleeve was tugged and then ripped swiftly away from the wounds. I screamed as fire roared up my arm.

The darkness won.

Something was wadded under me in uncomfortable lumps. I stirred, wriggling a little, but I did not have the strength to rearrange myself. I moved one of my arms and cried out when a white-hot pain spiked through it.

"Shh, Little Mistress." A soothing, familiar voice.

"Y–Youta?"

"How do you feel now?"

"I am not sure. What happened?"

"You must tell me that," he said, and he sounded sad.

With an immense effort, I forced my eyes open.

I was lying behind the stove on a tattered bundle of rags that I realized must be Youta's bed. My arms were thickly bound in soft, greyish-white bandages. A lantern was lit now and Youta was leaning over me, his back to the light. His face was too shadowed to make out. I was glad. I was remembering now why I was here, what I had done.

"I didn't mean to…" My voice trailed off.

"To kill yourself?"

"No." But I thought about that sense of relief I had felt the moment I believed I would die, and my denial had no conviction behind it. "I came to you. I came before it was too late."

"Yes, I suppose that is something." He reached across me and I heard clinking and things moving around. "I have made some tea – which you will oblige me by drinking."

He handed me a bowl of fragrant green tea and helped me to sit up, offering his shoulder to lean on. He smelled of sweat and charcoal, and old man. His arm behind me was as solid as a tree branch.

"If you did not mean to end your life, please will you tell me why you cut open your own arms?"

I sipped the tea, though my arms burned and my fingers shook. It gave me an excuse for silence. I had come here for help, and Youta had helped me. Yet I found I still did not want to speak of it.

"It ... was ... an accident..." The words came out slowly and heavily.

He refilled my tea bowl. "You trusted me to save your life. Trust me enough to tell me the truth."

"I need it," I whispered, tea slopping over the edges of the bowl.

Youta steadied my hands.

"I feel – I feel as if I am mad. I am so angry all the time, and so sad, and it screams inside me and never stops. Cutting is the only thing that eases me." I met his eyes pleadingly. "I usually only make a little mark – but ... tonight it was not enough. I did not mean to hurt myself. I swear it."

Youta did not react with shock or disgust. He helped me to lift the bowl to my lips again, saying, "I have heard of such things. Your feelings are natural, Little Mistress. It would be insanity if you were not angry and sad. But instead of being angry and sad with the men who hurt your family, it seems that you are angry and sad with yourself, and that is not right."

"It is not like that. I am not punishing myself. The cutting makes me feel *better*."

"Hurting yourself makes you feel better?"

I bit my lip. It was no use. He had not seen what I had seen. He had not watched them die. No one else could know how I felt.

Youta sighed. "You have made yourself very unwell. So much blood lost. And these wounds will leave scars. It will be hard for anyone to miss what has happened to you."

I went rigid with horror as I realized the truth of what he said. For a moment I wished that I had simply stayed in my room and bled to death.

"I can help you," Youta said, breaking into my spiralling panic.

"How?" I whispered.

"I will assist you back to your room, and clean the blood, and take your *yukata* away to be burned. If, when tomorrow comes, you are too weak to leave your bed, you must feign an illness. Young women of noble birth are notoriously delicate. The important thing is that you rest."

"What about the scars? How shall I hide them?"

"Let me ask you something. When Tsuki no Ouji-sama's men came to your father's house, they pursued you through the orchard. How did you manage to escape so many armed men?"

"I do not know," I said miserably.

"You do," he said, and his definite tone made me look at him in surprise. "Try to remember."

"I don't know," I insisted.

He gave me an impatient look.

I closed my eyes, forcing my mind back to that time of terror. So much fear ... so much pain ... running, seeing Aimi fall and then ... the light. I had reached out into the light, bent it around me like a shield, like a mantle. I had imagined myself invisible.

And I had run past the soldiers and they had not seen me.

"It was not real," I whispered. "It couldn't be."

"If you remember it, why should it not be real?"

That made me blink.

"And in the fireplace," he continued, "it was not really the ashes that covered you. I made a blanket of darkness to hide you from the soldiers, just as earlier you had made a mantle of light. You are Kage Oribito. A shadow weaver. One who can weave illusions from the threads of the world. When faced with death, you instinctively used your talent to save yourself."

"But I—I am not... Such things do not exist," I stammered, shaking my head. "You are speaking of—of magic."

"The skill is real. The men who taught me believed that Kage Oribito are favourites of the Moon, allowed to share in her special gift of concealment; for does she not cloak her face in the shadows of the sky? You may have been using this power in tiny ways, unbeknownst even to yourself, all your life. Or it may never have manifested were it not for those terrible events. I do not know. I do know that what you did was an extraordinary thing. To walk before those men in daylight, unseen, is a feat I could never have achieved, and you might never work such a weaving again. It was the Moon's protection – her gift – that saved you."

A sense of wonder filled me. "How do you know so much about this, Youta?"

"I was not always as you see me now," he said, his eyes turning far away for a moment. "Once I had a different life. I, too, was born with the Moon's gift, though it does not work so strongly in me. As a young man, I was sought out by a group of men and women who had this skill and who made it their mission to find others like them, and train them. It was done in secret, and I was told always to keep it so, except with others of my kind. We are drawn together. No one knows why. Instinctively we find one another. Instinctively we help one another. Perhaps that is another gift from the Moon. I do not know. "

"Then you did come here to find me?"

"Yes. I had to. One day you, too, will feel that *knowing*

and will be compelled to aid other shadow weavers in need."

"So when you said you would help me...?"

"I can teach you to use your skill again. A small illusion to cover your arms should be within your power."

"I have no idea what I did," I said warily. "You call it a skill but, for me, it just happened, as easily as reaching for a blanket in the cold."

Youta carefully drew my right arm out straight. "Watch what I do. Follow me not just with your eyes but with all your senses, and that extra part of you should be able to follow too."

I squinted, tensing as if my muscles could help me to see. At first I saw, felt, nothing. Then there was a strange sensation, not in my arm but in the air around it. A brightening of the light and an intensity of the colours: a sort of stillness in the air. I had an intuitive flash of understanding – I knew what was going to happen – and as the greyish lumps of bandage smoothed out into pale skin, I knew that Youta was right. I *could* do this. I did it all the time.

For weeks, whenever Mother or Terayama-san looked at me, I had been putting on the mask of Aimi's gentle smile without ever realizing what that mask was. A shadow-weaving.

Youta now supported a perfect, unblemished arm in his rough hands. It was not quite my arm. The faint patterns of hair, the tiny lines at the wrist, were subtly wrong. But the bandages were gone.

"Do you understand what I did?" Youta asked.

"Yes!" I said, hearing the surprise in my own voice.

I knew I could do this. In a strange way, it felt the same as picking up my shamisen for the first time. When my fingers had closed on the instrument, I had just known what to do.

I hoped I was better at this than I had been at playing, however.

"Let me try."

Youta laid my right arm down carefully and helped me to hold the other one out straight.

I stared at the lumpy bandages, then closed my eyes and imagined how my arm should look.

I sketched in my mind the skinny wrist, white but flushing to peach near the base of the palm. Faint lines ringed it, and there was a pattern of blue veins just under the surface. As my forearm thickened, the skin did too, hiding the veins. A gleam of soft hair on the other side, and a tiny mole, and then the sharp point of my elbow pushing against the skin. Just as I saw Aimi's smile as a mask, I saw the arm as a close-fitting sleeve that I pulled into place on top of the bandages. I felt a ripple of power, a tingling of pleasure and excitement that reminded me again of holding a musical instrument, and I knew, even before I opened my eyes, that it had worked.

There it was. My arm. Unscarred, unbandaged, mole and all.

"You have a good eye for detail," Youta said.

I touched the weaving gingerly, half expecting to feel skin – but my fingertips found the bandages, which my eyes insisted were not there. The difference made me feel queasy.

"We have the ability to only change what the eye can see," Youta said, noticing my grimace. "A shadow weaver's principle tool is misdirection. You must try to prevent anyone touching your arm, but if they do, simply act normally, and they will usually believe they have imagined it. That is the trick the senses play, you see. People trust their eyes above all else – but most people see what they wish to see, or what they believe they should see, not what is really there. It takes long study or intense desperation to overcome the illusions most of us carry in our own minds."

"Will I need to think about it all the time? To keep it there?"

"As you grow used to it, it will become easier, just as you barely notice the concentration it takes to sit properly, or to read. There are stories – my teachers told me – that at one time shadow weavers could fix their illusions in physical things so that the door in the wall would always be hidden or the piece of twine would always appear as a gold necklace. It was said that they could change the substance of things too: turn a stone into a flower if they wished or simply *wish* a flower into existence. I have never met one of those people, though." Youta smiled.

Hesitantly I reached out, wincing, and laid my small,

white hand on his large, sooty one. "I would be dead twice over if it were not for you. Will you be my teacher, Youta? Teach me to see things as they really are and to create more illusions."

His smile grew wider. "I will teach you everything I know."

Six

What Youta had said was true. Given a choice between what was real – but improbable – and what was false – yet expected – people really did see only what they wished to.

Although I had never been indisposed during the months I had lived with Terayama-san, when I laid in my bed the following morning, groaning that my woman's time had come and that I dare not move for the pain, Mai believed me without question.

The room was darkened, cold cloths were laid on my forehead, and I was left in peace.

Normally lying in bed without anyone to talk to or anything to do would have bored me into a restless rage within half a day. Instead I found myself dozing and daydreaming, too drained for temper. It was four days before I felt well enough to get dressed, and even then I was wan and listless: forced to move carefully for fear of dizzy spells. If my mother had observed my slow, careful movements, she would very likely have approved, all previous attempts to instil grace in me having failed.

Of course, Mother was not there.

The weeks that Terayama-san and my mother were gone should have been a miserable and lonely time for me. I took all my meals alone – except for Mai, sitting watchfully in the corner in case I choked on an eel bone or was attacked by spiders. If I needed something, Mai arranged it – but the sharp efficiency that Terayama-san inspired was notably absent, and I thought the servants must be treating it as a kind of holiday. I did not mind; it felt the same to me.

I read a little, walked in the garden a little, and tried to improve my painting skills once my arms had healed somewhat. Mostly I enjoyed the chance to be ... whatever I wanted to be. If I was sad, I could stare out of the window without guarding my face. If I was cross, I could stamp my way through the garden and throw stones in the river. There was no one to ask me what was wrong or to tell me that I must forget the past, be happy, be grateful.

Once I was strong enough, I made my way down to the kitchens each night, and sat cross-legged on the floor with Youta. I listened to him talk for hours, and he taught me to turn a drifting piece of ash into a fluttering black butterfly, to transform his wispy pale hair into a glossy wave that reached his waist, and to hide him with a cloak of darkness that turned him into nothing more than a shadow. The control necessary to keep my arms concealed soon became second nature to me. I also learnt to pierce Youta's illusions, to detect them and see through them, though I could never see through my own.

If there was a part of me that asked why, with such an astonishing talent, I had made no attempt to save my cousin, my father, my home … I tried not to hear it.

After nearly five weeks had passed, Mai woke me early one morning. Since I spent almost all my nights wide awake and talking to Youta, I normally stayed in bed until nearly midday, and Mai let me. On that day, mid-morning had barely arrived when shaking hands folded back my coverlet, and the screens at the window were pushed away to let in the sun.

"Nakamura-sama, the master and mistress are home. The mistress has sent a message for you to join them; she is anxious to see you."

Mai's face clearly demanded some expression of delight from me, so I smiled and thanked her, and let her dig me from my warm bed, while inside my stomach dropped. It might be disloyal and ungrateful, but seeing my mother suddenly seemed a poor exchange for my solitary peace.

The kimono Mai helped me into was a new one; a soft, pale pink embroidered all over with red and blue chrysanthemums and tiny brown thrushes. The sleeves were long enough to brush the ground as I walked. The obi and obiage that wrapped my waist and ribcage were crimson and pale blue, with patterns of tiny flowers, and a new red obi-jime belt was tied carefully over the top of these. My hair was coiled into a smooth knot at the base of my skull and held in place with more new things, a tortoiseshell-and-gold comb and an elaborate tortoiseshell pin that dangled tiny coral plum blossoms over my right ear.

"The honoured mistress sent these things," Mai told me, obviously giving up on me asking for myself. "She brought them back for you."

"They are beautiful," I said dutifully, but really I was surprised that Mother had thought of me at all on her trip. A sneaking twinge of pleasure found its way into my depression.

When Mai was finished, she helped me to my feet. I stood still a moment, gathering my balance – this had become a habit, even once the dizzy spells had passed – and then gathered my sleeves up carefully so that my hands peeped out and the long ends swept gracefully down to my feet.

"Oh, Nakamura-sama." Mai sighed, and I looked back at her in surprise. She was smiling, her hands clasped at her waist as if she wanted to hug herself.

"Yes?"

"If I may say, Nakamura-sama, you look beautiful."

I remembered a time when a compliment like that from such a lovely woman would have made me jump with glee. Now I just felt sorry for Mai, who cared so much about the surfaces of things. "Thank you, Mai."

She let out a tiny giggle, raising her hand to hide her mouth.

She walked behind me as I left the room. My steps settled into their now customary slow rhythm; it was a habit I had developed during my convalescence so that I would not fall too hard if I suddenly lost my balance. I took a turn in the corridor I had never taken before: the one that led to Terayama-san's rooms.

My breath was coming a little faster, despite my best efforts to appear calm. *I don't care if she wants to see me*, I told myself. *Why should I care? I'm just here because it looks right to have us all together.*

Mai stepped ahead of me to push open a set of shoji screens. Light flooded out, blinding me. I bowed my head rather than trying to squint against it, and when I looked up, my mother was before me.

Her face was flushed mottled pink, as if she was too warm. She smiled, her expression one of pleased surprise.

"You look so different, Suzume," she said. "So … pretty. I am very happy to see you."

All my resentment rushed away. I wanted to fling myself forward and embrace her. With an effort, I forced myself to bow politely.

"Thank you, Mother." I was surprised that my voice was even and calm. "You look very well. I am happy to see you too."

She blinked and her eyes followed the new grace of

my movements. "They told me that you were ill. I wish I had known – but you were probably better off with Mai and the others nursing you. Are you better now?"

"Of course. Thank you."

"Let Suzu-chan into the room, my dear." Terayama-san's voice, warm and amused, made Mother turn. As I stepped inside, I saw him sitting by the open screen at the window. The lake outside was shrouded in rising white mist, and I could see the silver gleam of frost everywhere and the glow of leaves just tinged with autumn colour.

"Your mother has missed you these weeks," he said. His eyes met mine and he smiled – a golden smile that matched his voice. "Come and sit with us, please."

I knelt before Terayama-san, and my mother sat opposite me. They smiled at each other, but it was different to before. The greed was missing from Terayama-san's face. The hungry look was gone. In fact, he was not even looking at her now but at me again. He *never* looked at me. I flicked a glance at Mother and saw her still watching him. She did not look well. I thought she had lost weight. *What has changed?*

"Well, Suzu-chan, you are growing up pretty, are you not?" Terayama-san said. I kept the astonishment and unease off my face, weaving a faint blush into place and ducking my head shyly – that was what Aimi would have done.

"Forgive me for keeping your mother away from you

for so long. I know it was selfish, and you must have missed her very much, but I wanted to take care of her."

"Of course, Terayama-san," I said, my unease growing. "I can only thank you for your kindness."

He laughed again and reached out to pat me on the cheek. The movement was unexpected, and I held myself still through willpower alone. His big, hard fingers were gentle on my face.

"Why did I never notice before how pretty you are?"

Because you never took your eyes off my mother before, I thought. My mother looked just as taken aback as I was. She frowned for a second, then, apparently deciding to be happy about it, smiled too.

"Shall we tell her?" she asked almost childishly, reaching out to touch his arm as he took his hand away from my cheek.

Terayama-san laughed. "Very well."

My mother leant forward eagerly. "Suzume, I am going to have a baby."

I felt my face go slack with shock, and there was nothing I could do about it.

"I intend to move the household to my city house as soon as possible, before the winter storms start. That way your mother can be close to the best surgeons. And there will be plenty of interesting things for a young thing like you to occupy yourself with in the city, hmm? We will have to look into that."

I barely heard him. My gaze was darting between my

mother's stomach and her face.

"Suzume?" She was looking at me, and I could see anxiety clouding her eyes. Had her face always been this expressive? I had once thought her so icy, so difficult to understand.

"Mother..." Without even realizing what I did, my hand reached out across the space between us. Hers rose to meet it, and as our fingers clasped, I felt tears prick my eyes.

I knew my anger, and my black memories, and my bitterness must still be inside me, lurking, waiting, but in that moment, with our fingers linked, I didn't feel them.

"I am going to be a sister," I said, my voice wobbling. "I am so happy. Thank you."

"That's a good girl," said Terayama-san. "Didn't I tell you she'd be pleased?"

"Yes, Shujin-sama," Mother said, using the most reverent term for husband. "You are always right."

Seven

The Terayama household departed in a long line of laden carts and snorting horses that trailed around the edge of the lake like a streak of spilled ink. For the first day or so, I enjoyed being out in the air and the light, doing something different. Then the disadvantages of the situation began to wear on me.

Even though we were now in the open, with fields and forests all around us, there was nowhere to hide. I could not say I would go for a walk in the garden. I could not plead tiredness and lie in my room alone. I was with my mother and Terayama-san all day long. Every day. Being back on my guard again all the time was tiring.

And I missed Youta. Although he was with us, somewhere at the back of the long, trailing caravan, there was no way that I could see him. Not even at night, once we

75

made camp. I slept in a different palanquin from Mother and Terayama-san, but they had given me another servant girl, and both she and Mai were to attend me while I slept.

Worse, Youta had warned me that in a city house there would be many more servants, and so he would be unlikely to be alone in the kitchens at night. I had grown tearful at the thought of saying goodbye to him, but Youta had taken my hands in his and squeezed them.

"I will always be here," he said. "Remember what I have taught you, and if you need me again, I am sure you will be able to make your way to me."

Knowing that Youta was around gave me a warm sense of reassurance, and I clung to it, telling myself that when we got to the city, I *would* find a way to see him, as often as I could.

We travelled for three weeks to reach the shore of the inland sea. There Terayama-san found a ship that would take us to the capital city of the Moonlit Land. It was not a regular passenger ship, but a huge, sleek merchant vessel called the *Row Maru*.

Mother and I watched through the pierced window-screen of the palanquin while boxes, bales and barrels of cargo were loaded alongside corded chests of luggage, many of them our own. Terayama-san stood near the gangplank, talking to a pair of richly dressed men who held folded cloths to their faces, possibly to guard against the strong smell that drifted from the nearby fishing boats.

Small children, bare-chested even in the chill, ran wild around the sailors and passengers boarding, earning coins for running messages and clouts on the ear for getting in the way. The children were ragged and dirty, but they looked as if they did not mind.

One of my long sleeves brushed my nose, and I realized that I was fiddling with the sharp *kanzashi* pin in my hair. I slapped the offending hand back into my lap and clenched it into a fist.

"You seem restless, Suzume," my mother said, not looking up from her embroidery.

"Nervous, perhaps. The ship is big, but the ocean is bigger still."

I had not been impressed by my first sight of the sea. It was a sort of dull greyish strip on the horizon, like an extra bit of land. The stretch of water must be very large, or else it would not go from one side of the horizon to the other, but then the sky did the same, and I saw that every day without getting excited.

"There is nothing to worry about. We will be perfectly safe," Mother assured me. Unspoken – but perfectly audible to me – were the words: *With Shujin-sama*. My attention wandered back out to the wharf, where grey-and-white gulls swooped and dived at the heads of fishermen unloading their catch. The fish were living silver, cascading down out of the nets, and as they tried to steal the treasure, the birds made piercing, mournful cries that I found strangely beautiful.

One gull, perhaps full from an early breakfast, declined to join its fellows and perched on a coil of rope near by. Its cold yellow eyes looked at me as if to assess whether I was food. Somehow it reminded me of Terayama-san, and I looked away. The cries of the other gulls now sounded less mournful and more menacing.

Suddenly there was a cry. Not human but animal, high and ringing. Mother and I both jumped. I leant forward, pushing the pierced screen out from the window, and saw another bird plummet from the sky. It was moving too quickly for me to see it clearly.

Before I could make out more than a colour – a dark slate blue – it plunged directly into the flock of gulls, and to my astonishment, the gulls, some of them nearly twice its size, scattered with harsh cries.

The slate-blue bird soared up, unmolested, with one of the smaller gulls dangling from its claws. The fishers dropped their nets and whooped and clapped at the sight.

"What is it? What is that noise?" Mother asked, clearly fighting the urge to gape out of the window herself.

I blinked, trying to make sense of something so strange and wondrous. "I … I don't know. It's a bird of prey – it attacked the gulls that were diving at the poor fishermen. It killed one. How could it kill a bird so much bigger than itself?"

The triumphant scream came again, and, turning, I saw the bird hover for a moment, its dark, pointed wings spreading to reveal white underparts barred with black.

Then it dropped the body of the dead gull onto the deck, almost at the fishermen's feet, and swooped away.

"It was as if it knew what it was doing. How is that possible?" I said, after telling Mother what I had seen.

"Ah. I knew I recognized the sound." She had picked up her sewing again.

"Do you mean that funny scream it made? It sounded like an owl. Only louder."

"When I was younger, many noblemen hunted with hawks and falcons. My cousin raised one from an egg. It was his pride and joy. But those birds went out of fashion; it was said the Moon Princess wouldn't have any animals at court. I haven't seen a tame falcon for years."

"A tame falcon? Like a pet? Do you think that is what it is?"

"I don't know," she said, rather impatiently. "You said it attacked the birds who were harassing the fishers."

The bird was circling now, its body just a dark shape against the clouds. It kept disappearing and reappearing as it passed between the intricate web of rigging and sails on the *Row Maru*. Then, more quickly than I could blink, it darted down and vanished. Where had it gone? Onto the ship?

"Come away from the window," Mother said. "It is ill-bred to be hanging out like that. You are not a child any more, Suzume."

I obeyed reluctantly, my thoughts staying with the flicker of bluish wings. Was its owner aboard the *Row*

Maru? I hoped so. If he was, I might get the chance to see the unusual creature again.

Shortly afterwards, Terayama-san returned to the carriage to tell us it was time to board. There was an air of tension about him – a tension that came not from anger but, I thought, from excitement. When he took Mother's arm to help her step up onto the gangplank, she winced, as though his fingers squeezed too tight.

One of the household men walked beside me, ready to catch me if I looked likely to tip off either edge of the narrow boarding plank.

"It is an incredible coincidence that they're taking this ship too." Terayama-san was speaking to my mother up ahead, his voice low and quick. "I am told they come from a country on the continent, and that their ruler has already been a guest at the Moon Prince's palace. There is to be a trade agreement – they have incredible amounts of gold but want timber and livestock from us. If I can make their acquaintance before anyone else at court, it will be a tremendous opportunity, not just in terms of money but also influence."

So that was why he was excited. Was this really a coincidence? Or were the foreigners the true reason we were taking the *Row Maru* instead of a proper passenger ship? I had read in one of Father's books that a man cannot be faulted for ambition – and Father had always said that his friend had enough for both of them.

I wobbled a little as one of my sandals caught in a

rough place on the gangplank, and grabbed at the servant to keep my balance. Suddenly that coppery foam below seemed far too close. I teetered for a moment, then drew in a breath of relief as I steadied.

Only then did I notice that the household man was not looking at me. In fact, although I was clutching his shoulder hard enough to bruise, he hadn't lifted a hand to help me.

His attention was riveted above me – over the heads of my mother and Terayama-san, who had both frozen too. As the shortest of the group, I had the worst view of the men they were all staring at.

I could only see them from the shoulders upwards as they walked slowly past the boarding area, but that was interesting enough. Their skin was *dark*. Not dirty dark, or tanned dark, but the deep brown colour of a piece of fine cherrywood. Their faces were shaped differently too, with prominent cheek- and jawbones and full lips.

Their hair was long and black, like everyone's I knew, but it was fluffy – no – fuzzy, like lambswool, and gathered into sort of ropes that fell down from knots or braids at the back of their heads. Golden ornaments, bells, charms and beads clinked and tinkled in those ropes of hair as they moved.

But the most interesting thing about the men – to me, anyway – was their scars. Each man had a pattern of scars on his face. On the closest, I could just make out dots and whirls and long, straight lines that scored foreheads and cheeks and glowed dark blue against warm brown skin.

These must be Terayama-san's rich foreigners; and they really were foreign, the strangest people I had ever seen. The men did not glance down at us. A sign of masterly self-control, since they must have felt our astonished stares.

Only one of them broke rank and turned his head. He was the youngest and the smallest. I could only just see him over Mother's shoulder. The marks on his cheeks were like storm clouds.

His eyes flickered over us all with what seemed like impersonal interest, but when his gaze met mine, his expression changed. I could not have named any one emotion that crossed his strange, beautiful face. A sort of recognition, perhaps? I felt I ought to respond but did not know how. Then a tiny smile twitched at one corner of his mouth and I was unable to contain the answering smile that crossed my lips.

One of the other men looked back and said something in a language I did not understand. The boy, for he was no more than a boy, turned his head abruptly and hurried after the rest.

I drew in a deep, slow breath. That was … odd.

The moment the men were out of sight, Terayama-san began talking to Mother again, his voice lower now. He glanced back at me briefly, eyes calculating, as if he too had noticed the strange look that passed between me and the foreign boy but did not know what to make of it.

The household man came back to himself with a start and, realizing that I was hanging onto him for dear life, looked mortified. He caught my arm and led me the rest of the way onto the ship with such tenderness and such deep protestations of regret for his inattention that I was worried he might cry. I turned my sweetest and most forgiving smile on him, while inside I wished him far, far away. I wanted to think about what I had seen. I wanted to remember those odd men and the boy's knowing smile.

They wear their scars on their faces. Right there on their faces. Where everyone can see...

Eight

Mother retched into the basin one last time and then fell back onto the futon. I brushed the sweaty hair from her forehead and wiped her face with a cool cloth. Her low moan might have been a thank-you. The ship rolled gently. I put my hand down on the floor to steady myself, and Mother groaned again.

"Shall I ask Terayama-san to fetch the ship's doctor?" I asked, already knowing the answer.

"Don't be silly," she rasped. "This is the way when women are having children. Especially if they are on a boat. There is nothing to worry about."

I was not so sure. Mother had been like this since the first night, but her illness grew steadily worse the longer we were on board ship. For the last week, I had barely been able to leave her side, and today she could not seem to keep even water down. The captain had told Terayama-san that at the very least we had four days left of our voyage.

"Then do you think you could get up for a little while? Walk on the deck, perhaps?"

"No, no." She tossed her head restlessly. "That doesn't work any more. Watching the water go up and down just makes the little one angrier."

One of her hands caressed her slightly swollen belly, gentle and soothing, even though her fingers shook from the latest bout of sickness. I propped the bowl of cool, lemon-scented water between my knees, to keep it from sliding as the ship rocked, and began wiping her face again, mimicking the slow movements of her hands on her stomach. The wooden walls and floors creaked and settled around us.

Then her face creased. I yanked the basin forward as she rolled over again and began to retch. There was nothing in her stomach now. She convulsed in horrible dry spasms for several minutes, silent tears running down her face, before lying back again and hiding her face in the sheet.

"I think I am done, for now," she croaked.

I pushed the basin away, rang out my cloth and laid it carefully on the back of her neck, untangling the long strands of her hair.

"Would you like me to tell Terayama-san that he can come back in?"

"Not just yet." She sounded a little sleepy now. I smiled with relief. I was not entirely immune to the seasickness, and the heat and the smell of sweat and vomit in the little cabin were more than enough to make my own stomach heave when the ship rocked. I desperately wanted to get out and breathe some clean, cold air.

Everything would have been a lot easier if the female servants who were supposed to look after Mother were not both prostrate with seasickness too. I did like being useful and feeling that I had a purpose and something to do. Still, there were times when, if I was to be fit to look after anyone, I needed to get away.

As quietly as possible, I shifted my kimono and began to stand up. Before I could get any further, Mother stirred again. "Where are you going?" she mumbled.

I kept a sigh inside with an effort. "I just want to clean things up a little bit."

"Not yet," she said as she pulled the cloth off her neck and rolled over. Her face, though sweaty and pale, still managed a smile. I fidgeted a little, anxious to get away but anxious not to let her know it.

"Are you feeling better?" I asked hesitantly, thinking that if I had been sick as many times as she had in the past eight days, I would probably never smile again.

"Not really. It's all right, though, Suzume. My mother told me once that the more illness the mother suffers, the better the baby will grow. She was terribly ill with me, and I was a big healthy child. I barely knew that I was carrying you, and look how small and delicate you have always been."

"It seems a heavy price to pay," I said without thinking. "I'd rather have a small baby."

Mother reached out to squeeze my wrist, and I wished I could call the words back. She was not angry, though. She made a little laughing noise and shook her head.

"You'll change your mind soon. When you have a baby of your own, you will realize that a mother is willing to put up with anything for a healthy child. Anything at all. It is what we are made for, to carry children. A woman cannot really be happy doing anything else."

I kept my face still with an effort. Was Mother's glowing happiness at whipping Terayama-san's household into shape and organizing this journey all part of her joy in having a baby, then? It had seemed to me that she revelled in it for its own sake. Couldn't a woman be happy doing a great many things, just as a man could? I had been happy when I was with Aimi, and my father. I had been happy playing the shamisen and singing. I had been happy when I was with Youta, shadow-weaving.

"Don't worry," Mother said, misinterpreting my expression. "We know you are not a little girl any more, and in the city, there will be lots of young men who will be interested in you. Now that our situation is different, there will be nothing to stop you from making an advantageous marriage. In hardly any time at all you will have babies of your own."

I managed to pull my mask-smile into place before she saw my grimace. "Yes, Mother."

I wished she had not said that.

I had always known what I would do with my life, of course. The same thing that my mother had done with hers, and her mother before her. What else could a woman do in this world?

Many things about my life had changed but that had not. Had my father been alive, it would have been no different, except that the selection of possible husbands would have been rather more limited. The choice would never have been mine. That was a parent's job: to pick an alliance that would be suitable for a girl and benefit her family. I was of age now, and the time was coming.

So why did Mother's words make me feel like I was being pushed out into a dark, narrow tunnel, where there was no room to turn around or even stretch, and no light to see where I was going?

"You know I loved your father, don't you?"

Her words jarred me from my reverie. "Mother—?" It was the first time she had even mentioned him since we had left the ruins of his house.

"You are old enough to hear of such things now, Suzume, and I might not have another chance before you leave us. Let me speak this once, and then we will not talk about it again. Agreed? You must not tell any of this to Shujin-sama."

I shook my head fervently.

"Very well, then. You know that I came from a good family – though not a wealthy one – and I was beautiful, as beautiful as you are. I had many suitors. Terayama-san was one of them, and my aunt and uncle wished for me to marry him. But I only had eyes for Daisuke. He was not like the others. He did not try to impress me, or brag to his friends about me. He wrote me poetry and talked to me. He seemed to truly see me, to love me. And I loved him in return. Eventually, after months of begging, I prevailed. We did marry, and we were so happy. At first. When I knew I was having you, I thought that I would die of happiness. But the labour was so difficult, and I bled so much, that afterwards the midwife told your father … she told him that to have another child might kill me. It was wicked of her. It was not her business to interfere."

She looked so fierce and unhappy that I made soothing noises and rubbed her forearm. After a moment, she relaxed and smiled.

"Your father listened to the midwife and told me that we would not have any more children. At first I agreed with him. I was frightened too, you see. After a while, as I grew stronger and you grew older, I began to realize what a terrible thing we had agreed to. It was not natural, the way we lived. I longed for babies. I longed to feel close to your father, as I once had. We argued about it again and again, and he began to hide from me in his papers. Sometimes I felt that I did not know him at all any more. He would not see how unhappy I was. All he would say

was that you were enough for him. He couldn't understand that you—" She cut herself off, paused and then
finished, "That one child was not really a proper family."

I heard that unfinished sentence. *You were not enough
for me.*

"I gave up. I cannot explain how awful it was, my love,
to give up. It felt as if something inside me had died. But I
have another chance with Shujin-sama. He waited for me.
He never married. He never looked at another woman.
And when I needed him, he was there. He has forgiven
me for choosing his friend over him all those years ago,
and now I am able to have the children I always wanted.
I am so happy, Suzume."

I stared down at her, trying to sort through the tangled threads of my emotions. One thread stood out above
all the others. "Mother, do you mean that you might die
having this child? And Terayama-san doesn't know?"

"No," she said, shaking my hand off. "I will not die
having this child. I was only sixteen when I gave birth to
you. A child myself. I had not even finished growing. I
am a woman now, and I am in no more danger than any
other woman. There is nothing for Shujin-sama to know.
You will not speak of this to him. Will you?"

"No, Mother."

"I have only told you all this so that you will know
I understand a young woman's craving for a home and
family of her own. I want you to know this happiness that
I have, and I am sure Shujin-sama does too. You are too

old now to live under a stepfather's roof, too old to need a mother any more. We will make sure you are happily settled."

"Thank you, Mother." The words felt like the prickly leaves of the aloe in my mouth. She was so eager to be rid of me. So eager to forget her old life and make a new one that had no place in it for me. I was realistic enough to know that once I was married off I would rarely, if ever, see Mother again. I dreaded this, but it seemed she looked forward to it.

How could I be too old to need a mother any more? It rather seemed as if I was too old for my mother to need me. In all her talk of children, she spoke only of babies, as if they were all that mattered. And suddenly it made sense. She had been different once, when I was very young. She was softer and happier, and as I had grown, so had her sharpness and anger and restlessness. And Aimi's arrival had made Mother worse. But I had never realized until now that some part of her blamed me for her inability to have more children. Maybe even blamed me for Father's distance.

And so she had turned to Terayama-san.

"Now you may go and clean up," she was saying. "Go up onto the deck, so that you might have some fresh air. You're looking rather pale."

I probably answered. I'm not sure what I said, but it got me out of the room.

I walked along the wooden corridor, my steps gaining

speed until the hem of my kimono snapped against my legs and my sandals slapped the floor. My thoughts and feelings were in turmoil.

I had often wondered when it had begun, that strange game between Terayama-san and my mother. The game of rejection and pursuit.

Now I had the answer. It had not been in the ruins of my father's house, or in the few missing days before that. The game had begun before I was even born, when Mother was the same age as I was now. It had begun when she had chosen Hoshima Daisuke instead of Terayama Ryoichi. And it had lasted all those years.

Mother seemed to think that it was devotion and love that had kept Terayama-san's interest. But I could not free my mind of the image of the cat at its mousehole, so still, so patient.

He had come to our house all the time. Laughed with my father. Eaten at our table. All the time, he had been looking at her. All the time planning, watching. All the time waiting, waiting, for his chance.

He had lost the first time.

He had never given up.

I burst out of the corridor, the door slamming back with a sharp crack that was hidden by the rush and boom of the water against the ship's hull.

It was overcast, the sky as white and hard as the inside of a tea bowl. The air was cold and tangy with salt. I stood for a moment, panting, my fists clenching and unclenching. After a couple of long, deep breaths, I pulled the door closed behind me.

A few yards away, a thin wall of wooden planks curved around the entrance to the deck. I could only look out by standing on tiptoe and peering through one of the moon-shaped piercings in the wood. A sailor went past carrying a coil of rope over his shoulder that was as big as my torso and a seagull flew low over the deck. I sighed.

I had hoped, since we all shared the same corridor and door onto the deck, that I might meet the strange foreigners here. However, so far they had managed to avoid not only me but also Terayama-san. He had been talking about it – *again* – last night, while my mother and I had pretended to eat. He had spoken of little else since we had come aboard. He was convinced that by gaining some influence over the men he would gain influence over the Moon Prince too – but it seemed to me that this was almost irrelevant now. It was the chase that consumed him. The more the foreigners evaded him, the more determined he became to corner them. The more he was thwarted, the deeper his obsession grew.

Just as it had been with Mother.

Yet once he had caught her, his frenzy had subsided. I saw the puzzled looks she gave him sometimes now, as if she, too, realized that something was different but could not understand what. He cared for her, treated her kindly, was proud of her beauty and the fact that she carried his heir, but his focus had shifted away from her. I believed he did love her, in his way, but his burning need to possess her had faded now that she belonged to him. She was his wife, and she could never leave him.

Once the mouse was dead, the cat lifted his paw.

I leant against the wooden wall and kept squinting through the little pierced moon shape. I wanted to get out of the enclosure and walk – pace up and down, stamp my feet and work off the unhappy, confused feelings that were boiling inside me. But I wasn't allowed to go out there, not without Terayama-san to escort me.

A tiny, rebellious thought flashed through my mind. I knew a different way to get rid of the confusion and restlessness. A quick and easy way. I had my own little cabin, adjoining Mother and Terayama-san's. I slept alone now. Mai was on the other ship. I would be able to pull the pin from my hair and make a quick, smooth cut…

I squeezed my eyes shut. I needed to get out and walk, now, before I gave in. I would endure whatever punishment my mother or Terayama-san meted out later.

I reached out for the brass latch of the gate, but before I could press it down, a shadow passed across the moon piercings and Terayama-san opened it himself. I snatched my hand away and dragged a mask of calm across my face.

Terayama-san stared at me, his eyes blank in the way that I knew meant anger. "What are you doing out here?"

"M–Mother is sleeping. She said—"

Just like that his face changed; the telltale stoniness was wiped away like grime removed by a wet cloth. He smiled his warm and charming smile.

"I am sorry, Suzu-chan. Of course you will be wanting some fresh air after being cooped up for so long. Come with me. You will feel much better after a walk."

He took hold of my arm and guided me firmly out of the enclosure. Having unexpectedly got what I wanted, I immediately wished that I was back in the enclosure. Alone.

The wind rolled over the deck with a low, wavering moan, bringing salt droplets to sting my face, and despite my double-layered kimono, I shivered. If Terayama-san had not had such a grip on me, I would have wrapped my arms around myself for warmth. The ship jerked and rocked more strongly, making me brace my feet, as a spray of grey-and-white water flew up the side of the deck.

Overhead, the sails made deep, booming noises as the wind dragged at them, and the ropes and rigging creaked loudly.

"Well, and how is your mother today, Suzu-chan?" he asked, pitching his voice over the ship's noises as he pulled me along.

My name is Suzume. It may mean nothing more than "little brown sparrow", but it is my name.

"She is very brave, but her health is not good," I said. "She is not eating. I am glad we will reach land soon."

"You have been a great comfort to her." He smiled

again, but his eyes flickered away from mine, his attention fixed somewhere over my head. What was he looking for? I refused to crane over my shoulder and look too, so pretended that I did not notice.

The ship bucked again, more strongly this time. Terayama-san's fingers tightened still further, keeping me from falling. I held in a sound of pain. I would have got fewer bruises from a tumble on the deck.

"Neither of my ladies has her sea legs yet," he said, indulgently. "Why don't we walk to the side, and you can lean against the rail? It is easier to keep your footing like that, and you can see the sea properly."

I didn't really want to see the sea. I was trembling with the cold, and my arm was throbbing, and I felt … uneasy. Something inside was urging me to shake off Terayama-san's hand and run back to the cabin. He didn't wait for me to agree, just manoeuvred me over to the side of the ship.

"Here, stand on this. You'll get a good view." His hand left my arm at last to grab my waist, and he lifted me onto a large coil of rope. I wobbled and found myself clutching at him. Standing like this, I was taller than he was, and the rail only went up to my hips. The sea was jumping and fizzling below, blowing spray up into my face until I had to turn my head away. I clutched at him more tightly.

"Terayama-san, I do not think—"

As I spoke, my eye was caught by a fleet, dark shape that swooped through the black tracery of the rigging, circling and diving as if at play. It was the falcon. This was the first time I had seen it since that day on the docks. Even above the sound of the sea, I heard my stepfather suck in a sharp breath.

At that same moment, the ship made another bucking movement. Terayama-san seemed to stumble. His shoulder drove into mine.

A scream wrenched from my lips as I was shoved forward, feet skidding off the coiled rope. My hips smacked into the rail, and I tilted like an acrobat about to do a cartwheel. I screamed again, slapping my arms down against the wooden planks. The silver-grey water reached up as if to grab me.

There was a flash of red on my left. A hand clamped down on my shoulder like an iron vise. Another hand grasped the back of my kimono. I was dragged back over the side, ribs grating painfully on the rail. Then I was falling again, backwards this time, onto the deck.

I landed with a sob, fighting to breathe. It took me a minute to notice that I had not landed on wood but on a person. My rescuer lay underneath me, his arm now around my waist. His heart was racing against my shoulder blade, chest heaving with shallow gasps like my own.

I turned my head and looked into the face of one of Terayama-san's foreigners. The boy.

This close, I could make out the patterns of dark blue dots that swirled across his cheeks. His eyes were not dark, as I would have expected, but a sort of brownish green, the colour of mulberry leaves. He smelled like cassia: the very best quality cinnamon.

The foreigner slowly pushed himself up, bringing me with him. His arm was still around my waist, and the heat of him seemed to pulse against my chilled skin, even through the layers of my clothes.

"Are you hurt?" he asked, his voice a husky, softly accented whisper.

"I—I do not think so," I said, taking stock of my aches and bruises. "Thanks to you."

He smiled, a crooked half smile that suddenly made me feel hot all over. "It was my pleasure."

Before I could reply, Terayama-san was leaning over us, pulling me away from the boy's warmth. I began to shiver immediately and barely heard Terayama-san's deep voice repeating, "Thank the Moon. You nearly went in. Thank the Moon."

Terayama-san put his arms around me. I found myself going still, like a tiny wild creature that plays dead in the hope it will confuse the hunter. Then the awkward embrace was over, and he was pushing me to sit on a wooden crate near by. "Are you well, Suzu-chan? Are you all right?"

I nodded, meeting his searching look for a second. My shivering was getting worse. I could feel my teeth chattering against one another. Terayama-san turned away from me and executed a perfect, elegant bow for the foreign boy, who still sat on the deck.

"I owe you a debt which I can never repay, honoured guest-san. I do not know your name, but please, you must allow me to thank you properly." Terayama-san held out his free hand to the boy to help him up.

The boy looked at the hand expressionlessly, then got to his feet unassisted. His voice was cold – almost belligerent – when he said, "Your daughter has already thanked me. I require nothing more."

No one had ever dared use that tone with my stepfather before.

Terayama-san rocked back slightly, and his hand dropped to his side. It flexed convulsively, the knuckles turning red, yellow-white, red, yellow-white. I closed my eyes, wrapping my arms around myself.

But when my stepfather spoke again, his tone was the same, humble and sincere. "Perhaps I have given offence? I beg your pardon. I meant none. But you are very young; perhaps I might speak to your father? I would like to tell him what you have done for me. We could drink tea in the captain's cabin."

"Thank you for the invitation," the boy said. "But I am afraid I do not care for tea."

There was a high-pitched shriek. I opened my eyes and saw the falcon glide down and alight on the young foreigner's extended forearm, which was bound with a brace of red leather. It had been the leather that had caught my eye as he pulled me back over the side of the ship.

Once again our eyes met. I mouthed *Thank you*, my throat too dry to sound the words. The blank look left his face, and he ducked his head, almost shyly. Then he turned to look at Terayama-san, and his face was cold again.

"You should take your daughter below decks. I think she is not well."

Terayama-san's hand flexed again. "Yes, of course. But first—"

The young man turned from Terayama-san's protests and walked away, his back very straight, the bird still on his arm. He passed the group of sailors who had gathered near by and were gaping at us as if we were a travelling spectacle which they expected to pay a copper piece for. The boy winked at them, and as if a spell had been broken, they began to disperse across the deck. One of them reached out and hit the boy on the back, almost sending him flying. The bird on his arm spread its wings and shrieked in protest.

Terayama-san watched for a second, and then swore once, softly and viciously.

I was dizzy. My head pounded. My body had gone as soft and floppy as melted tallow. Yet despite all that, I now realized two things.

The boy who had just saved me – and perhaps all the foreigners Terayama-san was so keen to meet – had some kind of shadow-weaving talent. The boy had been close enough to reach me seconds after I began to fall, and yet I had not seen him on the deck in the moments before that, not even a glimpse. More than that, though, I had felt his weaving shredding away as he laid his hands on me to pull me back from the edge. I had felt it but not understood it, just as one can hear speech in a strange language and not comprehend a word. Of course Terayama-san had never had any luck seeking them out. These men could make themselves invisible in plain daylight.

The second thing I knew was this: after seeing the falcon flying above the deck and realizing the foreigners must be near by, my stepfather had been so determined to get their attention that he had deliberately pushed me over the side of the ship.

Terayama-san had tried to kill me.

Nine

When he turned back towards me, I wanted to cringe away from him. I wanted to scream, accuse him at the top of my voice. Run to my mother and beg her to protect me.

I did none of those things. I leant against him and allowed him to help me back across the deck, through the rising wind, into the enclosure, then into the lamp-lit dimness of the corridor. I could not stop the shivering, but I prayed he would not realize it wasn't the cold that made me shake. He had his earlier frustration under control now. His attention was on me. I could feel his eyes searching my face.

Cat. No: gull. Cold and assessing. Wondering whether I was worth eating…

"You're still trembling," he said quietly. His fingers

tightened against the bruises he had made on my arm earlier. "We must have you lie down. It will be Yukiko's turn to care for you for a change, eh?"

He was a man who was willing to push his stepdaughter overboard in order to force a meeting he hoped would increase his political influence. What would he do to me if he thought I was a danger to him? If I allowed one tiny flicker of fear to cross my face, he would see it. He would know that I suspected him, and then—

"It's nothing," I murmured. "I am only cold. Don't wake Mother if she is sleeping. If you will help me to my cabin, I think I will be all right."

I truly believe that my shadow-weaving saved my life that day, just as it had when I had fled from the prince's soldiers. If Terayama-san had seen my true face, the terror that I knew was twisting my features, I do not know what he would have done.

Instead he saw Aimi's face, her serene expression. Pale with shock, and drawn with exhaustion, but smiling gratefully at him. His grip eased.

"You are a good, brave girl, Suzu-chan. When we get to the city, I will buy you a lovely new kimono. Several. You will like that, will you not? You will forget all about this."

I heard the odd mixture of regret and satisfaction in his tone, and wondered if he was sorry now, a little sorry, for what he had done. Maybe he really thought that a pretty new kimono would make up for it. In his head, my life was worth no more than a piece of embroidered silk.

After he had helped me into my tiny room to lie down and drawn the door shut behind him, I lay awake, staring at the patterns in the darkness, caught in a kind of trance. I didn't dare move, for fear that he might hear and come to look in on me, and see that I knew. I breathed slow, shallow breaths through my nostrils, because I did not want panicked breathing to catch his attention, should he listen at the door. I could not close my eyes, lest he creep in somehow while I was unaware.

All this time, ever since we had gone with Terayama-san, I had been standing on the edge of an abyss. I had been living with a man who was not mad, or insensible, but who would risk my life without a moment's hesitation if he thought he might profit from it, and I had never known until now. What was I to do?

I could not tell Mother. I knew that without a doubt. She might tell Terayama-san what I had said, and the only protection I had was my ignorance. I must pretend it never happened. Try to forget it ever had. I must be exactly as I had been before, so that he never had cause to look at me with suspicion.

With that thought came relief. I could do it. If there was one thing I was good at, it was hiding. Hiding my face, my thoughts. Hiding the truth. It was only one more layer of lies. One more mask. I rolled over onto my side, and sighed, and closed my eyes at last.

Four more days aboard the ship. I did not venture onto the deck again, not even when the rocking and swaying made me sick. Then it was onto solid land, staying at a little ryokan by the shore. Those two days did Mother much good, as did the fact that her experienced maid, Isane, was now well enough to care for her. She was able to eat again, and her colour came back.

Some other things had changed as well, but not for the better.

"Our daughter is an excellent little nurse, isn't she, my dear?" Terayama-san said, patting me lightly on the head.

Whereas before he had interspaced ignoring me with sporadic comments on how pretty I was and how good a husband I would get, now Terayama-san's attention had become almost cloying. I was not sure if he was trying to make me believe that he cared for me as a father would or if the change simply came from guilt, but in either case I did not like it.

And neither did Mother.

I cursed him mentally when he added, "You must look after me too, Suzu-chan, if ever I am ill."

"Is my care not enough for you, Shujin-sama?" Mother asked, her voice grave. Her eyes avoided me. I knew she was remembering times when Father had praised me, and, after our talk on the ship, I knew that the memory was bitter for her. "That is a *wife's* place."

To my relief, Terayama-san left me and went to sit by her, taking her hand. "I will be ill now, if you will promise to nurse me," he murmured.

Mother smiled, but she still did not look at me. I, who

had fought not to cringe from Terayama-san, now fought not to cry.

I turned and quietly left the room.

Another four days' travel brought us to the capital city of the Moonlit Land. The city was sometimes called Tsuki no Machi, sometimes the City of the Moon, sometimes just the city. It was where all the most important people lived, all the greatest artists and poets worked, where the Moon Prince had his palace. It had been the centre of all civilization in the world for a hundred years or more, ever since the faraway empire that had granted the prince's family their title had fallen.

The weather had turned wet and dark on our second day of travel. Terayama-san had given up riding his horse and now shared the palanquin with us. He was the one who threw open one of the shutters and bade us look as we crested the hill above the city – but our first look at it was not promising.

The city was embraced by the curved arms of the headland, so that the horseshoe-shaped bay was nearly at its heart. Countless docks and piers jutted out into the water, and ships milled in it. The many rivers through it had also become part of the city, criss-crossed by dozens of bridges made of wood, rope and intricately carved stone. Otsukimi no Yama – Moonview Mountain – towered over it on its far side. The mountain's verdant pine-covered sides gave it the appearance of a furry green monster that glowered down at the human scar at its feet.

In the dim dampness of the rain, the city itself seemed nothing more than a chaotic mess of whitewashed walls, grey slate roofs and bare black trees.

"So vast…" Mother breathed. "It has grown since I was last here! Do you know how many people live here now, Shujin-sama?"

"Over ten thousand, I believe," Terayama-san said proudly, as if he had birthed them all himself. "Excited, Suzu-chan?"

I could not help looking at Mother. She turned away before our eyes met. The more Terayama-san tried to pretend we were a happy little family, the more she pushed me away.

My voice came out very small. "Yes, Terayama-san."

Terayama-san banged on the wall. The palanquin lifted again with a lurch and a jerk as I stared at my mother, wishing I could reach out, wishing so desperately that I could speak.

I don't want his attention! He only pets me and notices me because he feels guilty for trying to hurt me. Why can't you see?

A fine mist of rain blew in through the open shutter. "Should I close the shutter, Mother?"

"If Shujin-sama wishes."

"No, leave it open – there will be many things to see. You'll only see the city for the first time once, you know."

I folded my hands neatly. The silence stung my face, making my cheeks flush. I gently wove threads of pale, smooth illusion to hide the angry colour. Out of the corner of my eye, I saw Terayama-san lean across and rub Mother's barely rounded tummy. Her hand came up to lie on his. Her eyes flicked towards me for a second, but I could not decipher her expression. I swallowed hard.

The palanquin moved down the hill quickly, and before any more was said, we had passed between the first buildings. I leant forward, gazing out of the window. Wooden houses, brightly painted in red and green and gold in the style of the Old Empire, mixed with others of plain wood and whitewashed stone. We climbed the steep bank of the river to a bridge of black wood and stone and, crossing it, reached the heavily forested opposite bank and Terayama-san's house. It looked much the same as his country one.

I glimpsed other, similar houses through the last of the red autumn foliage. I wondered if all the houses here belonged to country noblemen who liked to pretend they were still at home on their peaceful estates, despite having travelled to the city. If so, they had my sympathy. At that moment I was suffering from a wave of homesickness so intense that it literally made my stomach turn.

Only my longing was for a home that no longer existed.

Ten

A baby wailed, its tiny voice lifting up in a piercing shriek that shattered the unnatural stillness of the winter evening. I longed to sag, to give in to the ache of relief and fatigue that throbbed dully in my bones. Instead, I turned a calm face on Mai, and said, "Run up to my mother's rooms and find out from the surgeon how she is, please."

"Yes, Mistress." Mai's face brightened at the prospect of being the first to hear the news – *boy or girl, boy or girl?* – and she hopped to her feet, one of her long sleeves thwapping against the screen on her way out.

As the screen slid shut behind her, I finally allowed my head to fall forward onto my chest. My neck cracked, and I shrugged, trying to relieve the tension in my back and shoulders. More than twelve hours had passed, waiting, alone except for the servants. Terayama-san had quit the house shortly after Mother's cries began to echo through the rooms above, claiming that he could not bear it. What kind of man went hunting while his child was being born?

My thoughts were interrupted by a second high-pitched wail that drowned out the first. *Two* babies?

The screen slid back, and Mai almost danced into the room, alight with excitement.

"Twins," she said, clasping her hands under her chin. "Boys. Mistress is asking for you. Twins, Nakamura-sama!"

"I understood the first time, Mai, thank you. I will visit them. Please send word to the hunting party immediately."

The plaintive wailing of hungry infants began to quiet as I gained the next floor, and when Mai pushed open the screen to my mother's sitting room, only the occasional hiccup and whimper could be heard. The inner screen to the sleeping area was pushed shut.

I walked forward, calling out quietly, "May I come in, Mother?"

The screen slid open, and Mother's maid Isane bowed as I entered.

My mother lay in the centre of her futon, propped up on a mountain of pillows, with the sheet carefully smoothed over her. She wore a clean robe in a flattering shade of pink, but her hair was damp and frizzy around her forehead and her face was pale and exhausted. Her eyes were closed. I glanced at Isane, who bowed again with a reassuring smile and then seated herself neatly in one corner of the room.

Two lumps of swaddling cloth, not even as long as one of my forearms, lay on the futon with my mother, one on each side. They were not crying any more, though one of them was making worrying gurgling noises.

My brothers.

I walked over to the futon to get a better look. All that could be seen of them was a scrunched-up oval that held eyes, nose and mouth without really seeming to be a proper face. I had heard a great deal about how beautiful babies were, and I wondered if there was something wrong with me for thinking they looked like badly carved dolls.

"What do you think of them?" Mother's voice was a tired whisper.

I looked up quickly, and my mask slipped as I struggled for something to say.

"They are very … purple."

She laughed. I went weak with relief. Despite her exhaustion, she was not in her angry mood – which was the one I had seen most of over the past weeks. Then again, Terayama-san was not here.

"Come sit by me, and you shall hold them."

I quickly pulled a serene smile into place and sank down onto the woven mats at her side, watching with a mixture of interest and apprehension as Mother gently lifted one of the babies up.

"This is the youngest. His brother has just gone to sleep." She leant towards me, and before I knew it, the bundle was tucked into my arms, the hard little head rolling against the curve of my breast. The baby was alarmingly warm, and inside its wrappings, wriggly.

"Cup his head with your hand. That's it," she said softly.

"He's heavy," I blurted out in surprise.

She nodded, smiling. "He is strong."

One of my fingers brushed the dark pink of the baby's cheek. My touch left a pale mark that faded after an instant. His skin was so soft, like a cherry blossom.

We sat quietly, Mother's maid nodding off in the corner. Mother lifted the sleeping baby into her arms while the wakeful one lay in mine. He made little snorting, snuffling noises, and I found myself responding with nonsensical babbling. His little eyes twinkled at me like black pebbles under sunlit water.

"Will Shujin-sama be home soon?"

It was surprisingly hard to tear my eyes from the little face. "I am sure he is close by. We sent messengers as soon as we could. Do not worry."

A little while later, raised voices and the sounds of horses began to drift up from downstairs, and Mother's head lifted. Her face, though still pale and tired, suddenly shone.

I thought I knew what was going through her mind. She had produced a healthy male child. An heir. And a spare one too. This was her moment of supreme triumph. But it would not be complete until Terayama-san arrived.

The outer door banged open, and there were heavy footsteps. Then the inner screen was flung back. Isane woke and came to her feet in a reflexive movement as Terayama-san, dusty and muddy and reeking of horse, entered the room. There was a glow about him, a burning look in his eyes. He didn't see me. He did not see Isane. His eyes barely touched upon Mother before they went to the babies.

"They spoke the truth…" he said. "Two, and both boys. The Moon herself blesses my house. Leave us."

I exchanged a look with Isane. Presumably that last part was aimed at us. I carefully laid the little child down on the futon by my mother's leg and bowed to Terayama-san, who ignored me – thankfully. Then I followed Isane from the room.

As Isane drew the screen closed behind us, I was overcome with a wave of tiredness. I had not eaten or rested for half a day, and while my ordeal was nothing, I was sure, compared to my mother's, it had still left me weak and shaky. I just wanted to sit for a little while in silence, alone. Maybe when Terayama-san was done with his paternal gloat, I would have the chance to hold my other brother.

I waved away Isane's concerned look as I slid down onto the pillows by the little tea table, leaning my elbows on it. Isane hovered over me for a moment, then went reluctantly to the door, closing it behind her as she left.

The evening darkness was slipping over the walls, and the one lamp still burning in this room provided only a faint glow. Terayama-san and Mother were talking – I could not focus on the words – and I could hear the gentle shushing of the trees outside. I let my head fall down into my hands, a soundless yawn closing my eyes…

"Don't say any more!"

I started awake at the sudden exclamation from the other room. It was my mother's voice, choked with tears.

"Hush, Yukiko. Do you want the whole house to hear?" The words were stern, but Terayama-san's voice was low and pleading.

"How did you expect me to react, Ryoichi? How am I supposed to feel? I can't look at you!"

"Why not? Both our fondest wishes have come true. Don't hurt me by feigning ignorance now, my love. You knew. You knew when you took my hand that day, with Daisuke's blood not yet dry."

I flinched, my own hands covering my mouth.

"You're wrong." A sob. "I … I didn't. I told myself it was obscene to even think it. I thought it was a nightmare, nothing more than a sick fancy brought on by grief. I never really believed—"

"You're lying. To yourself as well as me." Terayama-san sounded weary. "You did not grieve for him. Does a grieving wife share the bed of her husband's friend just days after she is widowed? You loved me, not him. You wanted me."

"Of course I did!" Fierce now, tears gone.

A hot numbness suffused my body. My skin seemed to hum, the blood beating beneath it as if it sought escape.

"I loved you for years, hopelessly, faithfully," she said. "That does not mean I did not care for him. I would never have betrayed him."

"I know that. I know, my love. You could never have hurt him. That was why it fell to me. I could not see you suffer any more. I could not suffer myself. We would both have been miserable all our lives."

"Rather that than … than what you did. And what of Suzume? She nearly died. My child, Ryoichi!"

"I never meant to put her in danger. I swear to you. I had no idea that my information to the Moon Prince would warrant such an extreme response. I only thought they would arrest him, and when he was gone, you could obtain a divorce. You know they give the wives of traitors that option – if the wives themselves are not implicated. I took care to stress your innocence and that of the rest of the household. I never meant to bring death there."

My breath rasped and caught in my chest, painfully loud. I was surprised they did not hear.

"You killed him, as surely as if you had held the sword yourself," she said.

"I am sorry, Yukiko, but only for the sorrow it has caused you. I cannot be sorry for what I did. Look at our sons. Look at our children's faces. They would never have been born. Are their two innocent lives not worth Daisuke's sacrifice?"

"I—I do not know. Why did you tell me all this now? Now of all times? I cannot think."

"You do not need to think." There was a trace of arrogance in his voice now. "It is too late. I did everything – all of this – for you, to give you the life you dreamed about and wished for. The life you whispered about to me when you and I were alone together."

He paused for a second, and when he spoke again, his voice was soft, not accusing but gently chiding, the tone of voice one would use on a child. "You are the one who made the mistake, Yukiko. You are the one who chose Daisuke, when it should have been me. All I did was to set that right, to make things as they should always have been. You are happy now, are you not? You have everything you ever dreamed of. You are my wife. The mother of my sons. Think about what would happen to our life if this truth came out. Think what would happen to our sons. Think what would happen to you. Do you want that?"

Silence. In my mind I saw her shaking her head.

"Good." The word was satisfied, and final. "We need never speak of it again. Understand, my dear, that I did not tell you this to distress you. I had to know that we shared the burden equally. I had to know you accepted that you were truly mine."

There was another silence. Then Terayama-san spoke again. "Come now. Look at me. Do you forgive me? Do you still love me?"

One of the babies let out a plaintive mewl.

Her voice broke on the words: "I could never stop loving you."

Daisuke's blood…

A sick fancy…

I could never stop loving you…

Father.

Aimi.

I barely noticed the outer door open. I barely heard Mai's voice.

"Here you are, Nakamura-sama."

I could not look at her. My eyes could not leave the thin shield of paper and wood that separated me from the man who had murdered my father.

"Nakamura-sama? What is wrong?"

The inner screen flew back with enough force to echo through the room. Terayama-san stood there, his eyes, riveted on me, almost bulging out of his head. Behind him, my mother leant forward, open-mouthed with horror. Her hands hovered protectively over the babies lying on either side of her.

No one moved.

"T–Terayama-sama?"

Mai's tentative voice broke the stillness.

Terayama-san's fingers twitched towards the long knife at his thigh. Mother's voice rose in a wail of denial as I jumped up and ran.

Eleven

It was the wrong thing to do. I knew it, even as instinct moved me. My brain screamed at me to be still, but my legs reacted before I gave them leave, pushing me out from under the table and turning me to the door. I had no choice.

He would follow. I knew it. Terayama-san was a hunter, and from the moment he had seen me on the other side of that screen, I was his prey.

He would chase me.

He would catch me.

He would never stop until I was dead.

He was shouting, telling Mai to stay in the room. I cleared the doorway and was halfway down the corridor before he had finished speaking. The corridor was dark; the lamps had not yet been lit. My sock-clad feet made no sound on the tatami mats, but my long sleeves flapped with the movement of my arms, making a noise like the frantic beating of birds' wings.

The outer screen to my mother's rooms slammed shut behind me, and footfalls thundered across the floor. It was like being in a dream, except that I was sweating, my heart jumping with fear. No nightmare had ever terrified me like this.

I rounded the corner and flung myself into an alcove, tucking my body into the gap between the wall and a tall arrangement of spiny black branches and white flowers.

I reached for the threads of an illusion – a familiar one, of shadows and nothingness. Frantically I wrapped it around myself, weaving it so thickly that my own vision went dim and grey. It was clumsy, but I did not have time to pick it apart and begin again.

Terayama-san came into view, his posture tense and ready, leaning forward as if in anticipation. He was not holding a weapon. Not yet. There at the corner, not a full arm's reach from me, he stopped. His eyes searched the corridor ahead, and then he turned back to look behind him.

"I know you're here. Come out."

The gentle coaxing tone, the way his hands flexed and clenched, sent a sickening quiver through me. I bit down on my lip to hold in the whimper that wanted to escape.

"Little Suzu-chan, don't hide. Answer me. I don't want to get angry with you."

He turned, his gaze tracking slowly over the twilight shadows of the corridor.

I had used this weaving a dozen times and no one had ever pierced it. No one. He could not find me, because I was not there to be found.

Why didn't he walk away?

Why did he stand there still?

People see what they wish to see.

Terayama-san knew me. He knew my smell, the sound of my breathing, the feel of my presence. He knew I must be somewhere in this corridor. People saw what they wished to see – and right now, Terayama-san wished to see me.

His gaze came back to the alcove. The little space where the shadows were ever so slightly too dense and the flower arrangement was ever so slightly askew. The only place where a small, frightened girl might be able to duck out of sight.

He took a step closer, eyes narrowing. They did not focus on me yet, but one more step and—

"Terayama-sama?"

Lamplight suddenly fell on Terayama-san's back. For a dizzy moment, I thought, *She's come – Mother has come to save me.*

But the voice was male, the tone that of a servant. Terayama-san had told Mother to stay in her room. I should have known better than to believe, even for an instant, that she would disobey him. Not now she knew – by his own admission – what he was capable of.

She had made her choice.

Terayama-san jerked around irritably. "What, Shiro?"

"Lord, it is dark. Are you well? Do you wish me to bring you another lamp?"

"For the Moon's sake, stop bothering me. Get away – get out of my sight!"

As the roar left his mouth, he turned his back to me. I darted out of the alcove. His head snapped around and he reached out, his fingers closing on the trailing edge of my illusion as I pulled away. The mantle of shadows shredded under his touch like smoke, and he staggered, knocking the vase from its pedestal and sending flowers and branches flying across the mats.

"Terayama-sama!" The servant stepped forward and I was gone, turning the corner and leaving them behind.

A female servant folding cloths at the top of the stairs gasped and clutched at her chest as I flew past: a blot of shadow, moving as no shadow could.

I scrambled down the stairs. Above and behind me I could hear Terayama-san's voice raised in anger, and I raced for the door. I did not know where I was going or how I could hide, but I did know that it was dark outside, and darkness was shelter.

The garden was heavy with the perfume of night-blooming jasmine, spread out before me in a tessellate of silver and purple shadows. I rippled through them, leaping from stepping-stone to soft moss, avoiding the gravel with its telltale crunch. What was the use of illusion if you gave yourself away with noise?

What was the use of my illusions at all?

Terayama-san had seen through them. He would find me. I had to get away.

But where? This was his land, and beyond it lay a vast city where I knew no one. I had the clothes I stood up in and the few baubles of jewellery that I was wearing. I didn't even have shoes. Panic squeezed at my throat like a vicious hand. Like Terayama-san's hand.

I stumbled to a halt near the kitchen that was tucked away at the very back of the house. Lost in my panic, I had almost walked right through the doorway. I drew my weaving more tightly around me, but the brick wall was warm and I was so cold. I let myself stop for a moment, gasping, newly aware of the commotion coming from the house.

Terayama-san would be making up his story by now. He would be telling the servants that I was ill, or mad, so that he could send them out to hunt me for him. The only other person who knew the truth was Mother, and she would never contradict him.

An overwhelming surge of anger crashed through me, bursting in my head and chest and limbs until I stood up straight, vibrating with it. My body still trembled, but the fear – that fear which had choked me for so long – was gone.

They had done this to me. They were liars. Traitors, cowards and murderers, and yet I was running from them. They had killed my father. They had killed my cousin, the sister of my heart. They had taken every-thing – *everything* – I loved from me.

Why had I run?

What did I have left to lose?

I knew then that I would die that night. I did not care. I would die, but I would make them suffer first. I dropped to my knees, scrabbling in the dirt of the herb garden for the sharp fragments of stone that edged the borders. I would have used anything. Any weapon was good enough. I felt as if I could tear out my enemy's throat with my teeth, if only I could get close enough.

I would wait, here in the dark, hidden from everyone. The only one who could see me was Terayama-san. He would find me, and when he did, I would not run. I would not give him the satisfaction. I would let my weaving fall, and I would scream out the truth for everyone to hear. When he reached for me, I would put out his eyes.

For my father. For Aimi. For myself. For all of us.

Even when they killed me, and even if they all thought me mad, they would still hear the truth. Maybe they would wonder, and rumours would start. Or maybe they would all be too afraid to talk. It didn't matter. I would see him bleed. I would hear him scream. My face would be the last thing he would ever see. Just this once, Terayama's prey would turn on him.

Something moved in the kitchen doorway. I whirled, clutching a sharp lump of rock in each hand.

"Little Mistress?"

Twelve

I heard doors opening not far away, and saw light spill-
ing out into the garden. They were coming. I twitched,
but did not move.

"It is you under there, Little Mistress? Your weavings
have grown powerful since you visited me last."

Oh no. I let the shadow illusion drop as I stepped towards him. "Youta," I said urgently, low voiced. "Get back
inside. It isn't safe here now."

His head went back a little. "Why is it not safe? Why
are you holding those rocks as if you thought they were
knives?"

"Youta, go away. I do not want you in this fight."

The voices and the lights were moving. Not in this
direction yet – they were heading towards the trees – but
it was only a matter of time.

"Fight? Who are you intending to fight?"

I growled with impatience. "Terayama-san! I can't escape him, so I must face him."

"You want to fight him? He will kill you!" His voice shook. It was the most upset I had ever heard him, and part of me was sorry, but it was too late now.

"Listen to me: I know what I must do, and I am not afraid." I turned from him to look at the lights bobbing between the trees. "Go inside before he catches you out here with me."

A hand clamped over my mouth and an arm as thick and strong as a tree branch wrapped around my middle. The rocks dropped from my fingers as I struggled, trying to prise Youta off without hurting him. His breath barked in my ear, and I could hear the strain in his voice as he whispered, "Be still. If you do not wish them to find us together, be quiet. I will not let you go."

He dragged me into the kitchen, where the muted glow of the fires showed blanket-wrapped forms huddled in sleep. There was an open door to the right, and Youta pushed me inside. There were no fires within – only the moonlight falling through a row of small, high windows showed that we were in a storage space filled with barrels and firewood. Youta finally took his hand from my mouth as he turned to carefully pull the door closed behind us.

"How dare you!" I said, shoving myself away from him. "What right have you to interfere?"

"As much right as anyone in the world and more, you foolish girl," he said, leaning against the door. "I did not save your life so that you could waste it like this."

"Terayama-san betrayed my father and committed treason against the Moon Prince. He knows I have discovered it. He cannot let me live. Why should I not die with honour, fighting?"

Youta blanched, then shook his head. "He has not caught you yet! I can smuggle you away. He cannot search the whole city for you, not if he wishes to keep his secrets."

"Then what? Where can I go? Shall I beg on the streets? Sell myself to a brothel? I have no one to turn to."

"You have me."

"I do not want you involved in this. Please, my friend. You have helped me so much; I owe you more than I can ever repay."

He drew himself up, his shoulders straightening, his posture commanding despite the dirt and rags. "Very well. Repay me now. Leave Terayama-sama's punishment to the Moon or fate or the demon of the river, and let me hide you."

I shook my head slowly, sorrowful but determined. Every shred of honour I had – the honour of the House of Hoshima – told me what I must do. "I will not hide from my father's murderer."

"Then I will go to Terayama-sama and tell him what you have told me. Repay your debt to me, or send me to my death. Choose."

"Why are you doing this?"

He stared at me as if I were mad. "I cannot watch you die."

I let out a choked sob and slumped against the wall. The furious anger that had given me strength died down, sinking into my bones with a deep, sullen ache. The ache of failure. The ache of knowing that I would leave my father and cousin unavenged, and dishonour my house with cowardice, in order to save the life of this man.

"I cannot watch you die either," I whispered.

He breathed out slowly. "Then make your oath to me that you will not put yourself in Terayama-san's way. That you will not attack him or go after him. Promise me you will hide, and stay alive, and I will promise to do the same."

I squeezed my eyes closed. Fought against myself. Then, finally...

"I promise."

I opened my eyes to see Youta slowly slump down until his position echoed mine, relief carved into his face. It was done.

For another moment, I fought with myself, weary and heart-sore, but eventually, compelled by my sense of honour, I admitted, "I don't know how I can hide. Terayama-san can sense me, even when I use shadow-weaving. He almost caught me earlier."

Youta rubbed his face with his hand. "That is ... bad. He must be desperate to find you. Wait here." He left quickly, closing the door behind him.

What was I doing? I had made my decision, chosen my own fate – everything had seemed clear. Now nothing was. I only knew that I could not be responsible for Youta's death.

Youta returned with a bundle of fraying bluish cloth. He sat down cross-legged on the tiled floor and gestured for me to do the same.

"Take off your kimono and jewellery."

As I twisted and fumbled to undo the complex folds of my obi, Youta mixed water into a cup of ashes with a twig, creating a thick black paste. Then, when I wore only my under-robe, Youta took my kimono, obi, the garnet combs from my hair, even my filthy socks, and folded them into a tight bundle, parceling them up with dirty rags and stuffing them into a gap between the floor and the largest pile of firewood. He helped me don a thin, much-patched kimono, which he said he had taken from the garbage dump outside – it certainly smelled like it. He gave me his own grimy *haori* to wear over it. Both were shapeless enough to conceal my figure.

"Give me your hands," he commanded. When I obeyed, he slapped a dollop of the ash-and-water paste into my palm. "Work this into your skin – your nails, your arms, your neck and face. Your skin is too fine. If Terayama-san looks closely, it might give you away."

The stuff was cold, gritty and slimy. I cringed as I covered myself with it. Youta rubbed it into the spots I missed. Then he handed me a bone-handled knife. "I am sorry. No drudge has hair like that. It must go."

"Drudge?" I said, staring at the knife.

"A drudge is what you must be, for a little while. I will make up a story about who you are and where you come from. You are so small that you can pass for a younger girl – thirteen, perhaps. First, though, you must look the part. You must be so dirty and unappealing that no one will ever see the beautiful Suzume-sama hiding within."

I looked at my hair, which had fallen down when I removed my combs, and now curved, sleek and glossy, to my waist.

What did it matter? I took the knife. I gathered my hair into a thick rope and began to saw at it. It parted easily, long, silky hanks slithering down like ink blots onto my kimono and the floor. "I cannot hide forever," I said dully. "Tomorrow, or a week from now, or a month, I must be myself again. What will I do then?"

"Tomorrow, a week from now or a month can take care of themselves. We will talk of that another day, when the knife is not at our throats."

When a ragged shoulder-length curtain was all that was left of my hair, Youta gathered up all the cuttings and took them to be burned. I rubbed the remaining ash paste into my scalp. My head felt wobbly without the weight of my hair holding it straight. I was just finishing with the paste when Youta ran back into the storeroom, puffing. "Quickly! I can hear them outside."

He manhandled me back out into the kitchen and to

a blanket spread out on one side of the fire. I lay down, bringing my knees to my chest inside the over-large kimono. Youta put his back against mine and dragged another blanket over us.

"Stay down and out of sight," he whispered. "Keep quiet. Nod your head, but do not speak. Keep your eyes on the floor. The shadow-weaving ought to be enough to hide you from anyone except Terayama-sama, but there is no need to attract undue attention. You need a name. Something simple… Rin. Your name will be Rin."

Rin. It meant "cold".

As if it had been an instruction to my body, I began to shiver.

Rin

Thirteen

When, minutes or hours later, servants from the house came to wake the kitchen staff to ask if they had seen poor lost Suzume-sama, I could barely force my eyes open enough to look at them. A tall – or he seemed tall, from down on the floor – young man ripped the blanket from me and nudged me over with his foot, holding a lamp close to my face. I gaped vacantly up at him, a feat which took little acting skill. I was so exhausted.

"Moon's sisters! This one has a face like the back end of a boar. Why are we searching this dung-heap for the lily? Why would she be here?"

"Master's orders. Your lily is a bit weak in the head, if he's to be believed. Might be hiding anywhere."

"Nothing wrong with a weak-headed woman. Less nagging that way. Did you check that one?"

"Old enough to be my grandmother. Come on."

The noises died away and I wriggled back under the blanket and, somehow, fell asleep.

A kick in the ribs woke me. I jerked upright and flinched at the sound of laughter. "This is Youta-san's niece? She looks like a wet fish-owl!" someone said, sniggering.

"Quiet, Yuki." A tall woman with thinning grey hair bent over me. "Up with you, Rin. It is time to dunk your head."

Remembering Youta's words from the night before – he was nowhere to be seen now – I wrenched my gaze down to the ground as I got up.

"D–dunk?" I didn't have to fake the high, scared note that crept into my voice.

"Wash, *baka*," the woman said, not unkindly. "Face and hands and that mop of hair. I can't have you shedding dirt all over my floors."

She whapped me on the side of the head with one thick, callused hand. I staggered, eyes watering.

"Don't cry about it!" she said, catching me by the back of my kimono before I could fall. She began to tow me forward. "Clean water won't kill you."

Before I knew what was happening, I was out of the light and warmth of the kitchen and in the darkness of the pre-dawn morning, my breath clouding up before me. Frost crunched under my bare feet and I yelped.

"Ach, you'll need sandals too, or your feet will be walking

dirt everywhere. I will find some for you later. In you go."

My scream turned into a wet gurgle as my face was shoved down into a barrel full of rainwater.

Cold water rushed up my nostrils and into my mouth. My nose and cheekbones felt as if I had run headfirst into a wall. I flailed and pushed desperately against the hand clamped over the back of my head. I was finally allowed to surface, coughing and snorting, and now the hand that had held me down was holding me up as I stumbled about, blind.

"Anyone would think you'd never washed before in your life. Though, looking at you, maybe you haven't," she said.

She dropped a square of rough material over my head and rubbed my face and hair vigorously, scraping my numb skin until it caught fire. I made helpless squeaks of protest, which were ignored.

"Now, listen, Little Rin," the woman said, still rubbing my hair. "I am Madarame Aya-san and I am your boss now. We drudges live in the kitchen – which no one else does – so it's our place and we take care of it. Your job is to do what I tell you. I do what Chika-san tells me, and Chika-san does what Sumiko-sama tells her. Now Sumiko-sama takes her orders from Terayama-sama – which means if you give me any trouble, it is the next best thing to trying to disobey the lord. And what happens if you disobey a lord? You get your hands chopped off. Understand?"

For a second I tried to follow this dizzying line of logic, but my teeth were chattering too hard. I nodded anyway. It made as much sense as anything else in the insanity which had taken over my world.

"You make sure you don't give me trouble, and I'll make sure you get enough to eat and no beatings if I can help it. Sound fair?"

I nodded again, wrapping my arms around myself as she pushed me back into the kitchen, where another girl stood waiting.

"This is Yuki, Rin," Aya said. "Rin is simple but nice enough. I want this floor clean by the time the cooks arrive. Show her how to go about it."

Aya bustled away without waiting for a reply, and Yuki looked me over. I did the same. The other girl was about twenty, much taller than me, and had brown, muscular arms that were revealed by the kilted-up sleeves of her kimono. Her face was probably pretty, except that she was looking at me with such disgust, it made me want to spit like a cat. I forced my eyes down again.

"I hate simpletons," she said. "Especially filthy ones. Get to work and stay out of my way." She thrust a brush into my hand and dumped a wooden pail of water at my feet, causing it to slop over and drench my toes. She was gone before I could say a word.

Shaken and bewildered, I stood there for a moment. Then I remembered what Aya had said about clean floors. I knelt down and dipped the brush into the puddle of soapy water Yuki had left and began to scrub. I had seen women doing this back at home – my old home – before everything changed and went so wrong.

Dip, slosh, scrub, scrape, slide back and pull the bucket, then dip again. In seconds my kimono was soaked with grey suds, and within minutes my hands were sore. I kept my eyes down, only pausing if feet walked in front of me and got in the way of my brush. Scrub, scrub, scrub until you hit the wall and then shuffle around and go again.

"You can stop now."

I blinked and looked up through the sweaty clumps of my hair.

Aya was standing above me. "You don't need to scrub it twice. It's time to eat, before the cooks get here. Don't your shoulders hurt by now? Up you get."

She grabbed my wrists in her strong, rough hands and pulled me to my feet. I let out an involuntary grunt of pain as my shoulders, neck and back suddenly began to throb with pain. My knees let out sharp cracks as they straightened.

She tutted and took the scrub-brush away from me, then led me across the kitchen to where Youta and Yuki were sitting by the stove. She sat. Hesitantly I lowered myself to the ground beside her. My knees cracked again and Aya shook her head.

"It's good to work hard, but you should stop every now and again to stretch. I won't beat you for it."

"Why bother talking to her?" Yuki said. "She won't remember. She's a *baka-yarou*."

Youta flinched. I said nothing. Rin had nothing to say. Rin was *slow* and stupid.

"That's enough out of you," Aya said, her face suddenly stern. "There is enough cruelty in the world without adding to it for no reason, Yuki."

Yuki shut her mouth with a snap and looked away.

Aya whipped the cloth off a large plate, revealing *onigiri* – rice balls – wrapped with dried seaweed and filled with pickled plums.

"Eat up, now," she said, and before the words had left her mouth, everyone dived on the plate. Youta grabbed two *onigiri* and gave one to me, probably realizing I would not be fast enough without help. I took it and wolfed it down. I only managed to eat one more before they were all gone. I could have eaten twice as much.

"So," Yuki said, wiping stray bits of rice from her lips. "Does anyone know what that was about last night? I heard that Suzume-sama went mad and ran off screaming into the night. She just disappeared."

I forced myself to be still, letting a cloak of disinterest fall gently into place over my face. Aya said, "She's certainly run off, anyway, or else why would they have been searching? Though why they came bothering us in here, I don't know."

Youta's sigh of relief was audible, but I was careful not to look in his direction. The drudges spoke about

Terayama-san – and about me – in the same way that Mai and Isane gossiped about the goings-on at the Moon Palace, as if the people concerned were players on a stage. Characters in a story. Not real people. Certainly not people that they would ever meet, or who would be working and eating beside them.

Or so I thought – until I realized that Yuki was staring at my arms. I looked down at them in a panic. I had thought that the dirt would be enough to conceal the unusual whiteness of the skin, but what if it wasn't?

Did I dare try to pull a shadow-weaving over them with Yuki looking?

"You have a lot of scars," she said suddenly.

Oh. I looked at my arms again, and saw that, without the illusion of smooth, fine skin that normally hid them, my scars were very obvious. No one knew Suzume-sama had scars.

Youta cleared his throat. "Rin's father is … a harsh man. He was not always patient with her."

A flash of sympathy lit Yuki's eyes. Then she jerked her shoulder, her face closing up again. "Plenty of fathers like that in the world. At least no one here will cut her up."

Youta smiled at her. "That is right. We will take care of her, won't we?"

The door at the back of the kitchen opened and a crowd of men in white kimonos and white cloth hats began to pour in.

"Up, girls," Aya said, groaning as she pushed herself to

her feet. "Time for the real work."

The real work was assisting the cooks as the kitchen became a place of shouting and sizzling, chopping and bubbling, and great clouds of steam and smoke that carried scents which made my stomach cramp with yearning.

The cooks themselves did all the skilful work, their hands wielding knives as delicately as I had once held a pen. We drudges were expected to do any peeling, gutting or rough chopping, to fetch and carry firewood, to haul in the huge cuts of meat or the armfuls of vegetables or sacks of rice. Most of all, we kept the kitchen clean, scouring out the used pots and dishes as they were discarded, then wiping and stacking them, or gathering up the debris and scrubbing everything down.

By the end of that first back-aching day, it was known that Rin could not be trusted with anything more than the most basic of tasks. If someone handed me one of the huge white dikon radishes and asked me to peel and chop it, their dish would be complete – without radish – before I had even managed to get the tough skin off the thing. If I was given a pile of plates to wash, I would drop or chip half of them. If I was asked to carefully scoop an even portion of boiled rice into a series of small bowls, I would get the rice everywhere from my hair to the floor, but little would make it into the rice bowls.

I was glad when Aya threw up her hands and confined me to sweeping, carrying, hauling water and tipping out rubbish, even if they were the most physically demanding jobs. It suited Rin's personality, and made my fumbling incompetence easier to hide. Some things could be explained by Rin's supposed slowness, but I did not want anyone to notice that the hardworking peasant girl did not even know how to shell peas. Much better to pretend to be clumsier than I actually was, and to be banished from touching the food at all.

"One of you take that pail of garbage and tip it out," Aya said, yawning. "And be quiet on your way back in. I'm going to sleep."

Yuki looked at me. I groaned quietly and weaved to my feet. I was so tired that the ground seemed to quiver as I went to pick up the full bucket.

Outside, night had long since fallen, and it was cold. After the hot and sweaty day, I welcomed the chill on my skin, even if it made my joints ache all the more. Distantly I was aware that I needed a bath and to wash my hair, not to mention some clean clothes, but I was too exhausted to feel as miserable as I knew I should.

I reached for the wooden gate of the rubbish dump. It was hidden behind a stand of coniferous trees so that it would not offend the eyes of visitors to the garden. The piney scent of the needles could not quite disguise the stink of rotting food and worse things that rose from the trench inside the fenced-off area. A day ago, I had had no idea that such a place even existed.

Standing well back, I tipped the pail out over the trench, making sure to shake it well so that nothing stuck to the bottom. Aya had whacked me on the back of the head earlier in the day for that.

I jumped violently when I heard a quiet rustle – something was moving in the trench. I started to back away, then went limp with relief when I saw the trio of cats emerge to pick over my offering of scraps. They were skinny, rough-looking things. Strays.

Like me.

I left them to their feast and turned to walk back to the kitchen, slamming the gate behind me.

From my place, under the trees, I could see the whole house, lamplight shining golden through the wood and paper screens at the windows. The shadows cast onto the paper gave me a glimpse of what was happening in each room, like a real-life version of the shadow theatre I had seen once as a child.

In one room, a man reached up, and the room brightened. He was lighting lamps. In another, a woman stood with her back to me, and I could not see what she was doing, until she turned and stepped aside, revealing a vase with flowers that made long streaks of shadow on the screen. The woman nodded and picked the vase up. Her shadow grew larger and then disappeared as she walked away.

On the floor above, another female form stood in profile to me, her head bent. She was very close to the screen, and I could see the bony points of her elbows as she hugged her own chest. The pose was one of utter loneliness, of terrible sorrow.

A large male shadow approached her and held out his arms. After a moment's hesitation, the woman went to him. He gathered her up and embraced her.

It was the window of my mother's room.

A strange, high-pitched noise filled the air around me. A kind of keening, like some little animal caught in a trap. Dying.

It wasn't until my knees buckled that I realized the noise was coming from me.

My ribs seemed to clench around my lungs. I could not breathe. Sobs piled up in my chest like stones, unable to escape. I knelt there in the dark, in the dirt, alone.

I pulled at my kimono sleeve until my arm was exposed, and with dirty, ragged fingernails, ripped open my skin.

Fourteen

The days turned into weeks, the weeks into a month and then another. It was frightening how quickly time slipped away from me. It was frightening how, most days, I could not even bring myself to care.

I was a healthy young woman, but I had never in my life done anything like work. I had never risen before dawn and toiled until after the sun set again, and then tried to sleep on a blanket spread on a hard tiled floor. I had never gone without rest when I longed for it, or forced my muscles to keep moving when they cramped and tore. The drudgery wore me down until I had no room in my head for anything but an inchoate longing for respite; when I did find the energy to think about something other than food or my aching back, I did not enjoy it.

Everyone was always exclaiming over how clumsy

I was. Hardly a day went past without a new bandage appearing on some part of my body. The most common injury was a burn, because they were so easy to inflict, and no one ever looked askance at a burn on a kitchen worker's arm, even if she had had no reason to be near the fire. My favourite was still cutting, though. Nothing eased the crushing pressure of sorrow and anger in my chest like the sharp, bright spill of blood. I made sure that the cuts were jagged and irregular and looked as accidental as possible. I avoided injuring my hands and lower arms when I could, because wounds there took so much longer to heal.

Sometimes I could not help myself, though.

It didn't take Youta long to realize something was wrong. He had seen me as Suzume and knew that I could walk straight and move gracefully. Only a certain amount of my new clumsiness could be explained away as me playing the role of Rin. He sought me out constantly, trying in vain to pull me aside. I avoided him without guilt.

One day, nearly nine weeks after my brothers – now named Takeshi and Yoshiro – had been born, news came of a change. Chika-san, the woman who was technically in charge of all the kitchen staff, came waddling in, her square wooden sandals clack-clacking on the floor. She was fanning her red face rapidly with a paper fan. "Heathens! We're to have heathens here!"

The cooks ignored her, and we drudges stared at her blankly. The head cook snorted and muttered under his breath. Aya sighed. "What heathens are these?"

"Black-skinned ones, with faces like demons. I've just seen them, Aya, I swear to the Moon, with these eyes!"

Aya shook her head, apparently unable to think of a reply.

Yuki snorted and whispered, "Early in the day to be that much the worse for the sake."

"They're *foreigners!*" Chika-san insisted.

There was an audible, "Oh!" and suddenly everyone was crowding forward to listen.

"Foreign visitors?" Aya asked. "They really have black skin? Well, where are they from and why are they here?"

Chika sniffed. "Some nasty foreign place. They are here because Terayama-sama invited them. Their country is knee-deep in gold, so Sumiko-sama the housekeeper said, and the Moon Prince is friendly with them."

"Then it is a good thing they are here?" one of the cooks ventured, then quailed under the fierce glare that the head cook turned on him.

"Whether it is or it isn't, I can't see how talking on it makes this soup thicken," the head cook said. "That goes for all of you men. Get back to work!"

Although no further word came to us about the visitors after that, I found my mind straying to them several times, wondering if they could be the same ones I had seen on the ship, wondering if that boy was with them. That shadow-weaving boy, with his tame bird of prey and kindness in his strange eyes. Thinking about this, I finally let Youta corner me as I hauled water up from the well.

Before he could speak, I asked him, "Youta, can all shadow weavers see through other shadow weavers' illusions?"

He frowned, surprised enough by the question that he let himself be distracted from asking me about my new scars. "I am not sure. I have only met a handful of others. Each one was different in the way they used illusions and in what they chose to hide. I did find that the more I knew a person, the more easily I was able to pierce their weavings, but for all I know, I may have met a dozen other shadow weavers and simply not realized because their illusions were impenetrable to me."

"So if I could not see through another person's illusions, it is likely that they could not see through mine either?" I said, relieved.

"Probably. Why do you ask, Little Rin?"

I shook my head. I had told him about what happened on the ship months ago, on one of my rare trips to the kitchen after we arrived, but clearly he had not connected the foreign boy who saved me with the foreigners that were here now. Not long ago, I would have been only too eager to pour my concerns into his ears, but now I found I did not want to say any more. Part of me was still deeply angry with Youta for his refusal to let me avenge my fallen house. He had blackmailed me, and my sense of trust in him was ruined.

Youta stared at me, waiting for me to talk. I quickly

finished hauling up the water I had been sent for and escaped.

That night I lay awake next to Youta, looking into the orange-tinged darkness. My bones and muscles ached, and I was as tired as a winter cicada, but I could not sleep because Youta was staring at me. He had been staring at me since we both lay down that night, never taking his eyes away. I knew he was just waiting for everyone else to quieten down and begin snoring.

"What do you want?" I whispered eventually.

"I know what you are doing. You are hurting yourself again, aren't you?"

I did not answer.

He sighed. "Some people might call you mad for cutting and burning yourself."

"Some might. They might also call the daughter of the House of Hoshima insane for playing the part of a slow-witted scullion on the orders of an old man whose family name she does not even know. In both cases they would most likely be right." I stopped with a gasp as Aya coughed and shifted in her blanket not far away.

I waited until the older woman had settled again and then turned over myself, so I was facing away from Youta.

"My name is Takatsukasa Youta."

I rolled over again to look at him, surprised out of my anger. "That is the name of a noble house."

"I was the son of a noble house. Once."

"Once?" I repeated. "Like me?"

"Very much like you."

"What happened?"

Now it was his turn to roll away, though only onto his back. "I was a fourth son. In my family, such sons traditionally went to the Temple of the Moon to become scholars or priests. I was taken for a priest. For ten years, I lived in the main temple, here in Tsuki no Machi, and it was there that I learned to shadow-weave in secret."

"You were a priest?"

"Yes. When the ten years were up, I should have taken initiation to a higher rank. Instead, I was sent on a spiritual journey." He laughed, a humourless little huff of breath. "Which means they turned me out to be a wandering priest, because I had not pleased the right people. I could have gone back to my family, who would have whispered in this ear and put gold into that hand, and made sure I was accepted back again, but I was too proud. I did as I had been ordered, wandering from place to place, preaching for a bowl of rice, performing ceremonies for a place to sleep, writing letters for a ride to the next town. For ten more years, I never stayed in one place more than a month. Until I came to a little village not far from where you were born, and met a women there … and fell in love."

I gaped at his profile. Priests took the Moon as their bride when they were initiated, swearing faithfulness to her for all their lives. To fall in love with a mortal woman was to break those vows – a crime punishable by death.

"I cast away my tattered priests robes and, sick of

wandering, built us a little house in the woods. We had a daughter, and for a little while – such a little while it seems now – we were happy. Then word reached the main temple. I still do not know how. Perhaps someone to whom I had once preached recognized me at the market. Perhaps the temple kept a closer eye on wandering priests than I realized. All I know is that they found out, and they came to punish me."

He drew in a sharp breath that caught in his throat. "I was not there. I had gone to sell our piglets in the little village. When I came back, the house was gone. Only ash remained. I found Ayako's body in the woods. I looked for my daughter there, but I did not find her. I walked the forest for weeks, searching, returning to the burned remains of the house again and again, just in case she came back. She never did. I do not know what happened to her, or if she is dead or alive. She was so small, my tiny cherry blossom. She would have been eight that year. We called her Sakura."

He turned over to face me, his voice rough and choked now.

"If I had ever met the men who took away my family, I would have killed them, even if I knew it would cost my life. If someone had stopped me, I would have tried to kill them too. I understand what you want, what you feel. But *you* must understand that I cannot bear to have another person die and leave me as my Ayako did, disappear as little Sakura did. I have grown to care for you, as if you were my own, and I cannot bear to feel that loss again."

I laid my head down, so that my forehead nudged against his hand, and closed my eyes. "What am I to do, then? What am I to do, dear friend? I cannot stay like this forever."

"Maybe you can. Maybe we will think of something. I do not know. Only please do not be angry with me any more, Little Mistress." He sounded pleading, and I could not bear it.

"I am not angry with you." I reached up and laid my fingers on his, and felt them curl around mine.

Silence fell again. For the first time since I had become Rin, I did not sleep at all that night. I listened to Youta's quiet soft breath until morning came.

Fifteen

A day or so later Aya was wrapping a bandage around a burn on my elbow. The wound had refused to heal, and as a result, Aya had asked Chika-san for the key to the little medicine chest. She had applied a foul-smelling liquid to the wound that had made it sting fiercely. I winced as Aya gave the bandage an extra tug. She didn't notice – which made me realize that something must be bothering her.

Yuki, passing us carrying a large iron pot, stopped to look. "It's a wonder she doesn't just fall into the fire and put an end to her suffering, as often as she gets burned," she remarked. I didn't react, knowing that this was as close to sympathy as I could expect from her.

Aya snorted. "At least Rin can't help her silliness."

"Are you going to start telling me off again?" Yuki put

the pot down with a clang.

"And why shouldn't I, my girl? Last night was the third time. If you must roll around in the hay with your stable lad, why can't you do it at a safe time of the month?"

Yuki, who was already pale and wan, went even paler, her mouth drawing into a thin line. "I have to take my joy while I can. There's little else to look forward to in this life."

"Well, I don't look forward to nursing you through another bout of sangre-root cramps, Yuki. Anyone would think you enjoyed being sick for hours! Either be careful from now on or you'll have a bellyful of trouble, because I won't give you sangre again."

Seeing the look on Yuki's face, I quickly made myself scarce. I'd just found a convenient hiding place by a pile of dirty utensils when Chika san appeared in the kitchen, her paper fan flapping so hard that I almost expected to see her fat little feet leave the floor.

"Aya, you will never guess what is going on! Terayama-sama is setting up targets in the garden!"

"Targets?"

"For *kyūjutsu*," Chika said, naming the art of archery. "Apparently those heathens were boasting about their prowess with the bow, and Terayama-sama challenged them to a contest! They are doing it right now."

Aya's look of bored indifference disappeared. "You mean the lord is shooting in the garden?"

"Ho ho!" said the head cook – this news apparently

interesting enough to suppress his normal contempt for Chika-san. "Terayama-sama is a master archer. He will put those foreigners in their place."

Aya and the cook exchanged a look. He pulled off his white hat as Aya began to move towards the door.

"Hey, you," he said to one of the undercooks, as he followed Aya. "Don't take your eyes off that *nizakana*, and make sure you turn the duck—"

"Sensei! Where are you going?" the undercook cried.

"None of your business. You are not a child. Just supervise in my place for a few minutes."

"The same goes for you girls," Aya tossed back from the doorway. "I expect all those steaming baskets to be repaired and stacked when I get back, Yuki."

"Wait for me!" Chika-san said, pushing in front of the head cook.

The door closed behind them, leaving everyone else gaping. Then Yuki flung down the basket she was holding. "Pigs! Leaving me behind like that! And all this work to do, and me not well." She picked up the basket and flung it down again, harder this time. In a moment, she would probably stamp on it, and then she would look for me to vent the rest of her temper upon.

I reached for an illusion of smoke and weathered, oily red bricks. As I gently eased the door open with one finger, so that it might seem as if it was only swinging on a gentle breeze, I concentrated on the unfamiliar, clayish feel of the shadow-weaving. I had never used this one before, and it was hard because bricks need to be still to look right and I was moving.

"Rin! *Rin!* Did anyone see where the *baka* went?" Yuki shrieked, suddenly behind me. "I shall give her such a beating when I find her!"

I winced, but it was too late to change my mind now.

Without questioning my desire to witness the archery contest, I went quickly down the short corridor to the house and through the side door. There was a long line of closely trimmed, round juniper shrubs and I bent, almost crawling, so that my head would be hidden behind them.

The garden opened up before me as the junipers curved around. Where the veranda at the back of the house led onto the garden and before the formal arrangement of pools and bridges began, there was a clear area of mossy grass with a serpentine gravel path. It was here that stable boys were setting up the large round targets for *kyūjutsu*. Small groups of house servants were clustered at either end of the veranda, making themselves unobtrusive behind posts or pressing back into the line of shrubs. Chika-san, Aya and the cook were there too. It was like a festival day.

I crawled back around the hedge until I came to the stand of trees that hid the kitchen. I ran along behind them and came out at the edge of one of the ornamental pools. There, a vast and ancient weeping willow bent down to the water. It was a safe distance from everyone else and the view was good. Better, the long trailing branches of the willow provided excellent cover, so I would not have to concentrate on holding an illusion over myself as well, as long as I kept behind the trunk.

I made a weaving anyway, carefully tweaking and pulling at my normal shadow-cloak until I felt it become green and fluttering like leaves, with a long edge that was dark and rough like bark. I held it in the back of my mind, ready in case of emergency.

With a click, the sliding door on the veranda moved back.

Terayama-san stepped out.

My hands became fists. My lips peeled back over my teeth. More than anything – more than anything I had ever wanted in the world – I wanted to hurt him.

But I could not. I could not harm a single strand of his hair. I could not even draw his attention. I had promised Youta.

I leant against the tree, panting and shaking.

After a moment, I peeked out again, and found that Terayama-san was standing close to me now, at the opposite end of the path to the targets. I forced myself to examine him with some semblance of calm and noticed that he wore the traditional *kyūjutsu* costume: a grey *keiko-gi* top with short sleeves that would not impede shooting and the *hakama*, loose trousers. I had never seen him wear anything so plain. It suited him. He looked strong, honest and capable.

This was the Terayama-san that my mother loved.

More people began streaming through the door onto the veranda. High-ranking men dressed in the sort of rich clothes that Terayama-san normally wore. After them came the foreigners.

It *was* the men from the ship. Their behaviour was so different to those around them that everyone was staring. They swung their arms as they walked, shrugged their shoulders, waggled their eyebrows when they talked. Smiles flashed across their faces like the moon striking through ragged clouds on a windy night. They seemed like giants, standing there next to Terayama-san's friends and servants. The shortest of them was actually no taller than Terayama-san himself, but the broad shoulders and powerfully muscled limbs, accentuated by their simple attire, made them look twice as big.

The foreigners wore leather breeches and loose tunics that were bound at the waist with lengths of embroidered cloth. They also sported an astonishing amount of gold. Rings, bracelets, nose and ear piercings. Closer to them now than I had been on the ship, I was able to count eight earrings marching up the curve of one man's ear. The bottom one was a dangling pear shape made of amber. Most had thin gold collars at their necks, the metal formed into fine strands and braided.

Not one of them carried a bow, wore a glove or displayed any other sign of the archer. It seemed that Chika-san had been wrong. There was no contest to be held here today. Something else was going on. And the boy – my boy – was not among them.

There was a pang in my chest. I breathed out sharply.

Terayama-san bowed deeply to his foreign guests. They bowed back just as deeply, but somehow I felt that they found the ritual amusing. Despite Terayama-san's smile, I did not think he shared their amusement. Something had nettled him.

He motioned his friends and the servants to silence, and I wondered why he had not ordered the servants away yet.

"Here we gather, friends and honoured guests," he said. "We were speaking of archery, and we have disagreed on the subject. It will give me great pleasure to demonstrate to you *kyūjutsu* – or as some are calling it now, *kyūdō* – the Way of the Bow. I intend to prove to you that this is, indeed, an art. *Kyūdō* is based upon the three principles that all disciples must attempt to attain: truth, goodness and beauty."

My fingers tightened on the harsh bark of the willow until they went numb. I remembered my father and Terayama-san standing together in the *kyūdojo* in my old home, laughing because neither of them could beat the other. They had had the same teacher, had practised together all their lives, and their skill and technique were equal.

Terayama-san had said that he was sure my father could beat him, if only he had the ambition. He had seemed frustrated that Father would only exert himself to a draw. Father had said that Terayama-san had enough ambition for the both of them. He had never realized how true that was.

Terayama-san was made of avarice and desire and covetousness. What he wanted he must have, no matter how low he sank to gain it. There was no place for truth, goodness or beauty anywhere that he was.

That was what this so-called contest was about. That was why it was taking place out here in the open: for though the house had a perfectly good *kyūdojo* of its own, it was so small that only Terayama-san and his foreign guests would be able to watch the demonstration, and Terayama-san wanted witnesses, lots of them, even servants. He wanted to win against the foreigners, defeat them, and prove it to everyone.

Terayama-san spoke again, gravely. "For a master of *kyūjutsu*, there is only one target. The one within our own spirit. Some have called me a master of this art, but I will leave it to you, honoured guests, to judge."

The dark-skinned men nodded respectfully and I felt sorry for them. Terayama-san held out his hand. It was clad in a *yotsugake*, an archer's glove that covered all but one of his fingers. A servant came forward to hand him his *yumi*. The bamboo bow was taller than Terayama-san, with a slight recurve to the bottom third of its length. The servant had already strung the bow for him. My father would have frowned at him for that. He had said that a man who cannot string his own bow is not fit to shoot it.

Terayama-san already had three arrows thrust into

the back of his obi. Now he reached back with his free hand and carefully pulled one out. It was longer than the full reach of his arm.

Still holding the bow above his head, he nocked the arrow to the string. He slowly drew the string taut, bringing the bow down in the same measured movement so that the arrow lay next to his eye. He sighted and released.

The arrow hit the target dead centre. Terayama-san drew the next arrow from his obi. Again the arrow thudded home at the precise centre of the target. There was a low murmur of admiration and pleasure from his friends.

Terayama-san drew the last arrow from his obi and held it in his hand. "From the moment that I lay my hand upon my bow, I must know that the arrow is already in flight. When I touch my arrow, I must know that it has already hit the target."

He closed his eyes. Keeping them closed, he went through the movements of nocking the arrow and drawing the bow. He stood still, blind, waiting. I could see most of the people around him holding their breath.

Terayama-san loosed the arrow.

It hit the target in exactly the same place as the others.

The foreign visitors began clapping their hands noisily. Terayama-san opened his eyes and smiled. Then his friends stepped forward to congratulate him.

"Do you see now, A Suda-sama? Do you understand that this is an art?"

"Oh yes," said one of the foreign men. He stepped

forward, reaching out. Terayama-san seemed to expect this. He switched his *yumi* to his left hand and allowed the man he had called A Suda-sama to clasp his forearm.

"Then I have changed your mind?"

The foreign man released Terayama-san's arm and made an odd gesture, lifting both hands and laughing. The painted scars on his face were in straight lines across his cheeks, like a cat's whiskers, and his laughter made them move as whiskers do when a cat yawns or snarls.

One of the female servants made a frightened noise, and it struck me with a deeper awareness than it ever had before that what Youta had said was true. The servants here in Terayama-san's house had swathed their own minds in so many layers of illusion that they were incapable of seeing these foreign men clearly. They did not see the friendliness, the relaxed confidence, the life and joy that glowed around them, like sunlight reflecting from polished jet. Those serving girls, and probably everyone else there, thought the foreigners were ugly.

To me, they were the most beautiful men I had ever seen.

"I am afraid my mind is not changed, Terayama-san," A Suda-sama was saying regretfully. "I cannot deny that you have made archery into an art here in your garden. This does not change the essential nature of the thing. Archery is what we call *gan a hamat a hana*. A skill of killing, a way of death. It cannot be beautiful."

"I do not understand you, A Suda-san. You have said to me that your young people, even your young women, are trained to use a sword and bow. How can you call archery evil if you teach it to your children?"

"I do not say it is evil. I say it is not art. It is a necessity." A Suda-san shrugged. "We are a peaceful people and we abhor killing, but our lands are rich, and we must be able to defend ourselves. Our sons and daughters fight and hunt, and we honour them for it – but because we know what they endure to fulfil their duty, not because the hunting and killing are glorious things in themselves. To kill is to destroy, and destruction brings despair. That is why our people do not eat the flesh of your domesticated animals. If we hunt wild animals, we give them a fair chance to escape, and in taking down a stag or a boar, we know we risk our own lives too. To destroy a tame animal that does not even know it may run and that trusts the hand that spills its blood is sickening to us, as is all death."

The man spoke so passionately in his deep, accented voice, I could see that everyone listening had been unwillingly touched by what he had said, and their instinctive resistance made them resentful of him.

"Our greatest warriors," Terayama-san said, "believe that they are already dead. They live as if their lives are over, and so fighting holds no terror for them."

A Suda-san looked gravely at him. "That, Terayama-san, is one of the saddest things I have ever heard."

"I hesitate to disagree with such an honoured guest, but it occurs to me that with such sentiments ruling their training, your warriors may struggle to defend your prosperous land. Should they ever need to."

A Suda-san blinked slowly, his dark eyes glinting. When he smiled, he again reminded me of a cat, but a rather less friendly one this time.

"You have been kind enough to provide a demonstration of *kyūjutsu* for me and my countrymen today. Perhaps you would be interested in a demonstration of the way we train our archers?"

"*You* will shoot against me?" Terayama-san asked, surprised.

"Oh no, no. I did not bring any weapons to your house. I did not think I would need them. Luckily, there is one among us who is still in training, and so needed to carry his bow with him to practise."

"In training? Do you mean—" Terayama-san broke off as someone new stepped out onto the veranda.

Sixteen

It was my boy.

The boy who had saved me.

Only it did not seem right to call him a boy any more. He had grown. He was nearly tall as Terayama-san now, if not as broad. He wore the same leather breeches as his fellows but had stripped to the waist, displaying long, wiry muscles that flexed and bunched smoothly as he stepped down from the veranda to the grass. His long hair in its thin ropes was gathered into a horsetail on the back of his head and was free of the golden ornaments his countrymen wore. In fact he had on no jewellery, save for a long leather thong around his neck that bore a piece of some fine white stuff, bone or ivory perhaps, carved into the shape of a crescent moon. The pendant hung just beneath his breastbone.

Then he stepped out of the shadow of the house and I – along with everyone else in the garden – gasped. The boy's back was … marked. Like his face. The scars glowed against the skin, a deep, almost iridescent blue. The dots and lines curved and swirled, like storm clouds or the sea. His left arm to his elbow was also thickly covered in the marks, as was his left shoulder. The pattern ended in a single, delicate tendril that curled around the top of his right hip, as if it were beckoning. Only his right arm was bare.

I had heard somewhere that criminals wore tattoos to identify themselves to others of their kind, but I knew instinctively that these marks were different. They meant something not frightening or bad, but important.

"My son, Otieno," A Suda-sama said. "He is just seventeen, so please excuse his technique. He still has much to learn."

Terayama-san looked at the younger, slighter man and nodded affably. I wondered if anyone else could see the suppressed smugness there. "Of course. None of us would expect perfection from such a young person."

And the boy – Otieno – smiled. My breath stopped at the glory of it. It was a fearless, reckless grin. Not the expression of a boy who knows his mistakes will be forgiven but of a man who has a healthy interest in winning, and every expectation of doing so.

Terayama-san did not see it. He was too busy directing the servants to remove the arrows from the targets. "Come now, Otieno-chan," he said. "Where is your bow? Surely you have not forgotten it?"

"I have it here, Terayama-san."

And it was there, in his left hand, just as if it had always been. It was tiny, not half the length of Terayama-san's *yumi*, and with a sharp recurve that bent it almost exactly in two.

Terayama-san blinked. "What a clever trick. An odd bow, though, if I may presume to comment."

Otieno raised an eyebrow. "To me, your bow also seems strange. Please inspect it, if it interests you. There is no magic in it, I promise."

Terayama-san took the unstrung bow and turned it over in his hands. "It is heavy," he said, giving it a little shake, as if he expected to hear it rattle.

Otieno took the bow back from Terayama-san and, having been handed a coiled string by one of his countrymen, quickly tied a figure of eight loop to one of the white nocks, and then pressed that end to the ground, bending the bow so that he could slip the string over the other nock and loop it into place. The young man who had given him the string said something to Otieno in a different language, a quiet mouthful of melodious sounds. Otieno laughed and so did the others, apart from A Suda-sama, who clapped Otieno on the shoulder.

Terayama-san broke in on the moment. I could tell he did not like their laughter: not when he could not tell if it was directed at him. "Such a small bow must have rather a shorter range than we are accustomed to. It is not fair to expect Otieno-chan to hit the targets as I have done. We will bring them closer."

"You are very good, Terayama-san," A Suda-sama said. "But if my son is to improve, it is best for him to have targets which are a little too difficult for him, rather than a little too easy."

"That is very true," said the man who had given Otieno the string. "My father is wise. I recommend we move the targets back another length."

"Brother!" Otieno tried to cuff the man's head, but he danced away from the blow, smirking.

Terayama-san was not one to blow away gold dust when it landed on his palm. He nodded. "Very well. We will move them back."

As servants hurried to do his bidding, I could see Terayama-san calculating the odds of his making such a shot himself at this distance, and then, after glancing at Otieno's small bow and smaller frame, smiling. I bit my lip. I knew elder brothers sometimes teased their younger siblings, but surely not in a situation like this?

I looked at Otieno again. He was not laughing now. His face was serious, his eyes focused on the targets as he took up his stance. A Suda-sama and his countrymen moved away from Otieno, leaving him alone in position. They were no longer laughing either, not even the brother who had been smirking moments ago.

Something shimmered on Otieno's back, and then there was a black leather quiver there, the strap slung diagonally across his chest. I drew in a sharp breath. He was shadow-weaving, right there in public. I was astonished that no one had noticed it, but then, perhaps no one else had believed their eyes.

Holding his bow in one hand, Otieno raised his carved, moon-shaped pendant to his lips and let it rest there, his eyes closing as his chest filled with a deep breath.

Then he let the pendant drop.

His bow was in position by the time the pendant hit his chest. It had not bounced once before he had reached back, found an arrow and nocked it. The first arrow left Otieno's bow with a high-pitched whistling noise, and a second seemed to fly almost in the same movement. The final arrow was released before the first had hit the target. My ears filled with their screaming as, for an instant, they hung in the air together.

Thunk. Thunk. Thunk.

Three arrows stood in the targets, each one at the exact centre. Even from where I stood, I could see that they had sunk so deeply they would have to be cut from the targets, not pulled free. I clutched the tree for balance.

Otieno was the greatest archer I had ever seen. Better than Terayama-san. Better than my father. Better than my father's legendary teacher Honma-sensei. And he was still in training. No wonder the Moon Prince wanted these people as friends. They might abhor killing, but if they had a thousand archers like that, their enemies would die regardless.

No one clapped this time. Terayama-san and his friends stood frozen and the foreigners simply moved forward to surround Otieno, patting and punching him on his arms and back.

His father smiled at him and spoke in their own language. I did not have to know the words to understand what was said. *You shot well, son. I am proud of you.* They hugged each other, right there in public, with Otieno holding his bow awkwardly out to one side to avoid poking his father with it.

Otieno's brother shrugged. "You hesitated on the third shot. If the target had been moving, you would have missed it."

"I don't want to hear that from the man who shot our uncle for lack of hesitation," said Otieno. He held up his bow as a shield when his brother made a threatening movement towards him.

"I missed him! I missed him by a clear foot."

"More like an inch, Kayin. Ask him yourself."

"Enough, enough," said one of the other men in the group. His ropes of hair were mostly grey, and I thought he might be the oldest, though he stood straight and had no wrinkles on his face. "You are neglecting our host. You must thank him for letting you practise today."

Otieno turned immediately, bowing to Terayama-san.

"I thank you for the practice," he said. "My bow was growing brittle with disuse."

Terayama-san's free hand clenched and unclenched as Otieno's father stepped up to him with a broad smile. "Do you see now why I insisted that to us, bow and arrow are ... your word is ... business?"

Terayama-san stared at them both in silence for a second, eyes blank and glittering. Then he laughed, and I sagged with relief. I did not trust his look of resigned humour – but it seemed the immediate danger was past.

"If your son is representative of a mere half-trained warrior of Athazie, then I am certainly willing to consider your point."

"Oh, Otieno is not a warrior," A Suda-sama said. "He is a scholar! An Akachi. He is my cleverest son, far too clever to risk in hunting or battle. We teach him archery and other skills to force him away from his papers and out into the sun once in a while."

Terayama-san's expression flickered as he absorbed the implication that he had been beaten by a mere scholar. "Well, after such exertions, I think that some shade and refreshments might be in order. I am sure my wife will be interested to hear about Otieno-chan's studies," he said in a voice of strained patience.

Otieno did not move. He squared his shoulders and asked, slightly too loudly, "Before we go in, there is something I have wished to ask you since we became your guests, Terayama-san."

"Oh? Ask, then," Terayama-san said, a little too tolerantly.

"I wonder when I might have the honour of meeting your daughter, Suzume."

I nearly fell out from behind the tree and had to grab a low branch to steady myself. *Oh no. What on earth is he doing? Of all the questions to ask!* Yet, even as I tensed with worry, another part – a tiny, unreasonable part – was suddenly flushed with warmth. *He knows my name. He remembers me...*

Terayama-san's expression of genial enquiry did not change, but I saw his throat work before he replied, "Suzu-chan is my stepdaughter. My wife's child from her first marriage."

"Really?" Otieno's face was utterly innocent. His father closed his eyes as if in exasperation. "How strange. We do not make such distinctions where I am from. You called her your daughter on the ship."

"I am very attached to her," Terayama-san said. "She is visiting relatives of her father's in the country at the moment. She is much missed."

I was leaning out at such an acute angle now that only my desperate grip on the tree branch was keeping me from sprawling face down on the grass.

The servants and Terayama-san's friends all seemed to be echoing my posture, their faces rapt. So my sudden absence had been noticed and remarked upon, and not just within the household. People had wondered, even if they had not dared to question Terayama-san. Abruptly he seemed isolated, almost vulnerable, not lifted up by people's unspoken fear and admiration but pinned down by the curiosity of their stares.

"I have certainly been sorry not to see her again," Otieno said. "I was looking forward to it."

Terayama-san's eyes never strayed from Otieno. "Of course. Suzu-chan was very beautiful."

There was an echoing silence that seemed to go on and on, one that even the quiet sounds of water and wind song and birds calling could not touch.

"*Was?*"

Terayama-san's face twitched. A tiny, betraying movement of unease. "She is not well. That is why she is resting in the country now."

"And when will she be back?" Otieno asked.

Before Terayama-san could formulate another lie, the veranda door slid open.

I jolted as I saw my mother's slender form there, her face and hands intensely white against the black of her formal kimono. The bones of her face seemed to push sharply against the skin of her face, threatening to break through, and when she stepped forward, it was with the careful movement of one who knows carelessness will be painful.

"Yukiko," Terayama-san said, his attention leaving Otieno abruptly. He stepped up onto the veranda and reached for her arm. "You should not come into the sun in this heat. The surgeon said it would be too fatiguing."

My mother flinched when Terayama-san laid his hand on her, then sighed and leant into his support. "I am sorry, Shujin-sama, but I was curious, since all the servants had disappeared."

Terayama-san glanced around, as if noticing the clustered servants for the first time. A curt jerk of his head was enough to send them scurrying about their business.

"We are finished now, my dear," he said, voice tender. "We were about to come inside."

He gently guided her back through the opening, ignoring his guests, who slowly began trailing after him.

So Terayama-san still cared for my mother – as much as a man like him could care for anyone. And why would he not, when she had given him everything he wanted, his sons, and her compliance and silence? He was the picture of the devoted husband. Yet she was bone tired and ill, and her first reaction to his touch had been to wince from it.

Did she regret the choice she had made? Seeing her like that, I allowed myself to believe it. Allowed myself to believe that she thought of me, missed me, despite everything.

Otieno was the only one to hesitate on the veranda as everyone else slipped inside. He made as if to step through the doorway, but at the last moment turned back, as if he was unable to help himself.

Our eyes met.

My breath stopped. His did too. I could see it.

We each stood in the shadows, reaching for one other across the sunlit space between us. Without ever touching, we touched. I felt his hand on me, and it was warm and familiar and wanted.

Then someone on the other side of the screen caught Otieno's hand, and forced him to step inside, or fall. Otieno crossed the threshold. The screen slid into place, breaking our contact like a pair of scissors severing a stretched thread.

I sat down on the grass, my legs no longer strong enough to hold me.

Seventeen

I tipped the pail of rubbish into the trench and the skinny stray cats converged on it. My eyes did not really see them; instead I saw three black-and-white arrows finding their target, a pair of bare, determined shoulders covered in blue marks, and those eyes, those pale eyes that should have been strange in the dark face but somehow were not...

There was a footstep behind me.

I jumped and the wooden pail thudded to the ground, cats scattering as I turned.

Otieno A Suda stood in the gateway, arms crossed, one shoulder propped against the fence.

Awareness and elation burst over me, making every inch of my skin flush. Then I realized that my shadow-weaving was not in place.

I put my head down so that my hair fell everywhere and yanked Rin's grimy, blank face over my own. *Baka-yarou*, I cursed myself. This man was not like the kitchen staff. He would not see only what he wished to see. No, no, it would be all right. Otieno had glimpsed Suzume for a bare moment, a year ago. It was twilight now, and everything was smudgy and grey. Surely no one could make out Suzume in Rin's tattered and grimy form. He was not here for Suzume.

Then… Why was he here? Why did he look at me – at little, tattered Rin – as if he knew me?

"Honoured guest-sama." I let my voice rise into a timid treble. He was not to know that Rin did not normally speak at all. "How may this humble one be of service to you?"

Even in the dimness his eyes were uncomfortably sharp. I forced myself not to fidget, and after a moment he bent to stroke one of the cats, which had returned to cautiously sniff at his boots. "I am just enjoying the night air. What are they called, these creatures?"

"You do not know cats?" I heard the note of amazement in my voice and hastily cleared my throat. "I mean, they are called cats, honoured guest-sama."

"It may seem strange to you, but there are no such creatures in Athazie. There is an animal – a very large animal – that lives on the plains, and is much the same shape. We call it *gadahama*. The golden hunter. He does not say *meep, meep* as these tiny ones do. His voice is like this." He drew in a deep breath, then let out a deafening roar.

The cats fled again, their legs going in all directions at once as they scrambled away.

I did not realize I was laughing until I saw him smile in response. I turned away, putting my hand over my mouth, trying to push the sound back in. When I looked up again, Otieno was closer: no longer leaning against the gate but standing next to me.

"Your voice reminds me of a bird," he said, still smiling. It was a different smile to the one I had seen earlier. It was gentler, almost shy – but still just as dangerous. I backed away from him, the last of the sudden laughter dying away.

He said, "There is a small bird with a sweet voice called a pipit. That is what you are like, I think. A little brown pipit."

"No, I am – no, honoured guest-sama," I said, the words coming out so flustered that I did not even have to try to sound stupid. "My name is Rin."

"You call yourself Rin? What does it mean, this word? I have found that names here always mean something. Are you named for a flower? Or a star?"

I hesitated. "Cold. It means 'cold'."

"That will not do. It does not suit you." He stepped closer again as he repeated softly, "Pipit."

Unable to help myself, I met his eyes. The softness was there too, and without thinking, I took a step towards him. We were close now, almost touching. The air seemed to crackle between us, lit with that strange connection, with the need to reach out. One of his hands lifted. Mine rose to meet it.

Then a shudder of incredulity went through me. *What am I doing?* I shrank back, whipping my hand behind me. He moved as if to follow me, but froze when I shook my head.

"No. Please," I whispered. I hardly knew what I was saying. It didn't matter. I knew he would understand. And that was the most frightening thing of all.

"Do not fear me," he said. The words were a plea. "I will not harm you."

There was a sound of furtive whispering and muffled giggles. A light flared, and then the warm yellow of lamp-light shone through the trees not far away.

Yuki and her young man.

I felt as if I were waking from a dream. I was frightened again, and not sure why, but I was sure that I needed to get away. Away from this boy Otieno and the way he made me feel. The things he made me think and say.

"Good night," I mumbled, slipping past him.

"Good night, Pipit. Sleep well."

I tightened my grip on the mantle of illusion and ran.

I was good at avoiding people I did not want to see. But Otieno's talent for finding people seemed to be stronger.

After that night, he began to turn up all the time, wandering casually into the less glamorous parts of the garden just when I might be expected to be there. It didn't seem to bother him that I had little time to stand and talk, or that – in my quest to keep the distance between us – much of the time I was short to the point of rudeness. Five minutes talking to me as I drew up water from the well or coaxing a smile from me as I poured garbage into the ditch seemed to be enough for him.

His interest in me made no sense. Even if Otieno saw through my shadow-weavings – and I had no way of finding out without first admitting that I was trying to hide something – I very much doubted that he would be interested in me now. I had been called beautiful, but that beauty had been just as much an illusion as Rin's ugliness was. Soft living. Expensive clothes and jewellery. Cunning hair arrangements and, when needed, the gentle mask of Aimi's smile. Now I was sweaty and grimy, with red, cracked hands and jagged short hair. Who would find me beautiful now?

We were utterly different. And yet, still, there was that spark of understanding between us. An affinity that I could not deny.

I sighed, giving the bottom of the garbage pail an extra whack. Then I stiffened. He was here.

I always sensed Otieno before I saw him. His footsteps were silent and he was wearing his own cloak of shadows, but in the last two weeks I had learnt the feel of it. It was like a quiet, melodious humming in the air. I closed the gate before I turned.

"Does your father know you are out here?" I said.

There was a low, husky laugh that sent a thrill up my spine. "I cannot creep up on you any more."

The shadow against the wooden fence wavered and became Otieno. He was leaning one shoulder against the wood, smiling at me.

I refused to let my reaction to that lazy smile show. "Well? Does he?"

"Not exactly," Otieno said. "He knows there is someone I like. He knows when I go out, I go to see her."

"But not that she's a low, dirty drudge," I finished.

"You are not low," he said seriously. "So please do not speak of yourself like that. Neither are you dirty – or not any more than anyone would be after a hard day of work. I have been dirtier than you many times, and so has my father."

My shadow-weaving should have shown layers of sweat and muck. Otieno acted as if he did not even see it. While I could sense Otieno's shadow-weavings, I could not pierce them so easily.

"I am a drudge, though," I said. "And he does not know. If he realized who your 'someone' was, he would take you away from this house within the day."

"My father judges people on who they are inside, their qualities and character, not by their job."

"Then why have you not invited me in to meet him?" I

asked mockingly, knowing that if such an invitation were ever issued, I should run away for fear of discovery.

"It is not because I am ashamed to know you. We are guests, Pipit, and I know that Terayama-san's ways, and the ways of this country, are different from my own. I cannot insult my host openly, much as I dislike him. That would be to embarrass my family and my ruler. It would be different in Athazie. Besides, it is not as if you do not have secrets of your own."

"Tell me about Athazie," I said hastily, hoping to distract him. "What is it like?"

Otieno spread his hands, as if there was too much to describe. "It is beautiful. To me it is the most beautiful place in the world. The plains are golden at this time of year, with long grasses that sing when the wind moves them, but soon the dry season will end, and the sky will turn purple and fill with rain. You can see rain coming for miles. It sweeps along the plain like a great veil, and it is warm. It feels like an embrace."

"Is everyone there like you? So..." Now it was my turn to gesture helplessly.

He gave me a sidelong look. "So loud?"

"I did not say that."

"You have said it before. We are not so formal, not so restrained as the people of this country. We laugh if we are happy and cry if we are sad, and there is no shame in it. I often find it hard to understand what people here are thinking."

"You do not seem to find it hard to know what I am thinking."

He reached out suddenly and touched my face. I froze, my breath caught in my throat. "But I do."

"What are you...?" I whispered as he leant forward.

My body lit up as his lips pressed softly against mine. One long finger stroked slowly down my neck and lightning sparks of sensation sizzled across my skin. I gasped. He drew back a little, looking into my eyes.

His fingertip rested lightly on my throat. Unconsciously I reached up to touch it, and he caught my hand and held it to his heart. I could feel the rapid pulse thrumming there, just like the time he had saved me.

"Soon, Pipit," he said. "Soon I will be able to show you."

Before I could ask what he meant, he pulled away, his body disappearing into a ripple of shadow and then nothingness. He was gone.

I went into the next day in a kind of daze, unsure whether to be ecstatic or miserable. I bumbled and bumped and made such a mess of things that morning that Aya threw up her hands and assigned me tasks that would get me out of the kitchen and out from under her feet. "Before you kill yourself or someone else!"

Youta looked at me searchingly, but all I could do was roll my eyes. How could I describe what had happened, or how I felt about it? I did not know myself. What did Otieno mean to show me? Was I a naïve fool to feel that tiny fragile fluttering of hope?

Then, just before noon, as I carried two pails of peelings to the rubbish pile, I heard the faint echo of laughter from the garden. And I forgot all about Otieno. About Youta. About the need for secrecy.

A moth, its entire body from wings to feelers, is designed to reach out to the moon. It cannot help it. At that moment I felt like a moth, drawn by an instinct beyond its control. I put down my burden and turned towards the sound, following it through the cover of trees and out again into the humid warmth of the sun.

I found a place under the weeping willow once more, and pulled a shadow-weaving over myself. I became a blur of green. Hidden, I watched.

On the grass near the veranda, a soft blanket had been spread out. A little cloth awning had been erected above it, to shelter it from the sun. Isane sat at the edge of the blanket, smiling, holding a long wooden wand, from which pieces of glass dangled on fine threads. My mother and the two babies were on the blanket with her.

Mother wore a comfortable, informal kimono, and her hair was loose, streaming down her back like black water, rippling in the light breeze. Sunlight caught in Isane's glass beads and sent rainbows dancing over Mother's face. The babies gurgled and cooed, their little pink fists waving madly as if they wanted to capture the spinning lights.

She laughed again and reached down and lifted one into her arms. She laid the baby against her shoulder and rested her cheek on its almost bald head, closing her eyes.

The gossip in the kitchen was that Terayama-san's wife – I had tried to train myself to think of her that way – had not been well for a long time. Not since the babies had been born. Aya said that some women were like that, perfectly healthy until they bore children, and then never right afterwards. She said that the lady probably missed her daughter and was worried about her being unwell and far from home. The cook was under orders to create a specially nourishing menu for her. I told myself fiercely that her suffering was none of my concern. She had made her choice and must live with it.

This woman was not shattered and broken and in need of careful treatment to retain her sanity. She was a little thin, a little pale, true. But it was nothing a few more good meals would not cure. She looked ten times better than she had the day of the archery contest.

It was then that I realized the truth. Mother was not mourning any more.

She was not tortured over the deaths which were her responsibility. Nor did she pine for the daughter who had disappeared to no one knew where.

Instead of suffering, she was getting better. And she was *happy*.

Happiness glittered and sparkled on her face, as clear as the tiny prisms from the toy. Nothing mattered to her but the child in her arms. For that child, she had sacrificed Aimi and my father. For that child, she had sacrificed me.

I walked away, but I could still see, as if it had been imprinted on the back of my eyelids, the look on her face. If she had ever cared about me, she did not now. She had forgotten Suzume.

Suzume no longer existed.

Eighteen

I emptied the garbage from my pails. I went back to the kitchen and set about fulfilling the tasks which Aya had given me. I had done them a hundred times. I did not need to think. My back bent, my hands moved. Slowly, slowly, like scorch marks deepening on a piece of paper held near an open flame, the knowledge of what I must do was forming inside me.

I could not touch Terayama-san, or face him, or hurt him in any way. I had promised.

I had never promised any such thing about my mother.

The weapon I needed was directly before me. The next time I passed through the herb garden, I saw the tall sangre plants with their yellow flowers, swaying in the breeze. The plant which had made Yuki so miserably sick with cramps that Aya refused to let her take it any more.

I stooped and ripped one of the plants out, whole.

I quickly and furtively stripped away the leaves, flowers and stems until I held in my hand the soily root. I washed it well, then poured the water away into the dry earth and drew another bucket to take back to Yuki. I tucked the sangre root, tangled and white and clean, into the breast fold of my kimono.

Knowing it was there made me feel powerful and alive: light-headed with excitement. I wanted to laugh, to shake my fist at the world. I had been trampled and abandoned, but now I had a weapon, and no one could stop me using it. I would take that happiness from her. I would make her suffer, even if only for a little while.

Later, while supposedly scrubbing at a stained pan, I took the root out and shredded it, separating it into fine fibres until it looked like nothing so much as a half-handful of uncooked rice noodles. When I had finished scrubbing the pan, I made sure to pass close to the stove as I put it away. A small pot, filled with *oden* and fishcakes, bubbled there, and the food was intended for one person, and one person only, to eat.

I felt almost as if I watched myself from the outside. As if it was not real. How else could it be so easy? I was not even nervous. I reached over and dropped the shredded root into the pot and turned away, triumphant.

Finally I had managed to strike back. Finally I had done something, instead of letting things be done to me.

The evening meal was prepared and carried away. We

drudges sat down to our own meal.

"Are you all right, Rin?" Youta's voice took a moment to reach me, and it was another moment before I could remember the correct response. I nodded.

Aya caught his attention, and he turned away reluctantly. But he kept watching me all through dinner. When we had eaten, I lay down, but I did not sleep. I was feverish with excitement. Soon. It would come soon.

Perhaps an hour later, we began to hear voices outside, a commotion in the house. The noise may not have reached us in the kitchen but for the doors and windows Yuki had propped open in an effort to create a cool draft.

Everyone began to stir and murmur. Straightaway Youta turned on his side to face me, and I realized he had not been sleeping either.

"Did you do something?"

Defiantly, I answered: "Yes."

The others were waking around us, getting up and sleepily lighting lamps, exclaiming over the racket up at the house, but the only thing I could hear clearly was Youta's quick, harsh breath.

In a jerky movement, he heaved to his feet. Aya turned to him as if to ask him something, but he silenced her with a fierce shake of his head. I did not know what she saw in his face, but her eyes went to me for a second, wide and shocked, and then she stepped away, saying nothing.

Youta reached down for me and hauled me to my feet as if I weighed nothing. He pushed me into that little storeroom where Rin had first been born and slammed the door shut behind us.

"Speak."

I stared at him, refusing to be cowed. "She was happy. She did not care. She deserved to be punished, and I never promised anything about her. I didn't."

"Did you do something to your mother?"

"It's nothing. It will just make her sick, like Yuki. She deserves it!"

"Tell me what you did!"

"Sangre root. I put sangre root in her food."

He stepped forward and grabbed my shoulders, shaking me once. "How much? Where did you get it? Was it dry or fresh?"

"From the garden," I said. His intensity was cutting through my sense of triumph, making doubts and worry creep in. "I sh—shredded a plant root."

"How much of the root? How much did you put in?"

"The whole one. What does it matter?"

The fingers on my shoulders spasmed. "Little Mistress … do you have any idea what you have done?"

"No. No … I…" I shook my head, refusing to look at his white face. "It was only sangre. Yuki took it. It just made her ill."

"Yuki took a spoonful of powdered root in water. Not a whole, fresh root. That is a lethal dose. A lethal dose. Little Mistress, you have killed her."

I gaped at him in frozen silence.

"Terayama-san will murder us all. When he realizes that this is not some sudden illness but poison, he will slaughter everyone who was in the kitchen today." He shook me again, hard. "Do you ever think of anyone but yourself?"

"I will go to him," I said, and as the words left me I realized it was right. "I will go to him now, and confess. I will tell him that no one here knew who I was. He will only kill me."

"That will not work!" Youta said. "How could he believe that you hid here for so long without anyone's help? He will—" He broke off, and his whole body seemed to ease. "I have it. There is a way."

"What? What way? I will do anything, Youta."

"Good. All you need to do is leave."

He let go of me to rummage behind the stacks of firewood until he pulled out the grimy, long-concealed bundle of rags that contained my clothes and jewellery.

"Leave?" I repeated blankly. "How will that help?"

"Come on." He took my hand and barged from the room. In the kitchen, Yuki and Aya were huddled together, whispering. They broke apart as we emerged but did not try to stop Youta as he pulled me out of the kitchen door.

We hit the herb garden and broke into a run. It was almost completely black, the moon no more than a thin crescent above us, but we had both walked this path so often that we did not stumble.

"Please," I panted. "Tell me how running away will help."

"Because he will not realize who you are. You are just a child that showed up a little while ago, whom we took pity on. None of us knew where you came from; you were mute; you gave us no trouble. You disappeared tonight before we even realized you were gone. You could have come from any one of a hundred enemies of his, and he will have no reason to believe that any of us helped you."

"Everyone in the kitchen knows that is not true! You told them I was your niece!"

"Once I tell them what you have done, they will have no choice but to go along with it. If you are some shadowy assassin who is unconnected with any of us, then we have a chance. Otherwise, we are all dead. But for this to work, you must be long gone by the time Terayama-san comes to the kitchen."

I was panting, sobbing: tears splashing everywhere as I ran. I did not protest. How could I? It was too late now. Too late for anything. Too late to realize just what I had done. I had banished myself from this place of safety and hard work, where Youta had watched over me. I had banished myself from Otieno. There was no going back. I was alone from now on, and I deserved it.

I did not even deserve the luxury of tears, but I could not seem to stop them.

I was a murderer.

We reached the fence that hid the rubbish trench, and Youta bundled me through it. Our sandals squelched as we crossed the edge of the trench to the little gate on the other side, through which the rubbish collectors entered the garden at night. The scent of rotting garbage rose up around us in hot wafts.

"When you get outside, you must run as far and fast as you can. You must not be anywhere near this house when we tell Terayama-san our version of the story."

"I'm sorry, Youta," I said, scrubbing at my face with my forearm. "I am sorry."

"It is too late for that," he said, his voice remote. "I should have known that to keep you here was wrong. I should have taken you away. The blame is as much mine as yours."

I was stunned into silence. Then I shook my head, frantically. "No! No— It–it is not. You only wanted to help me; you saved me—"

He cut me off. "Take your jewellery. Go far away and find another place to belong. Forget your father, forget the dead. Let your anger go before it destroys you."

"Youta." I sobbed out the word, clutching at his hand. "I – why … why are you still helping me? Why have you always helped me so much?"

He closed his eyes. "For thirty years, I have tortured myself. I have wondered, if I had been there that day, could I have saved them? When you ran into my kitchen through the sakura, I thought … this is a sign. This is my chance to atone. I did nothing for them. I will do something for this girl."

To my astonishment, he suddenly put his arms around

me, his wiry strength pressing me into his chest. His lips were dry, whispering against my forehead. "I kept you alive. I may not have done it the wisest or kindest way, but I did keep you alive. My Suzume."

Then he let go of me and thrust the bundle into my hands. "Do not look back."

Before I could speak again, he had disappeared into the darkness.

Nineteen

Cold. I opened my eyes. Dawn was turning the sky iron grey and dew was beading all over me, trickling down my face and neck as I sat up, like icy sweat.

I looked around. I had not seen much of this little alley last night when I stumbled into it. There was not much to see now. A packed dirt floor, the lower walls of houses, thick stone without windows, on either side of me. I was hungry with a deep, gnawing ache in the pit of my stomach, and my throat scraped dryly as I swallowed. I ignored it.

I stared at the walls.

I noticed a loose thread dangling from the edge of my right sleeve. I wound the grey, frayed stuff around my index finger and pulled. The weave of the fabric bunched and caught. I could not pull it out. I twisted my head and bit at the thread until it came away. I pulled my sleeve straight and stared at the grey thread woven around my finger for a while.

Then I looked at the walls again.

A little while later I had to stop staring and search for another loose thread that I could feel tickling my neck. Then I had to pick away a scab from the side of my right wrist, leaving a sore red mark behind.

A strand of damp hair fell across my eyes. I pulled it out. My eyes watered, and I gathered the water between my fingers and rubbed at it until it disappeared. I wound the hair around my finger with the thread.

I stared at the walls again.

There were noises starting to come from the houses on either side of me. Voices, screens sliding. *Servants*, I thought, *getting up, lighting fires, scrubbing floors.*

I was a servant. I had been a servant. Before that, a lady.

Now I was a murderer.

I began to shudder. Feverishly I searched for something to distract myself – *the spicy smell of sangre flowers* – another loose thread? – *laughter drifting on the wind* – no, a scab, a scab here on my elbow – *the way the white roots shredded under my nails, damp and squirmy* – I prised at the scab, trying to focus on the itchy discomfort – *the soft, almost inaudible plop as the little bundle of roots slipped into the pot* – no, no, no, the scab – *you have killed her…*

I screamed, hitting my forehead again and again with

the heels of my palms until my vision went grey and my ears growled and it hurt so much that I could not remember, that I had to stop.

I put my aching head down on my knees and wrapped my arms around myself so that I could keep pick, pick, picking at the scab on my elbow.

"Eugh! Disgusting!"

The exclamation jerked me out of my huddled position. I scrabbled to my knees as a young man, dressed in the plain kimono of a servant, gingerly approached me. He held a broom in both hands like a sword. I cringed, only just remembering to grab my little bundle before I ran.

"Don't come back!" he shouted, sounding relieved.

The road on the other side of the alley was narrow. Small houses were jammed in together as if jostling for space, brightly painted wood rubbing shoulders with plain stone. Some were shops, the painted shutters still closed, colourful awnings still rolled up for the night.

Where was I?

I thought – maybe – I remembered crossing a bridge last night. More than one. There were many bridges in the city. I was far from home.

Home?

A harsh, hacking laugh escaped my throat, burning as it went. I clamped my lips shut. Hugging my little bundle to my chest, I wandered away from the road down another alley, and then another. One of the houses had a door here, and little windows high up, and there was a water barrel next to the door.

I cleared the floating scum from the surface of the water, cupped my hands and drank. The water ran down my face and onto the front of my kimono. I dried my chin with my sleeve and then, taking a deep breath, knocked on the door.

A towering woman, her face and muscular arms lightly coated with flour, answered the door and stared down at me. Behind her, there was the familiar chaos of kitchen sounds and smells. I found myself leaning forward.

I cleared my throat. "Do you have work? For a drudge? I know the job and I work hard."

She sighed and shook her head. "There's no work here for the likes of you. Wait." She reached back for something and then held a bowl out to me. There was rice and broth in it, and vegetables. I looked at it and then back up at her.

"Take it, *baka*!" she said, pushing it at me so that it slopped. "Don't you want to eat?"

"Th–thank you." I took the bowl, the heat of it scalding my hands. The food burned my lips and tongue as I tipped the bowl up to eat, and made a path of fire in my chest and belly.

The woman took the bowl back, careful not to let her floury hands touch my dirty ones. "Now get on. Mistress will have my skin if she finds out I'm feeding beggars."

She closed the door in my face.

I stayed there, leaning against the door for several minutes, longing for her to come back out, yearning for that brief, warm brush of kindness. Then the door rattled as if to open, and I skittered away. She would not be kind if she saw me a second time. She did not want me dirtying her clean doorstep.

I walked on. Shops and houses were coming to life around me now, screens and shutters opening, voices and everyday sounds filling the air. The sun was not high enough to warm me. I shivered in my damp things. My sandals crunch-click-scraped on the ground, rubbing my feet. I was getting blisters.

As I leant down to look at my sore foot, I noticed another kitchen door near by. I knocked. The door flew open to reveal a man with a red and shiny face. He was clearly in a rage and seeing me made it worse. Before I had even opened my mouth, the heavy wooden spoon in his hand lashed out.

I jumped sideways, and the blow that would have knocked the wits from my head connected solidly with my upper arm. Everything from the elbow down went numb. I yelped, dropping my bundle.

"How dare you?" he screamed. "I won't have beggars knocking at my door like visitors!"

He landed another hit on my shoulder as I cowered, trying to retrieve my bundle. I dodged the kick he aimed at my side, and my fingers closed on the knotted rags. I snatched them up and stumbled away.

"Scum!" he shouted as I left the alley. I kept running until the sound of his voice faded behind me.

Eventually, unable to go on any longer, I collapsed on a section of stone paving outside a closed shop, trying to catch my breath. I was more thirsty than ever, and my shoulder and arm throbbed.

Across from where I sat, men and women were moving purposefully around an open area, raising wooden stalls, unrolling awnings and setting out wares. I unwrapped my bundle. The grey rags parted to reveal the soft, fine fabric of the kimono I had worn the night I had run away. The cloth was crushed and crinkled, but still, no one would ever believe that a person like me could have come by such a thing honestly. Could I use shadow-weaving to fool someone into buying it from me?

Another of those harsh, braying laughs escaped me. Even at my very best, rested and calm, I could never have created an illusion good enough to hide the way I looked now. No, it would have to be something smaller.

I pulled out one of the combs and rewrapped the bundle. Looking at the delicate beauty of the tortoiseshell, coral and amber, I felt a pang of regret that I must part with it. Then the stupidity of that washed over me and I was furious with myself.

Resolved, I got up, the comb clutched in my fist. Anyone might lose a piece of jewellery like this on the streets, and any beggar might come across it and keep it. A stall that sold jewellery, and which was perhaps not too respectable, might buy this from me.

The market was open now, and already filling with customers. I roamed it for a time, too frightened to stop and look or meet anyone's eyes. It was sunny and noisy and full of laughing women, running children and determined sellers, who sang out the names of their wares like a song. On a normal day I might have enjoyed spending time here.

A normal day? For who? Suzume? Rin?

There was no such thing as a normal day for me, and there had not been for a very long time.

Brightly embroidered sashes caught my eye on a nearby stall. They were like the ones Otieno wore.

For a moment it was as if he was before me. I remembered the way he leant or lounged on the edge of the well or against the wall whenever he came to talk to me. He should have looked undignified but did not. I remembered his deep, almost lazy way of speaking with that soft accent. His long hair and its clinking hair ornaments. Most of all I remembered the way he had made me feel. Alive. Real. Loved.

What do you think of little Pipit now, Otieno? Do you hate me and revile me as everyone else does? As much as I hate myself?

I walked off, eyes dry and smarting as if I had blinked sand into them, and wandered again through the market, head down, shoulders hunched, tracing patterns in the dirt under my feet. I bumped into people. They cursed and shoved me, but I did not look up to apologize.

The day grew hotter. My throat was so dry I could barely swallow. My suffering forced me to pay more attention to my surroundings. I came across a small, tumbledown stall at the back of the market. Its sagging awning was propped up against the side of a building. When the owner saw me coming, he grimaced, revealing three teeth in varying shades of brown.

"No begging, no begging," he said, raising his hands. "I have nothing to give you."

I looked at the stall. Laid on a faded cloth were little clusters of semi-precious stones, small pieces of jewellery and some fragments of larger pieces, cheap combs and more expensive ones that had damage, and badly carved netsuke.

"Please, Oji-san," I said, giving him the title of uncle out of courtesy. "Do you wish to buy today?"

"No, no, you have nothing that I wish to buy. Go away. You are frightening off my customers."

There were no other customers. I kept my eyes lowered. "Oji-san, last night I found something outside a great man's house. It is very pretty. I want to sell it."

"Pretty?" A note of interest entered his voice.

I looked up and brought my hand forward to display the tortoiseshell comb, with its smooth cabochon jewels set in silver, resting in my dirty palm.

"Well, well," he said, his eyes brightening. "That is pretty. But—" Suddenly he moved back, his face blank. "Not worth much, I am afraid, a little piece of nothing like that. Worth very little."

He named a figure, and I ran into a problem I had not foreseen. I had never carried money, or bought anything for myself. How was I supposed to understand what he was offering? I stared at him, trying to work out how to ask.

"What? Do you think someone else will offer you more? All right, all right!"

Another, slightly higher figure was named. Again I stared wordlessly. Again he protested and fidgeted and slightly raised his offer. Emboldened by this success, I began to close my fingers over the comb, shaking my head.

"You want to starve my children? You want my wife to go out in rags? Very well!" His voice rose almost to a squeak as he named another amount, a little more than twice the original.

I had no idea if it was fair, but by then my hunger and thirst were such that I could not care. I nodded.

As I walked away a moment later with a handful of coins, I heard the man chuckling to himself, and knew that he had cheated me. I had sold half of everything I possessed, and been cheated. He was a thief.

But you are a murderer.

I sat down right there on the dirt at the edge of the market, shuddering, gritting my teeth. *Sangre flowers dancing in the breeze* – I did not want to see – *Mother's face dancing with light*— Stop it!

· I brought my fist down into the dirt, hard, panting and choking on my breath. I was going insane. No, I was already insane. I had not realized it until now, that was all. I was a beggar, a madwoman, a murderer.

I was no longer hungry. People were carefully walking around me without looking. I snorted with miserable laughter and climbed back to my feet.

I used a little copper coin to buy tea and drank it under the seller's watchful eye. When the cup had been refilled once – as much as a copper coin could buy – I returned it carefully. I was tempted to ask for another cup, but although I had five more coppers, the tea-seller did not look as if he would be happy to accept another from me. It was late afternoon now, and the crowds in the market had thinned. I could feel the stallkeepers' suspicious looks. Did they think I was here to steal from them? The bruises from the wooden spoon ached warningly.

I put the rest of the money into the bundle, shaking it well until I was sure that none of the coins would escape, and began walking again.

Twenty

This was my new way of walking: head down, shoulders bent, clutching my bundle to my chest. Walking with no idea where I was or where I was going.

I had a handful of coins and one jewelled comb that I could sell. When coins and comb were gone, I would starve unless I could find work. The only work I knew was drudge work, but even that seemed to be above my reach now. People thought I was a beggar. That was almost funny; I wished I knew *how* to beg. It might be a way to stay alive.

Was it possible, if I tidied myself up a little, that I could approach people for work without being turned away? I could not afford to replace my tattered kimono, or wash the dirt from it. I had heard that there were such things as public bathhouses, where men and women shared the same water, but I had no idea how to find such a place, or even if the owners would let me in, looking as I did.

I walked for a long time, thinking. The houses grew sparse around me, and the path under my feet grew stony, and grass and wild flowers sprouted along its sides. The air tasted of water. I saw the gleam of it between the houses, and then the houses were behind me and the river was in front. It was a wide tributary, wide enough that there was a bridge over it. It was a sturdy wooden structure, made in a gentle curve so that small carts and animals could be pulled or driven over it.

As I walked towards the bridge, not watching my steps, one of my sandals caught on something in the path. The cord which had been rubbing at my toes all day finally snapped. The geta went one way and I the other. I fell, grazing hands and knees on the rough ground. Something sharp jabbed into my left knee. I flinched and sat back, pulling my kimono up to see blood streaking down my leg.

There was no Mai here to fuss and flutter, and no Aya to bandage me up. I had thought before that my life was hard, but I had not realized until now that the greatest hardship, more painful to bear than any other, is to be alone.

I rubbed a little of the blood away from my knee with a fold of my kimono, but it just welled up again. The cut did not seem to be very deep, but if it was, what then? There was nothing to do but ignore it.

I got up, kicking the other geta away, and then, limping heavily, I made my way to the bridge.

The sun was setting now, and the water was gleaming bronze with crests of fire as it moved, deep and mysterious. Several fishermen were out on the water in little boats, hauling in their nets. A pair of cranes waded in the thick mud at the edge of the river, their bodies gleaming white and their black heads almost invisible.

Not really knowing why, I forced my tired legs to carry me up onto the bridge. The wooden slats had been worn smooth by hundreds of feet and were gentle to mine. An old man walked past me in the opposite direction, tugging a protesting goat behind him, and then I was on my own at the top, breathing hard.

I put my bundle between my chest and the handrail to cushion me and leant over, eyes drawn down to that dark water rippling so gently below.

I imagined the water was still warm from the sun. I imagined what it would be like to fall from this bridge, down, down, with the wind fluttering through ragged hair and ragged clothes, and be swallowed up by the river.

It would hurt, no doubt. The pain would be terrible as the water forced its way into mouth and nose, and you would likely struggle, unable to help yourself. But a girl who had never learnt to swim, who was tired and weak and dragged down by her clothes, would not be able to struggle for long. The water would close over her head and she would stop struggling and the pain would stop. A girl like that would go under very quickly.

The priests said that virgins who took their lives to avoid dishonour became stars in the Moon's celestial train. Such maidens were supposed to die by other means, though. Their father's sword, or sometimes poison.

My father's sword was lost. And I had given my poison to another, and thrown away my honour thereby.

Yuki would say that I would become a river ghost, drifting sadly about the bridge to warn others away from my fate. I did not believe in ghosts. I thought, *hoped*, that I might disappear. That everything would go away, and I would just cease to exist. I let out a long, slow breath. How peaceful that sounded.

I watched the very last fisherman making his way back to the bank. Once he had finished, and gone…

The wood under my feet vibrated with heavy foot steps. I waited for them to pass, keeping my eyes on the fisherman dragging his boat up onto the muddy bank. A man laughed behind me.

The laughter caught my attention. It had the same unkind note as the laughter of Terayama-san and his friends. I turned my head and just as quickly turned it back, staring blankly down at the river. Behind me were two guardsmen in uniform kimonos with swords thrust into their obis. I froze, and tried to make myself as small as possible. I felt rather than saw them come and stand one on either side of me, blocking off all escape but down, into the water.

My fingers tightened on the rail. Could I push myself up and over it in time? Would they follow me and try to pull me out?

"Good evening, Imouto-chan," the one on my left said, using the familiar term for little sister. A darting glance showed me that he was young, twenty perhaps. His hair was falling out of its neat topknot at the front, as if he had been rubbing or scratching at it. It showed me something else too. The man's face was not tense or grim; he did not look as if he had unexpectedly come across a criminal wanted for the assassination of a powerful lord's wife. He looked a little excited but relaxed, confident.

Relief made my voice tremble. "Good evening, guard-san." They did not know who I was. They would not drag me back to Terayama-san and expose Youta as a liar.

The relief died as the man said, "What is a young girl like you doing out here all alone at this time of the day? Don't you know that this is a bad area? Anything might happen to you."

Oh no. No, no. It could not be. All day long I had been treated with revulsion and now – now someone found me attractive? Was this man blind? Could he not see what I was?

"I live in this part of town," I said evenly. "I only stopped for a moment. My father is expecting me home."

"Really? Well, perhaps we should escort you back to him."

The other guard sighed impatiently.

The first guard let out another of those low, gloating laughs. "My friend is not as soft-hearted as me. He would let you walk home in the dark all on your own. You don't want that, do you?"

I clutched at the wooden rail. *Another few moments – just another minute – and I would have been beyond your reach. I would have been beyond this fear. Go away and leave me alone.*

"She isn't interested," the second guard said, stepping away. "She smells awful anyway. Let's go."

"Not so fast—" The first guard moved suddenly, sliding one of his arms around my waist and up to the front of my kimono. In rage and disbelief, I felt his fingers grope at my chest.

Instinctively I fought, digging my nails into his arm and jabbing one of my elbows back. The bony point sunk deep into his stomach. I felt him grunt against my ear. He shoved me away with both hands and I went flying, crying out as I landed hard. Sobbing with pain and relief, I got my hands under me and began to push up. *Run, run, get away…*

A foot slammed between my shoulder blades. I went down onto my face, still scrabbling to get away. The foot pressed down against my back, a steady pressure that kept me flat, crushing my lungs. I coughed, struggling for breath.

"That little—" I heard the first guard say.

"Stop acting like a fool for once and look at that bundle

she just dropped," said the other. It was his foot holding me down.

"What about ... well, well," said the first guard. "Jewellery, money and a lady's fine kimono. We've caught a thief."

Footsteps pounded up to me and a kick to my side made my ribs explode with agony. I gasped, unable even to scream. I wanted to curl into a ball, but I was already being hauled up. My arms were bent behind me and bound with something thin and strong that bit into the skin of my wrists.

"Not so icy now, are we?" said the first guard, leaning towards me, his hot breath puffing over my face. My stomach was cramping. If there had been food inside me, I would have been sick.

"I bet you wish you'd been a bit more friendly, eh? Too late now. You're going in a holding cell with all the other scum, and in the morning..." He made a crunching noise behind his teeth and then poked his tongue out as if he was dead.

I spat in his face.

He stumbled back. The guard holding my arms jerked me to the side and punched me, his fist smashing into my temple.

The blow knocked me silly. Everything swam dim and grey, as if I had jumped from the bridge after all and was slowly sinking through the water. Distantly I heard cursing and was aware that I was being lifted and heaved over someone's shoulder. The shoulder drove into my abdomen and I retched. I was not aware of anything more for a while.

I woke up when we stopped moving. There were voices, and then I was dropped. I slid to the ground with a bruising thump to my shoulder and hip. My head bounced off the floor. I was rolled roughly onto my stomach by someone's foot.

"That way if she pukes she won't choke on it."

Something heavy slammed down inches from my head, making me wince. A gate. A rattle: keys?

Then silence. Darkness. I was alone.

Why? I had been so close to escaping this, so close to escaping everything. Why must I be brought lower than I already had been? Why had the fisherman lingered? Why hadn't I jumped when I'd had the chance?

I would die tomorrow anyway, from what the guards had said. On the face of it, it made little difference. Yet once again the choice had been snatched away from me, just as with everything else in my life. Even my death was not to be my own.

Every bruise, cut and scrape began to throb in time with my heartbeat. I could not even hear myself moan over that thump, thump, thump of pain. My ribs seemed to grind against one another with every breath. It was almost as bad as the memory of that man's hands all over my chest. I could still feel them, clutching and rubbing. I retched again, gasping as my ribs protested.

Carefully I rocked and shifted until my bottom was

on the floor and I could stretch my legs out. My head and ribs both sent out warning jolts of pain, and I had to hold still and breathe slowly and shallowly for a few minutes.

It was only then that I noticed I was not alone.

The room was small and square, about as long across as twice my height. I thought that I would be able to stand upright in it, but most people would not. Three of the walls were packed dirt, and so was the floor. The fourth was made of thick, strong bamboo staffs, bound in a criss-cross pattern. There were no windows. Some light – orange and flickering, as if from tapers – filtered through the gaps between the bamboo bars, confirming what my nose told me, that the room was surprisingly clean and well swept. There was no furniture, not even a blanket to lie on.

In the furthest corner of the room, a man – a very large man – was slumped against the wall, unconscious. He had at least three chins, and his mouth gaped in a silent snore. I could not smell alcohol, but something about the boneless way he drooped told me he was drunk. Was that good or bad? I watched him warily, but he did not move at all.

Still, I shuffled back, ignoring the stabbing pains from various bits of me, until my shoulder blades were pressed against the opposite wall.

I began trying to free myself from the bindings on my wrists. Moving cautiously, I squirmed and wriggled, leaning forward and then back against the wall, forward and then back, until gradually I was able to work my hands under my backside. I knew I was scraping and bruising my fingers terribly, but they were numb enough that it did not stop me. I leant back again, using the wall for support, and lifted up as much as I could. Cold sweat was streaming down my face and back, and my legs were trembling. I yanked desperately, and my hands came up and hit the backs of my knees. I collapsed down again, still shaking, and slowly worked my hands out from under my legs.

My shoulders twinged, grateful to be in a more natural position. I rolled and shrugged them as best I could with my hands still tied together, but my ribs soon demanded I stop.

When I brought the bindings to my mouth, I could feel that they were leather, thin and flexible. I lost track of time as I gnawed at them, working at the same tiny piece until I felt it begin to fray and finally to part. I pulled my hands from side to side and tugged at the other ties with my teeth until they loosened, just a little, just enough to drag my hands free.

I flung the hated ties at the bamboo door and began rubbing the feeling back into my hands, gritting my teeth against the tingling agony of the blood returning to the cold flesh.

I was free from my bindings. There was no way to be free of this cell, or my fate.

I had only this last night to live.

For the first time I began to wonder why the Moon had been so swift in her punishment. It was not that I did not deserve it. I knew I did. But others had committed crimes as terrible as mine and had suffered no immediate downfall. Terayama-san had murdered his best friend and a defenceless girl and had gone on just as before.

The one punishment that Terayama-san had suffered had been the one I had inflicted. I had – I forced myself to think it – stolen his wife from him. He loved her in his way. He would mourn her. Yet he would still be Terayama-san, golden and proud, feared and admired. He had not lost all he held dear, been exiled from home, been brought lower than dirt.

My mother had died, but Terayama-san lived. He had not been punished nearly enough.

On these bitter thoughts I drifted into an uneasy sleep.

Twenty-one

A noise woke me. A low groan. It took me a moment to realize that the noise had not come from me.

I tensed as I looked up, expecting to see a fat drunken man.

There was no fat man in the cell with me. There was a woman, lying on her side near the back wall. I stared at her in astonishment. It was not just the fact that she had somehow entered the cell and changed places with the fat man without ever disturbing me.

Everything about her was wrong. Such a woman should never have been in a prison cell.

She wore a *kurotomesode*, the most formal style of kimono for married women. It was black with a stunning design of butterflies and dragonflies in red, gold and amber. Even in the gloom its colours seemed to glow. Her hair was long, as long as mine had been once, and just as glossy, even in disarray and cascading from a series of golden pins and combs.

Then she moaned again – no, whimpered – a sound of profound suffering, and all other thoughts left my head. She was clearly in pain. I was the only one there to help. Cautiously I shuffled closer to her.

"Onee-sama," I whispered, using the most respectful term for older sister. "Onee-sama, what is wrong?"

The woman murmured and stirred; her sleeve fell away from her face. It was too dark for me to make her out perfectly, but the shadows could not hide such beauty.

Enormous, cat-like eyes blinked dazedly out of a heart-shaped face. Those eyes – both the shape and the colour, an unusual pale amber – were so astonishingly lovely that for a moment I did not even notice the perfection of her cheekbones or the delicacy of her mouth. All I knew was that even to me, who had grown up with Hoshima Yukiko and Hoshima Aimi, two acknowledged beauties, this woman was overwhelming.

"My side," she whispered. She was struggling to focus on me, her slender brows drawing together. "Please…"

"Your side is hurt?" I asked, still dizzy with the strangeness of finding such a person as this in the cramped little cell.

She panted through her teeth, as if bracing herself, and then rolled onto her back. Her right arm fell away from her side and I saw a wet, spreading stain just below the golden fabric of her obi, where her ribs ended.

Alarmed, I reached out and then drew back again. I was not a surgeon. I would be more likely to harm than help. And yet I desperately wanted to help. The intensity of that desire surprised me.

"There is – a lot of blood," I said, my hands hovering over her. "I must call the guards." They would not let a woman like this die. It must have been a mistake that she was here in the first place.

"No!" Alarm seemed to rouse her a little, and she shook her head. "It is only a graze, but … I have enemies. There is a price on my life. If those guards know of it, and find me here, defenceless—" She made a jerky gesture towards the stain.

Which meant that it was up to me to do something. I did not think I could bear to watch anyone else die. She might be a stranger to me, but I was all that she had, and I knew I had to help her. I swallowed dryly, trying to remember any small snippets of information that Aya had let fall about treating wounds.

"We must stop the bleeding by applying pressure. I am sorry: it is likely to cause you pain."

"Thank you." The words came out as a cough, and she jerked, then tried again. "Thank you for helping me."

I bit my lip. What was the best way to get at the wound? Moving to sit behind her on the floor, I stretched my legs out on either side of her body.

"I am going to lift you now," I said, trying to sound

confident. "Try to help me as much as you can."

"You speak keigo…" she said idly.

I stiffened as I realized my mistake. Drudges did not speak keigo. It was one of the reasons Rin had spoken so little. Why had I let my guard down so easily? But it was not important now. She was surely in too much pain to care, and was just trying to distract herself.

"Yes," I replied shortly, and slid my hands beneath her, grasping her torso under the armpits. She pushed up on her hands, adding her strength to mine, then made a muffled sound and went limp.

I cursed, wrestling with her weight, using every muscle I had gained while working in the kitchen. Finally I had her in place, and braced her on both sides with my knees to keep her there.

"Apply pressure," I muttered to myself. Her obi was the obvious choice – it would have layers of fabric, including two padded *obimakura* to give it volume. I pushed my hands down between us and fumbled with the complex folds of fabric, unknotting the *obi-jime* belt and then pulling away the obi and *tare* – the outer wrapping cloth – and the first *obimakura*. They gave me plenty of fabric to use on the wound.

The fat, padded centre of the *obimakura* went over the wet stain on her side. I pressed it down, hard, and kept it in place with my knee as I pulled the long ties around her body and knotted them, making the wrapping as tight as I could. I checked her face for signs that I was hurting her.

Her head was lolling on my shoulder, and her eyelashes did not flicker.

I put the thin, fine cloth of the *tare* on top of the first makeshift bandage, wrapped it around her body twice and knotted it again. The outer obi cloth went last. It was long enough to wrap around her body twice and still have a lot of material left over, but it was too stiff to knot. I made a simple obi fold on top of the wound, hoping that the extra layer would create more pressure.

I checked that the binding was tight and secure and then, letting her settle sideways against my knee, slumped against the wall.

It felt like forever before she breathed in sharply and then groaned. "Oh … tight…"

"I am sorry," I said. "It must be tight to work."

"I fainted? I apologize for burdening you. Thank you for your efforts. "

"Onee-sama," I said, having been thinking hard while I was waiting for her to wake. "You asked me not to call the guards, but they are the only ones who could have put you in this cell. They must already know you are here. Will you please explain?"

She shifted uncomfortably. "What of you? There must be some strange tale behind your being here. Your appearance does not match your voice."

I refused to be distracted. "Onee-sama…"

"Please. I need to think, and your voice is soothing. Talk to me for a while, and then … I will try to explain."

I hesitated. She did not say anything else. Her silence had a peaceful quality, which reminded me a little of Youta, and the way he always waited for me to talk. They could not have been more different, and yet something about this woman called to me in the same way that Youta had. No matter how ridiculous it was, I felt as if she was a friend.

And after all, what did it matter now? Tomorrow would be the end of me anyway.

Softly, awkwardly, I began to speak of what had happened to me. I did not describe things in great detail. I merely said that my family had been destroyed, and that I had found out later my stepfather had been responsible, and my mother complicit. I told her about Youta and my shadow-weaving, though I expected her to think me mad, and even about Otieno.

I did not mention my real name or Terayama-san's name. And I did not tell her about the awful thing I had done before I left my stepfather's house. I did not want her to condemn me, as even Youta had done. Instead I said that my mother had died from an illness.

"I had no idea how horribly unprepared I was for life outside the kitchen," I said bitterly. "Now I can wish only for a swift execution. My father and cousin will never have justice, and our name will die with me…"

I fell silent at last, and the silence lasted for several minutes. I wondered if she had fainted again. When she eventually spoke, it made me jump.

"What is it that your cinderman called you, child? Rin?"

"Yes."

"Well, Rin, I believe that you and I were brought together by the Moon. You have said that you only want to die now. Is that really true?"

I sighed into the darkness. "It is. You might think me a coward, but I dread any more suffering in this place."

"What if the choice was not between death and prison, but between death and life? A new life? What if there was a way to escape this cell?"

"I … do not know," I said, then frowned. "There is no way to escape, so it does not matter."

She laughed, a hoarse little sound. "Very well, then. I shall show you. Look."

She lifted her left hand. She had very long fingers. I was looking at them, wondering if she was going to produce a set of keys or if the delirium had set in – for both of us – when suddenly there was no longer a hand extending from the end of her sleeve but a furry golden paw. The wicked black claws extended and then disappeared as the paw flexed.

The golden fur slowly melted back into pale skin, and I gasped. "You were the fat man in the corner, weren't you?"

"I was walking in the market, alone. It was stupid of me. A man tried to rob me, and stabbed me when I resisted. That was stupid of me too. I managed to get away, and flung an illusion over myself – the fat man that you saw. But the pain made me dizzy, and I stumbled into a guardsman. My third episode of idiocy. Taking me for a drunk, the guardsman threw me in here."

"Is this shadow-weaving?" I asked, awed. "I could see every hair on that cat's paw. I did not look at the fat man twice. I did not sense anything."

"You need further instruction," she said. "From what you have said, you know only the basics of the craft. The one who taught me to shadow-weave was a very learned man. He said that there is some force in the world – whether it is fate, or the Moon, or even an instinct of our own – that brings people like us together in times of need. We have both found that to be true in the past: you with your cinderman and your foreign friend on the ship, and me with others. Now you and I have found each other, and we must help each other as best we can."

"Onee-sama, I agree that it is strange and wonderful that we should meet in such a way, but I still do not see how we are to leave this cell. We cannot shadow-weave the door open."

"We will not need to. The guards will open it for us," she said, a smile in her voice. Then she told me what we would do. She finished by saying, "I must have your help for this. Though I am skilled at complex weavings, I am not used to maintaining such a large cloak of shadows for so long, and I am very tired and weak."

"I can do it," I promised. "But will you be able to run, or even walk, when the time comes?"

"I have no choice," she said. "Besides, I will have you to lean on."

Twenty-two

I helped her to rise, and we moved to stand against the wall next to the bamboo bars. This would be where the guards would come in, and hopefully where we would shortly go out. The light was stronger there. I would have to compensate for that, but, just as she had said, I had no choice.

"How are we to attract their attention?" I asked.

She settled heavily against me, one arm across my shoulders so that I could support her, the other clutching at the makeshift binding of her wound. "Leave that to me. First of all we must make the shadow-weaving."

It was a peculiar sensation, working with a shadow weaver who was not Youta. Her style felt very different. She pulled threads of darkness into being sharply, creating hard lines and folding them around us as efficiently as a good maid folds cloth. My weaving seemed soft and insubstantial by comparison. It drifted around her boundaries like cobwebs – but cobwebs that blocked out the light and filled every gap she had left, until my own vision began to dim. The hardest part was to prevent the illusion from becoming too shadowy, to preserve the impression of rough mud walls and flickering torchlight while at the same time completely obscuring our shapes. I knew it was working when she faded completely from my sight.

"Very good," she murmured. "Subtle. You are talented."

I could not remember the last time someone had praised me, and it made me glow.

"Now you must take it and hold the whole together by yourself. We cannot chance it falling apart at a crucial moment if the pain becomes too much for me." Her voice seemed to speak straight from the wall.

I felt the weight of the illusion pushing down on me. It was a heavy, even pressure that made me sag, like wearing a woollen cloak that was utterly soaked with water. My ribs chose that moment to jab at me sharply.

"Wait," I managed to gasp. It was strange how something I knew to be purely illusion could affect me physically, but I remembered that I had clutched at my blanket of ashes for warmth, and supposed it must always be that way. Another layer of illusion: my mind tricking my body.

I took a firm hold on the illusion, and, visualizing those hard and sturdy lines that she had laid out, used them to haul myself upright again. The illusion would support me instead of weighing me down. It resettled around us, and she made a surprised and approving sound.

"Do you have it?"

"Yes."

I both felt and heard her take a deep breath. Then the cell was filled with an unearthly, high-pitched wailing. It sounded like a demon rising up from the depths to claim its prey, and even though I knew where the sound was coming from, it still made the hairs on the back of my neck stand up. She interspaced the wailing with occasional, more human-sounding screams of "No, no, save me!" and "What is it? Moon, preserve me!" that made me want to look around and check that nothing really was attacking her.

Soon I could make out voices outside, and then running footsteps. The wailing stopped abruptly.

With a rattle and a creak, the bamboo bars slid to one side, making a gap large enough for someone to step through. The woman beside me was shaking with tension. I planted my feet firmly, determined to be ready.

One of the guards stepped cautiously into the gap, bending so that his head would not hit the low ceiling of the cell. He held a lamp out before him – close enough to make me squint. I pressed back further.

As the light showed him the empty corners of the room, he grunted. The lamp shook in his hand.

"Well? What's going on in there? Did they kill each other?"

The bamboo slid back still further and the other guard peered in. The gap was now wide enough for two people.

Her fingers dug warningly into my shoulder and I forced myself not to move. The first guard was still too close, and the second one was blocking most of the entrance.

"There's nothing here," the first guard said.

"What—" The second guard broke off as his gaze too travelled over the bare room. "There were two prisoners in here. *Two*. A drunk and a thief. I put them in here myself." He took another step forward, the keys jangling in his hand, and left the doorway empty.

But I could not move. Both men were now abreast of us, filling up the cell with their burly shoulders and muscular arms. There was not a hair's-breadth of room. If we tried to pass them, we would collide with the one holding the lamp and be trapped between him and the wall. I held desperately still.

If only he would move forward – just a little. One step closer to his friend… Just one step forward, and we could slip past. One step forward…

He stepped back.

My breath seemed to choke me as I watched him shake his head. "I don't like this," he said, inching closer to the door. "Something's not right. Let's—"

Beside me, the woman shifted. What was she…? Was she leaning forward?

She screamed, a bloodcurdlingly shrill shriek of terror.

I started so violently that I bit my tongue. The guard nearest us jerked away from the sound that must have come almost in his ear. He stumbled, knocking the other guard into the wall and sending the keys flying out of his hand.

I did not need her hissed "Now!" to make me move. I was already moving, clutching at her kimono to keep her with me as I plunged towards the door.

There was a jangle and a strangled shout. I glanced back as I crossed the threshold and saw both men plastered against the wall, their faces blanched with fear. The thick bunch of keys was hovering in the air.

She had caught them.

I held in a crow of triumph as I wrenched her past the bamboo gate and grabbed the closest bar, slamming it shut behind us. The keys jingled about, jumping in and out of the lock one at a time until I was in a fever of impatience, and then one of them turned with a click. The gate was locked, and we were outside it. Through the small gaps in the bars, I could see that both men were still pressed motionless against the wall, apparently frozen in disbelief.

A handful of flickering tapers fixed in a sconce in the wall showed me that we were in a tiny space, not even big enough to be called a corridor. A step to our left was an open doorway through which yellow lamplight glowed.

"Onwards," came the whisper in my ear, and I felt her take a firmer hold on my shoulder. The keys still hung conspicuously outside the weaving, but we did not have time to do anything about that now. The caged guards were starting to call, albeit in choked whispers, for help. If there was someone else in the end room, he would be coming soon.

We entered a tiny room with a low table on which there was a sake gourd and cups and evidence of a dice game in progress. A lamp burned on the deeply recessed windowsill of the one window, which also had bamboo bars. There was no one in the room.

"Nearly there," she whispered. We limped towards the door. It swung open when I kicked it. My bare foot left a dirty print on the wood.

And just like that we were outside in the fresh warm summer night air, under a lightening sky. A daylight moon hung almost overhead, its horns seeming as delicate as an ivory hair comb. The sounds of the guards yelling, in earnest now, could be heard behind us. With a sigh of relief, I let the weaving go, and the woman rippled into view next to me, her form swimming and then firming as if she was rising up out of dark water.

"Wait here," I said, helping her to lean against the wall. She complied, panting a little. I took the keys from her and closed and locked the door, muffling the sounds from inside, and then I walked around the little building until I found that deep window. It was far too small for anyone to climb through, and too high. I smiled grimly as I forced the keys through a gap between the bars. That would keep everyone busy for a while.

I went back to the woman, and we stared at each other, dazed, I think, by the speed of our escape.

"Did you see that guard's face?" I said slowly. "When you screamed in his ear?"

She nodded equally gravely. "His eyes … they did *this*…" She opened her own eyes wide and pulled a horrified expression.

A snort escaped me, and abruptly we were both helpless with laughter, clutching at each other and the wall. Gasping with pain – me from my ribs and her from the stab wound – we were barely able to stand but equally unable to stop.

"Like *this*…" she repeated. "Just … like … a fish!"

"*Carp!*" I sniggered, setting us both off again.

"Oh! Ow, ow, ow." She grimaced, her laughter fading as she wiped tears from her face with one hand and held onto her injured side with the other. "Oh, that hurt."

The lanterns planted near by gave a steady light, and I sobered as I saw that her skin was chalky pale and her eyes were lidded with tiredness and overly bright, as if with fever. She was older than I had first thought, too. Fine lines at her eyes and mouth told of a life filled with both laughter and pain.

"I have no idea where we are, or where we should go," I said, steadying her as she stepped away from the wall.

"Do not worry. This is the Perfumed District. I know it well. Let us go now, though. I am near the end of my strength."

My mind still spinning at that casual admission, I helped arrange her arm over my shoulder again, taking her weight with a grunt of effort and pain as my ribs protested. The Perfumed District was the area of the city where men and women would dance, play and sing to entertain people of the opposite – and occasionally even the same – sex, and offer more intimate services too. Such people ran the gamut of social classes from the well-educated, accomplished *oiran* who were sought after by lords and princes to lowly flower girls who walked the streets seeking custom from strangers.

As we stumbled along the well-paved road, through empty streets and past houses from which laughter, singing and music still sounded even at this hour, I remembered the one time I had seen an *oiran*. It had been during my first week in the city, and Mother had not yet been confined for her pregnancy. We had been going to visit a friend of Terayama-san's, when we had heard music, and found the traffic in the road going silent.

The *oiran* had been carried in an open, golden palanquin that rivalled Terayama-san's for showiness, with eight attendants besides the four men carrying her. The attendants were beautiful young girls who played soft, sad music on *shinobue* flutes and rang small silver bells. The *oiran*'s face had been hidden by a veil, but her kimono had been the colour of a night without stars, and her hair had been coiled up in a tall, elaborate arrangement of dozens of combs and pins that glittered with gems.

As she and her little procession passed, everyone had crowded back to the sides of the streets, watching respectfully, not jostling or jeering as they had been doing before she arrived. It was as if she were a princess.

"This way," the woman mumbled now, leaning on me even more heavily and drawing me down a side path. Here the houses were very large, with their red lanterns still glowing, and flowering trees and plants flourishing outside their doors. The grandest house was the one at the end of the path. A haunting tune, played on what sounded like a four-stringed *tonkori*, drifted out from one of the upper windows.

I looked down at myself with blurry eyes and saw the dirt-and-dust grey of my kimono and my bare, blistered feet.

"Onee-sama, I don't think—" I began.

"Too tired to think," she said, and before I could say any more, she let go of me and fell forward onto the porch on her knees. I scrambled after her, trying to pull her away – but it was too late. She had hold of the intricately carved outer screen, and was shaking it so fiercely that I felt sure the whole house must be rattling.

"Stop it!" I cried, horrified.

The inner screen slid open, and I looked up to see an older woman, her hair streaked with grey, step out. Her face, glowing like the moon under a light coating of white make-up, showed no emotion. She stared at us impassively, and I braced myself, groping weakly for one of the porch posts to hold myself up. Then the woman's eyes widened and suddenly she was flinging back the pierced screen and dropping to her knees, crying out, "Akira-sama! What has happened?"

My shadow-weaving friend – Akira, it seemed – crumpled down into the other woman's arms with a sigh.

The woman cast a look of horror and accusation at me. "What have you done to Akira-sama? What is the matter with her?"

I opened my mouth to reply, but only a dry croak came out. My knees wavered. Overcome with exhaustion, I slid down to sit on the edge of the porch, squeezing my eyes closed.

"Hush, hush," Akira said, her words slurring. "Not so loud, my dear, you will disturb your patrons. I have had an accident, and this child has saved me. Now take me inside, and bring her in too. She is … Yue. Yes. Yue, for the Moon. Take care of her, please, Mie-san. She is ours now."

Yue

Twenty-three

The next thing I remember is being hot. Sweating and confined and horribly uncomfortable, I struggled and squirmed, trying to get out from under what felt like layers of blankets. My ribs seemed to crunch against one another, and a wave of sickening pain ran over me. For a moment I went cold, and every droplet of sweat on my face was a chip of ice. Then the cold flushed back into heat.

There was a red light shining through my eyelids that might have been fire or lamplight. I did not know. It felt as if flat river stones had been laid on my eye sockets. I could not open them. Terrified, I began to make frightened bleating noises.

"Quiet, now." A shadow fell across the redness of my eyelids, and something wet and cool was put on my forehead. Trickles of moisture slid down the sides of my face into my hair. Someone took my hands and gently peeled them open – I had not even been aware of squeezing them into fists until then – and bathed them with cold water. Then they were dried and tucked back under the blankets, and a cup was pressed to my lips.

"Open up, now. This is medicine you must take," said the quiet voice. It was kind but determined, and I obeyed automatically.

The liquid that flowed into my mouth was sweet with honey, but there was a harsh, acrid flavour under the sweetness that burned my throat and made me choke. The medicine bubbled up out of my mouth and dribbled down my face. I moaned, and the voice hushed me again, and a dry cloth wiped my face, just as if I were a baby.

Is that what had happened? Was I a baby again? Had I died and been reincarnated, as the religion of the Old Empire had used to teach? Or had everything else, the life that I remembered, been nothing more than the fever dreams of a child? Perhaps I would wake up tomorrow and everything would be all right, and I would have a mother and father who loved each other again, and a cousin called Aimi-chan that I loved like a sister...

The next time I woke up, the first thing I did was to try and open my eyes. They did open, although stickily, and it was such a relief that I did not panic at the sight of the strange room, even though the whole place was bathed in a reddish light with golden edges, and the walls and the ceiling wavered strangely. People moved around the room: black, featureless silhouettes.

I turned my head with a great effort, the bones of my neck and skull humming and sending golden-edged waves across my vision. The waves seemed to go through me too, and the room became a strange froth of red and gold and black shapes, like a tiny pond full of bright fish that thrashed and struggled against one another.

When the rippling waves had settled down a little, I noticed someone lying on the futon next to mine. Their head turned restlessly back and forth, and they were muttering about the *yamatagoto* having a broken string, and how disappointed Ouji-sama would be if they could not dance tonight…

Ouji-sama? Who did I know that might dance for a prince?

Squinting made my head ache and all I could make out was a pale face and long hair straggling everywhere. I closed my eyes to make the ache go away, and fell asleep.

I had a strange dream. I was looking down at a small, skinny girl whose face was so thin and white that it might have been a skull, if it hadn't been for the half-healed grazes and bruises that ran down one cheek. Her face was all that could be seen, for the rest of her was swaddled in thick layers of blankets.

Two strange women were kneeling by the girl's futon, and a doctor was telling them that she was strong, and would be all right if she was looked after properly.

I realized that the skull-girl was me. I had got those

marks on my face when the guards had shoved me down on the bridge. I must have been ill a long time. The bruises were yellow and grey and brown now. It did not occur to me that staring down at myself from the outside like this was unusual. My eyes were closed, so how else was I to see what was going on?

As I examined my bony face with detached interest, I realized that the last thing I could remember was the woman, the beautiful woman who was a shadow weaver too. And as soon as I thought about her, I found myself standing over her.

She was lying on a futon next to me, and she too was swaddled in blankets. But her face did not look like a skull. Somehow, and I was not sure how it could be, she looked worse than I did. Her skin was the colour of cold wax and her veins showed through it, dark and bruised.

She was not mumbling now, or moving at all. Her eyelids did not even flicker, and when I concentrated on the sound of her breath, it had a wet, sucking sound to it, as if there were water bubbling in her chest instead of air.

"The wound weakened her," the doctor was saying sadly. "Or perhaps it was the exposure to the unhealthy prison air. I do not believe there is any more to be done. We must make her as comfortable as possible, and prepare for her to pass on."

One of the women covered her face with her hands, and the muffled sound of tears reached me.

The other woman reached out to touch the shadow

weaver's face. "Oh, Akira-sama," she whispered.

The two women stood – the first one still weeping bitterly – and led the doctor from the room, thanking him. I hovered over Akira-sama's bed, and if I had had hands in my dream, I would have held them over my face in sorrow too. Poor Akira-sama. To escape so bravely and then to die of fever. It seemed very unfair.

That was where the dream became even stranger.

I found myself back in my own body again, like falling from a great height and landing on a hard surface. Instantly everything began to ache, from my head to my hips to my toes. My ribs screamed, and I wanted to wake up, to escape from this dream that hurt. But I also knew that there was something important I had to do in the dream. Warmth was kindling within me – not the warmth of the fever but a bright, spreading heat that sparked and flickered in my hands.

Fighting with my covers, I at last succeeded in pushing them down and off. Sobbing with effort, I flopped over onto my stomach. The pain in my ribs made my vision go black, but the heat in my hand would not let me pass out. It itched and itched. I had something to do. I reached out blindly, groping across the tatami mat until I found the edge of Akira-sama's futon. Yes, this was it. This was what the heat wanted.

Akira-sama's hand was lying neatly across her breast. With a mighty effort, I heaved myself across and grasped her wrist.

Her skin was chilled and clammy, and her wristbone poked sharply into the centre of my palm. I was shocked to see that my hand was glowing, white-yellow and orange with burned black edges, like an ember. I could feel it getting hotter where it touched her, throbbing in time with my pulse. I wondered that I could not hear her flesh sizzling under such heat, but the burned edges of my skin seemed to keep the heat inside. That was no good. It needed to come out. *Out. Please come out.*

Come out.

There was a flash. It felt as if it was inside me, but it made the room go bright. Now I could see perfectly. The edges of my skin peeled away, and the heat spread outwards, pouring from my fingers.

Her wrist warmed and softened under my touch, like melting wax, letting the heat enter and sink down into her body. Part of me followed that heat, racing through veins and burning out the poison, blasting her lungs to dry them, scorching the seeping wound until it crisped into a hard, protective scab and warm, healing pink tissue.

Akira-sama shuddered and twitched and cried out, and as she opened her mouth, a long black trail of smoke left it. I was very glad this was a dream. That smoke danced and coiled over her body like some awful living creature. The shapes it made reminded me of claws and scales and lashing tails. I could almost see glinting eyes in the blackness, eyes that saw me too, and hated me. My imagination was more powerful than I had ever realized.

Go away, I told the blackness. *I want to wake up, and I cannot until you are gone. Go on. Disappear.*

The smoke writhed again and dissipated, leaving a sickly charred smell behind. Abruptly I was cold. Akira-sama's skin beneath mine felt warm and comforting.

She breathed in, and my whole arm was lifted up with the depth of that breath. As I lay there, hanging onto her wrist, she turned her head on the pillow to look at me.

"Yue? What is happening?"

I didn't have the energy to explain. I managed a sleepy smile. My dream was slipping away now, going grey and distant at the edges. In a moment I would wake up...

I opened my eyes.

It was daylight, but early, and a soft, yellow light was filtering through screens into the room. I felt weak and hungry, and there was a disgusting taste in my mouth. My eyes were crusted and flinched from the light, as if I had not opened them for a long time.

Next to me, Akira-sama was lying peacefully, her deep, slow breaths telling me that she was asleep. There was no one else in the room.

I lifted up one of my hands, and my arm felt slow and heavy. My palm and fingers were clean and the nails were neatly pared, and when I put that hand over my face to block out the light, my skin smelled of flowers. I had managed to get away from prison alive. I was clean and safe.

And I had killed someone. I had killed my mother.

My actions lay before me now, like a path of little white

stones on the surface of a still, dark pool. I made myself look.

She had chosen Terayama-san. Even after she knew what he had done, she had chosen him. She had betrayed Aimi and my father. She had killed my love for her, banished me and forgotten me. But I had stolen her life. I had committed a cold and cowardly murder, against a woman who had no way to defend herself. Just as Terayama-san had taken my family's lives, I had taken hers.

I did not have the right.

She had ceased to be a mother to me long before – but she had not ceased to be a human being. I had killed her.

I was a murderer.

Hard, dry sobs wracked my body. My ribs ached and jabbed. I endured it.

After a while my sobs died down, and I took my hand from my face. Akira-sama was still breathing evenly next to me, and the morning light was still yellow and warm. I felt as if I had run a long, long way and got nowhere. There was a kind of peace in that. I would never get anywhere. I would never get away from what I had done.

If there was justice in the next world, I would be punished. If not, then I would simply turn to dust. But I would not fling myself into a river to escape. I would not take refuge in madness.

I would carry this secret, this burden, for the rest of my life, and I would never forget.

I would live with it.

Forever.

Twenty-four

Akira-sama and I had been in the *okiya* above Mie-san's teahouse for over a week before either of us woke up properly. Mie-san said that we were both nearly unconscious with fever by the time she managed to get us upstairs that first night. She said that I had probably caught the fever while wandering the streets and given it to Akira-sama in the cell. Akira-sama said that she had been in the cell longer than I had and had probably caught prison-fever and given it to me while I was trying to help her. Either way, it had nearly killed us both.

What followed the illness was a strange, not entirely comfortable time, despite the fact that I was offered more physical comfort than I had known in a long while. Mie-san looked after us very well. She had a doctor in to examine us every day. She arranged for the young women living in the house to visit us, to play music for us and sing, and talk and play games if we wished. Mie-san's second in command, Yoshi-san, arranged all our material needs from clothing to food with a smile, and begged us to tell her if we ever needed anything. It was almost like I'd gone back in time and was Lady Suzume of Terayama House again and wanted for nothing.

I am not dishonest enough to pretend I did not enjoy being truly clean and sleeping on a fresh, thick futon. I enjoyed having comfortable clothes, even if they were borrowed. I enjoyed having all the food I could eat, and not constantly having to hurry about menial tasks. I especially enjoyed not worrying about starving to death, or where I would sleep when it got dark.

The problem was that all these privileges were lent to me by the goodwill of Akira-sama's friends, not for my sake but for hers. I knew it, and so did they. Akira-sama was the only one who did not seem to notice. I thought she was so used to being loved and wanted wherever she went that the idea of being a hanger-on and barely tolerated would simply never occur to her. Once again I was an outsider, lurking on the edges of a world which had no real place for me. The women who lived in the *okiya* were *gijo*, a kind of female entertainer, and their world seemed very strange to me indeed.

Because we were both aching and exhausted and forbidden to shift about and use up any energy during the day, we convalescents often sat up very late into the night, drinking tea and talking. It was during these night-time conversations that Akira-sama explained to me a little about *gijo*. The *gijo* had only recently come into fashion in the city, but had found favour with many because they practised shorter, less formal versions of many of the traditional *oiran* arts, like dancing, singing and playing musical instruments. They were highly skilled and the more popular ones were highly paid, but the *gijo* did not leave their *okiya* in grand processions to visit their patrons as the *oiran* did. Instead they entertained men in the teahouse attached to the *okiya*, and the tea ritual was part of the services they offered. Unlike *oiran*, who could take their pick of lords, and would not even see men of low rank, anyone with money was welcome to visit the *gijo* in the teahouse. However, like the *oiran*, the *gijo* often had *danna*, particular patrons with whom they had a special relationship.

These faithful patrons, most of them married, came to the teahouse not just to drink tea, watch fan dances and be soothed, but also to make love with "their" *gijo*. No *gijo* was obligated to offer herself to a man in such a way if she did not want to, but many of them did. Some had several such special men, others only one.

"I do not really understand it," I said slowly, leaning against the window frame and staring out into the busy night-time street below. Laughter and music was coming up through the floor and from the houses all around, but after what Akira-sama had said, it seemed to me that all of it had a sad, desperate air. "If–if I did not have to lie with these men, I do not think I *could*."

Akira-sama, who, still weaker than me, was reclining on heaps of pillows rather than sitting up, gave a husky little laugh. "*Gijo* are living, breathing women with beating hearts – and yet they may not take lovers, may not marry or fall in love. The *danna* visit them often, talk to them, bring them gifts … they grow fond of them. When they are alone together, holding each other, for a little while *gijo* and *danna* cease to be, and they are only man and woman. For a little while they can both pretend. Pretend to be in love."

She turned her head away. "You see, that is why it is so easy to fool people with our illusions, Yue. In this world, illusions are usually much kinder than the truth."

It was clear that she thought I was being either judgemental or dense. I did not have the words to explain what I really meant. How could a *gijo*, knowing that her *danna* would leave her in a few hours and return home to his wife, simply pretend? Wouldn't such an illusion, when it was shattered, cause more pain than the simple, bleak truth ever could?

Those stolen, golden minutes with Otieno … how they hurt me now, remembering … what if I had known all the time that by my own actions I would destroy that fragile relationship and be forced to leave him? What if I had known that every second was precious, and limited? Would I have had the courage to cherish my moments with him, or would I have cringed from the coming pain, and run all the sooner? I shifted uneasily, and winced as my ribs twinged.

The next day Yoshi-san came to sit and talk with Akira-sama, and to bring her a gift of a polished metal mirror – in case Akira-sama wished to brush and arrange her own hair. Later I gave into the temptation to look into that mirror, and wished that I had not.

It was a stranger who looked back at me: a gaunt, hard-faced woman with greyish skin and a look in her eyes that spoke both of fear and dissatisfaction. I wondered how anyone could ever have thought me beautiful. The knowledge that I could shadow-weave colour into my cheeks and sparkle into my eyes only made it worse.

"You are very unhappy, aren't you?"

I jumped at Akira-sama's voice. I put the mirror away and looked up to see her staring at me gravely.

"I do not know," I said. It was true. I did not know what I felt.

My sense of being lost and out of place was not helped by the discovery, a few days later, of who my saviour really was. Everyone who had visited us up until then had called her Akira-sama, as I did. Then a very young *maiko* – a trainee *gijo* – came to bring us our lunch one day and called her Kano-sama.

It took me several moments to make the connection in my mind. By then I had a mouthful of *gyōza* – a pan-fried noodle packet filled with pork and vegetables – and nearly choked on it.

"Kano Akira?" I sputtered. "You are—?"

Akira-sama, who was serenely sipping a broth of fish stewed in sweet soy sauce, smiled. "We never did properly introduce ourselves, did we?"

I gaped at her. Aimi's favourite story, the one that she had whispered about in bed at night before falling asleep. Kano Akira-sama was known to little girls all over Tsuki no Hikari no Kuni. Ten years ago, when I was a mere baby, the old Moon Prince had held the Kage no Iwai – the Shadow Ball – to meet all the most lovely and eligible women in the country, and he had chosen Kano Akira to be the Shadow Bride, his most favoured companion.

It had been a scandal.

Though technically the Shadow Bride was nothing more than the most prominent of the prince's lovers, her social status was second only to the Moon Princess, the prince's legal wife. It had even been known for a child of the Shadow Bride to become heir to the crown if the Moon Princess was barren. That was why it was an unwritten law that the prince should chose a wealthy, well-bred young woman. And also the reason that the Shadow Bride, once chosen, could never marry: the mother of a potential heir could have no other man in her life. Nor could the prince ever marry her himself, even if he chose her before he took a wife.

Kano Akira had not been the wealthy, well-bred

daughter of a lord. She had been a penniless entertainer of obscure birth, who was only at the ball to dance for the guests. What was worse, instead of retiring his scandalous Shadow Bride at the end of a year and then holding more Kage no Iwai to form new political alliances, as was traditional, Tsuki no Ouiji-sama had refused to give Kano-sama up. He had never held another Shadow Ball, and Kano-sama had stayed with the prince for the rest of his life, reigning as the Shadow Bride until he died in an accident four years ago.

It was then that the beautiful Shadow Bride had disappeared. Rumour hinted that the Moon Princess, enraged at the favour shown to a mere commoner, had done away with her rival by some secret means.

I remembered my father shaking his head over it, telling me that he had once, on a brief trip to the city, glimpsed the Shadow Bride, and that such a lovely young woman did not deserve such a fate. My mother, I remembered, had raised her brows and said, "Adventurers often meet untimely ends." There had been a frosty silence then, and no more was said of it.

Now it seemed that this woman, this legend, whose tale had made so many little girls sigh and weep, was alive after all. With all this in my brain, all I could think of to say was, "I am honoured to meet you, Ohime-sama." I used the honorary title of princess, since that was customary.

"Oh, for the Moon's sake!" she said, sounding truly impatient. "I am not a ghost, or a fairy tale. I am still that same person whom you took pity on in a dirty prison cell, whose wounds you bandaged and whom you almost carried through the city to safety. It is I who am indebted to you, child. And we are friends, are we not?"

I put down my cooling bowl of food and stared at my hands. "I had not thought of it … in quite that way."

"Had not thought of what?"

"I do not consider that you are indebted to me. Though I … should like to be your friend."

She reached out to me, with a hiss of effort, and took hold of my upper arm. "We can only be friends if you will stop acting like a shadow who is lurking at the door and might be banished at any moment. We are not waiting for the chance to get rid of you. You are not with me on sufferance. Not indebted to you? I would be dead if it were not for you."

"I would be dead if it were not for you," I protested.

She nodded. "Yes. The difference is that I desperately wanted to live, and you were already prepared to give life up. I know you escaped from that place for my sake, not your own, and that you do not know what to do with yourself now. That does not make your life worthless. Not to me. Now come. Call me Akira."

"Akira-sama."

"No. Call me as my dearest friend would. As a sister would."

"Akira." I stuttered over the end of the word, wanting to add the honorific.

She nodded again, sharply this time. "You will need to practise."

"I will, thank you Akira—sa— Akira."

She sat back with a tiny groan and picked up her broth again.

I gazed at my cooling *gyōza* with distaste. Akira caught my eye and gave me such a look that I quickly picked up the bowl again and began to eat, if not with enthusiasm then with determination. She smiled, and I felt comforted.

A few days later, when the doctor visited us again, Akira asked him if we were both well enough to travel.

"Only three more days," she said gleefully, when the doctor had gone. "Then we shall be able to go home."

I looked at her, and she sighed. "Of course you are coming too. Please rid yourself of the notion that I am itching for the chance to cast you out onto the streets. Where I go, you go."

While I was trying to adjust to having my thoughts read as easily as tea leaves, Akira went on. "You will like my house, I think. It is not large, but it is very beautiful. We live on the edge of one of the little tidal lakes, just outside the city. The views over the water and the mountains are so peaceful."

I smiled. "I will look forward to it." I did not ask: What will I do there? What use will I be? How will I make up for the awful thing I have done? Akira did not know the answers.

By the end of the week we were leaving. When we had been tucked tenderly into a carriage that had been hired by Yoshi-san, Mie-san and the other *gijo*, most of whom had got out of bed especially, waved us off.

It felt strange to smile and wave back at them, and even stranger, once the door was closed and the carriage had pulled away, to fold my hands in my lap and sit quietly, wearing the heavy, good-quality clothes Yoshi-san had found for me. Even my butchered hair, reaching now to just below my shoulders, had been drawn up and tied into a simple knot. Once again I felt that sense of having been thrust backwards in time, except that I was even less fit for the role of fine young lady now than I had been before. I was thinner and tougher and more wary, and that wariness was as much for the rest of the world as for myself.

Maybe that was all right. Akira had given me a new name, and who was to say that Yue should not be thin and tough and wary? No one. No one in my new life had known me before. No one even knew the name Nakamura Suzume now.

I could tell when the carriage left the Perfumed District – sleeping now in preparation for the night – by the sudden increase in noise. I wondered what part of town we were passing through and wished that we might have the windows unveiled. When I moved my hand towards the window and the gold pin that held the veil in place, Akira stopped me.

"This is the easiest way to conceal ourselves from passers-by," she said. "Your stepfather might still be looking for you, and I already know that my enemies look for me."

"Why do you have enemies, after all this time?" I asked. I was curious, rather than doubting. She had lain bleeding in the prison cell for hours rather than call for help. "Surely if those at court disliked you, they would be happy just to see you go."

"That would be true, if it were only ordinary dislike. Unfortunately there was one at the Moon Court who hated me with the kind of passion that does not dim with time. She will not rest until I am dead."

"The Moon Princess?" I breathed.

Akira bowed her head. The swaying of the carriage made the butterfly ornament in her hair dance gently.

"The tales do not lie about that. After Ouji-sama's accident I panicked, fearing she would do me harm. I ran in secret, and in doing so I made myself the perfect target, for everyone assumed that I was already dead. She had spies everywhere, including in the guardsmen. Once Ouji-sama was no longer there to hold her in check, and with the power of being regent until her son came of age, it was the easiest thing in the world for her to tell her spies that the man who brought her Kano Akira's heart would have a thousand jewels heaped upon him. I became hunted – but covertly, for a messy murder that could be traced back to her would threaten her position. If I had stayed at court, I do not believe she would have dared to destroy me."

"Then would not the solution be to return to court, to let everyone see that you are alive?"

"It would buy me back my safety, yes," she said. "But I have not yet found the courage. There are so many memories there. It is strange how grief turns happy memories to knives that pierce you. Satoshi-sama will be grown now. We were good friends, he and I. It was part of the reason the princess hated me so much. I wonder if he still remembers me…"

I gulped as I realized it was the new Moon Prince, who came of age this year, that she spoke of so fondly. But I knew what she meant about happy memories and knives. "Akira, did you love the Moon Prince, then?"

It was only when the reminiscent smile on her face froze that I realized how impertinent such a question was. Before I could stammer out an apology, the frozen look melted into a wry smile, and she laughed.

"Do you know, that is the first time anyone has ever dared ask me that? Not the first time someone has wondered, mind, but the first time someone has said the words. I think it ironic that with all the tales about me and the Moon Prince, none of them answer that question – the most important one of all."

She turned her hands over and rubbed idly at the long, strong fingers, an uncharacteristic gesture; her movements were always so graceful and deliberate. "Have you ever heard this haiku, Yue?

'Love comes like storm clouds
Fleeing from the wind, and casts
Shadows on the moon.'"

The noises outside the carriage increased as we entered some especially busy area, and our motion stopped with a lurch that made me catch at the wall for balance. I thought about the poem in silence. Was it saying that love was fleeting and unreliable, like clouds? Did that mean Akira had not loved the Moon Prince, after all?

Before I could decide, Akira, her eyes on the veil at the window, continued: "On the night of the Shadow Ball when I was chosen, I was so frightened. It was all a terrible mistake. I should not even have been there. The prince was supposed to pick a noble virgin girl, and when he realized that I was … well, far from that, he would have me killed. They put me in his inner chamber – the bedchamber that only the Moon Princess or a Shadow Bride may enter – to await him, and I sat on the floor at the hearth, weeping, because I knew that no matter what I did, I was going to die.

"When he entered the room, I cowered back. He came towards me slowly and gently like a man approaching some trembling wild creature, and knelt by me to ask me what was the matter."

She let out a long, slow exhalation, as if even remembering was a deep effort.

"So I told him. He smiled, and put out his hand – and

this time I did not cower back, for there was something in his face … something I did not recognize, but which did not frighten me. And he recited to me the haiku that I have just told you."

She looked at me again, her topaz eyes bright with more than the memory. "It took me a long time to understand those words, or even to see why he did not cast me aside in disgust. I hope one day you will have cause to understand it too."

As the last word left her mouth, the veil at the window billowed up in a sudden gust of sea-scented wind. Akira turned away sharply, lifting her hand to hide her face. I knew I should do the same. I did not.

In that instant, as the veil fluttered upwards, I had caught sight of a man standing on the other side of the road. The sea was behind him, glittering grey-gold in the sun, and as I looked, he turned and I saw his face.

It was a face of sharp, strong angles, chestnut skin, swirling blue-black marks, and a pair of mulberry-leaf eyes.

My breath became a stone in my throat as those eyes met mine and widened in recognition, and his lips moved, shaping the name of a tiny brown bird with a sweet singing voice. I leant forward, as if I would reach out of the window, across the street, across all the people between us, and touch him.

Then, with another lurch and a shouted curse from the driver, the carriage pulled away. The man and the sea behind him disappeared and were replaced by the wall of a house. The veil fluttered back down. I turned away, stricken. My breath was still a stone, but now it had slipped down my windpipe and sat heavy over my heart.

"You should have covered your face," Akira said, replacing the pin that should have held the veil, then tugging to make sure of it this time. "What if someone you knew had seen you?"

I swallowed. "No one knows me. Not any more."

Twenty-five

I knelt on the veranda, twitching my robe aside so that it would not be caught under my legs, and looked out across the gentle silver undulation of the lake. Its surface was pitted and pocked by rain, and its reflections hidden. The city was hidden from my view too by the trees, but the mountains were a cloud-shrouded blue-green shape on the horizon, a larger version of the delicate water-colour Akira was currently working on indoors.

I sighed.

The shamisen which Akira had given me a few days ago rested comfortably against my knee. I stroked the gentle curved rectangle of its bo, enjoying the silky smoothness of the wood. I wondered what had happened to my old shamisen. Did it moulder now in the ruins? It had not been anything like so fine as this one. It had been a child's instrument. I was no longer a child.

I sighed again.

My fingers had not quite regained their old skill, but one thing had not changed: the sense of peace playing gave me. Mother had always said that the only time I could be relied upon to stay out of trouble was when I was holding my instrument.

Hesitantly, I began to pluck out a sad, slow tune that I had learnt long ago, and when I felt I had got it right, I sang:

"Copper fish, dance, dance
Leaves falling on silver pool
Autumn rain, fall, fall.
Autumn leaves, dance, dance
Float in the pool of copper fish
Silver rain, fall, fall."

"You are not happy, are you?" Akira's voice behind me did not make me start. I was used to her catlike ways by now.

"You asked me that before," I reminded her, gently lying the shamisen down.

"And you never answered," she said, kneeling beside me.

The wind swirled around us. I shivered. Autumn was making way for winter now, although the winter here was much milder than in my old home. By this time on my father's estate we would have seen the first snow. I pulled my *haori* closer around my neck as I fixed my eyes on Akira – and stared. The breeze had plastered her thin cotton yukata to her form, revealing a flat chest. Not flat for a woman with small breasts. Completely flat.

As flat as a man's.

My gaze flew down to those strong, long fingers as I remembered Akira's words: *"I was so frightened … should not even have been there … supposed to pick a noble virgin girl … and I was … far from that…"*

"Akira. Are–are you an *oyama*?" I asked. It was the name for a male actor who plays female roles in the theatre.

"It has taken you long enough to notice," Akira said. "I have not bothered with my chest pads for over a week."

I blinked up at her, numb with shock. Now it was clear how and why she – and Akira was still "she" to me – had become such a skilled shadow weaver. She had to be. I had never noticed the faintest hint of a man's knot in her white throat before. It was there now, though it was not very prominent.

She had been the Shadow Bride! The whole court had followed her with their eyes, and the prince had loved her. Yet she was not a woman.

"How?"

She gave me an amused, sidelong look. "I was one of many, many children. Some strange accident of fate gifted me with this face and this slender frame, and my parents knew that a child who looked as I did would be valuable. Of course, I would have been more valuable as a girl … so they raised me to talk, move and even think as a girl would. I barely realized that I was any different from my sisters. When I was eight, they sold me to a kabuki theatre."

She sighed. "By the time I was twelve I was on stage as

a *bishounen*, one of the beautiful boys who take the female roles. I was much admired, and had many patrons. One of them was the Moon Priest who taught me to shadow-weave in secret. Yes, many Moon Priests love other men. They believe it allows them to remain faithful to their true wife the Moon, you see." She laughed. "I wonder if She agrees."

I thought of Youta, and the men who had killed his wife. How could they punish Youta for being unfaithful when they did the very same thing themselves? How was it different to love a man than a woman? "I hope not," I said grimly. "I hope She is very angry at them indeed."

Akira gave me a surprised look, but continued: "One of my patrons was a minor lord who thought it would be a very fine joke to arrange for me to dance at the Shadow Ball. He said I would be more beautiful than any 'real' woman there. He thought he was paying me a compliment and had no idea how those words pained me."

I breathed in deeply, awed. "You were chosen. Out of everyone there. I cannot even imagine how you must have felt."

"I have already told you that! Terrified! I was convinced I would die. A man pretending to be a woman in the Moon Prince's chamber." She smiled again, and its brilliance was like a warm golden dawn rising over newly fallen snow. "Later, when I knew him better, I asked him if he ever wished I had been born a real woman. He said that my heart was a real woman's heart, and that was all he was concerned with."

And you did love him, I thought. *You loved him with the whole of your woman's heart, Akira, you sly thing.*

"Was it a secret at court, then? Did anyone else know?"

She made a restless motion, as if shrugging something away. "Why do you think the Moon Princess hated me so much? That her husband should fall in love with his Shadow Bride was enough of an insult – that the other woman should be, in fact, an *oyama*? She loathed the thought that anyone might find out. That is why I would have been safe if I had stayed at court. If I had died there, the court doctors would have examined me, and court doctors are not known for their discretion. Half their income comes from trading gossip." She gave me a long look from those piercing eyes. "You still have not answered me. Are you happy?"

"No," I said, before I thought about it. Then, in a rush: "I do not expect to be. How can I, after everything that has happened?"

I do not deserve happiness.

She frowned, not in anger but as if she were thinking deeply. "If you could do anything now, Yue – have anything, change anything – what would it be? I do not mean impossible things, or wishes granted. I mean something you could work for and gain with your own efforts. What do you want?"

I stared out over the calm silver ripples of the lake and thought about her words. As I thought, something sparked inside me. Something I had pushed away because I had thought it impossible. Something I wanted. Something I would do, if only I could.

"Vengeance," I said finally. "I would avenge my family, and ruin my stepfather as he did us. If I could do anything, it would be that."

She nodded. "I suspected as much. I have been wondering for a while whether I should speak to you about this – but I do not think it will harm anything to tell you another secret. It is not even much of a secret really, since everyone at court knows of it. It is called the Shadow Promise."

"Promise?"

"Yes. It is the most ancient part of the tradition of the Shadow Bride. Ouji-sama believed it was originally a simple vow of fidelity between the Shadow Bride and the Moon Prince, but whatever its origin, this is what the promise is now: on the morning after she is chosen – the morning after she has lain in the prince's bed for the first time – the Shadow Bride is granted one boon.

"She may ask the prince for a promise, and by law he must keep it for as long as he keeps her. The minimum time is one year, but, as in my case, it can be much longer. You see how valuable such a thing is for a lord, if his daughter is chosen? That is why all the lords scramble for an invitation to the ball. If the girl is well coached, she can obtain any concession for her family that does not actually break the law. That is important. She cannot ask for her father to be made Moon Prince, or to have her father's enemy assassinated. If the wish is not legal, it cannot go ahead. But if she wishes to specify that all the government storehouses buy rice from her family before any other, it will be done, as in the case of Shimada Naoko-sama. If she wishes to charge tolls on every road in the nation and direct that money to her family's coffers, as Toyoda Ran-sama did, it can be done. For a minimum of one year. A clever person could become incredibly rich in such a year."

"And a girl who wished to destroy a man...?" I asked, feeling the spark flutter up inside me and become a flame.

"Could simply tell the Moon Prince all that she knew about her stepfather's actions and wish for an official announcement to be made to that effect. If Tsuki no Ouji-sama's seal was upon the announcement, it would be accepted as truth, even if there was not enough evidence to have the man arrested. It would ruin his house's name forever. His friends would turn on him. No one would ever be willing to deal with him again. He would lose all power and influence and probably his fortune shortly after."

The flame became a funnel of fire, sucking air down out of my lungs. I felt the heat of it thrumming through me, bones to veins. There was a way. There was a chance. I could do it.

"But—" And as she said the word, I knew what she would say next, and my elation was checked for a moment. "In order to gain the promise, you must first be chosen. You must attend the Kage no Iwai and be the most beautiful, the most talented and the most memorable woman there. You must force the new prince to forsake all the careful political alliances that his advisers and his mother will be urging on him, and choose you instead. More than that, Yue, if you are chosen, you must fulfil your duties as the Shadow Bride. You must be prepared to become the lover of a man who is a perfect stranger to you, and live in the court with the hangers-on and lords – many of whom will despise you – for at least one year. You will have to deal with the dowager princess. You may bear a child. I know ways to avoid this, but none of them are perfect. Once you are retired, you may never marry. I was born to such a life, brought up to accept such limitations. You were not. Can you bear it? Can you really make such a sacrifice with vengeance as the prize?"

The fire was back, and its crackling and roaring almost drowned out her words. I waited a few moments, so she would be reassured that I had considered what she said carefully, but inwardly I pushed it all aside. Akira did not understand what I had done, what I had to make up for. No matter what happened, even if I had to wade through molten rock, I did not care. I would live with it. For such a prize I could bear anything.

Slowly, pressing my hands down onto the veranda, I bent until my forehead touched the wood.

"I can," I said. "I can. Please."

One of her hands came to rest on the top of my head.

"Very well. It will be done."

Twenty-six

We started the next day. The schedule Akira made up for us was punishing and rigid, and I began to see how she had become the most admired and sought after *oyama* of her day. She worked at it. Hard.

"You have a lovely voice, and you play superbly. That will count for something," she said severely, as she seated herself opposite me in the room with its sliding doors and view over the lake that I thought of as the music room.

I concealed my surprise. How did she know I played superbly? I had not even known that she listened to me, let alone that she liked it. Had my skill improved so much since she gave me my new instrument?

"However, they do not forgive mistakes at court, so you will practise for between an hour and two hours a day. You must also learn to dance. That I can teach you."

"Wait— Why?" I asked. "Noble girls do not learn to dance. They will not expect me to dance at the Kage no Iwai, will they? Surely none of the other girls will be dancing?"

"You are not going to the Shadow Ball as a noble girl. You are going as Kano Yue, my sister – and any sister of mine will be expected to dance."

"I am to be your sister?"

"You are a little too old to be my daughter, and I cannot think of any other explanation as to why I should be escorting a young girl to the Shadow Ball, can you? I suppose we could tell them we met in prison, if you like…"

"Thank you, no," I said dryly. "I will be proud to be your sister."

"Which is as it should be. Something else I will teach you – or try to, as I have never attempted it before – will be to shadow-weave as I do. Your music and dancing will be important in gaining you attention, but that is not enough. We are working against the odds, my dear. You must be the most beautiful woman at the Shadow Ball in order to catch and hold Tsuki no Ouji-sama's attention. The only reason I believe it to be possible is that this is his first Shadow Ball. He has only just come of age and will have been very sheltered. This will make him much more susceptible to seduction. So you must seduce him. You must be a credit to me."

Her play-glower surprised a laugh out of me. She sat back, the glare turning into a look of pleased surprise.

Discomfited, I picked up my shamisen. I did not deserve to laugh. Akira did not know this, and hiding it from her made me sick, but the thought of telling her the truth made me even sicker.

"I had better begin my practice, then," I said.

She rose. "I will be back in two hours."

She kept her word, and I was very grateful to see her arrive, along with a servant who bore tea and plates of sweet *higashi* and *anpan*, for by that time my hands had become stiff and cramped to the point that playing caused me pain. I had never practised for such a long period before. I had never really needed to. At home, once my mother was satisfied that I had learnt the basics and had dismissed my teacher, no one ever listened to me play. Mother said I was not good enough for company.

Akira was sympathetic to my suffering but not very impressed. "*Gijo* do not stop for tea unless a patron requests it. And *oyama* do not stop at all, until their performance is finished. Be grateful."

I was, once the warmth of the tea bowl had eased my fingers. When I had finished my tea, Akira began to teach me the two dances that she said I must learn.

"There is no time for me to educate you properly," she said. "Instead I will drill you in just two, quite short, simple dances: a fan dance and a formal Chu No Mai. You will practise them until it will seem that you are a complete mistress of dance who has chosen simplicity only to display that mastery."

First of all we stripped off our heavy outer kimonos and put on thin cotton yukatas, although I would have to learn to dance in elaborate clothes later on. Then, taking up a rather beautiful pair of painted silk fans, Akira demonstrated a dance which seemed neither simple nor short to me.

There was no music. She moved around the room to a rhythm that was all her own, with such liquid grace that it was hard to believe there could be actual legs and arms beneath her yukata. The dance was delicate and joyful, and her face radiated peace. She threw, caught, fluttered and swirled her fans, making each one seem alive, but at the same time a part of her. I never, for a single moment, believed she would drop one. They flew back to her as if they were birds that she had trained to eat from her fingers.

"This dance is to symbolize a young girl finding joy in the warm winds of summer, and the fans represent both the wind and the girl's emotions," she said when she had finished. "It was a little stiff. My side still pains me rather, and I am out of practice. Now you will shadow my movements and begin to learn."

When we had finished, I was panting for breath and despairing. I was a rank amateur and it showed. I had barely managed to keep up with her, and I had dropped my plain wood-and-paper fans too many times to count.

"Well, that was a good first try," she said, apparently unfazed. "Now for the Chu No Mai. This is a little trickier.

I have thought about it and decided that this will be a sad dance. You have an air of … of not belonging about you. Cultivating it will add to your mystery and your allure. So you will be the ghost of a woman who longs for love."

And once again Akira demonstrated. The dance showed the ghost searching, with increasing sorrow and loneliness, for someone to see her, and love her. It began with broad, beseeching movements that moved Akira around the room, but gradually the gestures became smaller and tighter as the ghost lost hope, lost the ability to reach out, until she curled in upon herself, and sank to the floor. Such was Akira's air of misery and longing that I almost expected to see her crying. I wanted to go forward and comfort her, but held myself still, because of course the point of the dance was to make the watcher long to offer comfort. She held herself in the position of mourning for a moment, and then sat back and crossed her legs. "Well?"

"Perhaps it would be easier if you merely killed me now. Then I really could be a ghost, and would save myself the sorrow of trying to look as much like one as you did."

Akira laughed as if she had not been making my eyes prickle with unshed tears a moment before. "No, no, we of the Kano family do not take the easy way out. You will learn."

After Akira had finished torturing me, we bathed and ate another meal together – I noted that the cooks had prepared an unusually filling meal of beef *motsunabe*, and sent them silent thanks. Then we began shadow-weaving lessons.

We moved to Akira's sitting room for this, as the evening was drawing in. The servants came to light the lamps, and we made ourselves comfortable on cushions, facing each other.

At first Akira tested me by asking me to create simple illusions, much as Youta had done. Holding out my arms in front of me, I made my hands disappear into shadow, made them appear to be covered in coarse fur and then in white and pink cherry blossoms. I looked at my efforts afresh, realizing that to a critical eye they were crude indeed. They relied too much on people seeing what they wished to see – but as I had already learnt with Terayama-san, sometimes people wished to see exactly what you wished to conceal. And the only full body illusion I could do was my clumsy, though versatile, cloak of shadows.

As the petals melted back to plain skin, Akira ran her hands gently down my forearms. I realized she was tracing my scars, and I forced myself not to pull away.

"You must learn to hide these," she said finally. "A Shadow Bride's skin is flawless."

In answer I pulled that most basic illusion, the one of normal pale skin, over my arms. She nodded in approval and said no more, but I caught a considering look in her eyes and knew that she had not dismissed the marks from her mind.

"I do not think you will need much instruction from

me," she said, finally. "Your gift is strong, and so you have learnt to create illusions in broad strokes. You need only learn how to be more attentive to detail, and you will be able to create illusions that will fit a little better, that will be undetectable in the sunlight as well as in the darkness. And in making your illusions finer, you will be able to create larger ones, and maintain them longer."

I practised this by creating a single cherry blossom, this time concentrating intensely on each individual tiny detail, on the red veins in the velvety petal, on the golden fur of the stamens: its faint translucency and the way it trembled under your breath, almost as if it wished to fly away.

As I worked I felt a strange sensation of heat begin to flutter under my skin. I tried to ignore it, but it grew more and more intense, until I was sweating. Then there was a tiny spark – a flash of fire – and a cherry blossom was sitting in the palm of my hand.

My skin was chilled now. I could feel the slight weight of the blossom as it rested on my hand, although I knew it was impossible.

Wasn't it impossible?

Akira's hand was shaking as she reached out. Slowly, she laid her palm over mine, on top of the illusion flower. I could feel the petals spread out and press flat, soft and faintly warm against my palm. I heard Akira's sharp intake of breath and I reminded myself again that it was impossible.

"Yue, when I was ill, I had a dream…" she said, her

voice low and hesitant. "I dreamt that I could barely breathe, and that I knew I was dying. Then something hot touched me. It felt like a brand, and the heat of it should have set fire to my flesh, but it did not. Instead it swept through me, burning away the illness, and left me weak but healed. When I opened my eyes, I saw that the brand was your hand, and the heat came from you."

I stared at her, very aware of the silence and the shadows in the corners of the room. "I—I had a dream like that too."

Her eyes searched my face, her pupils huge despite the lamp burning near by. "Hundreds of years ago, when the Old Empire still governed Tsuki no Hikari no Kuni, there were men who had a power like ours, a gift… But these men could do more than weave illusions. They could change their shape, see the future, heal. They called these men 'Akachi'. It means 'Hand of the Gods'."

That word ran through me like a rumble of thunder. *Akachi*. That was the word they had used to describe Otieno.

I shook my head. "I am only a shadow weaver."

"How would you know that?" Akira asked. "If shadow-weaving is all you are trained to do, how would you know you could do more? Unless you reached out to a friend in need and somehow healed them? Unless you did things that you did not even know you were capable of until they were already done?"

"No," I said. "It was just a dream. A fever dream."

Even as I said it, there was another flash of brilliance in my mind – like a firework cascading against the night sky – and I remembered that day, in my family's orchard, when I had run from the soldiers. It had not felt like shadow-weaving. I had thought myself a white hare, had felt myself shrink and become light and small. *They could change their shape...*

Another flash. The day, on the ship, when Terayama-san had escorted me across the deck, and, without knowing why, I had felt so uneasy and frightened, even though I had longed to walk there before. It was almost as if I knew that he was going to hurt me. *They could see the future...*

"If you have such a gift, you must have training. Proper training. Who knows what good you could do? Or what harm, if your talent is left uncontrolled?" Akira looked away, frowning, already planning. "I knew someone once who travelled across the sea to a place called Athazie, and he said that there were still Akachi among the people there—"

The name of Otieno's country snuffed the flaring lights in my mind as quickly as a damp blanket snuffs out a flame.

Otieno had spoken of Athazie, that land of golden plains and hills, of sweet-voiced birds and warm, drifting rain. It was a beautiful place. A place where men like Otieno and A Suda-san laughed and smiled. Where no one slaughtered an animal unless it had a fair chance to escape.

What would such a land – such men – make of me? I would be anathema to them.

"Stop!" I shouted without meaning to, trying to cut Akira's voice off. My fingers curled around hers until she winced. I loosened my grip and repeated, more softly: "Stop. I do not have such an ability. I do not want it."

"But—"

"If you are my friend, then please, do not speak of this again. I want vengeance, that is all. Nothing more."

It was the first time I had ever seen Akira speechless. She opened her mouth once, twice, as if searching for the words to change my mind. But as she stared into my eyes, something in her expression altered. After a long moment she let out a sigh and bowed her head, the proud line of her back slumping.

"Oh, Yue," she whispered. "I thought... I thought that helping you take your revenge would set you free. I was wrong, wasn't I? It is just another prison for you."

She did not look at me. She expected no answer and I had none to give. I leant forward and pressed a kiss to her forehead – it was where Youta had kissed mine the last time I saw him. Then I released her hand. The brown, dried-up remains of a cherry blossom fell from between our palms, dissolving into dust before it hit the mat.

·

Twenty-seven

"Ow!" I flinched as the flexible willow wand snapped down on my toes.

"That is the third time you have placed your foot incorrectly," Akira said calmly from her place kneeling at the edge of the tatami mat. "You know the rule."

I grimaced. After I had learnt the basics of the two dances, Akira had started using the willow wand to drive the finer – and more easily forgettable – movements home. At first I had protested mightily. I had lost the argument, and the willow had stayed, and been used. Though Akira's blows were light and never broke, or even bruised, my skin, the swish and snap of the stick made me jump every time. But perhaps it did help me to remember; I did not usually make three mistakes in a row nowadays.

I thought, wryly, that once I had inflicted much

worse pain on myself without even blinking. I had not cut, scratched or burned myself for over four months, not since Akira and I had begun planning for the Shadow Ball. I did not know why. I had never really known why I needed to do it, or why sometimes I did not. It wasn't about being happy. I was not happy, though I had learnt to hide it from Akira as much as I could.

I loved Akira. Not as I had loved my father and Aimi, for I had owned a full and untroubled heart then, but as much as a person like me could love. As much as a liar can love the person she deceives. As much as a stray dog can love the woman who offers it scraps and kind words, though in its wildness it might still turn on her and bite her hand.

I comforted myself that I would not impose on her forever. Once I was the Shadow Princess, I would leave her to take a place in the court of the prince. I never allowed myself to doubt that it would happen. I never allowed myself to think any further into the future than that.

And I did not cut myself any more.

"Begin again." Akira broke into my thoughts. "Complete the dance flawlessly and we will stop for the day. If not, you will complete both dances again, and you will use the ceremonial fans, not the practice ones."

I groaned. I was tired and hungry and I knew I would not manage to get through the fan dance again – not using the heavy ceremonial fans, which had steel spikes in them – without landing on my face.

. I began the slow, deliberate motion of arms, fully extending my fingers into the soft fluttering movements that would tell the audience I was a ghost. The proud line of my back and raised head showed that I was a noblewoman. It was up to my feet, my face, my spirit, to show them that I was alone, desperately sad, and searching.

The dance grew gradually faster, a sense of desperation and despair drawing my movements back towards my body as I gradually realized there was no hope...

I sank down onto my knees, head bowed, bringing my arms together so that my hands were cupping my face by the time I was still. I held the position. My breath came in tiny pants, which I kept as silent as possible. Snorting like a horse would get me another flick of the willow.

"Good."

I would never have Akira's glowing expressiveness. That was her own particular genius, honed through years of professional practice. Yet in the past few months, I had heard "good" little enough to know it was worth a great deal.

"You are ready."

"What?" I yelped, then bit my lip. "I'm sorry, I meant, ready in what way?"

"Ready to take a place in the Moon Court. The news came yesterday, but I wanted to see you dance again before I told you. The Kage no Iwai has been announced. It will be in eight weeks, and the invitations will be issued a week before that."

So it would begin. We had discussed this at length,

and I knew that the next step would be to begin attending parties and functions – the first of which was to be a simple tea ceremony at Lord Takakura's house. If I did well there, more invitations would follow. I must do my utmost to impress, cultivating an air of mystery, charming everyone with my playing, and becoming fashionable, sought after, infamous. Then the prince's advisers would be forced to invite me to the ball; the only criteria for invitation was supposed to be beauty, after all, even if everyone knew it was really political.

Once I was at the ball, Akira would bribe one of the entertainers to let me take their place and dance for the prince. It would be shocking and scandalous and hopefully enough to persuade the young prince to choose me. As she had said: "You must cast him such glances that he will feel as if you lay at his feet. You must seduce him. Then, and only then, will you be chosen."

Thinking of that now, I rested my head in my hands. "Akira," I groaned. "It will be a disaster. I am not good enough. Everyone will be disappointed and you will be a laughing stock."

"No. You will keep practising, and by the time the Kage no Iwai comes, you will be ready."

"But—"

"Do not contradict your teacher. I know what I am doing. You will be good enough. If there is any doubt, you must remember the reason why you are doing this. You must remember what you said you wanted most in the world, and that this is your chance to get it. Dance with that passion and that commitment, and the Moon Prince will make you his."

"All right." My voice wobbled.

Akira tilted her head and then said hesitantly, "Yue, if ... if by saying you are not good enough, you mean that you are frightened or having second thoughts—"

"Of course I am frightened," I interrupted, and my voice was firm again. "Only a madwoman would not be frightened. But I am not having second thoughts. It is as you said. I want this. I will do it."

Akira looked at me again with the sad look she had given me the night we argued about my shadow-weaving. She had never mentioned the subject of that other power to me again, although she helped me to practise weaving every evening. Under her ruthless eye, my skill had increased at an astonishing rate, and I was now capable of creating the same detailed full-body illusions that Akira could. At a pinch I, too, could disguise myself as a fat drunk man, or a prosperous merchant's wife, or a farmer's daughter. Never again would I be turned from anyone's door because I looked like a beggar. That brought me fierce satisfaction.

If there was more I could do, I shut the knowledge away with every shred of strength I had. That path was not for me. It might have been for Suzume. Before Rin. But Yue had only one path to travel, and it ended with Terayama-san's destruction.

So when I created a glittering gown that looked like the night sky filled with stars, if Akira and I both noticed it drag on the ground with the same slight shushing noise as a real gown that had weight and substance, neither of us mentioned it. Neither did we mention the time Akira had a headache and I touched her hand and she instantly felt better. And we did not mention that after any such incident, I suddenly became tired and drained, as if I had used up more energy than was mine to spend, and had to lie down.

Still, Akira looked at me now with that defeated face. She had not forgotten.

I smiled. A smile of happiness and peace. Aimi's smile.

"So," I said cheerfully, "what shall I wear?"

Twenty-eight

I wore three layers – the outer one of a deep, dusky pink embroidered with red and pale pink blossoms, the next of red with pink blossoms, and the inner of white with red blossoms. My obi was made of cloth striped in red and gold, and red and pink. I wore three combs in my hair, which had now grown to the middle of my back and was long enough to arrange properly. One of the combs had little dangling pink and white mother-of-pearl flowers that clattered together gently above my ear. I ignored them with an effort.

My most important garment was my shadow-weaving. I had not altered my features in any way. I had polished them, as a craftsman takes a piece of dull wood and with his tools shapes and buffs, bringing out the rich colours and shine of the material. Deep within the normally unremarkable darkness of my eyes was a glimmer, a sort of iridescence, like the sheen on the black spots of a butterfly's wings. My hair shared that same sheen, while my skin had a fragile cherry-blossom glow that begged to be touched. Everything about me begged to be touched. I had already seen the looks in men's eyes – in the eyes of the servants who helped me from Akira's carriage, in those of the one who welcomed us to Lord Takakura's house – that told me they each wanted the hand touching me to be theirs.

I knew I had never looked more beautiful. I knew that beside me, even Akira could not hope to command all of any man's attention. And I also knew why Akira's plan had been to make me seem mysterious and silent – because under the weight of such a complex and subtle weaving, I could barely breathe, let alone speak.

After being ushered into Lord Takakura's house, we were led out, not into the magnificent gardens that I had glimpsed through the open screens but to the roji – the narrow, winding paths of the tea garden.

The day was bright and chilly. After passing through the outer gate of the roji, I slid my hands into my sleeves to keep them warm, concentrating on keeping my footing on the uneven white stepping-stones. The path was made like this on purpose, a tactic to prevent guests in the roji from dawdling or looking around too much. Likewise, the carefully maintained shrubs, ferns and trees that closed in around us blocked any view of the rest of the garden. The point of this narrow walk was to concentrate one's mind on the ceremony to come, and the principles of harmony, respect, purity and tranquillity that guided it.

The stones of the path and the little stone lanterns that lined it all glittered wetly – scattering water like this was the host's way of welcoming his guests and showing that he had prepared the way for them. At one point the path branched in two, but on the first stepping-stone of the left branch there was a fist-sized rock, wrapped carefully in black, bracken rope: our host's way of marking the incorrect path.

We took the right branch, and soon the trees parted to show us the *koshikake machiai* – the enclosed, outdoor booth where guests at a tea ceremony would wait to be summoned by the host. This was where we were supposed to say goodbye to the outside world and compose our minds to the solemnity and serenity of the tea ceremony, in order to honour our host. Directly behind it there was a tall, bamboo gate that would open to show us the teahouse itself.

The wooden frame of the booth, the stones outside it and the vibrant green ferns that grew around it had all been drenched in water too, making them gleam in the sunlight that shifted through the leaves. The water was still dripping gently from the ferns, a sign that we had arrived at just the right time, not too early or too late.

Akira and I both stepped carefully out of our zōri sandals and placed them on the stepping-stones in front of the waiting booth, where a shallow, stone-lined trench was filled with the washed branches and bamboo sticks that were used to collect garden trash.

The familiar sights of the ritual calmed my nervously skipping heart and made it easier to hold my composure, to keep my shadow-weaving perfectly in place. Akira turned to look at me, and raised her eyebrows, asking me if I was ready.

The first test, she had called it. There would be no turning back after this. I had come so far. I would not let myself fail now. I nodded, making the mother-of-pearl flowers tremble above my ear.

We stepped through the entrance into the *koshikake machiai*.

The booth was small and warmed by a tiny brazier. An ornamental alcove contained a painted wall scroll and a small vase with a single iris. A wooden bench, built into the wall, ran around the room. Akira was taking off her outer *haori* and carefully placing it in a shallow tray that lay on the bench. I followed suit, fussing a little as I folded my own *haori*, reluctant to turn fully to face the room. My sun-dazzled vision had already caught a brief glimpse of others in the opposite corner, and I could feel eyes on me. Despite the effort I had put into making myself as attractive as possible, it was still unnerving to be stared at wherever I went. I had been invisible, in one way or another, for a long time. But I would have to get used to it. After tucking in the edge of the *haori*, I allowed myself to look up.

It felt like falling. Like confidently stepping from the

last stair only to find that the ground had disappeared. I clutched at my weaving and forced my startled gasp back between my teeth. Two men stood on the other side of the small waiting space.

Otieno and his father.

I barely noticed A Suda-san, despite the fact that he was looking directly at me. My eyes were on Otieno. He had his back to us, and was examining the little tray of smoking implements that rested on a pile of square cushions in the corner.

No, I told myself desperately. *It could not be Otieno.* This man was too tall. Too broad. He was taller even than A Suda-san. He wore a pleated dark blue jacket with very long, full sleeves that clearly displayed powerful muscles in his shoulders and back. His full, pleated trousers were belted at a narrow waist with twisted silk cords. His hair was braided down his back, and gold and jade ornaments gleamed in the long dark rope. Surely Otieno's hair could not have grown so much.

It is not him.

It cannot be him.

It cannot be…

The strong, straight back stiffened and the head tilted as if listening for some faint, familiar sound. He turned.

It was him.

He stared at me, as if he could not believe his eyes, and stepped forward, reaching out to me. "Pipit!"

I cannot. I turned to ice inside, razor-sharp shards that

throbbed and burned in my chest. It took everything I had to turn a polite look on him and step back, avoiding his hands. *Oh, Otieno. I do not know what else to do.*

"I am sorry," I said coldly. "I do not believe we have met before."

His reaching hands slowly dropped back to his sides. "Do you not recognize me?"

"I am sorry," I said again, my tone making it clear I was anything but. "I have no idea what you are talking about. We are strangers."

His face was expressionless now, blank, as it had never been when he looked at me. It was the same face he had shown to Terayama-san. I clenched my teeth against the pain.

"Perhaps you have mistaken my sister for someone else?" Akira said smoothly, edging into the space between me and Otieno. "I am sure we would remember if you had been introduced to us before."

She bowed to him politely, and I copied her, grateful for the excuse to tear my eyes from him and look at the floor. Akira addressed a remark to A Suda-san – giving him our names and asking for his. Otieno was silent. After a moment I saw his feet move. He was turning away. Hidden by the sleeves of my *furisode*, my hands were knotted so tightly that nails gouged into skin.

"Yes, we will be returning home in little more than seven weeks," A Suda-san was saying to Akira. "We have been in your country for a long time, and much as we appreciate its beauty, we miss Athazie. Now that our ruler has concluded his negotiations with the Moon Prince, we are eager to begin our journey."

There was a sharp rattle, and we all turned to see a short, plump man putting back the pierced screen of the inner gate of the tea garden. Behind him, the path to the tearoom glittered and swam with green and gold light as the tree boughs danced in the spring breeze. He bowed silently to us, and we bowed in return. This was our host.

He turned and walked away, and Otieno and A Suda-san – the principle guests – followed him. Otieno paused at the entrance and turned back. I saw in his eyes everything I felt myself: sadness, pain, longing. And something more. Betrayal. He hesitated there, waiting. Then he shook his head, and the screen slid shut behind him.

I managed to stand tall for about a minute before I had to put my hands over my face.

"We should go out soon," Akira said softly, her hand resting gently on my back. She said nothing more. She knew who Otieno was; my reaction would have given it away even if I had never told her his name.

I nodded, straightened and took a deep breath. *Stop acting like a child,* I told myself. *Stop making a grand drama out of everything. Get on and do what you must do.*

We passed through the inner gate, stepping into the wooden clogs that had been left there for us, and closed the gate behind us. Then we rinsed our hands and mouths at the ceremonial stone basin, and proceeded along the gently winding path to the teahouse itself. By the time we reached it – a beautiful little house, with a thatched roof, golden walls and large, screened, round windows – the sharp iciness inside me had begun to spread, until my whole body felt numb.

We bent down low to pass through the *nijiriguchi*, the wooden-framed entrance, and I clutched my weaving to me still tighter, and tried, *tried*, to leave my thoughts and feelings outside.

Akira arranged us so that I was as far from Otieno as I could be, and I was grateful. I did not look at him as we ate the traditional meal of fish, vegetables and broth. But I was excruciatingly aware of each movement he made. I heard every breath he took. Sensed the tiniest shift in his position. I was more aware of him than of myself. Aware that even when we moved back to the booth to wait for the second part of the ceremony, and then when we returned and our host served the tea, Otieno never once looked at me.

That was good. Wasn't it?

Takakura-san, however, looked at me a great deal. From the approving expression on his face, it seemed that Akira's plan was working. So strange that to sit there, silent and unsmiling, feeling as miserable and thin as rice paper, was enough to make this man like me. *No*, I reminded myself. *It is the shadow-weaving he desires. Not you. No one could ever want you.*

Then at long, long last the ceremony was over.

Takakura-san escorted us back to the waiting booth, where he engaged in a whispered conversation with Akira that included many furtive glances in my direction. Akira was smiling and nodding. I pretended not to notice as I stepped out of the wooden clogs, entered the waiting booth and then stepped back outside to put on my zōri. The others were still in the waiting booth behind me, and I seized the moment of relative solitude to step away from the entrance. I tilted my head back so that the sunlight moved over my face. I would not cry. Not now.

"Rin."

I turned reflexively, and then cursed myself when I saw Otieno standing behind me, blocking the entrance to the booth. There was a look of grim triumph on his face, and I knew I had given myself away.

"You—you startled me—" I began. The words trailed off as I searched his face. There was nothing there: only smooth blankness that made the ice inside me burn with cold fire. It was as if my words earlier were the truth. As if we were strangers.

"I know I did," he said. "I meant to."

I looked away from him again, shaking my head. "Don't—"

"Don't what? There is no point in this pretence. Look at me."

"Stop it. Leave me alone."

"Not until you look at me."

"Please." I backed away from him, slipped off the path

and stumbled. Otieno's hand shot out and caught my wrist before I could fall.

"What has happened to you?" he murmured. "What went wrong? I looked for you for so long. Where did you go?"

Panicked, I just shook my head, refusing to move my eyes from the tips of his feet.

"Pipit," he said again, his voice soft.

He released my arm and took my face between his hands, gently tilting my head until I met his eyes. "Pipit. Pipit, do not deny me. I cannot bear it."

The ice shattered. My shadow-weaving shredded away like mist under a summer wind and I was exposed, weak and trembling and pitiful as I was. I could not speak. All I could do was look at him.

It was enough. The horrible deadness melted from his face and he was Otieno again, my Otieno. His arms came around me, almost lifting me from my feet. I pressed my face into the hollow under his shoulder, breathing in the smell of him — still the same, always the same — and felt his chin, ever so slightly prickly with stubble, rub against my forehead.

"Shh, shh." He stroked my back with his free hand. "It is all right now."

Just for a moment. Just this one moment. Surely a moment is allowed?

"This is not the place for this. Tomorrow," he said, his voice rumbling in his chest against my cheek. "Meet me tomorrow on the Red Bridge. You know it?"

"I cannot. You don't understand. I cannot—"

He pushed me away from him and shook me a little. "You can, and you will, Pipit. Do not argue unless you want me to hound you until your life is a burden. I will do it. Tomorrow at noon you are going to meet me and tell me the truth. Now go. Tell your 'sister' you followed a butterfly or something. I will wait until you have left."

He turned me around and propelled me forward with a little push. I went, dazed, with barely the presence of mind to draw the shreds of my discarded shadow-weaving back into place around me as I walked away.

Twenty-nine

The Red Bridge was one of the oldest bridges in the city and a well-known landmark. It was surprisingly small and shabby for all that, and nearly deserted this bright spring morning. The tributary that it spanned was deep and narrow; the trees on either bank towered above it, and the water looked almost black. I did not really need my painted parasol, but at least it gave me something to do with my hands. I sat on one of the little benches carved into the crest of the bridge and stared at the grimacing, scarlet-painted dragons – evidence of the fashions of the Old Empire – and wondered what I was doing.

"Good morning." Otieno's voice came from behind me.

I froze, feeling the tiny hairs on the back of my neck stand up, whether with fear or excitement I could not have told.

"Good morning, A Suda-san."

I forced myself to stand, bracing myself to meet his eyes, only to find that he was staring down at the dark river. Grateful for the reprieve, I let myself gaze at him. His hair was loose today, with just one strand of golden ornament braided next to his ear. He wore his normal Athazie tunic and breeches, with the addition of a long over-robe of deep blue. The cold manner of yesterday was gone, but his face showed caution, and a hint of reserve. That was my fault. The knowledge sent a pang through me.

"You did not bring your sister," he commented, still avoiding my eyes. "More secrets?"

"I do not keep secrets from Akira," I said, a little stiffly. "She brought me here and is waiting in the carriage on the other side of the bridge."

And as if my reply had answered some vital question, Otieno finally looked at me, smiling his sunlight smile. "I am glad for you," he said simply. "I am glad you have someone to confide in."

He caught hold of the hand that was not gripping my parasol and drew it through his arm so that it rested in the crook of his elbow. He kept his own hand firmly on top of it; warm skin and hard muscles shifted under my fingers as he guided me forward.

The heat of him seemed to radiate against me. If I moved a little – just a very little – closer to him, my breast would press against his arm. My body had its own will and it desperately wanted to make that tiny movement.

I had to hold myself completely rigid to prevent it.

"I can walk unassisted," I muttered.

"Oh, I know. And run too. You are always running away from me," he said. "If I have hold of you, you cannot get away so easily."

"Just ask your questions," I said. The effort to keep the proper distance between our bodies was wearing.

"All right, then. Tell me about your sister."

"She is not related to me by blood," I began obediently. "We met under difficult circumstances. I helped her as best I could, and she helped me. Afterwards we decided we liked each other, and to stay together as sisters."

"Amazing," Otieno said, after a long pause. "A succinct and factual account of events which tells me precisely nothing."

I came to a halt, wrenching my arm away from him. "If you only wish to mock me, why did you come here? What do you want?"

"*I want you to trust me!*" He reached out and grabbed my shoulders and held me still, forcing me to look at him. His face showed such a mixture of fury and anguish that it made me flinch. "Why are you being like this? We are not enemies, Pipit. I dragged you back over the side of that ship when Terayama tried to drown you. I kept your secrets at his house even when questions about how you came to be in the kitchen burned my mouth. I have never hurt you. I never would!"

A thrill of shock and fear – and flaring bright pleasure

– rendered me speechless. He knew who I was. He had always known. When he had befriended Rin the drudge, he had recognized her as the daughter of the house he visited. Yet he had never said a word until now. How very far apart we were! Otieno was good, truly good. I did not deserve a friend like him.

"You are right," I said bleakly. "You are right that you have been wonderful to me, but you do not understand – you cannot understand – what I am, what I have been through, the things I have done. Terrible things." My voice broke, and I bit the last word off sharply, forcing my rising emotions down. "We are too different now. You are like a great warhorse that tries to be friends with a mouse. You do not even realize how easily you could crush me beneath your feet."

The temper drained from Otieno's face and he looked appalled. "Yue, we are not animals. We are just people. A man and a woman who like each other. It is as easy as that. I promise you that I will never hurt you."

I took a slow, deep breath, and spoke to him as calmly and carefully as I would address a child. "Sometimes people hurt each other without ever meaning to, simply by being who they are, simply by existing. I know this. The fact that you believe such a promise could be kept shows that there is no common ground between us."

"That is a lie," he said. His fingers flexed on my shoulders, not quite bruising. "No, I do not know what you have been through – you have not trusted me enough to tell me, to make me understand. The truth is that you do not want to try. It is easier and safer to push me away. But if people can hurt each other simply by existing, then people can also make each other happy, if they want to. People like us. You and I are kindred. From the first moment we saw each other, we both knew it. We have always been reaching out to each other. We are the same."

A harsh, bitter laugh escaped me. "We are nothing alike!"

He made a noise of rage and snatched the parasol from my fingers, flinging it away, then seized my hands. I thought, for a dizzy instant, that he was going to kiss me.

Instead, there was a sharp crack, like the sound of an axe splitting wood, and the air around us changed, went bright and still. Heat began to gather in my hands, pulsing through my fingers where Otieno held them trapped. Otieno's face was intent, his eyes fixed on mine. I could not look away. The air between us was glowing, shifting, stretching out in long, golden strands like honey, filling my vision with a web of light that wrapped around us.

"Now," he said.

Instinctively I responded. I let go, not of Otieno's hands, but of something inside me. The heat in my hands flowed outwards, running along the golden strands of light. I closed my eyes at last, shielding them from the unbearable brilliance.

The light faded, and the heat was gone. Something cool brushed my face. I opened my eyes.

It was snowing.

I drew in a sharp breath. There was a column of spiralling snowflakes above us, coming down out of a cloudless sky. The flakes flashed and glittered in the sunlight, piling up on my head and arms, on Otieno and our joined hands, and turning Otieno's black hair silver.

His hands tightened on mine, bringing my gaze back to his face. "We are the same. Suzume. Rin. Yue. No matter what. We are the same."

"W—we did th—this?" I asked faintly, my teeth beginning to chatter.

"Yes," he said, with a trace of defiance that was ruined by a fat snowflake landing on his nose. He sneezed, then added, "Together."

I could not deal with that revelation at the moment. "Will it f—follow us if we m—move?" I was trembling now, as the cold penetrated the layers of my *haori* and kimono. The flakes were not melting yet, but it was only a matter of time.

"I am not sure." He tugged me down off the bottom step of the bridge. As we moved, the column of snow began to diminish, and by the time Otieno had shaken my *haori* out and put it back on my shoulders, and then brushed his own hair free of snow, the flakes had ceased to fall. There was still a rather large drift at the foot of the bridge, though.

Otieno took my hand again. His fingers trembled as they closed on mine. He started walking along the path, and I followed.

Hesitantly, I began: "I left Terayama-san's house. I had nowhere to go. I wandered the city for a while, trying to find work, but everyone turned me away…"

I told him the rest, though I excluded the hardest parts, such as what had really happened to my mother, and my plans for the Shadow Ball.

When I finished, he was silent, then asked, "Your name now – Yue – where did that come from?"

"I wanted to leave Rin behind. Akira called me Yue, and it stuck."

By now we had turned around and begun to walk back towards the bridge again.

"I have only heard half the story. Less than that," he said. "I never asked before, but I always hoped you would eventually tell me. How did you come to be working in Terayama-san's kitchens? Why did he tell everyone that his stepdaughter was sick? Did he even know you were there?"

"I do not want to talk about that."

He nodded thoughtfully. "Then I will ask again the next time I see you."

"Next time?"

He smiled, and it felt it like an ache deep inside me. "I told you that this time you would not get away so easily."

Thirty

"Sakura, sakura,
Covering the sky,
The fragrance is blown like mist and clouds,
Now, now, let us go now, to see them.
Sakura, sakura,
Covering the hills and valleys,
Drifting like mist and clouds,
Sakura, sakura,
In full bloom."

The last note died away, and I closed my eyes, the morning breeze ruffling the hair around my face. There was a footstep behind me on the veranda, and then Akira spoke.

"You have a guest."

I looked up to see Otieno standing with Akira by

the sliding doors. My suddenly stiff fingers fumbled the plectrum and forced a jangling discord from the shamisen.

"Good morning," he said, smiling. "That was beautiful. I've never known anyone use their gift like that."

I blinked at him. "What?"

"I will go and ask for tea," Akira announced. She went back through the doors and slid them shut behind her.

Otieno padded across the veranda and sat down close to me – far closer than I was comfortable with. His hair was loose again, and it danced in the wind. The trailing end of his turquoise sash fluttered. "What are you doing here?"

"Visiting you. You said you would talk to me again, so I thought I would call on you and make it easier. Is that not all right? Kano-san did not seem surprised to see me."

"I bet she didn't," I muttered. Then I went on, "What did you mean about a 'gift'? What gift?"

He raised his eyebrows. I laid my shamisen down, adjusted it a little to the left and rearranged my sleeve, and then looked out over the lake. I heard him sigh.

"I worry about you, Pipit. I sense that there is so much power in you. The fact that you use it without even realizing, and without ever having been taught, shows that. Powers that are denied and ignored can sometimes go wrong. I do not want you to hurt yourself."

I glanced at him from the corner of my eye. "My music has nothing to do with shadow-weaving."

"I know that, but most Akachi have some specialized area that their gift naturally seems to enhance. Mine is archery. I am not an expert, but it seemed to me that you were weaving power through your voice and playing to bring the emotions of the song directly to the listener's heart. It was a subtle and lovely enchantment. A wonderful way to use your gift."

My voice was pathetically small as I said, "Thank you."

It was hard to describe, even to myself, why I was so resistant to this extra ability that seemed to be trying to push its way out of me. Every time it emerged, I felt a strange fear, something telling me that you could not harness such a power without being changed, that embracing it would mean letting go of other things. Things like fury and sorrow, and the desire for justice. And without those things I doubted I would even exist.

"Tell me about your gift," I said impulsively. "You said it enhances your archery. I have seen you shoot, and it all seemed completely natural to me."

"Of course it is natural," he said indignantly. "My gift is as much a part of me as your big brown eyes are a part of you. Now, do not frown at me, and do not try to distract me either. You promised you would tell me a story."

"What story is that?" I asked, amused at the childlike expression.

"The tale of how you went from noble lady of the Terayama House to drudge in its kitchens. I shall not tell you any more about my gift until you have told me that."

My amusement vanished. "It is not a bedtime story," I said, turning away from him.

His hand came to rest on my shoulder, drawing me back until I came to rest against him, my shoulders encircled by his arm. It was warm surrounded by the haven of his embrace, and I felt … safe.

"Tell me."

"I cannot. Please accept that. I cannot bear to think about it."

We sat in silence. Otieno's fingers traced slow circles on my shoulder.

"You are a stubborn woman." His lips touched my hair. "My stubborn woman."

Held against him, I felt no urge to argue.

The sliding door went back with a sharp bang and I jolted, pulling away from Otieno. *What on earth was I thinking?* Every time he laid a hand on me, my common sense seemed to fly away like a swallow in winter. The man was a snake in cat's clothing.

"I am sorry I was so long," Akira said breezily, sitting down beside us. "I had to deal with a message. One of the servants is bringing the tea now."

As I sat in mortified silence, Otieno and Akira chatted happily. When the tea arrived, Otieno effortlessly ate his way through a plate of sweets, and had two cups of tea. Apparently I was the only one who was disturbed.

"*Gochisosama deshita,*" he said eventually, using the traditional words to thank a host for the meal, and bowing elegantly from the waist. "Kano-san, I wonder if I could request the honour of Yue's company for a little while?

Her beautiful music has made me wish to walk under the cherry blossoms again before I leave your country. I think I would enjoy visiting the West Park, if she will come with me."

"What a lovely idea!" Akira said, before I could answer. "I am sure Yue will be delighted to go, but sadly I am quite busy. You will manage without me, will you not? Such old friends as you are."

"Akira—"

Otieno cut me off. "You are very wise, Kano-san. Thank you." His grave tone was completely ruined by the twinkle in his eye.

Outside there was a dashing carriage, drawn by a pair of blood bay horses whose colour was an almost exact match for Otieno's skin. I noticed this particularly because his tunic had a deep, V-shaped neckline that gaped rather distractingly when he turned to open the carriage door for me. I tore my gaze away and, with some difficulty given my layers of clothing, climbed in.

I sat down – and gasped as a pair of pitiless black eyes met mine. Otieno's hunting bird was perched inside the carriage on a specially adapted framework that had been bolted into the carriage wall. There was even a lacquered tray at the bottom to catch the bird's waste. The polished mahogany perch was marked with glaring white gouges from the bird's extremely long claws. Those claws flexed as Otieno settled down next to it, in the seat opposite mine.

"Do you not hood and jess it?" I asked nervously.

"Sometimes," Otieno said, stroking the bird's sleek head with one finger. It bridled and shuffled sideways to get closer to him, apparently enjoying the attention. "When we are going somewhere very busy, like a market, or if I will have to leave her alone for a long time. She will be fine flying free in the park today. You will enjoy that, Mirkasha, will you not?"

The bird let out a muted chirping noise, as if agreeing.

"Mirkasha. That is a beautiful name."

Otieno grinned. "It amused me at the time – but I was only twelve when I got her."

"Why? What does it mean?"

"Sparrow."

"Really?" I asked sharply.

"Yes." He gave me a quizzical look. "Why does that surprise you?"

I shook my head a little. "It is a coincidence, that is all. My old name – Suzume. It means sparrow. My father always called me that. He said the noises I made when I was born reminded him of a little bird."

I could see the struggle in Otieno's face, curiosity warring with caution. I sighed with relief when he only said, "Well, perhaps she has some fellow feeling for you. It was her who called to me, that day on the ship, and attracted my attention to your plight."

I looked at the bird and then, on impulse, bowed from the waist. "Thank you, Mirkasha."

Otieno rapped sharply on the roof of the carriage at the same moment that the bird spread her wings and bobbed her head. For an instant I thought she was returning my bow. Then, as we rocked gently into motion, I realized that she must simply have been adjusting her balance.

"You said you would tell me about your archery," I said swiftly, hoping to keep the conversation off me for a change. Otieno gave me a sidelong look, not unlike Mirkasha's, and smiled, as if to let me know that he was aware of my strategy. Unable to help myself, I returned the smile.

"My gift helps with my archery," he said, "but in such a way that it is impossible to tell, most of the time, how much is natural talent for the bow, and how much is magic. The two bleed into one another. The world is … malleable to Akachi, in a way that it is not to others. It is as if the raw energy inside us – our souls – has an affinity with the raw energy of the world itself. Such a closeness brings gifts of talent, healing and foresight."

"You make it sound wonderful," I said, a little wryly. "I bet all the children in your country want to be Akachi."

Otieno's face became serious. "No. No more than all the children dream of being warriors, or hunters, or any other dangerous and exciting thing."

"Dangerous?"

"Yes. Of course. Nature is dangerous – think of hurricanes, floods, earthquakes. When we draw on that energy, we are capable of hurting ourselves, and others. It can be too much. My grandmother told me a story once, of a little boy who longed for a nearby lake to freeze over, so that he and his friends could skate on it. Every night for a week, the little boy added this wish to his prayers before he went to bed. Then one day, the family woke and found that the lake had frozen solid – in the middle of summer. The little boy was dead in his bed, his skin blue and frost around his mouth and nose."

"How awful. He died because of such a small thing? Is the story true?"

"I think so. Grandmother told me this when she was teaching me to control my gift. The boy died because his family did not realize he was an Akachi, and he had no idea that he really could change the world, just by willing it enough, or what the consequences could be. Mostly those of us with such a strong gift are caught early. The families notice strange things about such a child. That he or she can always find things that are lost, or that the dreams they speak of come true. Grandmother knew what I was because I loved birds, and there were always birds gathering around me, even around my crib when I was a baby. If I was put in a closed room, they would find ways in under the window screens or down the chimney. I would laugh and clap when I saw them. I called them to me, you see. If Grandmother had not been there, I might have died very young, without anyone ever realizing why. She said it was a sign of how powerful an Akachi I would one day be, that my gift manifested itself so early."

I nodded, fascinated but at the same time aware that he had not really answered my question. Somehow the conversation was back on the topic I had forced him to abandon the day before: the perils of ignoring a gift.

"How did you find out you had a special gift for archery? From what I overheard at the archery contest, it does not seem as if your father values such skills. I would have thought he would keep you away from weapons training, especially once he realized you had a special gift."

He frowned. "It is not that my father does not value such skills. It is merely that in our country we do not … glorify them. And you are right that I was kept away from the training grounds as a child. I discovered archery by accident."

He turned his face away, and Mirkasha made her soft chirping noise. He reached up absently to stroke her head again. I wondered how many handlers of hunting birds could take that kind of liberty and avoid the kiss of the lethal hooked beak. But Otieno made everyone love him. Or, everyone who had the wit to see him for what he really was.

"My mother died having me," he began hesitantly. "In every way that counted, my grandmother took her place, but she was already old when my mother was born and … she died when I was ten. Because I was the youngest, because I had never known my mother, and because of the gift we shared, she was very special to me. We spent so much time together, singing, laughing, telling stories – when she was gone it was as if … as if the part of me that could laugh and sing, and tell stories, had died with her. Everyone had loved her, and everyone mourned her, but I was … lost. My father let me wander for a little while, grieving, and then he decided to distract me. He dragged me and my brothers out to the village training grounds where the hunters and warriors were drilling. He knew I had never been there before. It was a good distraction: a place that was free of sad memories. The warriors and hunters knew of our house's loss – some of my aunts and uncles were in training there – and were kind to my brothers and me. We watched them dance with swords and throw spears, but my attention was caught by my uncle's bow work. Something about the flight of the arrow…" He shrugged a little self-consciously.

"Maybe it reminded you of a bird?" I said.

His eyes flashed up to mine, and he smiled, the shadow of sadness leaving his face. "Yes, it was that. I asked to hold one of the bows, and as a joke they gave me one that had been made for a teenager to train with, and told me to try stringing it. It was taller than I was. I should not even have been able to bend it, let alone string it. Yet I did. Easily. It was the gift, but I did not realize it then. I just thought it was magic, magic of the kind you hear about in children's stories. I can still remember how the training ground fell silent. How everyone came to watch me, so cautiously, not daring to let the excitement show, just as parents will bite their lips as a child takes his first steps, fearful that to cry out will cause him to fall. My aunt handed me an arrow. The skin of my hands seemed to sing where it touched the arrow; I nocked it, and drew the string on that bow which was made for a boy of eighteen, and it felt like the most wonderful, and the most natural thing, I had ever done. I let the arrow fly, and it hit the target. Not dead centre, but it did not matter. Everyone began yelling and hugging, and slapping me on the back. My father put me on his shoulders, though I was far too heavy for it by then. We had all come alive again. It was as if the laughter and singing and stories rushed back into the empty space my grandmother had left behind. I will never forget the way it felt as long as I live."

For a moment I felt lost in the world of his story. A noisy and chaotic world, to be sure, but one where grief and love were expressed freely and honestly, not repressed. In such a world, a girl who had seen her father and foster sister die, and whose home had been lost, would be allowed to speak of them, and cry for them, and admit that they had existed. She would not need to hide her pain – her lostness – behind the mask of a dead smile, and cut herself, just to survive.

Then Otieno said: "For a long time that was the best day of my life, Pipit. I thought I would never know such a joyous sense of rightness again. But I did. The first day I saw you."

I drew in a sharp breath. "Oh, Otieno—"

The movement of the carriage slowed and then stopped. Otieno pushed the door open from the inside instead of waiting for the driver and jumped out. He called out a word in a soft, musical tongue, and Mirkasha shrieked in answer and spread her wings. The tip of the left one brushed ever so faintly across my cheek as she flew out to land on Otieno's gauntlet.

Was there something wrong with me that, after the draining emotional talk we had just had, I still found myself distracted by the way his upper arm bulged when he took the weight of the bird?

I made myself look down at my own feet as I moved to the doorway, but I had to look at him when he took my hand to help me down. The carriage had obviously been constructed with long-legged, athletic men in mind. My short limbs and three-layered kimono made getting out a rather more tricky exercise than getting in had been. I envied the easy way he bounded around. It had been a very long time since I had been able to do that. Even when I had, I had usually been caught by my mother and punished.

The day was warm: filled with gentle breezes that stirred the wild sweet scent of sakura around us, mixing it with that perfume of spring, which is less a smell than a sort of freshness, telling of sunlight and growing things.

We had drawn up by the park's entrance, where a wide gravel path led between wrought iron gates. We crunched slowly along the path, Otieno eyeing me for a few moments before repeating his gesture from the bridge and drawing my hand through the crook of his elbow so that I could lean on him as I navigated the uneven surface. He clucked at Mirkasha, and she let out another of her piercing shrieks and leapt from his arm into the air.

"She has spotted her lunch," he said.

"I pity it," I said feelingly, watching the bird transform into a dark lightning bolt as she darted into the shivering cherry blossoms.

We walked side by side in the sunlight and the shadows of the trees, enjoying the almost unearthly beauty of the flowers and nodding politely at those we passed, though many of them stared at Otieno. I did not care; I was proud to walk with him for however long he wished it.

"What of you, then?" Otieno asked. "What happened the first time you picked up an instrument?"

He sounded so eager that I hated to disappoint him. "I do not have a story to tell, Otieno. Nothing happened the first time I had a music lesson. I knew straightaway that I loved to play, but unfortunately I was not really very good at all. Because it was a proper activity for a young woman, and because I begged my father, my mother allowed me to continue despite my lack of skill. That is all."

He looked at me sceptically. "Lack of skill? I do not believe it. I heard you play. It was beautiful. Are you saying you never showed any extraordinary degree of talent as a child? Never astonished your teachers, or brought your friends and family to tears with your performance?"

I frowned. "I do not think my teacher was allowed to— I mean he never praised me. He never spoke to me at all, really, apart from to instruct me. My mother probably asked him not to. All the servants had orders about that. I was rather wild and unruly – my mother said that my father indulged me too much."

"What about your father, then, and the rest of your family?"

"I was not allowed to play for them," I said uncomfortably. "Well, not for my father and cousin. Mother listened to me a few times and said … she said I was not good enough. I would have to spend less time running around like a savage and more time practising…" My voice trailed off.

"Was your mother tone-deaf? Did she hate music for some reason?"

"Not–not that I know of." I looked up at him. "Do you mean that she did it on purpose?"

"I cannot see any other explanation." His brow wrinkled with confusion. "Only it makes no sense. She must have been proud of you. Why would a mother who knew her daughter was so immensely talented try to hide it from everyone?"

I squeezed my eyes shut as my memory jumped back eight years. I remembered that first lesson, when the teacher had called Mother in to hear me play. I remembered his face, with its wide, excited eyes, and hers, so set and white that she looked quite ill. She had taken him out

of the room, and when he came back, he had been rubbing his hands nervously over the threadbare edges of his
kimono and would not look at me. And Mother had said
that she did not think I needed any more lessons, that I
should learn embroidery instead. I had burst into tears.

For a week I pestered Father to intercede, and begged
and cried and begged again, and finally – when Father
said that perhaps he should hear me and judge for himself
– Mother gave in. I could keep my shamisen, and have my
lessons, if I promised never to play where anyone could
hear, until she told me I was good enough. Father, with
his desire for a quiet life, had accepted it, and I had been
so happy that I had not questioned it. And after that I
had had a different teacher. A stern-faced one, with much
nicer clothes, who hardly ever spoke to me at all...

"It makes perfect sense. It makes perfect sense if you
knew her," I whispered.

Father would have been so happy, so proud of me. He
had loved poetry and music. But Mother had no talent for
those things at all. In finding that connection we would
have excluded her. No wonder she never let Terayama-san
get me a new instrument. He would have wanted to hear
me play, and she was frightened it would take his attention away from her.

"Yue?" Otieno's hand on my face recalled me to myself. "What is wrong?"

"Nothing. Or rather something I should have seen for
myself a long time ago. It does not matter."

It didn't, did it? Not now. Once it would have broken my heart, but what was that small betrayal so many years ago compared to the great one later? And what were either of them compared to my own betrayal, my ultimate crime?

"You have that look on your face again," he said softly.

"What look?" I asked, playing for time as I tried to rearrange my expression. He saw through my shadow-weavings too easily. I almost wanted to curse him for it.

"The sad, lost look. It makes me think of a little girl, abandoned in a crowd, who cannot find her parents."

I felt my eyes widen, and only just managed to keep my hands from rising to my face, to hide me. "I have such an expression?" I made a strange noise, a strangled laugh. "You must be the only one who can see it."

"Perhaps. I am sorry. Sorry that your life has been so full of unhappy things, and that I reminded you of them again now."

I sighed. "You are not responsible for any of it. Not even my feelings."

"That does not mean I do not care about them. I want to chase that lost look away, so far away that it can never come back."

"Thank you. But I do not think you can."

He smiled, and it felt like the warm light of a lantern banishing the chill of a dark, lonely room somewhere inside me. "Well, I am going to try," he said. "And I might surprise you."

I looked away, and we kept walking. Gradually my tumultuous feelings quietened, and calmness returned.

"I think I must be boring you." Otieno broke the companionable silence.

"Why?"

"One of my uncles said, when I told him I was coming here, that it is traditional when viewing the cherry blossoms to compose haiku in honour of its beauty. He said I ought to make some up beforehand, in case you expected it."

It was too much. After the morning I had had – the tension, the revelation – the image of Otieno squinting at a page with a puzzled frown on his face, scribbling away, was too much for my self control. I burst out laughing.

"Oh, oh, I cannot – I—" I gasped helplessly.

"Why is that funny?" he demanded. "I am not an idiot. Do you think I am incapable of writing a simple poem? I can play poetry games as well as you can!"

I rubbed my streaming eyes with the heel of my free hand, sniffed, and finally managed to answer. "Can you, indeed?"

I stared up at the trees consideringly and then said:
"Cherry blossoms dance
Shiver and sigh with the wind
Like maidens in love."

Otieno stared at me. "Was that— Did you really just make that up?"

"You challenged, I answered," I said. "Now, in order

to play the game correctly, you should take the last line of my haiku and use it to begin a new one. Go ahead."

He made a noise of disgust, which started me giggling again. "My father was a poet," I said, surprised that I was able to mention him so easily for the second time that day. "Perhaps I have an unfair advantage."

"Perhaps we should just admire the scenery. Quietly. With no talking."

"Very well."

"And no laughing either," he said pointedly, as he took my arm again.

"I do not think I can promise that."

"Shhh."

I snorted and giggled my way around the park for another ten minutes. Then Mirkasha flew back and horrified me by dropping a dead finch at our feet. After my time in the kitchen, there was little that could make me squeamish, but the surprise of the little body hurtling past my face made me squeak like a trapped mouse, and this time it was Otieno who was helpless with laughter. He had to stumble off the path and lean on a tree, my support being insufficient.

He only managed to recover himself when I walked off down the path without him, and nearly turned my ankle.

"I am sorry," he said. "Do not injure yourself on my account."

When we reached the main gates again, Otieno let out a deafening whistle that made everyone within sight start violently, and Mirkasha came hurtling back, this time with no presents for us. As she took her place on the perch inside the carriage, Otieno asked, "Your name now means 'moon', yes?"

"It does. Why?"

He shook his head. "Just curious."

He spent the rest of the journey staring pensively out of the window. I did not mind. I had more than enough to think about.

We arrived at the house to find Akira working in the garden, her skin shielded from the sun by a straw hat, a basket full of spring flowers in her hand.

"Hello," she called out as I clambered out of the carriage, wishing for some steps, or even a box, to make the process easier. "Did you have a nice time?"

"Very, thank you," Otieno called back. "Excuse me a moment."

He caught my arm as I passed and drew me to him with a gentle but implacable grip. "I had a very nice time," he repeated. "Thanks to you."

Then he kissed me, warm lips parting mine. His hand slid possessively down my spine, making me arch like a cat begging to be stroked. I gasped and felt his smile against my mouth. The caress of his tongue made me gasp again.

Then he stepped away, holding my shoulders considerately until I caught my balance.

"That's the look I want to see," he whispered. He took one of my hands and pressed something into it. He had turned away and was back in his carriage and rattling down the drive before I had even managed to close my mouth.

"Such a nice young man," Akira said from somewhere close by. I hadn't noticed her approach. "So polite."

"Polite," I echoed, staring at the retreating shape of the carriage.

Paper crackled in my hand. I blinked a few times, then brought that hand up and managed to extract and unfold the note.

Scratched out in tiny, painstaking characters, were the words:

The night sky weeps snow
Heart pierced by the moon's beauty
Just as you pierced mine.

"Oh," breathed Akira, reading over my shoulder. "I am very glad Otieno came to call on you. Very glad, indeed."

"Anyone would think you want my heart broken," I whispered.

"Anyone would think I want your heart saved."

I pressed my lips together on the various retorts that wanted to spring out. Despite everything, Akira was still a romantic. How she envisioned a happy ending here I did not know, but I could not repay her genuine kindness and concern with spite.

Instead I asked, "Have you heard anything from Lord Takakura yet?"

"How funny you should ask," she said. "That was the message which delayed me earlier. You have been invited to view the sakura in Lord Takashi's gardens, and to play for his guests if it pleases you. Tomorrow night. Excited?"

I clasped my hands neatly, ignoring the crackle as the haiku was crushed between my palms. "Of course."

Thirty-one

By the time we reached the sakura viewing at Lord Takashi's house, I was trembling with nerves. It did not help that Akira insisted we be the very last to arrive, and time our entrance so finely that just one more minute of delay would have made us horribly rude.

This was my second excursion into society, and, from what Akira had said, the most crucial one. Lord Takashi could make or break a girl's reputation with one sarcastic comment. If I did well here, I would be a success. If not... I did not even want to think about it. And I was required to do much more tonight than simply sit and look pretty. I had to play my shamisen in public for the very first time. I was worried about Akira too.

"This is not too dangerous for you, is it?" I asked. "I know you said being back at court would probably be safer, but this is not precisely court—"

"Do not worry. I have let it be known that my mourning period is at an end and I intend to take a place in society. My return after all this time, alive and well, has created quite a stir. If I were to be murdered now, the old princess's reputation would be horribly damaged. She is unpopular enough anyway, and now that the prince is old enough to take power, her influence is on the wane. She cannot risk it."

The sun was setting as we entered the gardens, and the stone lanterns placed along the paths had been augmented with paper lights that hung from the lower branches of the trees to illuminate the delicate shades of the petals above. Shin, one of Akira's servants, followed behind us, reverently carrying my shamisen. I had to stop myself from looking back to check on him.

We greeted our host. Lord Takashi was a tall, thin man who had no doubt been good-looking in his youth. Now deep, harsh lines carved his face into haggard sections, giving the impression that he was constantly hungry. He spoke to Akira politely enough, but the way he looked at me made me worry that he was about to try and squeeze me to check my ripeness. He directed us to a tiny pagoda at the centre of the garden, exquisitely carved in the style of the Old Empire. This was to be my stage.

Blankets and silk pillows had already been spread over the grass beneath the trees so that my audience could sit in comfort while I played. Not many people were in this area now, and none of them paid us any attention. Akira sent Shin to place the shamisen on the stand in the pagoda, but instead of staying with her, I followed him, and carefully checked the instrument.

"Stop," Akira said after several minutes. "If you fiddle with the strings once more, I may give in to the temptation to snip them all off, just to give you something real to fuss over."

"I am sorry." I wished I could get the performance over with, but it was to be saved for later, when full dark had fallen. Lord Takashi wanted to make a spectacle of me.

"Do not be sorry – but do come along," she said, fluttering her fan, which was painted to look like a lupine butterfly, in shades of indigo and yellow. It matched her *kurotomesode* kimono, which was embroidered with butterflies in blue, yellow and grey. Her obi was the same deep blue as the fan.

For the first time it occurred to me as odd that Akira wore the formal kimono of a married woman, since she did not have the status of a widow in law. Of course, as a former Shadow Princess, she was not allowed to marry, making a *furisode* – the unmarried woman's kimono, with its very long sleeves – inappropriate. I looked at the yards of material trailing from my own sleeves and wondered if there was some kind of Shadow Bride etiquette that I would need to learn. I would ask her another time. A time when she was not leading me out of the deserted little clearing into a twilight garden filled with chattering, laughing strangers who held my revenge in their hands.

"Remember, your watchwords are silence and mystery. You show up perfectly against the shadows in that outfit. Everyone will be horribly curious about where I've been for the past few years, so I am going to mingle and subtly spread tales of your perfection, and you are going to glide over there and wander through the trees like the essence of spring. Try to avoid talking to anyone. Yes? Good."

"Glide—?"

But she was already turning away, making her way through the guests and turning heads as she went. *She has no difficulty gliding,* I thought. However, unlike me, in my ice-blue kimono and white obi, with white cherry blossoms in my hair, Akira blended into the darkness quite well. I felt a rush of gratitude and affection towards her. Although she was less and less enthusiastic about the plan, she was still doing everything possible to keep her word.

I knew I had not earned such loyalty. Anyone would have done what I did for Akira that night in the cell, while few people would put themselves to such trouble as Akira did for me now. I was reminded of another friend. Quiet, bent old Youta. He had risked so much to save me, time and again. I had not even been grateful much of the time. I wondered if he ever thought about me, or if remembering what I had done was too painful. Would he disapprove of what I was doing now? Perhaps. Or perhaps he would understand it. I hoped so. I hoped he was well, in spite of me.

I took a deep breath. Very well, I would do my best.

I arranged my mask into an expression of grave contemplation, and walked slowly along the outskirts of the lighted area, weaving in and out of the trees, letting myself be seen only in brief, enticing glimpses. I wove the warm lantern light into my illusion, creating a faint glow to my skin and hair that I hoped would shine against the gathering darkness.

It was working. As I passed, conversations faltered. Heads began to turn. Eyes followed me. It made my skin prickle with a strange combination of excitement and unease.

"Who is that…?"

"Hmmm. Pretty girl."

"Who is she?"

I kept my expression of melancholic contemplation in place, but internally I grinned. Akira was right. She really was a genius.

I told her as much a little while later when she rejoined me. The two of us walked together now, through the crowds instead of around them. No one approached us, but everyone seemed to be looking.

"I know," she said. "You have created the perfect impression. It needs only your performance to set the seal upon it."

My stomach lurched. How odd that music – always a

source of comfort and peace to me – was now the cause of my anxiety. Otieno's words had unsettled me. Although I felt reasonably confident of the skill of my fingers and the clearness of my voice, I was worried about that other ... thing that Otieno had hinted at. More than hinted at. The danger of ignoring my so-called gift. I did not understand how I used that gift when I played, and was anxious that now I was aware of it, I might stop doing it and ruin everything. It was an unhappy thought.

"You are worrying," Akira said, her sharp eyes resting on the movement of my hands, which were gripping and regripping each other under the cover of my sleeves. "There is no need. Yue, in my former life I listened to hundreds of professional musicians. Ouji-sama had the best that the Moonlit Land could offer. And I have never been as moved by any performance as I have been listening to you pick out a simple lullaby on my veranda. You will enchant them."

My stomach lurched again at the use of that word. I nodded, pretending to be reassured, and tried to distract myself by running mental fingers over the material of my illusion for the hundredth time, checking that no wrinkle or blemish marred it.

I approached the little stage on unsteady legs, the curious whispers rising around me like the roar of the high tide. I pretended that I did not see them stare. I pretended that the way they parted before me was only my right. Akira selected a blanket close to the front of the stage and sank gracefully down onto it. Our host moved to sit next to her.

I walked past them and climbed the three low steps to where my shamisen waited under a cluster of paper lanterns. My shadow was stark black on the light, polished wood. I bowed to my audience, took my instrument from its stand and knelt in the formal *seiza* position, laying the bowl of the shamisen against the outside of my thigh.

The guests did not quieten down as I pulled the ivory plectrum from my hair and lifted my hands to the strings of my instrument. If anything, the voices grew louder and more speculative.

You know how to do this, I told myself firmly. *These people are important, yes, but no matter what happens, we will not give up tonight. This is not the end. Just play.*

I closed my eyes and breathed in the wild scent of sakura.

I let my fingers move, the poignant notes trembling out through the darkness and over the rustling and muttering of the crowd. I let myself flow out with that sound, let it carry me as I began to sing. My audience ceased to exist. I played in silence, in darkness.

"*Sakura, sakura, covering the sky…*" I thought of the way the spring breeze had tangled Otieno's hair, of the sunlight and shadows dappling his skin as the canopy of trees danced overhead.

"*Drifting like mist and clouds…*" Leaning on him as I laughed, knowing he would not let me fall.

"*Sakura, sakura…*" Otieno's warm, spicy cassia smell mixing with the sweetness of the cherry blossoms.

I reached the end of the song in that quiet, protected place inside me. The last note seemed to linger for a long time. Finally I laid my hand over the strings and brought their vibration to an end. I opened my eyes, expecting the noise and movement to rush back.

It did not.

The silence had not been in my head. The guests were still, wide-eyed, staring as if mesmerized. I flicked a look at Akira. She was smiling, eyes closed, as motionless as the others. They were all under a spell.

My spell.

A woman near the front shifted, wiping tears from her cheeks. A gentle sigh seemed to ripple through the clearing, and more people began to shift, slowly, dreamily. Then someone started clapping, and soon everyone joined in. The applause had a hushed quality, and carried on for a long time. It stopped only gradually, slowing a few times before coming back in little spurts and then finally dying away. When they were quiet, I rose and bowed again, and placed my shamisen back on the stand.

Akira stood and came to meet me as I left the little pagoda, and the gathering began to break up. People rose and moved about, though their voices were still hushed and their faces were still peaceful. Had *I* really done that?

Lord Takashi appeared beside us. The change in his face was remarkable. He looked like a man who had just woken from a beautiful dream; the deep lines were smoothed and his expression was calm and refreshed. Yet more striking was the change in the way he looked at me. It was no longer the speculative gaze of a man who is inspecting an object he might wish to buy. Now he seemed certain he wanted to buy, and that the merchandise was of the highest quality too. He looked at me the way my father had looked at his beloved scrolls and papers.

"My very deepest thanks," he said to me, bowing. "I am honoured to have had my home graced by such an extraordinary talent."

I gathered myself to reply, bowing formally as I said, "It is my honour to have provided some small measure of entertainment to your distinguished guests."

"Lord Takashi, thank you for a lovely evening," Akira said, subtly nudging him back and away from me. "Yue is tired now from her performance. I think we should return home."

We both bowed to him again, and he returned the gesture. "I hope you will visit my humble home again. Soon," he whispered as I passed him.

Rumbling home in the carriage, I cradled my shamisen safely in my arms while Akira burst into delighted laughter. She tossed her fan up, catching it on one finger and flicking it open in the same movement so that it spun around in a blur of blue.

"Takashi has fallen in love!" she crowed. "It was a triumph. I have never heard you play like that before. Your voice was… I felt as if I was your age again. I cannot describe it."

"I accomplished what was needed, then?"

"More than. Much more than! No one who was there tonight will ever forget you, or how you made them feel. You will be the talk of this city by tomorrow morning." She paused, as if struck by a sudden idea. "Have you ever tried playing any other instruments, Yue? You have such a strong talent, you might enjoy developing it; I would love to hear you play a thirteen-stringed *koto*. Or perhaps a *shakuhachi* – the flute would be something completely different."

I blinked, taken by surprise. I had never considered taking up any other instrument than the shamisen. What would it be like to be able to play others? To be able to pick up any instrument I wanted and express all the feelings in my heart? I could see myself doing it. I could imagine years of blissful study, perfecting my music in different mediums. It would take up all my time.

I felt that instinctive tug of fear, the same one I felt whenever Otieno or Akira mentioned the "gift" they were so sure I had. I only had room for one obsession.

"I— Maybe," I said, shaking my head to rid it of the images of new songs, new instruments. "Maybe I will have time after. I cannot think about it now."

"Of course." The animation left Akira's face. She snapped her fan closed. "After."

Thirty-two

The performance at the cherry blossom viewing had served its purpose. Akira was deluged with invitations, some for me to play and others simply begging us to attend various gatherings.

As I played and sang for people more and more often, I began to understand just how much pleasure it brought them to share my music with me. After a couple more public appearances, my nerves completely disappeared; with my shamisen in my hands, I was as comfortable surrounded by a hundred people as alone on Akira's veranda. At such gatherings, I felt that I had a purpose, and was valued.

The invitations to tea ceremonies, parties or dinners where there was no music seemed strange to me, though. Obedient to Akira's rules, I spoke very little, never laughed, rarely smiled, and for the most part ignored people unless they spoke directly to me. I thought I must be the most intensely dull guest that most of them had ever entertained, but Akira assured me that everyone found me charming. Weeks passed, and the invitations continued to arrive. My hosts grew steadily richer, and their parties bigger, and I knew that Akira's plan was working; I was becoming famous. The more famous I became, the closer I drew to my ultimate goal, the Kage no Iwai.

"Are they truly satisfied simply to stare at my face?" I asked. "I cannot comprehend it. Perhaps I would feel better about it if it were really my face, and not a mask, but still—"

"Here, eat," Akira interrupted, passing me a full rice bowl.

"*Itadakimasu*," I said absently.

"No, they are not merely captivated by the way you look, although your weavings now are so skilful that it would not be surprising if they were. It is the mystery of Kano Yue that intrigues and enchants them. You reveal nothing; they imagine everything. Real love is hard because it requires one to know and accept another person with all their faults. This kind of infatuation is easy because, as far as they are concerned, Kano Yue has no faults. They love everything about you because they know nothing about you."

I sighed, catching a piece of stewed pork belly in my chopsticks and popping it into my mouth.

"You already know all this," Akira said, chasing a slice of boiled egg. "Why so cross? It is working, which is what you wanted. You are well on your path to receiving an invitation to the Shadow Ball."

I nodded, and slurped some soup.

"Yue?"

"I hate that name," I whispered.

"What?" Akira dropped her chopsticks. "Why did you not tell me before? We could have picked another—"

"No, no," I said. "It is not that the name is bad. I just—" I broke off, stirring my food around, then finished, "It is harder than I expected."

"What is, Pipit?"

She too had picked up Otieno's pet name for me. Hearing it again made my voice wobble as I said, "Everything."

There was a pause. "This is about Otieno?"

I gave up on my *kukuni* stew and looked at Akira. "He goes home soon. One week."

Akira's expression was unexpectedly stern. "Would you have him stay, then?"

I shook my head violently. "No. He has been in the Moonlit Land for two years, and although he does not admit it, it has been hard for him. He does not belong here. He is not happy here. He must go home."

"Besides which," she said deliberately, "in two weeks he will have no reason to stay. You will belong to someone else."

※　※　※

The next day Otieno did not come to see me at the normal time.

Over the last few weeks Akira had relaxed her rules on my music practice a lot. I played and sang every day but some days only for half an hour before Otieno arrived. Providing I put in my full dance practice later on, Akira did not scold me. Dancing for an hour was an inflexible rule; just as I was determined to attend the Shadow Ball, Akira was determined that I should not shame her with my dancing.

Otieno always came somewhere in the middle of my playing. Sometimes he simply sat on the veranda and listened, sometimes we talked. Other times he would whisk me – and occasionally Akira too – out on some planned trip to the market or park or another special place that he had heard of. There were even times, more often lately, when Otieno stayed with us for the whole day, blending seamlessly into our normal activities, drinking tea with us, lying lazily on his side on the tatami mat watching Akira arrange flowers, or laughing at me when I tried to imitate one of her fan tricks and hit myself on the head.

Yet today, he did not come.

I spun my shamisen practice out, digging the recesses of my memory for half-heard tunes to reconstruct and then resorting to simple children's songs. Eventually Akira came to collect me and force me inside. We drank tea, and then our day continued just as it normally would have. As if that gap in routine had never happened. Except that it had. I felt the gap inside me; it was a void, an aching emptiness. *Where is he?*

Melodramatic. Foolish. Childish. If his absence for a single day felt like a wound, how would I manage when he was gone forever?

"You must get used to this," I muttered.

"Did you say something?" Akira asked, looking up from her letter. Her eyes widened. "You are pale. Are you ill? Moon in the sky, you are attending Lord Yorimoto's party in two days! He is the Moon Prince's principle adviser; he is the one who will get your invitation for you."

"I am not sick. I was just thinking about something."

She tapped her fingernails against her brush, and finally said, "Tomorrow. He will be back tomorrow."

I refused to look at her. After a moment I heard her sleeves swishing and the movement of the brush again, and relaxed. I went back to listening intently for the sound of carriage wheels approaching.

That night I had a dream. I was fourteen, a child again, standing under the cherry blossoms in my father's orchard, hearing the screams. I dreamed of the fear clogging my throat as my father fell. Aimi was pulling at me, dragging me away, and as I turned to run, I saw Otieno.

He was lying in the grass. One of his own black-and-white fletched arrows was buried in his back.

I woke miserable, shivering and sick. I felt more sick

when I had to look at the miso soup, rice and vegetables that were served for breakfast.

"I am not hungry," I mumbled, getting up and going to sit on the veranda.

Otieno was not thoughtless. He knew we expected him to visit. If he had not been able to, not wanted to come, he would have sent a message. Yet there had been no message. Something was wrong.

So many things could happen to people. I had seen most of them first-hand. So many ways to die. Arrows. Swords. Poisoning…

If he did not come today, what should I do? I had no idea where he was staying. He had never taken me to his home. Who would know where his family could be found?

I began to make bargains in my head. I would not mind if he had simply grown tired of us – of me – and did not want to see us any more. If, now that his time to leave was drawing near, he had decided to distance himself, I would accept that. If all we got was a little, polite note that said goodbye, that would be good enough.

So long as he was all right.

That was all.

That was all I needed to know.

I did not take my shamisen out. I did not see the lake or the sky or the mountains, though I stared at them until my eyes watered. I just sat there, and waited. Making promises to the Moon, or fate, or anyone else who would listen.

It took me a moment to hear the impatient footsteps

in the house behind me. I turned as the screen door flew back. There was Otieno, framed in the entrance. Breathing. Alive.

Bandaged.

I took in the raw-looking grazes on the right side of his face, his purpling and swollen eye, and the clean white wrappings that covered his right hand. He was hurt. But he was alive. I stared, torn between joy and horror, unable even to move. I felt the tears well up in my eyes. They burned as they spilled down my frozen cheeks.

Otieno's expression went from smiling to shock. In an instant, he was on his knees beside me, gathering me against him. I clutched at his solid arms and breathed in his comforting cassia smell.

"Yue. Do not – do not cry." The soothing murmur rumbled through this chest where it pressed against me.

But I could not stop crying. Sobs ripped from my body and left me weak and shuddering in their wake.

"What happened?" I asked. The words were so thick and muffled by tears that even I could barely understand them. "What happened to you?"

"I had an accident on the way here yesterday. My carriage overturned. I was unconscious. Even when I woke up, I am afraid I was knocked a little silly, and did not remember that I had missed my visit here until it was too late to send a message. I did not want to wake your household just to apologize, so I came here as soon as it was polite."

"*Wake the household?* Do you think I care for that? Do you know all the terrible things I was imagining? *Seeing*, in my head? I thought you were dead!"

Otieno ignored my weak struggles until I gave up and laid my head against his chest, letting him support my weight. I sniffed soggily. My nose was blocked and I knew that by now my face was swollen to twice its normal size and blotched red.

"Would you please explain what this is about? Why would you think I was dead? Did you have a vision that harm had come to me?" Otieno asked hesitantly.

"No – I – no, I do not think so. I felt something was wrong."

"Is that why you panicked?"

"No!" I said, jerking against him. He winced, and I felt remorseful. I rubbed gently at his side. "You do not understand."

"Yes, but I have already admitted that," he said, his tone a mixture of irritation and amusement. "I cannot read your mind, though believe me there are times when I would trade all I own for that ability. You must tell me. Tell me why I found you sitting here this morning as if you had already bid me goodbye."

I drew back from him and rubbed my fingers over my stinging, puffy eyelids. "Otieno, you have never seen anyone killed, have you?"

I could hear the frown in his voice when he said, "I saw my grandmother, after she died."

338

I drew in a slow, jerky breath. It hitched in my chest, but I fought the tears down. "That is not the same thing. Not at all. I have seen people *killed*. They were gone in a moment, an instant. I could not even try to save them."

I pulled my hands away from my eyes and looked at him. "You think you are immortal. Everyone does. Only those of us who have seen – have really seen – how easy death is, can understand. Life is the improbable thing. It is so fragile that it can be taken away at any second, without reason or logic or warning. My fears may seem foolish to you, but I know how easily you could be taken from me. I know how it would feel."

Otieno took my hands, leaning forward until our foreheads touched. "Pipit. It is time. You must tell me now. Tell me everything."

I swallowed, wanting to deny it. Only how could I, now? I had made it his business.

"Soldiers came to the house and accused Father of treachery. They cut off his head and brought my cousin down with an arrow. She died trying to save me."

I tilted my head to look at Otieno and told him the rest in as few words as possible, right up until the time when I ran away from the kitchen. As with Akira, I did not mention my mother's poisoning. When I was finished, I felt exhausted.

"You wanted to know what happened, and I have told you. Now you must give me something in return."

He nodded. "Very well. What would you like?"

"Promise me you will never leave me like that again. Arrange with your father so that no matter what happens, I will know you are all right."

"We are leaving in less than a week. It will hardly be necessary after that."

I flinched at the reminder, everything inside me cringing back. I ploughed on, determined not to let him see. "Until then. Please. I cannot live through such a day, or such a night again."

He smiled, and before I could stop him, he kissed me, a sweet, soft kiss that made me sigh.

"I promise," he whispered, "you will never have such a day or night again. I will make sure of it."

Thirty-three

"There is something we must speak about before we attend Lord Yorimoto's entertainment tonight," Akira said.

I turned away from my comparison between a silver and mother-of-pearl *kanzashi* pin and a tortoiseshell and coral one, and looked at her. She was pale, and very serious.

"What is it? Are you well?"

"Do not worry about me," she said. "I have told you that Lord Yorimoto is the key to gaining your invitation, but I also said that all you need to do is be your usual charming self and the invitation would be yours. That may no longer be true."

"Why?" I asked, although I was not sure I wanted the answer. It was no minor problem that put such a look on her face.

"I have just received word that Lady Yorimoto is ill. She will not be presiding over the party tonight. She will not even be in the house, in fact. She is staying with her daughter."

I frowned. "Does that make such a difference?"

"I am afraid so." She drew in a deep breath, as if bracing herself. "Lord Yorimoto is a handsome, charming and intelligent man. That is why he is a valued adviser to the prince, and why you need his help if you want to attend the Shadow Ball. He is also a notorious seducer of young women – though seducer is not precisely the right word, as I have it on good authority that many of his victims are less than willing. His wife is a formidable woman, and a friend of the old princess; having her there tonight might have made your role a little more difficult, since she does not like me, and would not have approved of you. However, her presence would have kept Yorimoto in check. With her safely out of the way, he may feel free to act in ways that you will not like."

I swallowed and looked down at my hands, clasped neatly and calmly in my lap. "We will be in public, though, and you will be with me."

"You cannot rely on either of those things to keep you safe. He could arrange to have us separated in any of a dozen ways, and getting you alone would be child's play for him. The higher people rise in court, the more they excel at such games. Besides…" She hesitated.

"What? Tell me. I need to know."

She made a gesture of frustration. "If Yorimoto is pleased, he can arrange to have that invitation in your hand by this time tomorrow. With his wife at the party, it would have been easy to please him: a little flirting, a smile, a touch of a hand. But without any restraint placed on him, he will expect more. If you offend him, he may withhold the invitation out of spite, and with both he and his wife as your enemies, it will be much, much harder to gain an invitation through someone else. Not impossible. You are Kano Yue. Someone will probably help you."

"Probably," I said, my voice hollow. "The ball is in a week and three days. Have we any invitations from other advisers to the prince before then?"

"No."

I let out a long, slow breath. "So the question becomes – just how much is the invitation worth to me?"

I had steeled myself to the duties of the Shadow Bride. I could and would go through with it in order to get the promise. Now I had to decide if, in order to get to the ball in the first place, I could allow another stranger to lay his hands on me, simply because he was despicable enough to be my enemy if I refused.

Akira looked away. "You are not the daughter of a nobleman. You are the sister of a notorious courtesan, of murky past. He will not expect you to be a virgin. He may feel that, even if you are to attend the Shadow Ball, there is no harm in sampling the goods. Or he may not

343

go that far, but he could still expect you to show him 'favour', shall we say. Yue, I know that you and Otieno have grown close these past few weeks. Have you—?"

"*No,*" I said.

Akira rubbed her forefinger in a gentle circle on her smooth forehead, a sure sign that a headache was building. "I am not sure if that makes it better or worse."

In the midst of my own dismay, I felt a flash of compassion for Akira. This was hard for her. Perhaps it brought back memories of her own past, of being sold to the theatre. They had expected her to take on the role of a grown woman not just on the stage but in the pleasure rooms behind it, when physically and mentally she was still a child. At least I had a choice. She had never had one.

Without thinking, I shuffled forward and laid my hand on her knee. It rested there a moment before it began to heat and tingle, bringing to me the awareness of the uncomfortable pressure behind her left eye and the thudding in her skull. This much of her distress I could alleviate, at least. I let the heat spread from my skin to hers, soothing the pain away.

Her tense shoulders relaxed, and her hand fell away from her head. I pulled back, closing my eyes against the wave of dizziness that came when I moved. It passed almost straight away. I was getting better. Stronger.

And less and less able to resist the temptation to use this new gift.

I pushed that thought away and opened my eyes to see

that the delicate colour had returned to Akira's cheeks.

"Thank you," she said, smiling. "I do not know what I ever did without you."

"If it were not for me, you would not have had the headache in the first place," I pointed out.

"Nonsense. Now listen to me, Pipit. We do not have to attend tonight. I can send a note to Yorimoto claiming a sudden indisposition, and then we will just have to work harder and try to get an invitation some other way. You need not do anything you do not wish to do."

I shook my head decisively. "There is no time. I will just have to do my best to stay with you, and charm him while keeping him at a distance."

"And if that does not work?" she asked, eyes huge. I wondered again at the memories that caused her face to fill with such emotion, and took her hand.

"Then I will have to make another choice. I cannot know yet what I will do. I will survive it, Akira, no matter what. I have chosen my own way, and I will see it through. Do not worry about me."

Brave words. Even I did not believe them, really.

Akira fussed over me more than normal as we readied ourselves for the party. She sent her maid away and dressed my hair herself. She brought some of her own pins for my hair, long ones with dangling beads of abalone and freshwater pearl.

"These pins are very sharp," she commented casually.

"If you were to stab someone with them, it would hurt a great deal."

I nodded, making the beads clank together. I wanted to tell her that I would not need the pins, that I could look after myself, but I was afraid of what might come out instead. I had used up my store of bracing speeches. Instead I took a sip of the tea that Akira had brought for me and gagged.

"What is this?"

"Just tea. Why?" Akira said, still busy with the pins.

I peered into the cup. The tea looked normal, but it was intensely bitter and had a faint spicy smell that was familiar. Then I realized where I had smelled it before and gagged again, pushing the cup away so hard that part of its contents slopped onto the lacquered tray.

"That is sangre tea!"

"Yue—"

"Why are you trying to make me drink this?"

"Calm down." Her hands left my hair and came to rest on my shoulders. "You said yourself that you cannot know what you will do. This is just a precaution."

I shook my head, wanting to refuse, to reject the tea utterly. "It is dangerous, this stuff!" I knew it was. None knew better than I.

"Not taken like this. It is heavily diluted, and you are not pregnant. I know it tastes bad, but it will not harm you. The worst that can happen is your monthly bleeding will be a little heavier. Yoshi-san and her girls use it often.

You know I would not put you in danger."

I took a deep breath. I knew Yuki had taken sangre without any real ill effects; it was the amount I had given my mother that had been fatal to her. And Akira was right. It would be stupid to take risks.

I picked up the now lukewarm tea and drank it down in one gulp, coughing and sputtering as the bitterness hit my throat.

"Good girl," Akira said, and went back to arranging my hair.

Eventually we were both ready, and we left home, not speaking much in the carriage. This was the event we had both been working towards almost since I had first come to live with Akira, but it brought about no feeling of excitement. I just wanted to get it – whatever it was – over with.

From the moment we arrived at Lord Yorimoto's home, I could see the truth of what Akira had said. Ostensibly it was to be an evening celebrating music, dance and the other traditional arts, but the boisterous voices and brittle laughter nearly drowned out the sweet tune that a pair of *gijo* were playing on *biwa* – four-stringed lutes – near the entrance. Many men and women were gathered around them, but no one seemed to be making an effort to listen.

In another area of the large room – which had been created by pushing back or partially pushing back all the dividing walls on the lower floor of the house – more *gijo* performed. Two of them danced with fans, while a third provided music on a shamisen. I could not hear enough of her playing to know if she was good. The girls were beautiful dancers, but their movements were much more openly sexual than the dances I had seen at Yoshi-san's teahouse. The girls wore heavy white make-up and had red lips, something I had never seen before either, and instead of keeping their eyes fixed on the distance, they cast laughing, flirtatious looks at those watching them, many of whom made lewd gestures in return.

Akira hissed quietly. "This will degenerate into an orgy before the night is through. Yue, I do not think—"

"Ohime-sama!" A hearty voice broke into Akira's words. A tall, solidly built man approached us, smiling. Akira moved, and I found myself half-hidden behind her as the man continued, "Your beauty graces my humble home. I am glad that your long period of mourning is, at last, at an end."

"I am Kano-san now, Yorimoto-san," Akira said, smiling. It did not touch her eyes. "It is no longer necessary to address me as princess."

"You will be a princess in my eyes as long as you live," he said. Though the words were flattering on the surface, they seemed like a threat to my ears. It had been a while since I had thought about the danger of the old princess's hatred for Akira, but he made me remember it now. He went on, "However, I will be obedient to your wishes, of course, Kano-san."

There was a high-pitched trill of female laughter behind me, and when I glanced back, I saw that one of the dancing *gijo* now sat in the lap of a man who had been watching her dance. She struggled a little, playfully threatening to bat him over the head with one of her fans, before he released her and she stood up again. I suddenly realized that the man was Lord Takashi, and I whipped back around before he saw me staring.

My movement caught Yorimoto-san's attention. "Ah, who is this? Can it be your famed sister? I am told that she might outshine even your legendary beauty."

Akira beckoned me forward, and I thought that no one but me could have detected the reluctance in the lines of her shoulders and back.

"This is Kano Yue. She is making her first appearance in society. Since you have the prince's ear, I have told her that she must meet you."

I bowed to Yorimoto-san, and he to me. He was handsome, as Akira had said, and his smile held a great deal of confidence and humour. Then I looked into his eyes, and saw not the frank appraisal that I had become used to, but a kind of calculating coldness that reminded me abruptly and unhappily of Terayama-san. As we both straightened, he moved a little closer to me, and his breath – not bad smelling, but warm and unpleasantly intimate – washed over my face.

"The stories do not do you justice," he murmured, more for effect, I thought, than because he was really impressed by me. "Kano-san, you have presented me with a jewel."

"Actually," Akira said, moving to separate us, "I hope to present Tsuki no Ouji-sama with a jewel."

"Oh?" He quirked an eyebrow, not looking away from me. "The Shadow Ball? No one ever faulted you for lack of ambition, Kano-san. It was a pleasure to meet you, Yue-san. If we have the opportunity to speak later – in private, perhaps – then we must speak of the Shadow Ball."

We bowed to each other again, and he moved away, smiling and talking to his other guests.

Akira swore viciously under her breath.

"It was no good, was it?" I said.

"No. He was telling us – not very subtly – that he will not even talk about invitations unless I let you go off alone with him. Most likely he will give you some time to think about it, and approach you again later."

"What if I go with him but make sure to stay in this room? Within your sight? Do you think that would be enough for his pride?"

"Possibly, if you flatter him," she said, unwillingly. "You must not let him take you outside, though, Yue. He will not want to be seen doing anything too outrageous here in public, because the gossip would get back to his wife. If he can get you really alone – that would be bad."

Akira moved deeper into the room to an alcove behind an ivory and mother-of-pearl screen. Another heavily made-up *gijo* was serving tea there, and a small group had gathered around her. We took a place among them. I was grateful to be allowed to kneel in silence while Akira chatted to everyone pleasantly.

"How do you feel?" she asked, turning back to me.

"Nervous," I whispered, and then, wanting to change the subject: "Curious too. Why do the *gijo* wear such strange cosmetics?"

"It is a new fashion among them," Akira explained. "The city guard demanded that when inhabitants of the Perfumed District leave it to attend parties such as these, they wear clothes or make-up that make them easily distinguishable from the normal inhabitants of the other districts. The *gijo* decided that instead of wearing a small badge or some other discreet thing, they would take their example from the *oiran*, and flaunt their profession. Hence the make-up. It has become popular. Some patrons even ask for it when they visit the *gijo* in their teahouses. It makes them look different, and the customers find it exciting."

"More illusions," I muttered.

"I find it amusing that the guards have not realized how easily a girl who wished to blend in could simply wash her face."

A little while later Yorimoto-san appeared in the alcove.

"Yue-san, I wonder if you would like to take a turn around the room with me? I am intrigued by what your sister tells me of your ambitions and would like to discuss them with you further."

I cast a look at Akira, whose expression was carefully blank. She nodded to let me know that she would keep her eye on me, and I turned back to Yorimoto-san, giving him one of Kano Yue's rare smiles.

"Thank you. I would be honoured."

I stood, aware that dozens of pairs of eyes flew to me with the movement. Yorimoto-san seemed aware of it too. He drew me away from the crowded centre of the room to walk next to the wall, and I found that screens and flower arrangements had been cunningly placed to shield the room's outskirts. I felt suddenly isolated, and though a few moments before the noise had been wearing on me, I now found the relative quiet just as oppressive.

Calm down, I told myself. *There is no point in panicking before anything even happens.*

"I assume," Yorimoto-san began, "that your object in wishing to attend the Shadow Ball is to win Tsuki no Ouji-sama's favour?"

"Yes, Yorimoto-san," I said quietly, keeping my face downturned. I watched the tips of my zōri peek out from under my kimono and then vanish, peek and then vanish, as I walked.

"You want me to help you achieve this goal?"

"If it pleases you."

He made a restless movement. "Why do you think I should help you?"

"I do not think that you should, Yorimoto-san. I merely hope that you will."

Yorimoto-san laughed, a sound of surprise. "I begin to see the resemblance between you and your sister. You both duel with your words – but where her tongue pierces, yours turns the blade aside without cutting, does it not?"

I did not reply. I already had the feeling that I had stumbled somewhere, and was frantically trying to work out where it was. I kept myself calm by regulating my steps, so that a perfectly even distance remained between us, and his longer strides did not force me to skip to catch up.

"A woman who does not chatter," he said after a moment. "I believe there is a saying that such a woman has a price beyond rubies."

"It is commonly held that a virtuous woman has a price beyond rubies," I said. "But, of course, that would depend entirely on your taste in women."

"How unexpected. Mysterious, serious Kano Yue has a sense of humour. I wonder how many men know that?"

He came to a halt, forcing me to stop too and face him. My eyes were still downcast, but I peered carefully at our surroundings. He had positioned us behind a tall arrangement of spiky black branches which had hundreds of tiny bluish-purple flowers fastened to them with threads. The arrangement was large enough to conceal us from any but the most determined of searchers. I spared the verbena flowers a wry look. The significance of their traditional meaning was not lost on me. Verbena meant cooperation.

Yorimoto-san placed his hand on the screen door next to me – which I assumed led to the gardens – and leant forward. "How many men have known you, beautiful girl?"

"None," I said flatly.

My brusqueness obviously took him by surprise. "None?"

"No. And I intend to keep it that way. I wish to be the Shadow Bride, Yorimoto-san, and my virginity is a precious offering on the altar of that hope. I will not surrender it to anyone other than Tsuki no Ouji-sama."

He stared at me in open-mouthed shock. I watched him from beneath my lashes, fearing I had been too bold, too blunt. Then he nodded. "I salute your honesty and good sense."

I had just begun to sigh with relief when he added, "Now that I understand you a little better, perhaps you would like to step into the garden with me, and discuss these matters more privately?"

He smoothly slid back the screen on which his hand rested, letting in a gush of night-scented air that felt icy on my cheeks, making me aware of how overheated I had become in the stale atmosphere of the room. I would have breathed the fresh air in gratefully, had I not been gripped with irritation and defiance. I had not known what I would do before; now I did. I had no intention of going anywhere with this man.

"No," I said. "I am, of course, delighted to have been asked, but I do not believe that leaving this room with you would be at all helpful to my goal."

He clicked his tongue mockingly. "Perhaps your sister has not explained the rules of this game thoroughly?"

"My sister plays by her own rules. So do I."

I intensified the beauty of my weaving, heightening the soft glow of my skin, deepening the rose colour of my lips, the dark lustre of my eyes. I lifted the terrible beauty of that face and looked him full in the eyes for the first time. "I will be Shadow Bride, Yorimoto-san. If you help me on that path, I will remember, and be grateful. But if you do not help me, I will also remember. My memory is very, very long."

Before I could press my point further, there was a commotion behind me in the room. I looked over my shoulder and gasped aloud.

It was Otieno.

Thirty-four

Otieno was standing near the two *gijo* at the entrance. His father was with him too, along with all the rest of the group from Athazie that I knew. There were also several men I had never seen before, including one wearing a gold circlet around his forehead. He was the tallest of all the men there, and his hair was mostly white and startlingly pale against his skin. It was hard to make out clearly at this distance, but I thought that his face was much more heavily tattooed than any of the others. Was this the man Otieno's father had called their ruler?

"Ah, the Athazies," Yorimoto-san said, interrupting my thoughts. "Their timing is exquisite."

His arm clamped around my waist from behind. My breath left me in a surprised huff and I stumbled back into him as he took a step out of the open screen door.

Before I could struggle, we were on the veranda and he was slapping the screen shut behind us.

His arms were like iron bars: one still at my waist, the other across my chest, pressing into my breasts painfully. I was pinioned against his front and could not move. His breath was hot and wet against my neck, and I was horribly conscious of his body pressing into mine. I let out a sound of disgust, digging my nails into the arms that held me, scratching as hard as I could through layers of fabric.

"Let go," I hissed, trying to sound angry instead of frightened.

"After all the trouble I have been to? I think not."

It was completely dark outside, with not even a lantern lit. The light from the room beyond was nothing more than a dim orange glow that hindered my night vision. It was like being blind.

"If I were you," he said, sounding calmly amused, "I would be careful not to make too much noise."

I stamped down – but missed his foot.

He chuckled. "In anticipation of meeting you tonight, I did a little research, and I happen to know that you spend an uncommon amount of time with a certain young foreigner. Now if you kept fussing, and your friend were to come out and catch a glimpse of us, what do you think he would see? You, tenderly held in my arms, in this deserted spot. That kind of situation would make any young man react somewhat impetuously. I suspect that you have been cultivating his acquaintance in order to take advantage of

357

the Athazie's remarkable cache of gold – and I applaud your pragmatism, my dear – but I feel I should point out that the boy is going home in a few days, taking his gold with him. While I will still be here, and still, I assure you, your most devoted admirer. I do not ask anything of you that would … devalue the gift you wish to offer my prince. Not at all. A mere token. How could there be any harm in that? No one could possibly have any objection."

His arms tightened. I could not fill my lungs to answer him. I could not even scream. All I could do was dig my nails deeper into his flesh and silently struggle.

"I object."

The screen slid back, and Otieno appeared as a silhouette in the gap. His face was lit for a moment – hard and furious – then the screen banged shut behind him, and his expression was hidden again. But I felt a tingling thrill that made all the small hairs on my body stand up, and I knew that he was using his power somehow.

"I object very much," he continued. "I think you are probably venomous. Most snakes are."

Behind me, Yorimoto-san seemed frozen. He had not drawn breath since Otieno began to speak. Not since I had felt that surge of power.

"What makes you even worse than a snake, though, is that you have disgusting, slimy fingers. At the moment you are touching Yue with them, which, believe me, is a mistake. You are going to take them off her, and they are never going to touch her again. If they do, I will come and find you, and snap each and every one of them right off your hands. Do you understand? Nod if you do."

I felt Yorimoto-san's jerky nod.

"Good. Now go."

The tingly, powerful feeling disappeared and Yorimoto-san released me so suddenly that I lost my balance again. Otieno caught me. His arms came around me and I clung to him, so relieved that I only distantly heard Yorimoto-san crashing off the veranda into the darkness, cursing as he stumbled around. The noises faded and disappeared completely as he rounded the corner of the house.

"Are you all right?" Otieno asked, his voice a growl.

"Yes. He did not hurt me."

I felt him relax. "Thank God. He will never dare to look at you again."

In an instant all my relief at being dragged from Yorimoto-san's arms evaporated. Akira had told me I dare not offend Yorimoto-san if I wanted the invitation. Offend him? Otieno had eviscerated him. The man had fled into his own garden as if demons from the dark of the Moon were after him. He would not forget this. He would not forgive me.

I would never go to the Shadow Ball now.

I wrenched myself away from Otieno so abruptly that I stumbled off the veranda.

"Yue? What are you—?"

I landed on my hands and knees on a gravel path,

scrambled to my feet and began to run. But I did not follow the veranda as Yorimoto-san had. There was no point going back into the house now.

It was too late.

Everything was ruined.

Otieno's feet landed on the gravel with a crunch as he followed me. "Where are you going?" he called. "What is wrong?"

I could not answer. I went towards the gibbous moon that hung over the garden. It was waxing tonight. Bright. In a week it would be full, and that would be when the Shadow Ball was held.

The Shadow Ball where I would not dance. Where I would not meet the prince. Where I would not finally redeem myself. Not ever.

My eyes had adjusted to the darkness now. I kept them on the moon. Leaving the path behind, I went through flowers that sent up clouds of perfume as I trampled them, and forced my way through bushes that ripped my skirts and sleeves.

"Answer me! Come back!" Otieno shouted.

The moon was tangled in tree branches overhead now. I had stumbled into a little coppice and found myself walking uphill. My breath was wheezing and my limbs were trembling.

"Yue, come back!"

Driven beyond endurance, I shrieked, "Go away!"

"Do not be stupid!" he shouted back, somewhere near

by. He was not even breathless. "I will not leave you out here alone."

I came to a halt, and in stopping I knew that I had come to the end of my strength. I could not take another step. I heard him moving about, not bumbling and thrashing through the trees as I had, but methodically searching. I considered weaving a cloak of shadows around myself, but discarded the idea straightaway. He would see through it. I simply had to wait for him to find me.

"Go away," I said wearily. "Leave me alone. You have ruined everything."

"What did I ruin?" he asked, directly behind me. "You were so happy to be set free that you nearly threw yourself at me. What could I possibly have ruined?"

I kept my face turned away from him, though it was doubtful he could make out my expression in the shadows. "What were you even doing out there?" I asked, my voice a weary rasp. "What did you do to him to freeze and terrify him like that? Why?"

There was a long pause, and when he spoke, his voice held an edge I had never heard before, not even when he was talking to Yorimoto-san. "I saw Kano-san at the party; she was worried because she had lost sight of you and thought that disgusting Yorimoto might have forced you outside. When I found you, I bound Yorimoto-san in place with my gift because I wanted to get you away from him without a struggle and I wanted to frighten him. There, I have answered you. Now it is your turn to answer questions, and I swear to heaven you will answer me, even if we have to stay out here all night. What is wrong with you? Tell me!"

"It is nothing to do with you!" I snapped, heart aching. "None of it is anything to do with you. We have made no promises to each other. I owe you nothing. Leave me alone!"

"I won't." He seized my shoulders and dragged me into his arms, crushing me against him.

I screamed with rage, punching and kicking, barely even knowing it was him I fought against. "Get off me! Let go!"

One of my fists hit his ribs and he jerked at the blow, arms tightening around me. I went still.

He had been in an accident only the day before. He was bruised and hurt.

"Oh, Otieno," I whispered. "Sorry. I am sorry."

"I do not care," he said, his voice a husky whisper. "You can hit me if you wish. Only do not run away any more."

He kissed me, and I responded as if I had no will of my own, my lips opening, my body moulding to the shape of his. I found the places I had hit, touching them gently now, carefully running my fingers over his face. We kissed until we both ran out of breath.

"Tell me you love me," he said, voice ragged.

I drew in a shaky breath. Something in the back of my

mind was screaming, telling me that this could not happen, that Otieno was not meant for me. At that moment, I could not make myself listen. For once, the truth was stronger in me than the lies.

"I love you."

He let out a short gasp of relief, his arms tightening around me again. "And you will come with me, come home to Athazie with me?"

"What?" I croaked.

"I love you. I have been in love with you since that day when I saw you hiding under the willow tree, with dirt on your face and hair like a porcupine. Maybe I loved you before that, from the day you smiled at me on the ship. You slipped away from me both those times. Now that I finally have you, do you really think I could get on a boat and leave you behind? I have not spoken because it might have taken more time. My father and I wrote home immediately after I saw you again at the tea ceremony, and we have been waiting for the reply from our king. I had to have permission to bring you to my country. Kano-san too, in case you both wished it. The letter has not come yet, and I thought we might have to delay our departure, but the ruler of our province, who came with us, has said that he will vouch for you and your sister, and we believe that this will be enough, if my uncles and brother vouch for you as well."

"They do not even know me," I said, dazed.

"They know me," he said simply. "They know I love

you. I intended to tell you all this tomorrow. It is short notice; we could put off leaving for another few weeks, if you need it. Anything you need. I love you so much. I do not think I can ever be happy without you again. Please say you will come with me."

Laughter escaped me, uncontrollable, slightly hysterical but real. I did not recognize the emotion that came with it. It was golden and warm, and bright. It burned away that screaming voice in the back of my mind until I could not even hear it any more.

"Yes," I said, through my laughter. "Of course I will."

He picked me up again, despite his sore ribs, and swung me around, his laughter joining mine. Then he laid me down on the spongy, cool earth beneath the trees. We both stopped laughing then. Things became slow and careful. It felt like the trees closed around us, as if we were hidden and protected, with all the time we could ever want. With shaking hands, we helped each other undress, spreading our clothes out on the slightly damp grass.

In the bright moonlight I saw Otieno's eyes go to my arms – to the pale skin with its livid scars. Burns, cuts and grazes long healed, representing pain that still lived inside me. I had always hidden them from him before, under dirt or sleeves. I did not try to hide them now. I offered them to him. "They are ugly, are they not?"

"Yue…" His hands wrapped carefully around my wrists. One of his palms was almost big enough to cover all the marks. "You think that?"

"I know it," I said.

He bowed his head, the soft coils of his long hair falling across my thighs as he kissed my arm, kissed a long purple welt, then a short red one, then a scaly brownish burn scar.

"The marks I bear were given to me by my family. They are a sign of the trials I have endured, the skills I have gained, the respect I have earned. They say who I have been, and who I am. Yours are the same," he whispered. "They are not ugly. Nothing about you ever could be."

With his hands still holding my wrists, I reached out and touched his shoulders, the thick ridge of muscle there, then the hard curve of his pectorals. I skimmed my fingertips slowly over his abdomen. His head fell back, tendons standing out in his neck.

"You like that," I said, feeling sly and smug.

He slid one of his hands along my arm, the light touch almost ticklish, bringing gooseflesh and bright shocks of sensation that made me gasp as his hand found my spine and caressed it, a long smooth stroke.

"You like that," he whispered.

"Let me put my arms around you," I said, suddenly desperate to be closer, to hold onto him.

I embraced him, held his weight with the cradle of my body, held his lips against mine. I enveloped myself in him. I would not let go. I would not let go of this happiness. No one could make me.

I stirred, lifting my head from its resting place on the broad plane of Otieno's chest.

"Otieno – what will Akira think? She must be worried. We just disappeared."

"It is all right, Pipit," he said a little sleepily. "I told her when I went looking for you that I would bring you home."

"Oh, did you?" I said, smiling, framing his face with my hands. "That was presumptuous of you, was it not? You are too sure of yourself, Otieno A Suda."

"No," he said. "I am sure of you."

He turned his head to press a kiss to the centre of my palm. A deep shudder of pleasure ran through me, even as the niggle of uneasiness emerged at the back of my mind. *If he knew what I had done—*

I forced the thought away. He did not have to know. All that was over. There was nothing I could do about it, and I would not allow such memories to taint this moment.

He sighed, sitting up and pulling me with him. "I think it might be time to keep my word now, though. I must take you back to Akira.

"Spoilsport," I said, nuzzling my face into his neck, just to feel the shiver he made. "I could stay out all night."

He laughed. "I have always thought of you as a bird, but I see now that I am wrong. You are much more like a cat, a little soft creature like the ones you used to feed in the garden."

A snake in cat's clothing. Again the uneasiness twinged. "Then you must be that golden hunter you talked about," I said, trying to drown the feeling out. "You certainly roar loudly enough."

Teasing, kissing and touching, we put each other's clothing to rights as well as we could. We searched for Akira's hairpins for some time, and finally found them in the grass. I managed to twist my hair up with them, but I could tell from Otieno's muffled snigger that the result was not ideal.

"We do not have to go back in again, do we?" I asked.

"Looking like that? I am not sure if they would bar the door to you, or take you prisoner and never let you out," he said, straightening the front of my kimono. "No, you are not going back in. I will walk you around the side of the house to the stables, and we will call for my coach, and you will go home in that."

"What about you and the rest of your group?"

"Oh, no one will notice if I am a bit dishevelled," he said. "And now that they have seen the dancing girls, no doubt the rest of them will want to stay all night. There will be plenty of time for the carriage to get back from your house before we need it."

We bickered playfully all the way back to the house – a journey which seemed much shorter this time. When we arrived at the stables, though, the light of hanging lanterns revealed Akira about to climb into her own carriage. She paused when she saw us, and although her face was obscured by the shadow of the carriage door, I could tell she was tense and unhappy.

I felt awful. Despite what Otieno had said, she had been worrying, no doubt imagining all kinds of horrible things. She stepped down from the doorway of the carriage, waving away her coachman's help, and came towards us, shock flickering across her face as she took in the state of my clothes and hair.

"Perhaps I had better leave you here," Otieno said. "The stable boys are staring, and Kano-san does not look happy. Explain things to her, please? Tell her she is very welcome with us. She made a great impression on my father."

I wondered if she would make an even greater impression if A Suda-san realized exactly what was under her kimono. Now was not the time to go into that, but from what Otieno had said in the past, I knew that people in his country were free to love those of the same sex without fear of prejudice, so I was not unduly concerned.

"You will visit us tomorrow," I said, not quite making it a question.

"As sure as the sun will rise," he said, risking a fleeting caress of my cheek. "Sleep well, Pipit."

He turned away, and I turned too, watching him until he left the lantern light and disappeared into the shadows at the side of the house.

Thirty-five

"Well," said Akira as she reached me. "You look…"

"I know how I look, thank you," I said, unable to suppress the smile spreading across my face.

Akira smiled back, but there was something beneath the smile that made mine fade a little. "Things have changed," I said. "I have not been hurt, though. I will explain on the way home. You do not have to fret."

We climbed into the carriage – me averting my eyes from the coachman's face because I did not want to see if he was smirking – and lit the lantern, and when the light was swaying gently with the movement of the vehicle, I faced her.

"Otieno found me and Yorimoto-san in the garden. You were right about Yorimoto-san: when I would not go outside with him, he resorted to force, and I could not get away."

I went on, telling her about the way Otieno had threatened and insulted Yorimoto-san, and my conviction that the man would die before he allowed me to attend the ball now. Then I told her that Otieno had asked both of us to leave the Moonlit Land with him and make a new home in Athazie, and that I had said yes.

She remained still and quiet throughout the story, nodding occasionally so that I knew she was listening, but not asking questions or showing any obvious reaction on her face. I leant forward, bracing myself against the seat with one hand.

"Akira, I know this is sudden, but please will you consider coming with us? You would be leaving your home, but I think there are people in Athazie who would prize you and value you. Including me. Will you think about it?"

She put her hand up to her head as though in pain. I reached out to help her, but she avoided my touch. "Not now. I have to— I do not know what to do for the best. I do not know if you will hate me for this. I just … I cannot keep the truth from you."

She reached into the top layer of her kimono and drew out a folded piece of red paper. There was a seal of golden wax on it impressed with the symbol of a crescent moon rising over a mountain.

I stared at the paper. "Is that—?" I could not finish the question.

"Yorimoto-san found me at the party and told me that

you and he had been about to reach an understanding when Otieno interrupted you. He blamed Otieno for everything, and said that since 'the boy' was leaving before the ball, he saw no reason why you should miss it because of 'Athazie barbarism'. This is only an informal note, but he promised to add your name to the official list tomorrow."

She held the paper out to me, but it slipped through my nerveless fingers and landed on my lap. On the rumpled, grass-stained kimono that Otieno had smoothed into place with loving hands just a few minutes before.

"Yue, you are invited to the Shadow Ball."

We went into the house in silence. Akira was waylaid by a servant; I walked into my room, closed the door behind me and sat down on the mat before the shrine.

Shrine was too grand a name for it, really. It was only a tiny alcove in the wall. The finest thing there was the silver crescent that Akira had given me. It hung on a red thread, to represent the Moon watching over the spirits of my father and cousin. There was little else to see. I had written their names neatly on paper and hung them on the wall, above a pair of cheap incense burners. I had placed flowers here for them that morning: dried lavender for faithfulness, bright yellow *suisen* for respect, dried white *tsubaki* for waiting. They were still waiting, I knew.

I had no likenesses of them, or stone tablets inlaid with precious metals or jewels and inscribed with their names. I did not even have a ribbon, an old pipe, not so much as a scrap of cloth, to evoke them. All those things had been left to rot in my father's house.

Just as their bodies had rotted in the grass where they fell.

"Forgive me," I said. "Forgive me. I shall not forget again. I shall not forsake you."

I heard the screen slide open but did not look up.

Akira asked, "What are you going to do?"

"You already know the answer," I said. My voice sounded dead.

"What about Otieno?"

"He will forget me."

"No, he will not," she said, and her voice broke, though there was no reproach in it. "You know he will not. You promised him, Yue."

I leant my forehead on the edge of the shrine, pressing until I felt the bone of my skull grinding against the wood. "They have no one but me. If I do not remember them, they will not be remembered. If I do not punish Terayama-san, then he will never be punished. I have no choice."

"You do have a choice. If you want to go with Otieno—"

"It is not a matter of wanting!" I banged my head down so hard on the edge of the shrine that the little incense burners rattled. "I do not want to go to the Shadow Ball and dance, and give myself to the prince. It makes me sick to think of it now. Sick. But I cannot abandon them to pursue my own selfishness. I cannot do what my mother did."

Akira came to kneel beside me, placing her hand on my back. "This is completely different! You are not your mother. You have done nothing wrong. Your family would not begrudge you your own life, your own happiness."

I lifted my head from the edge of the shrine but could not bring myself to look at Akira. I wanted to tell her; I felt as if I would burst from the wanting that swelled up in me. But if I did, she would turn from me, just as Youta had, just as anyone would. No one could trust and help a girl who had murdered her own mother. And then I would be alone again, and I would never be able to attend the Shadow Ball.

"I do not deserve happiness, Akira. I have done something … something so terrible…"

"What did you do, my dear?" Her voice was hushed.

"I cannot tell you. I will not. But you must believe me. This is my chance, my only chance, to atone for what I did." I turned to look at her, at her unhappy, white face. "Will you still help me, Akira?"

"I will always help you, no matter what," she said, squeezing my shoulder. "You are my sister. I love you."

I turned my face into her neck and remembered with a piercing ache doing the same thing to Otieno. *Oh, Moon, what have I done? Why must I break his heart too?*

"I cannot see him again," I said, my voice low. "I know what I must do, but if I see him again… I cannot."

"All right." She nodded. "You must write him a note. I will give it to him."

"He will not accept it."

"We must not give him a choice. It must be a clean break; a swift, sharp pain that will heal quickly. I will send you back to Mie-san's place. You can practise your dancing with them and Otieno will not be able to find you. I will stay here until he gives up."

"Yes. Thank you," I said, relief and agony mixing inside me.

He would be disbelieving at first, as he read the note. He would fling it aside and push past Akira to search the house. Walking from room to empty room, the sense of betrayal would creep over him. It would be so much worse than that time at the tea ceremony. I remembered the way his big hands had touched me so gently, and saw them bunching into fists of anger, and denial. He might shout at first – that soft, beautiful voice that had whispered loving words against my skin – and demand to know where I had gone, why I was doing this. There would be no answer.

He would shake. Not as he had trembled when he lay with me, from happiness and nerves and excitement, but with the pain and the rage. Then he would turn away from Akira and leave, because he would not want her to see him break down.

I thought of the words of an old song, a sad song, that I had sung for him once: *Oh, my love. I would shatter my own heart a thousand times before I hurt yours.* But I had already shattered my own heart, and it had made no difference.

I felt my control begin to splinter and I said quietly, "Akira?"

"Yes?"

"Could you make me another cup of that sangre-root tea?"

She flinched as if from a blow, but gently patted my head. "Of course. I will be back in a few moments."

I waited, just barely managed to wait, until she had left. Then I lay down on the ground before the shrine and cried. Miserable, painful tears that shook me from head to foot but made no sound. The tears of the hopeless.

Akira, when she returned, picked me up and made me drink the tea, and then held me, saying nothing, though tears streaked her own face. I cried for a long, long time. I could not seem to stop. Perhaps I did not want to stop.

But when morning came, and brought Otieno with it, I was gone.

Thirty-six

Even through the fog of misery that clouded my mind, I noticed Mie-san and Yoshi-san's surprise when they saw me again. I was expected, of course; Akira had sent a message in the middle of the night, reasoning that they would be awake anyway. Only, they had expected to see an urchin, tattered and dry and yellow as a blade of winter grass. With my hair elegantly arranged, skin glowing with life and good health, and subtle shadow-weaving enhancing everything, I must have looked to them like an entirely different person.

The pair greeted me enthusiastically and drew me inside with real happiness, and I realized that this was how it would always be from now on. People would see the mask I wore and react to that, even if they had some idea that the person inside did not match. It ought to have been pleasant to confound their expectations, but it only made me feel more lost, more lonely.

For every increase in the beauty of my illusions, there had been a deepening in the shadows within me. Inside I was uglier then than I had ever been.

Yoshi-san went to arrange tea for us while Mie-san sat down with me in a pleasant room which I suspected she normally used to entertain patrons. I gave her the longer note that Akira had hastily penned before I left and asked me to present on arrival.

Her cheeks flushed and her breathing quickened, and I guessed that Akira had written to Mie-san about our plans for the Shadow Ball. When Yoshi-san returned, and she read the note too, her eyes shone with identical glee.

"We will arrange for you to have the same room as before," Mie-san said. "You must tell us if you need anything at all, Yue-san. It is our honour to help you."

I tweaked the face of my mask into a smile. It was good to know that I was not a completely unwanted burden, but I did hope Akira would arrive soon. I needed her to shield me from them and their interest and excitement, which felt like rough sackcloth scraping over grazed skin.

"Perhaps if I could rest a little?" I said, knowing it was feeble. "I was awake quite late last night, at Lord Yorimoto's party."

"Of course, of course," Yoshi-san said. "Such fine, fair skin needs a great deal of sleep to keep its brilliance. I will take you up now."

After they had petted and fussed me onto a futon, they drew the screens, placed some scented oil in the room and left me alone.

I cried again then – but the tears brought no relief. My eyes were sore and swollen, and despite the drag of deep exhaustion, sleep would not come, either. I could not stop thinking about Otieno and what I had done to him. I tried to tear my mind away from my betrayal, but it merely strayed to Father and Aimi and the last time I had seen them. Then I thought about my mother's babies: the twin boys who would now be a little over a year old. I wondered what would happen to those half-brothers of mine when I used the Shadow Promise to reveal Terayama-san as a traitor. I wondered if it made me weak that I did care a little, or monstrous that I did not care enough to let it stop me destroying their father.

Then I went back to thinking about Otieno. I ground the heels of my palms into my eyes, trying to drive his image out of my memory. Finally I got up and crept across the room, searching. I found what I wanted in the form of a sharp set of hair pins that had been left by some previous occupant of the room.

I hesitated. It had been a long time since I had done this. I knew that Akira would not be happy if she found out. I could not afford to make any obvious marks. Not here among strangers, not so close to the Kage no Iwai.

But I could not help myself. I picked an area on my upper thigh and pressed the point of the pin to my skin, then drew it slowly across in a straight line.

The pain made me grit my teeth. Blood welled up, and with it, that almost forgotten sense of relief, as the stinging pain became comfort. I sighed, feeling some of my tension leave me. It was hard to resist the urge to mark myself again. The desire to keep cutting, to scratch and scratch, was frightening in its intensity. That was selfishness. I knew that this one line could be passed off as an accident; two or more would give me away.

Feeling dull and dim now – and glad of it – I dabbed at the blood and lay down again, and after a few minutes, I slept.

It was two days before Akira came to join me at the *okiya*. I hurried down to greet her, and clung to her, and she shushed me gently, and soothed me. I drew back a little fearfully, wondering if she would tell me anything, or what I might see in her face.

She looked away, as if bracing herself. Then she spoke. "He is gone."

It was as if she had struck me through with a blade. Pain rushed out through an invisible wound, dripping and spreading through me as blood would pour from a mortal injury.

Gone.

I had known it must be true. That was why she was here. But it hurt. It hurt. So much that it scared me. It felt like dying. I turned away from her, my hands knotting together as I forced myself to stay upright.

There was no hope this time that Otieno would arrive, bruised but grinning, in my doorway. There would be no big gentle hands, no cassia smell, no strong arm to rest against, to make me warm again. He was really gone, for always.

I would never see him again.

That night I curled my chilled limbs around the one thing I had left, and clutched it to me. Revenge. That was the meaning of my life now.

If you do not avenge them, no one will.

If you do not destroy Terayama-san, no one will.

Forget everything else, and remember that.

The next day Akira said she wanted me to show my two dances to Yoshi-san and Mie-san, so that they could offer me advice. Inevitably I found myself going over each dance again and again while both women called out blunt and sometimes obscene comments on tiny faults like the position of my index fingers, the angle of my jaw and the expression on my face. Akira observed, wincing occasionally.

"Something—something is not quite right," Mie-san said. "I cannot pinpoint it."

"She is not putting her heart into it," Yoshi-san said decisively. "That is what is not right."

I bit down on my lip and worried it between my teeth. I was sweating, panting and so limp I could barely lift my head, and yet I knew Yoshi-san was right. I no longer had a heart to give.

"Yue, the reason I asked Mie-san and Yoshi-san for

their help is because I learnt something worrying at Yorimoto-san's party," Akira said. "Do you remember that when I told you I wanted you to learn to dance, you protested? You said none of the noblemen's daughters would be dancing. Well, apparently, this is not true. Since the last Kage no Iwai, it seems there has been a fashion for the city's nobly bred young women to attend dance lessons, and learn all the traditional dances that might be performed by *oiran*."

"No wonder," Mie-san said. "You were magnificent, Akira-sama."

"I was certainly *successful*," Akira said dryly. "Which I think is more to the point. And, also probably as a result of my success, when organizing this Shadow Ball, the princess decreed there would be no *gijo* or other entertainers dancing. There will be musicians, but the only dancers will be those invited to the ball as potential Shadow Brides."

I forced myself to pay attention, and frowned as I turned over her words. "You always intended me to dance, did you not?"

"Yes, but I intended you to be the only potential Shadow Bride doing so. It would have made you unique and captured the prince's attention, if for no other reason than because it was shocking. Now there will be several other potential brides dancing. The prince will apparently be free to choose whichever girls catch his eye. Considering your beauty, and the fame that we have created in Kano Yue's name, I think it certain that you will have your turn to perform. The problem is that the others will also have their turn, and many of them will have been dancing since they were able to walk."

"You think I will humiliate myself," I said flatly.

"Not that," Yoshi-san broke in. "Your performance is technically very good."

"It is?" That got my attention.

"Yes, but your dancing does not have that extra quality which will make it stand out from the others," Yoshi-san said. "Not even your Chu No Mai, which is what I would recommend you perform. If there is a girl there who has the soul of a true dancer, she will outdo you, and probably ruin your chances."

"Then what am I do to?" I asked.

"Costume!" Mie-san said. "Do you remember that seven-layered costume I had, Yoshi-chan? Each layer was inspired by a line from the poem 'The Mountains of the Moon'."

"Yes, yes!" Yoshi-san said excitedly. "It would not have mattered if you had fallen over your own feet that night. All anyone remembered was the costume."

Mie-san looked affronted and Yoshi-san quickly added, "You danced beautifully, though."

"Yoshi-san is right," Akira interrupted. "The other girls will not think of costumes – they are noblewomen, not *gijo*. I imagine they will simply dance in their formal kimonos. This is a way for Yue to stand out. We do not have time to create a seven-layered costume, but perhaps … three layers?"

"Inspired by a haiku?" Mie-san asked.

"*Love comes like storm clouds…*" Akira said. "Perfect."

Within minutes, what seemed like all seven of the *gijo* who lived in Mie-san's *okiya* had been unearthed from their rooms and given instructions to open their clothes-chests and search out suitable kimonos for alteration. The little sitting room where Mie-san and Yoshi-san took their tea became a sewing room, and we all lived in it for the next five days, working feverishly to transform the borrowed kimonos into a costume so beautiful that it would hide the performer's missing heart.

I would arrive at the ball in the kimono which Akira had already had made: a demure, pale pink one sewn with flowers and birds. It was the sort of kimono that most of the girls would probably be wearing. All the better, said Akira, to highlight my uncommon beauty. On top of that I would wear an *uchikake* kimono – a very long robe with a padded hem that would be left untied and allowed to trail behind me. That was in a deep pink and was covered in a pattern of daisies and songbirds.

Unlike the rest of the girls, though, I would be wearing another costume beneath that first one, hidden from view at the neckline and hem by a plain white *nagajuban*.

The first layer of my dancing costume was black; shocking because it was a colour never worn by unmarried girls unless they were in mourning. We sewed tiny sparkling fragments of metal to its surface in patterns that resembled the constellations of the stars, and embroidered the sleeves and hems with silver-thread clouds in billowing swirls. This was the night sky with clouds from the first line of the haiku. Rather than an obi – which would be impossible to untie during a performance, and would be too bulky anyway – it was held closed by a sash of flame-red. For maximum effect, Mie-san suggested flinging it away into the audience once it was no longer needed.

The second layer of the costume was a gown of silver gauze which I believed was actually a piece of nightwear. The *gijo* to whom it belonged had not been glad to give it up, but her protests were hushed by the others. The fabric was incredibly fine, fluttering and catching the air as I moved. It represented the "wind" of the second line, and to make this clear we made curling leaves from gold and red and copper silk and fastened them to the hems and cuffs, where they drifted and rustled just like real ones. The sash for this one was gold, and again I was to send it flying as I untied it.

The final layer represented the moon. It was pure white – a colour reserved for brides, just as black was reserved for mourning – and it had no ornamentation. The shadows of the haiku would be created by my hair, which now reached the middle of my back, and by the movement of my body as I danced, shifting the sheer fabric across curves and lines it did not quite reveal. This kimono had to be pulled on over my head because it was sewn shut.

My final sash was also white, but it was embroidered

with yellow camellias for longing, blue forget-me-nots for true love and red zinnas for loyalty. The sash belonged to Mie-san, who surrendered it to the cause willingly. Yoshi-san, who was the best seamstress, carefully added one yellow chrysanthemum to the design. This was the flower of the Moon Prince's crest and would be the equivalent of sewing his name on the sash. It told him I longed for him, loved him, and would be loyal to him.

"You must aim this at Tsuki no Ouji-sama," Yoshi-san said. "Let it fall at his feet. He will pick it up and read its message, and feel the warmth of your body in it and smell your scent."

I nodded and smiled, pretending to admire the beauty of the sash and the cleverness of Mie-san and Yoshi-san's plan, when truly her words made me feel ill.

That night, while everyone slumbered, I slipped out of bed and down to the sewing room, and lit a lamp there. The costume, complete now, lay on the table, its various layers tenderly folded, glowing and glittering in the golden light. Waiting.

I picked up that last, flowery sash, and took a needle and threaded it with orange thread. I was no master seamstress, but I had just enough skill to add a tiny, tiny star of orange in the top right-hand corner of the piece of fabric. That star represented the many delicate petals of an orange lily. The flower that stood for hatred, and revenge.

When my work was complete, I refolded the sash and

placed it back in its position of honour at the top of the low table. Then I blew out the lamp and sat quietly in the moonlight that filtered through the lattice window screens.

All the preparations were complete. The decisions had been made – the melancholy Chu No Mai was to be my dance – and there was nothing left to be done. In under two days I would attend the Shadow Ball and spend every particle of my will to capture a prince.

I looked again at the stunning costume. There had been times over the past few days, as we worked our fingers to the bone, when I had wanted to laugh at all our efforts to make it fit the haiku. Not because it was funny, but because it was so desperately sad. Of course, my costume must be inspired by that poem now, of all times, now, when I finally understood it.

When Akira had recited the haiku to me the first time, I had been confused, thinking it compared love to storm clouds because they were capricious and fleeting. Perhaps love was capricious and fleeting, but that was not the true meaning of the poem. The true meaning was this: that love, when it came, was powerful enough to transform everything. Anything. Even the unchanging, ever-changing face of the Moon herself.

Youta's story had proved that. Akira's story had proved it. But I had needed to fall in love myself before I could truly understand. I had needed to meet someone so precious that he had the power to transform me completely.

I had thrown my love away like trash on the wayside.

I hated myself for it, and yet I knew that it had been inevitable. Such a precious thing could never have been meant for someone like me. If I had tried to keep it, I would have destroyed him.

I had been telling myself all week that I wanted nothing more than revenge now, that it was my only desire, and my only wish. It was not true. In the aching emptiness of my soul, there was room for one more wish, just as powerful as the first.

I wished that Otieno would be happy. That despite all I had done to him, the way I had betrayed him, he would recover and go on with his life. I wanted him to heal cleanly as Akira had said he would. I wanted him to be the same bright, shining person he had been before we met, and I wanted him to fall in love with someone else, and be happier with them than he ever had been with me.

"I love you, Otieno," I whispered. "Goodbye."

I bowed my head, sending my wish for him out into the world. Then I closed that part of me, the part that was Otieno's, folded it up like a piece of paper and tucked it away.

No more. That life was over.

Finally I got up, and left the room, and went back to bed.

As Yoshi-san had said, I needed plenty of sleep to look my best.

Thirty-seven

The day of the Shadow Ball came.

After breakfast I wanted to practise my dance again, but Akira told me it was more important to rest my muscles. She said I could play if I wanted, but I refused. I had not touched my shamisen for over a week. Not since… I blinked, and the thought fled. I was getting better and better at pushing such thoughts away. The coldness inside me made it easy. The colder I got, the less I seemed to need to think at all.

Akira brought out the *Igo* board, with its black and white pieces, and challenged Mie-san to a game. Yoshi-san was working on a piece of embroidery, though judging by her muttering it was not going well. I sat calmly. The nervous tension that thrummed in the house did not touch me.

This might have been because of the private few minutes I had taken before breakfast to scratch several small lines on the inside of my knee. Yet it was not just that. There was a sort of stillness inside me now. The clearness of ice. I felt like one of the warriors from the ancient poems, on the eve of battle. I was prepared. I was resolved. I was not afraid.

When afternoon came, I took a bath – alone, despite offers of assistance – covered myself with scented oils and washed my hair until it was as smooth as threads of unwoven silk. When I emerged, Akira was waiting. She urged me to drink a little tea and eat a light meal of clear soup with fish and rice. Silently she dried my hair and rubbed a sweet-smelling pomade into it to give it gloss. She made me rub creams into my face, hands and feet to soften and brighten the skin.

"Now rest for a while. I must attend to my own bath."

She drew the screens and I laid down on my futon and dozed, without dreams. When Akira came back, she was fully dressed, resplendent in a formal black kimono that had designs of red-and-gold birds across the sleeves, chest and back. It reminded me of the gown she had been wearing when we first met. She brought Yoshi-san and Mie-san with her, carrying between them my many-layered outfit for the ball.

They rolled up my futon and had me stand naked in the middle of the room. The moon kimono went directly over my skin, with no underwear, so that the effect would be perfect when I danced. All I was allowed to wear beneath it were my tabi socks. The white sash was carefully tucked around my waist so that it was secure but easily unfastened for my dance. The silver and the storm-cloud kimonos went over the top, each secured with their own sash. Next came a long, plain white under-kimono. It was to shield the exotic costume from peeking out at collar and sleeves. Then came the pink kimono with a formal obi and belt, and the final layer, the trailing, deep pink *uchikake* robe. They had me walk across the room, and turn and bend, in order to check the ease of movement, and then I was made to sit again, so that Akira and Yoshi-san could start work on my hair. Since I was supposed to wear it down during the performance, it was important that the arrangement could be easily disassembled, but it must still be beautiful and intricate and – most importantly – sturdy enough to last for the first part of the evening.

I endured it all without speaking. They smiled and rubbed my shoulder reassuringly, but they did not make me talk, and I knew it was because they thought I was nervous and trying to compose myself. I was not. I felt as peaceful and distant as I had all day. I watched the sky grow dim, blue shading into grey, into deep blue, and sat as still as doll, letting them work.

"We cannot improve you any further," Akira said finally. She looked into my face. "Yue, are you ready to go?"

One question that hid a hundred questions. I answered them all with a word:

"Yes."

One by one the *gijo* – most of them just waking up – came into the room, each giving me a lucky kiss or a touch on the head, even Haruhi-san, whose beloved silver gown I had stolen.

"Do your best. You are representing all of us, remember," she said, and then yawned and went back to bed.

I collected my kiss of luck from Yoshi-san and Mie-san, smiling and thanking them for all their help. Then Akira and I climbed into the carriage, and left them behind.

Akira opened the screen at the window, letting in a breeze to dispel the close, warm air inside. I had expected to be too warm in my many layers, but I still felt cold. When I brushed a fluttering moth away from my face, my fingers felt like ice against my cheek.

The journey, which took us across the entire city, seemed to last only seconds. We arrived at the massive gates of the Moon Palace before full dark had fallen. Akira held the official invitation – a long scroll of paper with red and green and gold seals and two long tying strings with gold tassels – out of the window to be checked by the guards, one of whom then opened the carriage door and helped us out.

As the light from the lanterns at the gate fell full on first Akira's face and then mine, the guard's impassive gaze altered, and his bow was reverent.

"Your first victim of the evening," Akira remarked quietly when we were out of earshot.

"An equal victory for both of us, I think," I said, unruffled.

We stepped through the gates into the prince's garden and onto a path paved with tiny white stones shaped like diamonds, which glittered even in the twilight. Pine trees hugged the path closely on either side as we walked, blocking out the sky twenty feet above, and the only light was that of the lanterns behind us at the gate.

Then the trees parted, and we were looking down a gentle slope at an immense garden, dominated by an irregularly shaped lake. Dozens of tiny streams flowed from the lake, criss-crossing the garden, circling banks of ferns, raked gravel and miniature mountains, so that the white path became a white bridge in several places. The way was carefully lit by stone lanterns or, where there was not room, paper lanterns that stood on poles.

To the north, the full moon had risen above the palace. Most of the building was screened from view by trees, but I could see its peaked roofs.

"Look," Akira said, voice hushed. "The Procession of Shadows."

I followed her gaze, and for the first time noticed others travelling along the glowing white path to the Moon Palace. Girls were walking with their families, transformed into black shapes outlined against the pale stones in the gathering darkness.

"Ouji-sama – my prince – said that this was probably how the Shadow Ball got its name all those many years ago," she continued. "For the ball – as for the prince's marriage – no one may drive or ride on the grounds of the Moon Palace. But a marriage is a thing of daylight. The Kage no Iwai is of the night. And tonight every woman who wishes to seek the favour of the prince must walk this path on her own two feet and become part of the Procession of Shadows."

The noise of another carriage arriving spurred us forward, and we took our place in the procession.

As we crested the last bridge, the trees again parted before us, and I saw the palace properly for the first time. It was three-storeys high, with a great hall from which many other wings stretched out. All the screens and doors of the lower floor had been thrown open onto the central courtyard so that music and the sounds of voices spilled out.

Ahead of us, I could see other girls – some with parents, others with larger groups of relatives – entering the courtyard and approaching the raised mound of earth at its centre. The mound was surrounded by a circle of water and had its own little bridge. An ancient fir tree grew from the mound, bent double with the weight of its own branches and thick needles. Lanterns hanging from the branches cast light on the girls that stood at the base but did not illuminate whatever – or whoever – was sheltering beneath the tree. The girls and their families each stood there for a little time, and then bowed and moved away towards the open palace.

We came down from the bridge, and suddenly we too were in the courtyard, and Akira was leading me towards that shadowed place beneath the tree. Now I could see what was beneath the branches. A throne.

It was tall and narrow and carved with patterns that my eye could not follow. At the top was a round crest inlaid with gold that represented the phases of the moon. The wood of the throne was so black with age that the two soldiers on either side, in their black lacquered armour, seemed to meld into the design. They were standing still enough to be made of wood.

Around the throne were several men and two women. Of the group, I recognized only Yorimoto-san. Seeing us approach, he nodded but did not smile, and then instantly turned back to the woman who sat beside him. She was tiny, with iron-grey hair and a fierce expression. Lady Yorimoto, apparently recovered.

As we came closer, I turned my attention to the occupant of the throne. Tsuki no Ouji-sama was very slender, though tall enough for his head to reach the crested moon on the back of the throne. His face was ordinary, not unattractive, but not memorable in any way. The most eye-catching thing about him were the layers and layers of brilliantly coloured clothes he wore, thrown back to reveal a stiff black chest-plate. The style seemed to be influenced by the fashion of the Old Empire –

the dragon motif and the crested moon certainly were – but instead of conveying power or grandeur, they just made him look lost.

He might be the only one here tonight wearing more clothes than I am, I thought wryly.

The second woman in the group moved closer to the throne, her posture protective, and my amusement vanished as I realized who she must be. Only one woman would dare claim the place on the prince's right. Akira's enemy, and mine too.

The Moon Princess.

She was tall and dressed in a sombre black kimono, with very simply dressed hair. Her only adornment was an ivory fan, which she held, closed, between her hands. Her face was striking, strong, almost beautiful. Almost, because it was completely expressionless, as blank as the stones I walked on.

I bowed deeply, aware of Akira doing the same beside me. I kept my eyes downcast, and spent all my concentration on making my shadow-weaving the most glowing, the most perfect, it had ever been.

"Ohime-sama," a light, young voice said happily.

I glanced up to see that the prince was not even looking at me but at Akira. His face, now that it was animated, was startlingly young and quite charming.

"Ouji-sama," Akira said, her face filled with equal pleasure, "I did not know if you would recognize me."

"No false modesty, please," he chided with a laugh.

"How could anyone ever forget you? I have missed you! I was very glad to see your name on the list of guests – but I hope you realize that you cannot be a Shadow Bride twice?" He laughed again. Beside him, the old princess was motionless.

"Much as it grieves me, I have accepted this fact," Akira said, her eyes twinkling. "I am here to escort my sister, Ouji-sama. Here she is."

"Oh yes! That was the other name on the list. You know, I never realized you had a sis—"

His voice trailed off as he finally turned his gaze on me. I met his eyes, holding them for a long moment, and then smiled. A smile of sweet shyness and innocent pleasure. The smile I had taken from Aimi.

He blinked, dazed, and I modestly lowered my eyes again.

At the corner of my vision, I saw the old princess's knuckles turn red and then yellow as they gripped the fan.

"Ohime-sama," said the prince, his voice hushed as a boy who has caught sight of some rare animal and does not wish to frighten it away. "Your sister is lovely."

I felt a surge of pity for his youth, and firmly squashed it.

Suddenly the old princess spoke. "You should not use the title Ohime-sama, my son," she said, her voice as toneless as her face. "It is not polite to remind Kano-san of the position she has lost."

"Oh, I did not consider that. I am sorry if I have offended you, Kano-san."

"Not at all," Akira said warmly. "You may call me whatever you wish."

"And what should I call your sister?" he asked eagerly.

I looked up again, and again smiled. "My name is Yue, Ouji-sama. But you may call me whatever you wish as well."

The prince stared at my lips, and sighed. There was a tiny, almost inaudible crack, and the fan in the old princess's hands came apart in two pieces.

The prince did not notice. Behind me, I could hear another group of people moving restlessly, awaiting their turn.

The prince looked over my head, and grimaced. "Ah, well. I must let you go now – but I have enjoyed talking to you both. Very much. We will see each other again later. I will make sure of it."

We thanked him, bowed, and moved away towards the palace. I heard Akira let out a deep, slow breath. "That went well."

"Was it difficult for you?" I asked.

"A little. The last time I saw him, I was with his father, and so happy. The last time I saw her, we were both standing over my prince's deathbed. It is hard to remember that." She smiled suddenly. "That fan belonged to her grandmother, you know."

"Perhaps she will be able to get it mended," I said, straight-faced.

Akira snorted, and then we stepped up into the hall and were enveloped in the crowd.

Thirty-eight

The central room was crammed with guests: two hundred or more. Immediately I began examining the other females, deciding which ones were potential Shadow Brides and which were mere guests – which ones were real rivals and which could safely be ignored.

I was surprised. I suppose I had expected all the other girls to be stunningly lovely. To be sure, there were a great many beautiful girls present, but there were a great deal more girls who were ordinarily pretty or even plain. If I were to cast off my glamour and appear as I really was, I would not be out of place in this company. I whispered this to Akira.

"Those are the daughters of families with whom it would be wise politically or financially for the prince to ally," she said. "No doubt his mother asked for them to be invited. And there are many people here who are already married, or engaged, or know they have no chance of being chosen but came simply to enjoy the spectacle."

We moved around the room, me hidden by my silent and mysterious mask, Akira greeting her acquaintances, many of whom I had already met. They looked at me with fresh speculation tonight – and those with daughters attending did not seem pleased. Most of the young women I was introduced to gave me the impression that they would have gouged my eyes out without a second thought.

I found it amusing that they all wanted to be Shadow Bride so intensely. What compelling reason could any of these pampered young women have to fight for the prince's favour? The glamour of the title? Because their parents wanted it? Well, they would just have to find something else to dream about.

I marked one girl in particular as a rival. She wore a pale yellow kimono, and I judged her to be a year or two older than I was. She was introduced as Sasaki Hinata-san, and was the daughter of a friend of Akira's, who greeted her with genuine pleasure.

"It brings back many memories to see you here tonight," he said, apparently without any double meaning. He and Akira chatted pleasantly while I covertly studied Sasaki-san. Her face was a perfect oval, with softly glowing skin, and her expression was of overwhelming serenity and kindness. She was the sort of person who could make a room feel happier just by smiling, and she reminded me a little of Aimi.

After we had walked away, Akira pointed out another girl, who was standing near the open wall of the room. This one had a striking, angular face with sharp cheekbones and a lush red mouth. Her hair was dressed with an oversized comb of gold and coral with tassels, and she wore a flamboyant *uchikake* robe in scarlet and white. She was speaking to a woman who seemed to be her mother, eyes brilliant with excitement.

"Ito Natsuko-san," Akira said. "She is nearly as famous as you – said to be a wonderful dancer, but apparently her temper is uncertain and she must have her own way in all things."

"That sounds familiar," I said.

Akira cast me a quelling look. "Her family are not of the highest rank, but they are very wealthy. She bullies her father into refusing any offers made for her hand; she wants only to be the Shadow Bride."

"Then she is a serious rival."

As if she sensed our regard, Ito-san's head lifted. Our gazes met. She looked me over with narrowed eyes, then gave me a challenging smile. I returned the smile with one of straightforward friendliness, and watched her hostile look turn to confusion before I turned away.

"Well played," Akira said.

Now that I had assessed the other girls, I turned my attention to the rest of the room. I noticed something strange: the guests were the only females present. Every servant that lined the walls or moved through the hall – including the group of musicians playing on the raised dais at the far end of the room – was male. The Moon Princess was certainly not leaving anything to chance at this ball. I wondered aloud how much real power she had now that her son had come of age. Enough to ban female servants and entertainers from the ball, but not enough to have Akira and I removed from that guest list.

Akira nodded. "She has enough influence to have been allowed to decorate this room to her own tastes, too. I cannot imagine anyone else would have arranged for these hideous things to be here." She averted her eyes from the fountain in the middle of the room. It was a grimacing dragon in the style of the Old Empire, with water trickling from its whiskers and long fangs. Several filigree bowls filled with brightly coloured fruit perched on the coils of its feathery tail. Elsewhere in the room, other bronze dragons supported more fruit, or bowls filled with flowers. I had certainly never seen decorations like them.

"It does seem strange when she is so very restrained in her clothes and hair," I said.

Akira sighed. "When she first came here to marry Tsuki no Ouji-sama, she was fifteen, and he fourteen. They had never met before, and although their families were cousins, they had been raised very differently. It is hard to find wives of high enough rank for a Moon Prince, you see; that is why the current prince is not yet married.

Only another princess will do. My prince was very conscious of his dignity then, as the young often are, and although his wife was a princess in her own right, she was loud and merry and much enamoured of garish things in the style of the Old Empire. She adored him, but he was embarrassed by her. He told a friend that it was like having a parrot for a wife. Unfortunately they were overheard, and the remark became a court joke. My prince was sorry then, but it was too late. The Moon Princess left court for a long time, feigning illness, and had her son while still hiding. She would not see my prince, even though he followed her, sending her apologies again and again. When she eventually returned to court, she had become as you see her now. No one ever laughed at her again – my prince made sure of that – but she never forgave him. He never forgave himself either. I think that was the true reason why when he met me, he was willing to look beneath the surface to my heart. He had learnt a hard lesson on what happens when you judge another person only on appearance."

"How sad for them both," I murmured. "I feel sorry for her now."

"Do not feel too sorry," Akira said. "She may have been wronged, but she made him suffer for his foolishness every day for the rest of his life. She will make you suffer too, if she can. She clings to her resentment, that one. I hope it is a comfort to her."

"She will not find it easy to visit suffering on me," I

said, with a small smile. "I am not at all sensitive to it any more."

Before Akira could answer, there was an excited stir in the crowd. The prince came into view, conveyed on his throne, on the shoulders of the two guards we had seen with him earlier. His advisers trailed behind, headed by the old princess – who I now realized was not old at all, but only in her mid-thirties. Her eyes were fixed on the back of the carved chair. They forged through the room towards the raised dais. Behind us, servants were drawing the screens and the doors of the hall closed.

The guards hefted the throne up the steps of the dais with no difficulty, and the princess followed, though the advisers stayed in the crowd. The guards put the throne down, and the princess took her place beside it.

The prince raised one hand, smiling into the sea of faces, but it was the princess who spoke.

"Welcome, honoured guests, to the Palace of the Moon. You are gathered to witness an ancient tradition, which is at the same time the very first of its kind. The first Shadow Ball of the Twelfth Prince of the Moonlit Land. You are the finest and best of the prince's subjects, and your daughters are the most virtuous, accomplished and beautiful women of our country. They have each had the chance to meet and speak with Tsuki no Ouji-sama tonight. A very few will be lucky enough to dance for him. One alone will be chosen as the Shadow Bride – the Kage no Ohime. May the Moon smile on the prince's choice, and may we all pray that she be worthy."

Her eyes settled on me, but her expression was as blank as ever. She looked away and continued, "If the prince wishes you to dance for him, you will be given a little while to prepare. The first girl chosen will dance in half an hour." She inclined her head, and the guards picked up the throne again, carrying it back down the stairs and positioning it directly before the dais. Servants appeared, and tall, painted screens of wood and paper were drawn into place before the dais, hiding it from view.

"No servants are coming for me," I observed.

"Silly," Akira said. "You are the most beautiful girl in the room. He will save you for last."

Within my voluminous sleeves, I ran my fingers over the scars that no one but me could see.

At that moment Sasaki-san walked past us towards the dais, following a servant. Her father walked behind her, looking proud and nervous.

"Ah," Akira said, leading me towards an ornate, carved bench. All around us other people were finding places near the stage to sit and wait. "I do not think you have much to fear from Hinata-chan."

I thought about Aimi, and how much she had loved to dance. "She might surprise us," I said.

When the music started, it was soft, a sweet trill on a flute that sounded like birdsong, a brush of notes from a *biwa* that reminded me of wind moving through trees. The paper screens were carefully drawn back to reveal Sasaki-san facing the crowd. She held a deep orange-and-gold fan in each hand. With a slow, teasing movement, she brought one of the fans up to shield her face – telling us that her character in the dance was a shy maiden – and stretching her other arm out to flutter the second fan gracefully in the air. These were the same gestures that Akira had taught me to begin my fan dance. The dance of a young woman, alive with joy in the warm winds of spring.

Sasaki-san was a much more precise dancer than I usually managed to be. Each hand and foot was placed perfectly, each tilt of her head exactly timed. She handled the fans with confidence and complete skill. Straight away, though, I could tell that she did not have what Mie-san would have called the soul of a dancer.

Watching Akira go through this routine had made me feel her joy, had made me want to get up and dance with her, had made me imagine those soft breezes on my own skin. Sasaki-san was very enjoyable to watch, but she did not share any emotions with her audience. Her face stayed in its unchanging expression of sweetness throughout. I decided that she was not so like Aimi after all. Aimi had always shown just what she thought on her face.

Sasaki-san threw both her fans up and, as she caught them, spread them out to cover her face again. She held the posture, and the music came to an end.

The audience applauded enthusiastically. Sasaki-san

moved a little closer to the edge of the stage and bowed deeply to the prince, and then the painted screens were drawn back into place, concealing her from view.

"She was better than I expected," Akira said. "But not so good that I think you need worry particularly."

"You have a great deal of faith in my costume of many layers," I said.

"I have faith in you."

I watched the prince, who was talking to Lady Yorimoto about the dance – if the fluttering fan-like gestures of his hands were anything to go by. I knew I should be quivering with nerves, but I still felt as calm as ever, and I was glad. The numbness helped. Doubts would only distract me.

Moments later Sasaki-san reappeared, her face pink but free of sweat. She was escorted to the prince. The two talked for a little while, with Sasaki-san turning even pinker and blinking shyly, and then she bowed and left him.

"He has not yet made his choice," Akira said. "I wonder who will be next."

"Ito-san," I said.

"Oh? What about Arakaki-san? Or Oshiro-san?"

"No. It will be Ito-san," I said. "She is more beautiful than either of them, and he has just glanced at her from the corner of his eye. She is next."

I felt instinctively that she was the one I needed to be careful of. Sure enough, Ito-san passed us around a quarter of an hour later, again following a servant towards the dais. As she passed us, she cast me a triumphant look. I pretended not to see it.

Ito-san's music began with the low, haunting cry of a flute. Bells chimed mournfully, and then the screens were pulled back.

"Chu No Mai," Akira said.

Ito-san danced the part of a noblewoman who has lost the one she loves and is driven mad with longing for him. The look of sorrow on her face made the skin on the back of my neck tighten; there was no doubt that she was sharing her emotions with her audience. The way her movements became frantic as her character lost her grip on sanity, the way her long red *uchikake* swirled around her – she was magnificent.

I managed to take my eyes off her for a moment to look at the rest of the audience. Where Sasaki san's performance had produced smiles and approving nods, Ito-san had her audience rapt: saddened and wide-eyed. I glanced at Akira. I was surprised to see that rather than looking either spellbound or perhaps worried on my behalf, she instead looked interested but cynical.

"What is it?" I whispered.

"She is carried away by her passion," Akira whispered back. "She is very talented, but she does not have enough discipline for such a dance. Look at the way she places her foot – there. Oh, look at her *arm*. That is an ugly angle. It is important to use one's emotions in dance, but equally important not to let them overwhelm you. Technically

Sasaki-san is better. So are you."

"Will anyone care?" I asked. "She has won them over completely."

"They will care, if you combine the strengths of both Sasaki-san and Ito-san. You can be as careful and precise as the first, when you really try. And as for the second – what can she know of sorrow that you do not? What can she know of love that you do not? You have the skill and the heart to defeat both of them, and if you do, the prince will be yours."

I bit my lip, feeling the first thrill of nerves as Ito-san's dance came to an end. Could I do that?

Ito-san emerged from behind the screen, her *uchikake* robe discarded, her hair smoothed back into place. She was flushed and smiling, and this time she did not even bother to look at me as she passed. She spoke animatedly to the prince, holding his attention for rather longer than Sasaki-san.

I watched the two of them so intently that I did not notice at first when the servant appeared before me. Akira pinched my arm, and the servant bowed as I looked up.

"Tsuki no Ouji-sama requests the pleasure of a performance from you, Kano-sama."

Nerves squeezed my breath again. It was time. It was really happening.

"See?" Akira said. "The best for last. I will speak to the musicians for you."

As I stood, she caught my sleeve, making me look back.

"Good fortune, sister."

I nodded. "Thank you."

I followed the servant towards the screened area, feeling dozens of pairs of eyes – covetous, envious, hostile, curious – fix on me. At edge of the dais there was a tiny gap between the wall and the edge of the screen, and a set of wooden steps. I went through the gap, and the servant pulled the screen closed behind us.

"Is there anything that you require, Kano-sama? A drink of water, or some other thing to help you prepare?"

"Take this," I said, already out of my *uchikake*. "And this." I grunted with effort as I began unwinding my obi, flinging the material at him. He caught it reflexively, and then stared at it as if he thought it might bite him.

"What would Kano-sama wish me to do with these things?" he asked, averting his eyes, but holding his arms out for more layers.

"Keep them safe, of course," I said. "I will need to put them back on again after the performance."

I took off the pink kimono and the *nagajuban*, and bundled them into his arms, and then reached up to pull the two tall combs and their matching pins from my hair. It fell down around my face, soft and wavy from the pomade, and slightly wild. I shook it out, and then put the combs on top of the pile in the servant's arms.

"Will … er … that be all, Kano-sama?" he asked. He was staring at the winking swirls of stars and clouds on the black kimono and its brilliant red sash.

"Yes, thank you," I said as I turned away and ran up the stairs onto the stage.

I positioned myself not in the middle of the dais, as Ito-san and Sasaki-san had done, but at one end, and took my beginning stance there. I went through the movements of the dance in my head one more time. No room for mistakes now. Akira had said I could do it – that I could be as precise as Sasaki-san – and I had no intention of proving her wrong.

There was a high-pitched cry from somewhere beyond the dais. A bird's cry.

Mirkasha?

I started, losing my stance as the sound brought with it a flood of memories.

The eerie cry came again. But – it was not quite right. The sound was too low, too musical. It was not the noise of an animal, I realized, but of a flute, skilfully played. Then the slow, solemn beat of the drums began, and I understood. Akira. She had told them to do it. She was telling me what I must do. I shuddered, forcing my arms back up into their correct position.

The flute cried out again, mixing with the sounds of the familiar music as the screens began to draw back. *What can she know of love that you do not?*

I closed my eyes and let myself remember.

The crowd murmured when they caught sight of me, but I was not thinking of them now. I was only thinking of him.

I hardly knew it when I began to move. Distantly I was aware of the singing in my body, the exultation of arms and legs as at last I let them do what they had always wished to do. I let go of my control and allowed them to lift and twist without hesitation or fear. The music wrote paths of sorrow in the air, and my body followed them, flowing seamlessly from shape to shape, writing my own message of mourning in the space around me for all to see.

My body said:

I still belong to him.

I will always belong to him.

I reached for the red sash and pulled it away, stretching out my arm as I let it go so that it billowed up above the heads of the watchers like a living flame. They gasped, and gasped again as I shrugged off the black-and-silver gown and left it behind. The leaves fluttered around my face, mingling with my hair as I raised my arms.

The audience let out exclamations of shock when the golden sash flew above them and I stepped out of the silver gown. Now I danced before them clad only in shining white.

I had reached the last movements of the dance, the moments when the ghost accepted that she had lost life and love forever, and would always be alone. My back arched into a line of unutterable pain, a physical representation of a cry of agony, and I pulled away the white sash. In too much turmoil to even aim it, I let the piece of fabric fly.

It seemed to hover above the prince, shifting in the air like a cloud. One of the guards made to catch it. He was too slow. The prince's hand shot up and it landed in his grasp, seeming to curl around the exposed skin of his forearm and embrace it.

I sank down into my final pose as the music ebbed and faded away. The flute cried out one more time, and then the music stopped. I drew in a deep breath. The intense emotions that had taken control of me began to drain away into the pit where my heart had once been, and left me cold and empty again. The emptiness ached now. It was a hundred, thousand times worse than it had been before, and I knew in that moment that just as I no longer played the shamisen, I would not be able to dance again either. This was the last time. Any more would destroy me.

I held my pose in those seconds of ringing silence that followed my performance. Almost without interest, I watched the prince. He had spread the sash over his lap, and was running his fingers over the flowers and smiling. He picked it up and lifted it to his face, closing his eyes.

I let my own eyes close. It was as Akira and Mie-san had said it would be.

The crowd began to clap – thunderously, deafeningly – louder than for Sasaki-san and Ito-san combined. I unfolded myself and stood, and bowed to them. I let my gaze meet the prince's, and he smiled rapturously, as delighted as a little boy with a new toy. I felt again that twinge of pity.

He was older than me, and yet he was so very young.

Well, if he is mine now, I told myself tiredly, *I suppose I will just have to take care of him.*

I looked away. Behind the throne, the Moon Princess was the only person present not staring at me. Her face was downturned, her gaze on the floor. At the front of the crowd was Akira, tears on her face, glowing with pride. She nodded at me vigorously, her hands a blur.

And then, as the screens drew into place and hid me from view, there was a stealthy movement on the stairs at the side of the stage. For a moment, even though I had just seen her in the audience, I thought it must be Akira; it was a woman in a formal black kimono, a woman that I instinctively realized I knew.

Then the woman turned her head to look at me and I saw a face that had haunted my dreams. The face of a dead woman.

Mother.

Thirty-nine

Breath turned to stone inside me. The blood stood still in my veins.

She was dead.

I had killed her.

But she was there. Standing before me. Walking across the stage with her own graceful walk. She had a red lily *kanzashi* in her hair that matched the red flowers on her dress. She was a little plumper, a little pinker than when I had last seen her, her cheeks rounded now instead of sharp. She looked well. Better than she had before – before – I killed her.

I had *killed* her.

"Suzume."

The sound of her voice – the voice I knew best in the world, the very first voice I had ever heard – made me realize that what I saw was not a dream, or a hallucination. She was real.

Youta had been wrong.

"I thought you were dead," she whispered, and I swayed as it seemed that she plucked the words from my mouth.

"I thought the same of you," I said through numb lips. "How did you survive?"

Her brow wrinkled with confusion. "Shujin-sama would not harm me. He would never—"

I cut her off, uninterested in the blatant self-deception. "You were poisoned."

She gave me a dazed look, as if I were speaking in riddles. "Do you mean – you mean the sangre? It was only a careless mistake in the kitchen. I was ill, it is true, but I was not pregnant, so I was not in danger. How do you know about that? You had already run away when that happened."

"Run away?" I demanded, incredulous. "I fled for my life, with Terayama on my heels like a hunting dog."

"No," she said, wringing her hands as she moved closer to me. "You were frightened. You misunderstood. If you had come home again, we could have explained: he did not want to hurt you. He only wanted to stop you. To make you listen and understand."

I stared at her in disbelief. "Understand what? That he is a murderer?"

"He is not a murderer!" Now temper flushed her cheeks. "He never meant for your father to die!"

"No, he only meant to ruin his name, destroy his life and steal his wife. And he succeeded, with your help. If you think you could have persuaded me to keep silent about that then you are far more stupid than I ever believed you to be."

She started back – I had never spoken to her so – but that only drove me on. "He had already tried to kill me once and you didn't even notice. He intended to kill me that night. He would have, if he had caught me. And you did nothing to stop him. Nothing."

She unclenched her hands, making a beseeching gesture that I flinched away from. "I wanted to go after you. I had just given birth! I was too weak and exhausted to move."

"What if he had threatened one of your babies, Mother? Would you have been able to move then?"

She hesitated, her face stricken.

I nodded, bitterly satisfied. "You could have defied him. But you were frightened. You knew that if you defended me then you would be at risk. You watched him go after me without a word, and somewhere deep inside I think you were relieved. Relieved to see me go and take all your old memories and jealousies with me forever."

"No. *No.* You are my daughter and I love you. I thought of you, mourned for you each day you were gone. When I recognized you here tonight, saw you dancing, I was overjoyed, but I had to be sure—"

"So you crept up onto the stage, alone, without telling

your husband, without telling anyone? That is hardly the action of a woman with a clear conscience. It is hardly the action of a woman who does not fear her husband's wrath. But what you tell him does not matter any more," I said triumphantly. "He cannot reach me now. In a few moments I will be safe from him forever."

She gasped, her eyes widening. "Safe? What… Is that why were you dancing, Suzume?" And now realization filled her eyes, and the very beginnings of fear. "Why did you come to the Kage no Iwai? Why did you dance like that? What are you going to do?"

"I am going to be Shadow Bride," I said proudly. "Most favoured, most desired, most beautiful. And when I have spent the night in the prince's bed, I shall use that power to finally claim justice for the House of Hoshima."

"What do you mean?" she breathed. Again she reached out as if to touch me. Again I avoided her hands. "You cannot … you would not…"

I felt dizzy, unreal, as if everything had been turned upside down, back to front. For so long I had begged for her approval, for her affection. Now she pleaded for mercy from me. It was both disorientating and exhilarating, and filled me with a sense of power such as I had never known before.

"What would I not do, Mother? Would I not avenge my murdered father and sister, and my home? Would I not destroy Terayama-san as he has destroyed everything I have ever loved?"

"What about me? What about your brothers? You have three brothers, Suzume. Shujin-sama and I have just come back from the country, where I had my confinement for the youngest. They are your family now, too. They are just babies, as innocent as you were once. If you destroy Shujin-sama, you will destroy them too, and leave them – us – with nothing."

"Why should I care for them?" I asked, brushing aside the brief memory of the helpless, gurgling baby I had held in my arms for so short a time. "Why should I care for you? Your love has brought me nothing but sorrow. If you wish to avoid your husband's ruin, take whatever money you can find, take your precious sons and run. It does not matter to me, and by this time tomorrow he will have more important things to do than come after you. But no matter what you decide, you will not stop me from fulfilling my destiny. This is the only warning I will give you."

There was a discreet throat-clearing from the stairs, and I saw the servant from earlier standing there uneasily, holding the pile of clothes I had given him.

"The prince wishes to see you at your first convenience," he said, bowing his head respectfully when he saw he had my attention.

"Of course," I said. I brushed past my mother without another look. Taking my *uchikake* robe from the servant, I pulled it on over the moon dress. I could not do anything with my hair now, and with just the robe on I was barely decent… But then, I was to be Shadow Bride. I was not bound by the rules laid down for respectable virgins any longer. I did not have to be decent. It was a thrilling realization.

"Suzume," my mother whispered behind me, clearly constrained by the presence of the servant. "Please."

Now I did look back at her. "Suzume is dead. I am Yue. And you are nothing to me."

I walked down the stairs, past the servant, and out into the main room.

I was greeted by a spontaneous burst of applause from the guests. Everyone was looking at me, bowing and staring – their eyes filled with admiration, lust, anger, speculation. For a second I wanted to back away, but why should I hide? This was my moment of triumph, of victory: the culmination of everything I had worked for.

Akira stepped forward, her face alight with enthusiasm. That light waned as she took in my expression, though I do not know what she saw there. She shielded me from the crowd with her shoulder as she said, "Congratulations. You were magnificent, sister. I was so proud I could not even be jealous." And then, lower, more quickly: "What is wrong? What has happened?"

"Nothing," I said, meeting her too perceptive eyes with all the bravado I could muster. "Nothing. Take me to him."

She gave me a searching look, then glanced back over her shoulder. "Very well. We cannot keep him waiting."

She took my icy cold fingers in her warm ones and led me into the crowd.

The prince caught sight of us and stood up, taking a step away from his throne. He raised his hands to silence his guests. His presence was surprisingly strong and commanding. Only the barely suppressed smile on his face hinted at the excitement of a young man about to choose between three beautiful women. The room fell quiet, the air singing with a deep expectancy, with anticipation.

"My subjects, I thank you all for your attendance tonight. I have been honoured by the presence of so many very beautiful young women, and I would have been honoured to choose any of them. Most especially I must thank Ito Natsuko-san and Sasaki Hinata-san and their families for providing us all with entertainment of such a superior nature. My choice has been difficult – but that is as it should be, for the decision is an important one. It is now made."

We reached his side, and as Akira dropped my left hand, the prince caught hold of the right. His fingers squeezed mine too tightly, and were slightly moist. I turned my head to look at Akira, seeking reassurance.

She was no longer by my side. She was nowhere in sight.

She had gone so quickly that I knew she had to have used a shadow-weaving to disappear. But why? Had something happened that I had not seen? Surely it had been too fast for that. The weaving must have been pre-prepared in order for her to wink out of existence so instantly.

Why would she desert me? Had her misgivings finally been too much for her? I forced the sudden swirl of anxiety away. I could not be distracted now. I turned my head to look at the prince again, my eyes riveted on his lips as they opened to speak the words I – and everyone in the room – had been waiting for all night.

"I have chosen," the prince said. "Kano Yue-san will be my Shadow Bride."

There was a hushed moment, and then the applause began again, loud enough to make my ears ring.

I was whisked out of the hall. Three black-armoured soldiers – my guards from now on – followed as one of the servants led me up two flights of stairs and down a long corridor to the prince's chambers. His rooms made up the entire top storey of the central hall of the palace.

The soldiers took up their places along the corridor as the servant opened the door for me, bowing deeply.

"The prince will come to his rooms as soon as all of his guests have departed. Hot water is waiting for you in the bathing room, if you wish to wash, and there is a selection of clothing also – although of course you will choose new clothes for yourself, when you have time. Is there anything else you would like, Ohime-sama? Something to eat or drink?"

Ohime-sama. Princess. "No. I do not want anything, thank you."

"If you should change your mind, simply inform one of the guards, and we will instantly do our best to comply with your request. Welcome to the Moon Palace, Ohime-sama."

He bowed again and stepped out, closing the door behind him.

I turned in a circle, looking at the enormous room with its exotic red and gold furnishings, its high, sloping ceilings, its wall of screened round windows, and its towering Old Empire-style bedstead with draperies embroidered in yellow chrysanthemums and red dragons. This was the place where, ten years ago, Akira had sat by the fire and wept.

There, at last, my legs gave out and I fell to the floor, gasping for breath.

My mother was alive. *Alive.*

I was not a murderer.

Had Youta made a mistake? He was a man, after all, and might be confused about the potency of a woman's drug like sangre root. But Youta had worked among drudges for a long time. He had known what sangre was when I spoke of it. Surely then he must have known enough to realize that what I had done was not fatal? Moon-curse it, if I had not trusted Youta so much, had not been so filled with horror at my own actions, I would have questioned it myself.

No. There had been no mistake. He had lied to me.

In the darkness and fear of that night, as I confessed to him, he had seized the chance to get me out of Terayama-san's house. Out and away, before I did something else – something worse. He might have thought that cutting all ties to my old life, to Mother and Terayama-san, even to himself, would finally allow me to leave the past behind.

He had tried to give me a gift. He had tried to set me free.

Only it had not worked. Believing I was responsible for Mother's death had only confirmed something that, deep inside, I had already felt for a long time.

There was a roaring inside me, a screaming, a wailing, as all the hidden voices, all the denied emotions that I had closed off broke free. I crumpled, curling into a ball on the floor, pressing my face to the mats, sucking in deep breaths as I tried to stay conscious. Finally I was forced to see the truth.

I had thought it was my fault.

What had Youta said to me, all those months and years ago, when he first taught me to shadow-weave? That I had a right to be angry – but why was I so angry with myself? I had ignored him, brushed those words aside without answering because *he was right*. I had blamed myself. I had survived when they had not. The youngest, scrawniest, least clever. The least beautiful. Why me? I had no right to have lived. I ought to have saved them, or died with them.

I had buried those thoughts so deep that I never even acknowledged they existed, but they had informed every choice, every decision I had made since my father and cousin died. Beneath my mania to punish Terayama-san was an even deeper one: the need to punish myself. That was why I had leapt at Akira's suggestion to attend the ball and win the promise. It was the only way I could destroy Terayama-san and myself at one stroke.

By the Moon – how could I have been so arrogantly, so monstrously, stupid? I had been just as powerless against the soldiers as Aimi had been powerless against the illness that had killed her family. To blame myself for not fighting that company of armed men was the same as blaming Aimi for not discovering some miraculous cure for red water fever.

Feelings were surging back into me, filling the empty pit that had opened up when I sent Otieno away. What had I done? Oh, what had I done?

At that moment, the ending of my life would have seemed a blessing.

I, who prided herself on piercing illusions and seeing things as they truly were, had clung to this one illusion as a child will cling to its favourite toy. The illusion of control. The illusion that in this terrifying, chaotic world, I had some vestige of choice. I had not wanted to admit that nothing I did could have saved my father and Aimi. I had not even wanted to admit that poisoning my mother had been a moment of thoughtless stupidity, and that I had never really meant to hurt her.

It was easier to hate myself, hurt myself, slice open my own flesh and bleed, than to face the fact that I had been powerless.

Just as I was powerless right now.

Forty

"No." The word echoed around the big, empty room. I would not accept it. It was no good to come to terms with myself – to finally see my own folly, and the truth – if I simply lay there on the floor, whimpering, and let disaster take me anyway. I was not a killer. I had not damned myself forever. I had a right to life and happiness, just as Akira and Youta – and Otieno – had told me.

It might be too late to undo all I had done, to retrieve the love I had spurned. But it was not too late to escape being a Shadow Bride. My father and cousin would not have wanted this life for me. I did not want it for myself.

I must save myself.

I scrambled up, shrugging away the long, heavy *uchikake*. Clad only in the white kimono, I went to the long wall of windows and threw back the closest screen and

the pierced-wood shutter and leant out. This was the back
of the palace, and there were no lanterns lit in the garden
below. I could only just make out the shapes of the trees
where they blocked out the stars and a hint of the trellis
below, covered in large white wisteria blossoms.

I gulped. I hated heights. My fingers were damp and
trembling as I reached for the window frame and hauled
myself up until I was astride the curved edge of the
window, a leg dangling either side. Another glance down
made me clutch at the frame in panic; my legs kicked
reflexively and the sandal on my left foot slipped off and
disappeared into the bottomless darkness.

That is all right, I told myself with false confidence. *I
am better off without shoes for this anyway.* I kicked the other
one off too, and watched it roll across the polished wooden
floor. What would the prince think when he came here
and found that a single shoe was all that was left of me?

Still holding onto the window frame, I began to feel
below me with my toes for the top of the trellis. *I am light
and scrawny,* I told myself. *It will hold my weight easily.*

But I could not find the trellis. My searching foot found
nothing but the wall, which offered no holds for a climber.
I pulled my foot back and leant out again. I had not imagined it. The trellis was there. It was simply too far away for
me to reach. My short legs had betrayed me.

My only way out of the room was down the corridor
and past the guards.

"Halt!"

I jumped, almost falling out of the window. My hands latched onto the screen in a death grip and I caught my balance with a gasp, my eyes searching the room. There was no one there. I was still alone. The shout must have come from the guards outside.

The guards who are here to protect me.

Instinct raised the tiny hairs all over my body as I strained my ears, trying to filter out the muffled noises of revelry from the floor below. The silence in the room seemed like a pall now, suffocating me. My nerves told me to hide, to find some dark place and curl up inside. But the noise had come from the corridor that was my one escape from the room. If I wanted to leave, I must go out there.

Working quickly, I drew threads of darkness around myself, weaving an impenetrable cloak of shadows, as dark and dense as the night outside. I went to the door of the prince's chamber and slid it open a little way, peeking out carefully. I expected to see at least one of the guards by the door – but there was no one there.

I slipped through the gap in the door and closed it silently behind me, drawing my cloak of shadows tighter around my body. My feet moved soundlessly as I turned the corner.

I screamed. I knew the noise would betray me and still I could not help myself. At the end of the corridor, three guards lay dead, blood and vile-smelling fluids pooling around them on the rush mats.

Terayama-san stood over them, just lowering his

katana. The blade was a dull black in the dimness. Black with blood.

My stepfather's head snapped up at my hastily bitten-off cry, searching the darkness. Slowly, unbelievably, his eyes focused on me cowering under my cloak of shadows.

"Up to your little tricks again, Suzu-chan." His eyes gleamed dully, like the blade. "I can see you, though. I could always see through you. It was never any good to run away from me. It only delayed the inevitable."

His eyes narrowed, and he shifted, moving his sword into a defensive position. "Come out from under there. It hurts my eyes to squint, and it will do you no good. Face me. Show a little of the spirit your father was always talking about."

Terror had sucked the strength from me. I clung to the shadow-weaving with everything I had, but under his eyes it had become heavy, unbearable. I watched my own arms swim into view, glowing white in the dim corridor.

Terayama-san's eyes widened. Then he smiled. "How appropriate. White for a virgin bride – a Shadow Bride who will die untouched. It is your own fault. You should not have told Yukiko what you planned to do. You do know that it was your mother who gave you up to me?"

He paused, waiting for me to speak – to cry, or to deny his words. But I could not speak. I could not even breathe.

After a moment he continued: "She told me of your plan, begged me to find you; she knew that when I found you I would not use words to persuade you but my sword.

She always knew it. I hope you did not believe that she would protect you over our sons? She is loyal to me. To our family. And it is for her sake that you must die. Take comfort in that, if you will."

"I shall not die tonight," I said slowly, forcing the words out into the air between us.

Terayama-san's smile got bigger. "Easy to say, Suzu-chan, but these three soldiers, armed and trained, could not stand against me. I am a master of the sword. Even poor Daisuke admitted it. I always won against him, did I not?"

"You are not fit even to speak my father's name," I hissed. And just like that, fury drove the weakness from my limbs. Power pulsed up along my skin, crackling through my hair and under my clothes like invisible lightning.

Terayama-san arched a brow, seemingly amused by my display of defiance. "Your father was a penniless provincial poet. It amused me to befriend him, to let him think he was my equal, but he was nothing."

"*Liar,*" I said, and as I spoke I knew that it was the truth. "You have spent years scheming and plotting – and for what? Why, when you are the great Terayama-sama, with your money and your title and lands, would you go to so much trouble to betray a *provincial poet*? Why? Because you know – you have always known – that my father was your superior. That is why you turned on him, and that is why you have hunted me." I sucked in a deep breath, feeling exultation sweep through me as I was finally able to speak the words that had been locked inside me. There was a storm of power swirling in the air around me, arcing from finger to finger, sparking on my tongue. It felt like being in the centre of a hurricane.

His face had lost its mocking expression now. "Watch your mouth, you stupid girl."

"Why? You plan to kill me anyway. Why should I not speak the truth at last? Or are you afraid to hear it aloud? Afraid that if I say it, you will have to admit it? Nothing you had, not the wealth or power or name, could match what he had. You could not buy his integrity, his kindness or his beautiful soul. My father might have been a mere scholar and poet, without riches or a title, but he was a better man than you will ever be. He could have beaten you whenever he chose and you knew it. You never won. He just let you lead because he felt sorry for you."

Terayama-san let out a great roar of rage and swung back his blade.

Sparks of gold broke out from under my skin, lighting the corridor like an exploding firework. I said: "Stop."

The light fell on Terayama-san, covering him for an instant like a golden net. There was a blinding flash – I turned my face away, closing my eyes – and when I opened them again, the light had disappeared, sinking into Terayama's skin.

His voice cut off in mid-shout.

The dull eyes bulged. His mouth strained as if trying to close but remained open. Snorting breaths puffed from his nostrils. His hands, clasped around the sword hilt, shuddered and trembled as he fought to bring the blade down on my unprotected neck.

Some instinct prompted me to speak, the words leaving a strange taste in my mouth.

"You are bound here by my will," I said formally. "And bound you will stay. You shall not stir from this spot, or speak, or move at all except to breathe, until the moment that someone discovers you here and sees what you have done."

Terayama-san's breaths were shallow and rapid now, and the blind fury was fading from his eyes, replaced with dawning horror and fear. I looked at him, searching my feelings.

"You have no doubt killed many people, as you did my father and cousin," I said. "Taking their lives without dirtying your hands. It is a shame you cannot be held accountable for all of their deaths. However, I think that your murder of three royal guards and your breaking into the prince's chambers, when linked with the mysterious disappearance of the Shadow Bride, will bring a severe enough punishment to satisfy their spirits. This is the end for you. Perhaps my father and Aimi will be able to forgive you now, but they always were better people than me. I will not forgive you. I will forget you."

I saw the rage flare up in his eyes again, and nodded, knowing that what I had said would haunt him for however long – and it would not be very long – he had left to live. Then I turned away. Carefully I drew a new cloak of illusion around me, and left the corridor behind, and with it the monster who stood frozen over the bodies of his victims. I did not look back.

I opened the door at the top of the corridor and walked down the stairs, my cloak rippling and changing with the light, hiding me from the blurry eyes of the guests below. I slipped through the crowd with nothing more to show for my presence than a slight breeze here or an uneasy feeling on the back of a neck there. The room was hot, filled with the smells of alcohol and sweating bodies, and loud enough to almost deafen me. I did not search for Akira; if she was there, I knew she would not be visible to me. I did spare one look for the prince, who sat in his throne again, flushed pink and bright-eyed, surrounded by his courtiers.

He would not be broken-hearted, that charming boy. He might be a little sad to imagine that his Shadow Bride had been hurt, or had fled, but he would not mourn me long. I would not pity him.

Behind the throne, his mother was staring into nothingness, eyes blank. Her I could pity, even if fleetingly. But she would have her wish now. I was leaving her and her son's lives forever. I would be nothing more than a strange mystery, a suspected tragedy. A name for little girls to whisper to each other, snug in their beds, before falling asleep, dreaming of the Kage no Iwai. Kano Yue-sama, the most beautiful Shadow Bride who never was.

I slid back the screen, and stepped outside.

The air was cool and sweet. I took a long, deep breath, letting my eyes adjust as I walked slowly into the deserted gardens, feeling the cool grass under my soles. I sought the shelter of the trees. There were still lanterns lit here and there, and the moonlight was strong, but from this angle the shining white path of the Shadow Procession was hidden. Should I search it out and follow it? Was Akira out there somewhere?

I shook my head, pausing to lean on the rough trunk of a tree, shivering a little.

It didn't matter. I would find my way, and I would find her again. No matter what, I would be all right. After everything I had faced this night, I knew that.

I was free.

And if my freedom was lonely that was my own doing.

"Where are you going?"

The voice came from behind me. Slowly, disbelievingly, I turned.

He stood in the open, the silvery moonlight illuminating his face. I could see, just, that his eye was still a little bruised, and the scrapes on his cheek were scabs now, but the bandage was off his hand. He was wearing black – the first time I had ever seen him in such a dark shade – and his hair was drawn back severely, emphasizing the prominent bones of his cheeks and jaw. He almost blended into the shadows. Almost.

Otieno.

He reached out and jerked me off my feet, into his arms, and I wrapped mine around him with a sob. "Got you," he whispered.

I ran my fingers over the beloved lines of his face, breathing in his cassia smell, trying to make myself believe that he was real. Cupping his face in my hands, I pressed my lips to his.

"Well," he murmured into my mouth. "That was the sort of welcome I was hoping for but not what I expected."

"You are here. You really are here," I muttered, still touching him, testing the planes of his shoulders and the rounded muscles of his upper arms.

"Where else would I be?" he asked, voice husky, as he gently set me down on my feet. "I said I would not leave you behind again."

I was laughing and crying at the same time, hiding my face in his chest, hiding myself in the wonderful relief of feeling him against me again. "But after what I did to you— Oh, Otieno, what are you doing here? You were supposed to be on a ship by now. I cannot believe you stayed."

"Akira-san told me the truth. That morning, after we—" He broke off, his face turning a ruddy shade that I could see even in the half-light as he cleared his throat. "She gave me your note, and let me read it, then she told me that every word of it was a lie. She said you loved me, that turning from me had nearly killed you, and that you had spent the whole night crying fit to break your heart. She told me that you felt you had to avenge your family, even if it meant being miserable for the rest of your life."

"Did you not hate me for choosing my revenge over you?"

"No, though I did think you were being... How to say it?" He paused, as if lost for words, then suddenly grabbed my shoulders and shook me, his next sentence emerging as a restrained roar. *"A half-witted, moronic, cake-brained fool!"*

He stopped. Taking a deep breath, he carefully loosened his grip on my shoulders. "I was all for storming the city and dragging you out of your hiding place by your hair. But Akira said that she was sure you would not be able to go through with it, not if you saw me again. We agreed that I would wait until tonight and confront you at the end of the ball. My plan was to come as a guest, but I could not get an invitation. I think our friend Yorimoto blocked me. So instead I snuck in wearing a cloak of illusions. I was about to try to get upstairs – and then you walked right past me and out the door! After I had spent half the night hiding behind one of those drooling lizards!"

I covered my mouth with my hand, unable to hold in a snort of laughter. "That is just what they look like!"

"But you looked beautiful," he said, voice softening. "I saw you dance. I did not know you could dance like that, Pipit."

I wanted to sink into his arms again, but this was not the place. "Otieno, we must go. If the prince catches me – us together – we will both be killed. I am the Shadow Bride now."

"What are you talking about?" said Otieno, squeezing me tightly again. "You have already escaped them, even without my help. You are Akachi. You can hide from anyone."

Except you, I thought.

I clasped his hand, and we mingled our gifts, weaving a dense illusion that hid us even from each other.

"Keep hold of my hand." His voice came out of the shadows. I could see the shape of him there, a darker shade of black in the night.

"Otieno," I said abruptly, "what would you have done if you had come here but I had not changed my mind and agreed to go with you?"

"Gagged you, thrown you over my shoulder and taken you anyway," he said promptly. "I have some ropes braided around my waist. Actually, I do not know whether to be relieved or disappointed that it is not necessary."

And I did not know whether to laugh or hit him. He would not have needed the ropes; I was not strong enough to have rejected him a second time.

"I think we should hurry now," Otieno said. His voice was casual, but when I reached up to touch his throat with my free hand, I felt his pulse galloping there. I flushed, imagining I could hear my own heart speeding up to match it. "Akira-san is waiting for us at the other end of garden with my father, and they will both be worried."

"Akira? Thank the Moon. Is she coming with us?" I asked, feeling a rush of relief.

"She slipped out to find me as soon as you were made Shadow Bride. She would not let you go alone. You are her family."

"We are her family," I whispered, tightening my grip on his fingers.

And together we disappeared into the darkness, swift and silent as shadows on the moon.

Otieno and Yue's love poems

On the journey across the sea to Athazie, Otieno and Yue pass time on the ship by writing love poems to each other...

Otieno:
Frightened little bird,
Trembling on the edge of flight,
Fly safely to me.

Yue:
As your arrows fly,
So your words seek out my heart,
And pierce it straight through.

Otieno:
Drifting shadow hair,
Flashing eyes like dark of moon,
Catch fire in my arms.

Yue:
Ink curls across flesh,
Moving with each breath you take,
And I am jealous.

Otieno:
Darkness is banished,
World alight with flame colours,
When my love dances.

Yue:
Loneliness is gone,
Blood and tears forever dried,
By your smile, my love.

The Rainy Season

A short story that occurs in Athazie
after the events of Shadows on the Moon

"Oh, what was I thinking?" Akira groaned. Her feet scuffed over the vibrant jewel-tones of the rug Otieno had spread over the floor when they first arrived here, to welcome them to their new home. "What am I thinking?"

"You were thinking that A Suda-san is an intelligent and interesting man, that he has always been kind to us, and that spending the evening with him watching the young men race on the lake would be fun," Suzume said, not looking up from the scroll of paper where she was using a fine brush to carefully inscribe the musical notes of her latest composition. "That is what you told me yesterday. As for what you are thinking now ... who knows?"

The younger woman's face was tense with concentration, and her hair, carelessly bundled back, was falling down her neck in an arrangement startlingly like a bird's nest. The summer heat of Athazie was intense, and Suzume's slim arms, bared by the tied-up sleeves of her plain cotton dress, shone with sweat, emphasizing the fading scars that rippled across her fine, pale skin. Akira paused in her restless pacing, struck. She had never seen her adopted sister look more beautiful. No, no – nothing so shallow as that. Not beautiful.

Happy.

Beauty was distressingly easy to buy. Happiness ... happiness was infinitely rarer, and more precious.

When Akira failed to respond, Suzume lifted her eyes from the paper, a wrinkle of concern passing across her face. Akira loved to see those tiny, almost imperceptible changes in Suzume's expression. It wasn't very long ago that Suzume had refused to let any emotion disturb her true face. All her smiles and frowns had been carefully constructed masks.

But that had been before Otieno, the beautiful, laughing, stubborn young boy who had barged into their lives and upset all their careful plans. Before Suzume learned that some people – the right people – can see through any mask, no matter how lovely. Before Suzume fell in love.

"What is it?" Suzume laid her brush down and swiped at her damp forehead with the back of one ink-stained hand. "You are not really frightened?"

"A Suda-san is very like his son," Akira said softly. Then she pursed her lips. I didn't mean to say that.

Suzume looked at Akira for a long moment. When she spoke, her voice was softer and more gentle even than Akira's. "You do not fear Otieno's father. You fear what he makes you feel."

Akira turned away to the window, forcing her movements to remain slow and graceful even though her body longed to jerk and stomp. Beyond the intricately pierced screens of perfumed wood, a plain of ripe golden grasses stretched out as far as the eye could see, interrupted here and there by the dark, angular scribbles of thorn trees. In the distance, low blue mountains dreamed under ragged veils of ever-shifting cloud.

A Suda-san called those clouds rain-singers. Soon their long shadows would begin to drift over the plain, bringing the autumn wind and storms. Bringing this long summer, Akira and Suzume's first in Athazie, to an end.

The season was changing. Everything was changing.

Everything always changed.

"Your silence speaks for you," Suzume whispered. "It hurts, does it not? To feel. To know that you have given some part of yourself, however small, to another – and now you are vulnerable again after so long."

"I have given nothing to A Suda-san." Akira said shortly. "I barely know him. Most women are never lucky enough to have true love. A great love. I have. I had mine. And he was..." She drew in a short breath, halting the too-fast flow of words. "He is gone."

"You are still here, Akira."

Akira forced out a light, tinkling laugh that cascaded from her lips like broken glass. "Suzume! Anyone would think you want my heart broken."

"No. No, my dear, dearest sister. Anyone would think I want your heart saved."

There was a polite knock on the carved wooden door of their rooms. Akira let out a tiny, involuntary gasp, turning to face the entrance as if it was a hungry lion.

"That will be A Suda-san," Suzume said blandly, making no move to get up from her writing desk.

Akira ran steady hands down the front of her new dress, and took a deep breath. "Sometimes, my little one, you can be the most annoying sister in the world."

She stalked to the door and threw it open.

Suzume felt the cool breeze of the coming rainy season wash into the over-heated room, and smiled.

Acknowledgements

Just when I thought I had figured out how to go about writing a book, this story came along. I blew two deadlines, one computer and probably more brain cells than I'd like to admit while working on it. Sometimes I would stare at the screen and think, with complete certainty: this book will never be finished.

The fact that it was eventually finished is down to a diverse network of people whom I will now attempt to thank. My sincere gratitude goes to:

The Royal Literary Fund – in particular, Eileen Gunn – for their astonishing generosity, which allowed me to write and take care of my family without being crushed by debt and financial hardship.

The Society of Authors and the Great Britain Sasakawa Fund, for making me the recipient of the Sasakawa Prize, as a result of which I was able to conduct vital research and create a much more realistic and textured story than I could otherwise have afforded to do.

Dr Susan Ang, who always knows just the right book to send at just the right moment, and Dr Mei Hiramoto, who looked at my sketchy Japanese translations, laughed heartily (I suspect) and did them again properly.

The intensely intelligent and well-read Furtive Scribbler's Club, who offered me such levels of support, inspiration and advice on every bit of this book that it was like having my own team of part-time muses on hand. So many people helped me that it would literally be impossible to print everyone's name here, but Pembe, Skippy, Sniffemout, Hobbitlass, Bookherder, PhoenixGirl, Bookbean, Miyu, Kehs, Diana, Holly, Tina, Rachel and Barbara especially deserve my gratitude. Not to mention Ruby, my one girl focus-group. I love you guys (sniff).

My editor, Annalie Grainger, who, with tact, persistence and insight, turned my bloated first draft into this book of which I am so proud. Special thanks also go to Gill Evans for her extraordinary support and kindness though a very difficult period. To my agent, Nancy Miles, for engulfing me in a sense of safety and well-being, and to Maria Soler Canton, for the cover art I love so much.

Finally, David and Elaine Marriott. My first and still favourite readers.

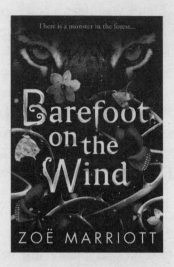

There is a monster in the forest...

Barefoot on the Wind

ZOË MARRIOTT

**A beautiful and thought-provoking retelling of
"Beauty and the Beast" set in a fairy tale Japan.
A companion title to Zoë Marriott's critically
acclaimed *Shadows on the Moon*.**

Everyone in Hana's remote village knows that straying
too far into the woods means certain death. When
Hana's father goes missing, she is the only one who
dares try to save him. Taking up her hunting gear, she
goes in search of the beast, determined to kill it – or be
killed herself. But the forest contains more secrets, more
magic and more darkness than Hana could ever have
imagined, and the beast is not at all what she expects.